The Prequel To The Legend Of Korra Meets Allegiant

Chapter 1

I walk around Chicago and duck under cars or into bushes, anything to try not to be caught by The Earth Empire Soldiers. Who knows what will happen if they found me. I run down Michigan Ave and turn left, diving into a nearby ally, just as Kuvira turns to walk down the same street. I look at my clothes, I'm wearing an old Earth Kingdom uniform. But if Kuvira caught me, well then that's the end of the line for me. I walk slowly at first not wanting to draw attention to myself, because by then Kuvira had turned to walk down the same ally. No one else but me and Kuvira are walking down the ally way. I turn my head and notice that she's still following me. I reach the end of the ally and then break into a sprint. I hear footsteps behind me and I know that Kuvira is following me, I try to run faster but I can't because I'm running at my max speed. I run for what seems like a while, until I turn another corner. Then I come to a sudden stop and see a few of the soldiers from her army and turn around and sprint back in the same direction at I had come from. Seconds later the soldiers come chasing after me. I continue running. I turn another corner and skid to a stop. I also try not to breathe too loudly. Kuvira stands in that exact same ally looking in the opposite direction. I start to back up slowly, but then I accidently hit something hard and I let out a groan—louder than I meant for it to be. I turn around and see that the soldiers have caught up to me and that I had backed into one of them. He puts a pair of metal handcuffs on me and pushes me forwards.

"Kuvira." one of the soldiers says.

"Yes." Kuvira says, without turning around.

"We caught someone." the soldier says.

At that statement Kuvira turns around slowly and looks at me.

"That's the girl I tried to catch earlier," Kuvira says. "Great job guys."

I just stare at Kuvira and it feels like someone has their hand wrapped around my throat. I let out a wheezed breath.

Finally Kuvira smiles and says. "Hi, sweetie, what's your name?"

"Christine." I say quietly.

"That's a wonderful name, now what brings you to Chicago Christine?" Kuvira asks, raising an eyebrow at me.

"Well...Um." I start to say, but then I start to cry.

Kuvira looks at her soldiers and nods. They let me go, take off the metal handcuffs and walk away. Kuvira walks over to me and puts a hand on my shoulder.

"Come on, what is it? You can tell me. I won't hurt you. Where are your parents?" she says calmly.

I wipe my eyes, look at her and say "Well... I'm all alone, I don't have a family."

"Oh. Well how about you come live with me, I can help you." says Kuvira.

"Really? Are you sure?" I ask.

"Of course. Come on." she says with a small smile.

"Okay." I say calmly.

Kuvira and I walk together towards her camp.

Chapter 2

We reach a part of Chicago that I recognize. We are near Erudite headquarters and my heart jumps a little. We walk to Kuvira's house and when we get inside, we walk to the living room and there is a man with black hair, a goatee and glasses sitting on the couch reading a book. I stand behind Kuvira, I'm still unsure about everything.

"Baatar. I have important news." Kuvira says and she smiles at me. I stand beside her and hold onto her arm.

"Alright what is it? I'm kind of in the middle of something." Baatar says without looking up.

"Junior look at me when I'm talking to you." Kuvira says, sounding irritated.

Baatar Jr. looks at Kuvira and says. "I told you never to call me that."

"I know, but it's the only way I can get your attention these days." Kuvira says with a sigh.

"Alright I get your point, so what is it?" he asks.

"I found this little girl wandering around Chicago, so I stopped her and asked her where her parents were and you won't believe this but she doesn't have a family." Kuvira says.

"Really? Oh, I'm sorry to hear that," he says. Then he adds with a smirk. "Then you two will get along greatly."

Kuvira's face turns red and she says. "Baatar, now's not the time."

"Oh right sorry," he says. Then he adds. "Are going to introduce me?"

"Oh right.," Kuvira turns to me and motions to Baatar and says. "Christine this is Baatar Jr.," Then she turns back to Baatar, motions to me and says. "Baatar this is Christine."

I walk over to him, shake his hand and say. "It's nice to meet you."

He nods and then says. "Alright, well I'm heading to bed. I'll see you two, in the morning."

"Where am I going to sleep?" I ask Kuvira.

"There is a house next door to this one. No one's in it, you could stay there."

"Thank you." I say and I give her a salute.

"Goodnight Christine." she says.

"Goodnight Kuvira." I say and I walk out of her house and next door to mine. I open up the door and walk inside. I close the door and lock it. I walk up to my bedroom and close the door, but then my doorbell rings. I walk back downstairs, open up the door and see Kuvira standing there.

"I forgot to give you more clothes." she says, as she hands me a bag full of Earth Empire uniforms.

"Thank you, but why are you giving me the Earth Empire uniform?" I ask.

"I'm giving them to you, because I would love it if you were part of The Earth Empire army. What do you say?"

"Yes! I would love to. Thank you." I say happily.

"No problem," she says. "I'll see you tomorrow. Goodnight."

"Goodnight." I say and she closes the door and locks it.

I walk back up to my bedroom, close the door, set my alarm, hop into bed and fall asleep.

Chapter 3

My alarm goes off at six in the morning. I hop out of bed and and put on one of my Earth Empire uniforms, walk downstairs and have breakfast. Once I'm finished, I walk over to the door and open it. Kuvira stands outside, with her hand on the door.

"Good morning Great Uniter." I say with a smile.

"Good morning Christine," Then she adds. "Please, just call me Kuvira."

"Okay," I clear my throat and say. "So Kuvira. What do we have planned for today?"

"Well, I was thinking that since you're going to be part of my army, that I was going to teach you how to metalbend." she says with a small smile.

"Yes, I would love it. Thank you." I say.

"Well let's get started." she says.

We walk out of the house and walk to a sparing circle, when we get there Kuvira bends a piece of a metal meteor into her hand.

"These metal meteors have a unique bending property, making it easier to bend." Kuvira says, as she bends it into a star, then she passes it to me and I try to bend it. But nothing works. "Try to focus on the small pieces of earth, within the metal." she says calmly.

I take a deep breath, drop into my metalbending stance and focus my energy on the small pieces of earth in the metal, soon I feel a connection and I move my hand and the metal forms into a ball.

I look at Kuvira and say. "It worked!"

"Great job." she says.

"Now, lets try something different." Kuvira says as she puts two spools of metal cables on each side of my uniform. I take a deep breath and fire out both of my metal cables and Kuvira dodges the attack. She then fires a few metal strips at me and I yelp and dive out of the way. The strips fly past me.

"Okay, that will need some work." Kuvira says as she walks over to me and helps me up.

"Sorry about that." I say.

"No. It fine, I just kind of got lost in the moment, it's been awhile since I've trained someone." she says, smiling.

"You're a great teacher for metalbending you know that." I say, with a smile.

"Thank you, I had a great teacher as well." she says.

"Who was your teacher?" I ask.

Kuvira looks at me and says. "You can't tell anyone, okay?"

"Okay."

Kuvira sighs and then says. "My teacher was the leader of Zaofu. I was the captain of her guards."

"Su Beifong was your teacher. Wow, that must have wonderful," I say, unable to contain my shock. "Is that why Baatar Jr. is with you?"

"Yes, he came with me to help stabilize The Earth Empire and it was wonderful having Su as my teacher."

"What happened? How did you end up in Chicago?"

Kuvira looks away for a second, then says. "Three years ago, after the fall of the Earth Queen. Raiko and Tenzin came to see Su, I attended the meeting as well. Raiko expressed his concerns on what might happen if no one took control of the problem in The Earth Kingdom. I tried to persuade Su to take control and she refused. I decided to help by bringing back order in Chicago and then expand from there. Baatar decided to come along to help."

"Wow. Well you're doing a great job at stabilizing the Earth Empire." I say with a smile.

"Thank you." she says.

I nod.

"Alright I think that's enough training for today."

Chapter 4

We walk back to Kuvira's house and when we get there, Baatar is standing in the living room with his arms crossed and a scowl on his face. "Where have you been? I was starting to get worried."

"We were just practicing metalbending Baatar, there's no need to get angry." Kuvira says calmly.

Baatar gives me a dirty look and I hide behind Kuvira. "Yeah sure. If you say so." he says bitterly.

"What's the problem Baatar?" Kuvira asks, sounding upset.

"Oh nothing. There's no problem." Baatar says rolling his eyes.

Kuvira turns to me and says. "Why don't you go back to your house, alright. I'll see you in the morning."

I nod and walk out of her house.

When I get back to my house. I sit on the couch for a few minutes and stare into darkness. Then I walk upstairs to my bedroom and fall asleep.

The next morning, I wake to my alarm going off. I sit up and then hop off the bed to get dressed. Then I walk downstairs and walk to the door and open it up.

"Good morning Kuvira." I say with a salute.

"Good morning to you too Christine," she says, then she adds. "I brought you something." Kuvira hands me another bag full clothes.

I take it from her and then say. "You know that I still have the other ones you gave me right?"

"Yeah, I know. Just have a look at the uniforms." she replies.

I take out a pair of the uniforms and look at the metal pads on the the shoulders and the two chevrons on the right arm and notice that there are two chevrons on the right arm of the uniform.

"Why are you giving me a Corporal uniform?" I ask. "I've only been part of your army for like two days."

"Because you've proven your worth. You're very determined, smart and I think that you should be a Corporal in my army. Not to mention the fact that you're a excellent metalbender." she smiles a little.

"Thank you," I say, with a smile, then I add. "Just let me get changed into my new uniform."

"Of course." she says

I nod and run upstairs to my bedroom and put on my new green uniform. I put on my new black boots, which have metal rings on the edges of them, next I put on the green shirt which has a belt and the two spirals of metal cables. The green shirt also has two markings on the right arm, saying that my rank is of a corporal. There's also metal shoulder pads, three rings of metal strips that have several layers on both arms and finally I put on my gloves which of course are green. Then I walk downstairs again and join Kuvira at the breakfast table. We sit there in silence for a few minutes before I say "I like this new uniform."

"I'm glad you like it." Kuvira says with a smile.

"Me too." I reply.

The Legend Of Korra Meets Allegiant
(Book 1)

Chapter 1

I woke up this morning in Chicago, Illinois in my house near Erudite headquarters. I had heard a loud ruckus outside and went out to investigate it. When I reach the door I heard a familiar voice telling everyone to stay inside their homes until further notice. I was just about to go back to bed when I had heard two knocks and then four knocks on my door, that told me someone from Kuvira's army needed me for something. I quickly change from my gray PJ's and into my Earth Empire Uniform and walk to the door. I was still groggy from sleep, but when I opened up my door, my heart leaped at the sight of who it was. Who I saw was not the normal soldiers that came to wake me up in the morning. For this time I was in the presence of someone more important.

"Great Uniter Kuvira!" I exclaimed with a quick salute.

"Morning Christine."

She returned the salute and we both stand in silence for a few moments.

Then she clears her throat and starts speaking again. "So I wanted to talk to you about something."

"Okay," I say as steadily as I can. "What is it?"

Chapter 2

*She wants me to be part of what?* I stare at her blankly as she finishes, I'm still processing what she just told me in the last five minutes. "So... you want me to be part of your inner circle?, wow... I... um... I don't know what to say." I say.

"So what do you think? You can think about it." she says with a slight smile that disappeared as soon as it started.

"Yes of course, I would love too." I reply with a smile.

"Well come on then, let's get started." She waves her hand towards the door motioning for me to follow her. I don't hesitate, we walk out of my house side by side.

---

"So where are we going?" I ask as we hop onto the train that connects Chicago to the rest of The Earth Empire.

"Just wait and you'll see." She says looking out the train window.

I nod, then ask. "Where is Bolin? Baatar? and the rest of your army?"

She finally looks at me with both eyebrows raised and says "Christine you ask a lot of questions. But I will answer some of them. For your first question: Bolin and Baatar have to stay and make sure our camp is safe from people who wish to destroy it, for your second: My soldiers are still there to make sure there is peace and order within the Earth Empire."

I nod and we both look out the window again. When I look out the window this time though, I see silver metal domes that are just opening up to signal to its people that it is morning and safe to come out. Then I realize where we are going: Zaofu.

Chapter 3

By the time we reach the home that belongs to Suyin Beifong and her family, I am too confused by what we are doing here to say anything about it. We travel through the corridors of their house until we get to the living room. Kuvira opens up the doors without knocking and walks in, with me following behind her. Inside of the living room is Baatar Sr, Su, Opal and the twins Wing and Wei, I look from Kuvira to the rest of the Beifong family.

"What are you two doing here?" Su says as she looks from me to Kuvira and back again.

Kuvira just simply states. "Have you had time to re-think my offer, because I would hate for you to say no."

Su starts to speak but I interrupt her and say. "What offer?"

Then I look at Kuvira and say. "What is going on here?"

Kuvira looks at me and finally says. "We are uniting the Earth Empire, you know this Christine."

I nod and smile. "Right I keep forgetting about that."

Su looks at me with a shocked look and says. "Christine you have no idea what's going on."

"Of course I do!" I say. "You have no idea what we've been doing Su, we are making the Earth Empire a better place to live!"

I look at Kuvira and say. "Maybe we should go and let them think about your offer a little more."

Kuvira nods and walks out of the room, with me following right behind her.

---

When we get back to Chicago we don't go back to our camp, instead we go to Erudite headquarters and straight to the lab. Inside the lab, Kuvira walks over to the panels on the wall, she opens one up revealing different colored serums and pulls out several red colored ones and then closes the panel on the wall, she sets them inside a black box and puts it down on a table.

Then turns to me and says. "There we go. Alright let's go back to our camp and get some sleep, we have busy day planned tomorrow."

"Okay," I say. "Let's go then."

We make our way back to our tents, but before I turn towards mine, I look at Kuvira and give her a worried look.

"Kuvira," I say. "I have a bad feeling that something is going to happen tonight, so be careful."

Kuvira takes her time responding.

"Oh quit being so paranoid Christine, nothing is going to happen, I assure you that I'll be safe, but if you think that something is going to happen, then you have to be on alert tonight to make sure nothing does happen. But only if you so choose to. If not then goodnight Christine, have a good sleep."

I take my time responding "Okay, but just to make sure you're okay, can I stay near your house until I feel like you're safe. Please?"

Kuvira laughs a little and says. "Well you're a little funny girl aren't you," Then she adds. "Just go back to your house I'll be fine, plus I have Baatar with me—oh wait he's on break—anyway you should get some sleep. It's almost—holy crap it's three in the morning."

"Okay," I say "I'll go back to mine, but if you need anything just call me from yours."

Chapter 4

When I reach my house, I go to my room and close the door. I don't bother getting changed, I just get into bed and try go to sleep.

---

That night I'm unable to sleep, I just keep tossing and turning. Eventually I get up and walk downstairs to my living room, unlike the tents the other soldiers have, mine and Kuvira's are houses. I sit down on the couch and stare into the pitch black living room, out of the corner of my eye I see movement outside and look out my window. But by then, whatever I'm seeing is gone, so I walk towards the door, put my hand on the doorknob and take a deep breath. I open the door and walk towards Kuvira's house.

When I reach Kuvira's house, I knock on the door but get no answer. It's not like her to not answer the door when someone knocks. I try the door and find it unlocked. I walk into her house and hear muffled shouts coming from one of the closets and open the door, Baatar Jr. is there with his hands tied with rope behind his back and a cloth wrapped around his mouth.

I take the cloth from his mouth and he yells. "They have her!"

I see a flash of light out of the corner of my eye and look to my right. Three figures are running away with a fourth figure slung across a shoulder. I see one with gray hair, two boys with dentical faces and the fourth figure—who is slung over a shoulder—has black hair and is wearing a forest green uniform, with its normal metal plates on the shoulders and back. Kuvira.

Chapter 5

I run through the camp and after the people who have Kuvira, they run faster, even though they con't know that I'm following them. When they get near the train, I yell. "Let her go!" The one with the gray hair turns around and I let out a startled gasp. "Su!"

The two other boys—Wing and Wei—who have Kuvira start to run again and I don't waste any time I bend the metal cable from my uniform and it wraps around the twins and they drop Kuvira to the ground, Su bends her own metal cable at me and I dodge the attack and reverse her cable so it flings back at her. Kuvira is still laying on the ground motionless.

"Su, Why are you doing this?!"

Su doesn't respond, she just stares at me with a glare in her eyes. Then she turns towards Kuvira and slowly bends out a small plated sword from her metal armor. I pick up my radio and send a message to the other soldiers at the camp. "We're under attack, Kuvira has been captured just north of the camp, send reinforcements quick. Until then I'll hold them off." I turn back to Su and say. "You're making a mistake, if you lay a hand on Kuvira, I'll wipe out your entire city," Then I add. "Then your entire family."

Su turns around slowly, looks at me with a panicked look in her eyes and says "What! No you wouldn't!"

I nod and say. "Of course I would, you need to remember who you're talking to. Now you can attack Kuvira and risk losing your life, your family's life and your city or you can let Kuvira go and surrender the city. Now what are you going to do?"

Su starts to bend the metal sword back into her armor but I stop her and say. "Give me your sword and metal cable, in fact give me all your armor including your sons armor."
She doesn't hesitate, she hand over all their armor until they have nothing but their clothes and by then the soldiers have shown up.

"Take Su and the rest of her family and put them in the prison. Make sure it's either a wooden box or a platinum cell. Though I think the platinum cells will do. Don't forget platinum handcuffs and don't take them off until they're in there cells and one last thing put Su and the rest of her family in separate cells far away from each other. Go now!" The soldiers take them to the prison and as soon as they leave, I walk over to Kuvira, swing her over my shoulders and run back to her house.

When I get there I find Baatar Jr. and lay Kuvira down on her bed in her room. Then I look at Baatar Jr. and say. "I'm sorry I left you in the closet. I should have let you out before I ran off. I'm so sorry."

Baatar looks at me and says. "No. It's alright, you had to stop Su and her family from killing Kuvira, it's okay, I understand."

I look at him and smile. Then I say. "Thank you for understanding. How about you get some sleep, I'll look after Kuvira for you. Plus now I can't sleep because of what happened.
He nods and goes to sleep on the couch. I stay by Kuvira's side and watch her to make sure she's safe. As soon as Baatar Jr. is asleep I hop on the bed and lay down next to Kuvira and eventually drift off to sleep.

Chapter 6

I wake up in a unfamiliar room, laying on a bed next to Kuvira. *Kuvira!* I lurch to the left and nearly fall off the bed. I catch myself before I do and lay back down.

"Uhh, what happened? I feel so weak." says a voice. I roll over and notice that Kuvira is waking up.

"Morning." I say as I get off the bed and walk to the other side of it.
She opens her eyes and tries to sit straight up groaning in pain in the process.

I lightly lay her back down on the bed again and say. "It's okay, you're safe. I had to get you out of there."

Kuvira rests her eyes on mine and weakly says. "Christine, wh- what are you doing here and you had to get me out of where?"

I take a deep breath and after a few minutes I say. "You were almost assassinated by Su and her family, but I stopped them and saved your life."

"Wait," she says "Su tried to kill me, why?"

"I don't know." I shake my head.

Then she says. "Where are they? What did you do to them?"

"I put them all in separate cells far away from each other in the prison," I say calmly. "Oh and by the way, after the attack, Su surrendered Zaofu."

"That's good," she says "That's very good. Great job Christine."

I smile and say. "Well I should go, you need to rest."

Just before I leave though, I feel something tug on my arm and turn around to see Kuvira holding on to it. She looks up at me and says. "Can you stay with me? Just for a little longer?"

I smile and lay down next to her and say. "Always. I'll never leave you. I promise."

Chapter 7

Later that day when Kuvira is fully rested and is able to walk, we go visit Su and her family in prison. We walk down corridor after corridor.

Kuvira gives me a puzzled look and says. "Christine, where you keeping them?"

I keep walking. "They are all in separate cells."

"Platinum cells?" she asks.

I shrug. "It was that or a wooden box, but we only have the one box and I wanted to keep them separate from each other. Plus we have a dozen platinum cells."

Kuvira was about to say something to me when we walk passed Wing's cell, then Wei's cell and finally Su's cell. Each cell is guarded by one of the soldiers.

I stop in front of the door, the guard nods to me and walks away. I slide the little slot on the door open. "Su hope you had enough sleep, because you have a visitor."

I open the door and Su just glares, first at me, then at Kuvira. Kuvira doesn't say anything she just looks at Su for a few minutes, then glances at me and says. "Alright close it up."

After the visit with Su. Kuvira and I take a trip back to Zaofu to let the people know that Kuvira and I are now their rightful leaders. We walk to the town square and Kuvira makes an announcement to the city.

"Citizens of Zaofu," Her voice is loud and clear and echoes throughout the city. "Late last night your leader Suyin Beifong attempted to attack me last night while I slept, rest assured, I will not take it out on the peaceful citizen of Zaofu, as long as your remaining leaders meet me tonight for the unconditional surrender of your city. That is all."

Later that night me and Kuvira walk to the battlefield where we will meet whoever they send. Ten minutes later Korra shows up with Jinora and Opal.

"Release my family now!" shouts Opal.

"I've already have laid out my terms." Kuvira says.

"Where's Bolin? I know he would never go along with this." Opal says.

"Bolin is with my fiancé making sure there is order in Chicago, you two have been apart for sometime, and I can assure you he's on board with my plans." Kuvira states.

Opal looks over to Korra and says. "Just go into the Avatar State and get it over with."

Korra looks back at Opal and says. "No. I'm only going to use that as a last resort." Then she turns back to Kuvira. "I can't just let you take the city."

"Avatar Korra you are interfering with Earth Empire business, the only way to keep me from marching into Zaofu is if you physically stop me. Now what are you going to do?"

"I guess you're not giving me a choice." Korra says.

"Fine." Kuvira says.

Then she turns to me. "I want you to know that, I would never ask you to do something that I'm not willing to do myself, so rather than risk your life, I will fight the Avatar one-on-one," She turns back to Korra and says. "Korra if you win, you can do whatever it is you want with Zaofu. But after I beat you, I want you out of my way for good."

"You want to fight the Avatar," Korra says. "Then let's finish this. Right here, Right now."
Chapter 8
Jinora and Opal look at Korra and say. "Be careful." They walk back to the other end of the field.

Kuvira turns to me and says. "Why don't you sit this one out. I can handle Korra on my own."
I give her a quick salute and walk toward the opposite side of the field.

She turns back to Korra and says with a smirk. "Use whatever you want, all the elements, The Avatar State, anything you need. I know you're a little rusty."

"Enough talk." Korra says as she lets out a stream of fire blasts. Kuvira evades all the attacks and then shoots two metal strips at Korra, one on her left hand and one on her right ankle and flips her over on her side. Korra slams into the ground.

"Looks like the Avatar is a little off her game." Kuvira taunts as she readies herself for another attack.

Korra pushes herself off the ground and fires both air and a rock at Kuvira as to which she evades quite quickly and as soon as Korra lands on the ground, Kuvira launches a rock at Korra's stomach. This goes on for several minutes, Korra throwing attacks at Kuvira and Korra always getting hit either with rocks or metal.

At one point Korra get knocked to the ground and Kuvira taunts her again. "Come on Avatar get up, show me what you got."

At another point when Kuvira had knocked Korra to the ground and runs at her to finish it. Korra looks up at Kuvira and quickly entered the Avatar State. Korra let out two blasts of air that knocked Kuvira off her feet and sent her flying backwards. Kuvira fell to the ground and Korra hovered over her with a giant boulder. Kuvira slowly moved from off the ground and looked up at Korra. Korra lets out a yelp, exits The Avatar State and falls to the ground.

Kuvira didn't do anything for a few seconds, then looked at Korra and said. "I knew you were weak."

Korra tries to run towards Kuvira. But she didn't get far because Kuvira lifted her off the ground with the metal strips that were wrapped around Korra's wrists and then slammed her into the ground, to which she incases Korra with rocks and earth. She was just about to end Korra with her metal blades which she had sharpened to a point, when both Jinora and Opal blasted Kuvira with their airbending. To which I watched with horror as Kuvira went flying backwards and I run over to catch her before she hits the ground. I lift Kuvira up and let her go.

"You broke our agreement." she says to Opal and Jinora, then she looks at me and says. "Attack!"

I run toward both of them and they create a giant tornado to keep us at bay.

A few moments later Korra wakes up and breaks through the rocks and earth that is surrounding her body, then all of a sudden an air bison swoops down with Meelo at the rains. They lift Korra from the ground and put her in the saddle on the bison and fly away from us. As they leave I walk up behind Kuvira and we both cheer and yell. "Zaofu is ours!"

We announce the news to the people of Zaofu, who now kneel before their new leaders.

Chapter 9

Later we go back to our houses in Chicago, then we take another trip to visit Su and her family in the prison.

We stop at Su's cell first and we are greeted with scowls and hateful looks. "I can't believe you work for her Christine, thought you cared for the Beifong family, now I can see that you don't."

"Well you see Su, I say. "I do care, but you and your boys were the ones who tried to assassinate Kuvira, which is what caused her to attack Zaofu. She did say she wasn't going to make any moves until Korra got back to her. So you can't blame it on us, it is your fault after all. If you had just surrendered none of this would have happened."

Then me and Kuvira walk away from the cells, but as we leave I grab one of the soldiers. "I have a bad feeling that something is going to happen tonight so keep an eye on all the cells, okay?"

He nods and gets two more soldiers to watch each of the cells.

---

When Kuvira and I reach her house again we go to the living room and collapse onto the couch and lean into one another.

Then I look up at her and then say. "Oh shoot."

She looks back at me. "What? What is it?"

"Remember the red colored serums that we left in the black box at Erudite headquarters."

"Yes. The memory serum," she says. "What about it?"

"Well I was thinking if we used it on the people in Chicago and the people in Zaofu, then they won't remember a time that you weren't in charge, just a thought, I'll let you think about it. In the meantime I'm going to find Baatar Jr. and tell him what we are thinking of doing. Okay?"

"Okay." she says.

I get up and walk out of the room, I hope to find him soon.

Chapter 10

I walk around the camp for a little bit, looking everywhere for Baatar Jr. When I'm unable to find him, I walk up to one of the guards.

"Have you seen Baatar Jr.? I can't find him anywhere."

The guard thinks about this for a moment and says "I think he went to the lab in Erudite headquarters to get something."

"Oh," I say. "Well thanks."

"No problem." The guard says.

---

I run back to Kuvira's house and burst through the door.

"Kuvira!" I yell.

She jumps up off the couch.

"What is it?" she says.

"We have to leave right now."

"Why?" she says.

"I think Baatar is going to use the memory serum on Chicago and Zaofu I think he overheard our conversation last night and took it seriously. So we need to leave right now."

"No," she says. "he wouldn't. Would he?"

"Come on." I say. I tug on her arm, but she stays put.

"I'm not going anywhere, I'm staying here." she insists.

"Fine." I groan.

---

Later I go to the lab in Erudite headquarters only to find Baatar taking out all of the memory serum from the wall panel. I stand just outside of the room. Just in case he decides to close the door and lock it.

"What are you doing?" I ask.

Baatar jumps and nearly drops one of the vials he's holding and looks at me. "Oh Christine, you nearly gave my a heart attack."

"What are you doing?" I ask again.

"Nothing. I'm... not doing anything." he says, trying to keep his voice steady.

"Uh huh," I say. "Then why do you have *all* the memory serum out?"

Baatar Jr. doesn't say anything he just glares at me and I notice another serum in his pocket, this one is purple. I look over at the table and notice more of the purple colored serum, I instantly recognize it as the death serum. He notices that I'm looking at the death serum and says. "Ah so now you know what I'm up to."

"What are you doing with both the memory serum and death serum?" I ask carefully.

"Well I'm... you'll find out soon enough." he says.

I quickly run into the room and grab one vial of the death serum and one vial of the memory serum and sprint out of the room and metalbend the door closed so he can't follow me. Then I turn and run down the hallway towards the prison.

Chapter 11

I run faster and faster until I get to the platinum cells, I stop in front of Su's cell first. I unlock the cell and open the door. She gives me the same look she gave me last time and says. "What are you doing here? Get out!"

"Su," I say. "Listen to me, I'm going to get you and your family out of here. But we need to be careful."

She scoffs and says. "Since when does that matter to you?"

"Su look, we can either do this the easy way or the hard way, your choice."

"No!" she says. "I'm not coming with you!"

I let out a frustrated yell. "First Kuvira and now you! Come on let's go. If we don't leave now either we will be dead or we won't remember anything!"

"Wait, what do you mean?" Su asks.

"Your son, Baatar Jr. wants to release the memory serum and the death serum on the city. So unless you want to be here when that happens then I'll leave you and your family in the cells. If not, then I suggest you come with me."

I lock her cell again and start to walk away, when she yells. "No wait Christine, I want to come with you. Don't leave me and my family here!"

I turn around and say. "Now that is what I like to hear."

I unlock Su's cell and we walk towards the other cells. First I unlock Wing's cell and then I unlock Wei's cell and give them back all their armor.

---

As we walk towards the living room I look back at them and say. "I'm sorry for all the pain me and Kuvira caused you and your family."

It takes them a few minutes to respond. "It's okay. We knew you and Kuvira didn't mean it."

I'm just about to respond when we reach the living room door. I open it up and Kuvira jumps off the couch and gives me a questioning look. "You'd better have a good explanation for this."

"Of course I do," I say. I pull out the two vials that I had in my pocket. "I was telling you that Baatar was up to something, but you didn't listen." I hand her both vials and she takes them and looks from the red serum to the purple serum, then back at me.

"What is this?" she asks.

"Well the red one is the memory ser—"

She glares at me. "I know the red one is memory serum, but what about this one?" She holds up the vial with the purple serum inside.

"That is the death serum." I say.

"Why do you have death serum with you?" she asks raising an eyebrow.

"As I been trying to tell you, Baatar wants to use it on Chicago and—" I look back at Su and her family. "And Zaofu."

"What?" says Su and her two sons. Kuvira looks at me in shock and so does Su and her boys.

"Why?" They all ask.

"I don't know," I say. "All I know is that we need to get everyone out of Chicago and we need to get them out fast, before Baatar releases it."

"When do you think he will release it?" Kuvira asks.

"I don't know."

"Alright," Kuvira says to the rest of us. "Let's go."

Chapter 12

We make our through the camp in Chicago, going door to door, telling the people to evacuate quickly and quietly. After our camp has been evacuated, we move onto the rest of the city and do the same thing. After half of the city is out, we walk towards the edge of the city and towards the train station to get a ride out of the city. I realize that in order to save Zaofu from the serum, that we need to get someone to operate the train so we can get there in time.

"Oh shoot!" I yell. "Oh crap!"

"What?" Everyone looks at me with concerned looks. "What is it?"

"I forgot that we need to get everyone out of Zaofu and we have only evacuated half of Chicago."

"What are we supposed to do?" Wing and Wei ask. "The train operator isn't here, so unless someone knows how to drive a train, then we are stuck here?"

I nod then I look at Kuvira and say. "I think you know how operate the train, am I right?"

Kuvira looks at us nervously. "Uhh. No. I don't. Sure I spent most of my time on the train during my campaign for uniting The Earth Empire, but I have never driven one before."

"Great," I sigh. "Now what are we going to do?"

"Oh I have an idea," says Su "Actually never mind. I was going to say that I know how to drive the train, but I don't sorry."

I sigh again. Then an idea pops into my head. "Wait," I say. "We don't have evacuate Zaofu, all we need to do is stop Baatar Jr. from releasing the serums, so while I go try to stop him, you four continue to evacuate the city, okay?"

I start to walk back to Erudite headquarters, but something tightens around my arm and I look back to see Kuvira gripping my arm.

"No! Christine I won't let you!" she says and I see tears forming in her eyes.

"I'll be fine." I say and I try to start walking again, but she is still holding my arm.

"No!" she says. "I won't let you go, never!"

I glare at her. "We're running out of time! I can do this, just trust me."

"Okay," she says. "Promise me you will be alright and you make it out in time."

I look at Su and her family. "Go now and start evacuating the rest of city."

They nod and run into the city.

After their gone I turn back to Kuvira. "Promise me you will make it out in time." she says again.

I take a deep breath. "Yes. I will make it out in time."

But her grip doesn't loosen.

"I promise." I finally say.

She lets go of my arm and gives me a hug and I return it with a tighter hug.

She looks at me and says. "Go save the city!"

I nod and she runs into the city to help Su and her family.

I take a few deep breaths and start my way towards Erudite headquarters.

Chapter 13

As I make my back into the city, I start to think about what I'm going to do when I get there. *Am I going to use the memory serum on Baatar so he doesn't remember who he is or am I going to use the death serum on him to end his life?*

I shudder at the thought, but keep moving forward. When I get close, I have trouble breathing, so I just breathe shallow breaths, soon I'm in front of Erudite headquarters and I stand outside for a few moments. Then I push the doors open and I walk inside.

Once I'm inside I look around and notice that none of the guards are there. *Where are they?* I think. *It doesn't matter.*

All that does matter is me getting to the lab and stopping Baatar Jr. from releasing the serum on Chicago and quite possibly on Zaofu. When I get to the lab though it's empty, I walk inside and the door behind me closes and locks. I try the door but it doesn't budge. I look around and I don't see anything.

"Well, well, well," says a voice. "Glad you could make it. Though I am surprised that you came alone, not very smart of you now is it?"

I see a dark figure with glasses and short black hair come out from the corner.

"Baatar." I growl.

"Hello Christine. What brings you here?"

"I'm here to stop you from releasing the memory and death serum on Chicago." I say as I drop into my metalbending stance.

"Oh are you now?" he says with a smirk. "You came here with nobody to help you. Plus you have no weapons. So I don't what you are going to do."

I laugh. "Just in case you have forgotten, which I think you have, but I can do this."

I take a deep breath and fire out two strips of metal from my uniform and aim them at him. He dodges the attack and runs toward the machine will release both the memory and death serum. I throw some more metal in his way to block his path so he can't release it. By the time I actually hit him with a metal strip, I'm to tired and weak to continue. Baatar lets out a scream as the metal strip strikes him in the chest, but he keeps moving. I lean against the wall and he uses that as an advantage and to run over and hit a button on the machine and the serum starts to fill the air. I try not to breathe it in.

Baatar smirks at me. "Now you can stay here and try to stop me and die trying or you can go save your friends and maybe get out of alive. What will it be?"

I gasp and breathe in the death serum more than I do with the memory serum. I nod towards the door and with a smirk he says. "Good choice."

He opens up the door and I fall to the ground and crawl out of the room. Once I'm in the hallway I run through the building until I get outside and I take deep breaths of clean air, seconds before the serum fills the air, making it smell like smoke and spice. I run through the city trying to avoid the airborne serum. I know what I need to do, I need to find Kuvira and Su and her family before it's too late.

I keep running.

Chapter 14

As I run through the city I call out for Kuvira, Su and her family. *I might not make in time.* I think as I run.

"Su, Kuvira where are you?" I call out and I start to cough as more serum fills my lungs, making it harder to breathe.

I call for them again and get a response this time. "Over here!" says a voice.

I look to my left and see Kuvira standing with Su and her two sons, I run up to them and give them a hug. I try to breathe, but it comes out as a cough.

"Oh god!" says Su. "Are you okay?"

I nod.

"Are you sure?" Kuvira asks.

"Yes." I say weakly.

Seconds later I fall, but before I hit the ground Kuvira catches me and holds me in her arms. I let out a pained breath as my lungs start to shut down from lack of oxygen.

"It's okay, you're all right, you'll be fine." Kuvira says as her eyes fill with tears that are more visible now, than the last time she almost cried.

"K-Kuvira?" I look up at her.

"I'm here, I'll always be, I'll never leave you." she says as the tears in her eyes get bigger.

"I'm sorry…" I whisper, leaning my head against her chest. "I left you and I promised… that was the one thing… I wouldn't do…"

Kuvira starts to cry and says. "At least we tried to save Chicago and Zaofu."

"Yeah," I say, then I add. "Don't break your promise…" I continue my voice getting softer and weaker by the second.

Kuvira let's a tear drop. "I won't."

I smile softly and my eyes close. I was still dying slowly, but I could still tell what was going on around me.

"Christine?" Kuvira says. But I was too weak to say anything. As the serum was shutting my body down faster and faster by the second.

"No… Christine… you promised you wouldn't leave me!" Then she whispers one last thing that I could hear which was: "Please… wake up…"

My body goes limp in Kuvira's arms and that is all.

Epilogue

*Two years later…*

Kuvira stands by Christine's grave site in Chicago, It's been two years since her death and that was the hardest day of Kuvira's life. When Kuvira had lost Christine forever. Kuvira will always remember that day; the day they had stopped Baatar from releasing the memory and death serum on Chicago and Zaofu.

*Why did Christine have to leave me like that?*

"Why did you leave me like that Christine. Why?" Kuvira shouts. "You said you would never leave me and yet at the time I need you most, you decide to."

Kuvira starts to cry.

*Kuvira, Su, Baatar Sr. and the twins Wing and Wei, all stand around the casket that holds my body.*
*My ghost stands behind Kuvira, who is crying because of my death, I've never seen or heard her cry that hard before.*
*"Why did you leave me like that?" Kuvira says.*
*"I'm sorry," I try to say, but I know she can't hear me. "I never meant to leave you."*

---

Kuvira is still standing by Christine's grave. But just before she gets ready to leave, she hears someone say. "I'm sorry I left you, I never meant to."

Kuvira wipes her eyes and says. "Wait do I hear someone talking or have I been here too long?"

The voice responds with. "You heard someone talking to you."

"Alright enough." says Kuvira as she launches a rock at the source of the sound.

"Whoa easy!" responds the voice. "It's just me don't worry."

"Wait I know that voice..." Kuvira says.

She turns around and sees someone who is ghostly pale and is wearing an old Earth Empire uniform and is standing behind her.

"Christine!" Kuvira says.

"Hello," I say. "Its been a while, almost two years."

"How are you here?" Kuvira asks.

"Well," I say. "You wanted to see me, so I thought I would come by and visit."

"It took you long enough." Kuvira says with a laugh.

"I'm sorry I left you."

"Its okay at least you're here now... sort of."

"Anytime you need me just call."

"Okay." she says.

"Okay."

Just like that Christine was gone. Kuvira stood by her grave and smiled, she knew one day that Christine would be back.

I Will Try To Fix You
(Book 2)

Prologue
*Two years earlier...*
Kuvira stands by Christine's grave site in Chicago, Its been two years since her death and that was the hardest day of Kuvira's life. When Kuvira had lost Christine forever. Kuvira will always remember that day; the day they had stopped Baatar from releasing the memory and death serum on Chicago and Zaofu.

*Why did Christine have to leave me like that?*

"Why did you leave me like that Christine. Why?" Kuvira shouts. "You said you would never leave me and yet at the time I need you most, you decide to."

Kuvira starts to cry.

*Kuvira, Su, Baatar Sr. and the twins Wing and Wei, all stand around the casket that holds my body.*

*My ghost stands behind Kuvira, who is crying because of my death, I've never seen or heard her cry that hard before.*

*"Why did you leave me like that?" Kuvira says.*

*"I'm sorry," I try to say, but I know she can't hear me. "I never meant to leave you."*

---

Kuvira is still standing by Christine's grave. But just before she gets ready to leave, she hears someone say. "I'm sorry I left you, I never meant to."

Kuvira wipes her eyes and says. "Wait do I hear someone talking or have I been here too long?"

The voice responds with. "You heard someone talking to you."

"Alright enough." says Kuvira as she launches a rock at the source of the sound.

"Whoa easy!" responds the voice. "Its just me don't worry."

"Wait I know that voice..." Kuvira says.

She turns around and sees someone who is ghostly pale and is wearing an old Earth Empire uniform and is standing behind her.

"Christine!" Kuvira says.

"Hello," I say. "It's been a while, almost two years."

"How are you here?" Kuvira asks.

"Well," I say. "You wanted to see me, so I thought I would come by and visit."

"It took you long enough." Kuvira says with a laugh.

"As I said before: I'm sorry I left you."

"Its okay at least you're here now... sort of."

"Anytime you need me just call."

"Okay." she says.

"Okay."

Just like that Christine was gone. Kuvira stood by her grave and smiled, she knew one day that Christine would be back.

Chapter 1

*Four years later...*

Kuvira walks towards Su Beifong's house in Chicago, they had moved here after Christine's death. She let out a depressed sigh as she walks into the house, its been almost four years since, she and Christine had saved Chicago and Zaofu from Baatar Jr., who had released both the memory and death serum, Christine had died in the process of stopping him. After her death, all of the memory and death serum in the air had disappeared completely, so no one else was affected by it.

*Great. I've lost Christine and then I had lost Baatar Jr. Well that doesn't matter I mean he's the one who killed Christine after all.* Thought Kuvira.

Kuvira continued her way into Su's house, well technically it was her house too. Su was nice enough to adopt Kuvira and now she was officially a part of Su's family. It was the one thing Kuvira had hoped for. To be part of the family, I mean Su had gotten Kuvira adoption papers and all that was needed was

Kuvira's signature, she only wished that Christine was here to be a part of her family as well. She pushed the thought out of her mind for the time being. When Kuvira reached the doors that lead into the living room, she stopped suddenly and put an ear against the door to listen to the conversations that were being taken place on the other side of the door.

"...took you long enough to show up." says Su.

"I know I didn't mean to be late." says a voice.

"Well I'm sure Kuvira would freak out if she knew you were here." Su responds with a laugh.

"Or maybe she would she would be happy." says the voice.

Kuvira stood in confusion for a few seconds and then walks away from the living room door and goes for a walk around the Beifong estate for a little bit to calm herself down, but that didn't work, she was still thinking about the conversation that she had overheard.

*Who was Su talking to on the other side of the door? Why would I freak out if I knew who was there?*

These thoughts haunted Kuvira for about three weeks and she would often walk towards the living room doors and try to see if she could hear anything else, but there was nothing. Kuvira started to think that she was going insane, and after two more weeks of hearing conversations on the other side of door, Kuvira decided to ask Su about it. But Su had declined any knowledge of such conversations taking place. Kuvira decided that she's had enough of Su lying to her. So she would wander the halls after everyone but Su had gone to sleep and decided to listen in on the the next conversation that would take place.

So later that night when Su had walked to the living room and closed the door. Kuvira would linger outside until, she hears Su and the other voice start to talk again.

"Sorry I'm late," Su says. "Its just that whenever I try to meet with you I always run into Kuvira and I don't want to tell her about this."

"I know," says the voice. "I mean it would be nice if Kuvira knew that we were talking, but it would either freak her out or she would be heartbroken."

"Yeah, you're right." says Su.

*Alright enough of this.* Kuvira thought as she opened the door to the living room without knocking. "What is going on here Su?" she says. "Why do you keep coming in here and..." She looks over Su's shoulder at the person standing there. "Wait I recognize you," she says as she takes a closer look at the person who is standing there. "Christine?"

I smile. "Hello, it's nice to see you again."

## Chapter 2

*Christine is here? No that can't be right, she died six years ago. Did she die? Or did she fake her death and if so, then where is Baatar Jr.?* Kuvira thought.

"Alright," she says. "What is going on here?"

"I'm alive. That's what's going on here." I say.

"Okay," she says. "If you're here, then where is Baatar Jr.?"

Su and I look at each other and sigh, before looking at Kuvira again. "He's dead."

"Wait," she says. "How can you be alive and how can Baatar Jr. be dead?"

I sigh and say. "Remember how you came to visit my gravesite, six years ago and I started talking to you."

"Yes. I remember because I had throw a rock at you that night." she says.

"Yes. I will always remember that because...," I take my arm out of my shirt sleeve and show her the scar on my arm from where the rock had hit me. Both Kuvira and Su both just stare at the scar on my arm in shock. "Yep," I say. "I'll always have that now."

"You threw a rock at Christine!" Su says. "I thought at least when she showed up you would be nice to each other."

"Wait, you've known that she's been alive for six years and you never told me?" she says to Su.

"Yeah." Su says with a sigh.

"Mom!" Kuvira says. "Why didn't you tell me?"

"I didn't want to hurt you, so I kept it quiet." Su says.

"Wait, did Kuvira just call you "mom?" I ask Su.

"Yes she did," Su says looking at me. "Soon after you had supposedly died, I had got her adoption papers, to which she signed and now she is a part of our family."

"What do you mean "our family"?" Kuvira asks. "Is Christine a part of the family to?"

"Not exactly, " Su says. "she's one of my guards. "

"Well as long as she's alive, I love it." Kuvira runs up to me and gives me a tight hug, picking me up in the process.

"Its... nice... that you... like it," I say between breaths. "Okay... you... can... put... me... down... now."

"I'm glad you're here. I missed you." Kuvira says as tears start to roll down her face.

"Well I did say that I was never going to leave you and I kept that promise."

"I know," she says. "I know."

Chapter 3

"So the coffin that supposedly was holding your body was actually holding Baatar Jr.'s body?" Kuvira asks me as we walk around the house.

"Yeah." I say.

"So where have you been for the last six years?" Kuvira asks.

"I've been here. In Chicago the entire time."

"How?" she asks.

"Did you notice that Su had recruited a new guard for her security force, six years ago?"

"Yes, I did," she says, then she asks. "Why was that you?"

I nod.

She takes her time responding."Okay so be clear: So you had never died, the coffin that was supposedly holding your body wasn't holding it, it was Baatar Jr's body, you've been working here the entire time, also every time I would walk to the living room and I could hear her talking to someone, it was you and when I was talking to your ghost supposedly by your grave, that was you?

"Yeah," I sigh. "I'm sorry. I never meant to make you feel so depressed."

Kuvira turns to look me. "So what you did to me was pretty much like what Korra had done after Zaheer had poisoned her, the only difference was: You faked your death, and you were here for six years and never told me or came to visit."

"I'm sorry," I say. "I didn't mean to hurt you."

"Well you sure did, I mean what person would fake their death and not come to visit the one person that cared about them?" Kuvira says angrily.

"I'm sorry." I say again.

"Sorry won't cut it Christine. Kuvira says as she starts to jog down the hallway.

"Wait!" I call.

"Just leave me be!" shouts Kuvira as she turns a corner.
I stop trying to following her and stand in the hallway at a loss.

Su walks up behind me, puts a hand on my shoulder. "We need to be patient with her, it will take time for her to accept what has happened."

"Maybe if you had told her sooner, we wouldn't be in this mess!" I yell. Then I start to jog down the opposite hallway.

"Wait Christine!" Su calls after me.

"Just leave me alone!" I yell as I turn the corner.

Chapter 4
I walk around the garden for a little bit as I try to cool down. But I have too many thought coursing through my mind, along with a dozen other emotions like: Sadness, Happiness, Anger and Loneliness.
*I should've told Kuvira that I was alive, I should've.* I think. I drop to the ground and start to cry. I cry until I feel sick.

"You feeling okay?" says a voice.
I turn my head to the side and see Baatar Sr. standing beside me.

"Yes." I say as I wipe my eyes and take a few deep breaths.
He sits down on the ground beside me and I look down at the ground.

"Oh come on," he says. "Everyone with eyes can see that you're not okay. You can tell me, what is it?"

I look at him and say. "Well its been six years since I supposedly died and did I ever tell Kuvira about it? No."

"I understand that it would've been hard for you to tell Kuvira, that you had faked your death. But now she knows and it will time for her to come around." he says.

"Maybe if I had just stayed with you guys and hadn't tried to stop Baatar Jr. from releasing the serums, none of this would've happened." I say with frown.

"But if you hadn't stopped him we would all be dead." he says.

"I know," I say and I look away again. "But it seems that no matter what I do. I only make things worse."

"We'll work through it as a family." he says.

I look at him again. "Thank you."

We get up and I give him a hug.

"Thank you." I say again.

"Your welcome, if you need anyone to talk to, then you can come talk to anyone of us. You're "family" after all."

---

That evening, when everyone else is asleep, I walk towards my bedroom, when I get there I notice that my door is closed and the light is on inside. That's odd. I thought that I had left my door open and turned the off the light before I left this morning. I open up the door, walk inside and close the door, then I turn around and see Kuvira sitting on my bed and she is staring at the floor.

I walk over to my bed and sit next to her, she continues to stare at the floor.

"Hi." I say.

She lifts her head to look at me. "Hey."

"What's on your mind?"

"I've been thinking about how you had faked your death and that you've been alive this entire time. At least you're here now." she says.

"I'm sorry if I hurt you."

"Its okay," she says. "I'm sorry that I yelled at you today."

"Its alright. I deserved it." I say with a small laugh.

"Yeah you kinda did." she says and she smiles.

Kuvira gets up to leave, but I stop her. "Hey, can you stay with me tonight?"

She smiles again and lays down next to me.

"Thank you." I say.

"Shh, just close your eyes and go to sleep." she says in a soft voice.

I nod and close my eyes. Moments later I fall asleep.

Chapter 5

I wake up in my bedroom in Su's house or should I say our house, I try to roll over on my side but I find that can't because Kuvira is holding onto me. I smile and lay back down. Kuvira's grip on me loosens as she starts to wake up. Then I roll over so we are face to face, Kuvira pops one eye open and then the other.

"Morning." I say.

"Hey." she says.

"How was your sleep?" I ask.

"Wonderful," she says. "Yours?"

"Great, I haven't slept like that in ages." I say, cracking a smile.

She lets out a laugh.

"Well I think we should go downstairs for breakfast," I say. "What do you think?"

"That sounds like a great idea." she says as we get out of bed.

---

Once we are dressed and ready to go, we walk downstairs. We sit side-by-side at the breakfast table, along with Su, Baatar Sr, Opal, the twins Wing and Wei and finally Huan who is now Su's oldest son, now that Baatar Jr. isn't here. We have pancakes and orange juice for breakfast. I turn towards Su and say. "So what do we have planned for today?"

Su looks at me. "How about you practice your metalbending, I know that it does need work."

"Sounds wonderful," Then I turn towards Kuvira and say. "Why don't you come practice with me, I know that you're a master metalbender but maybe we could spar with each other."

Kuvira looks at me and says. "Okay if you say so, but just so you are warned, I'm very good at it. So don't cry if I beat you."

I laugh. "You have no idea what's coming to you."

Kuvira raises an eyebrow at me. "Oh alright, bring it on."

Chapter 6

After breakfast we go outside, once we reach the sparing circle both me and Kuvira drop into our metalbending stances.

"Alright so Kuvira what you need to do to help—" Su starts to say but I cut her off.

"Su unless you've forgotten, Kuvira is a master metalbender." I say.

"I know but I was going to instruct her to instruct you on what you need to do." Su says.

"You do know that I know how to metalbend right, you should remember that." I say with a smirk.

"Oh okay. Then start." Su says.

Me and Kuvira circle each other for a few minutes. I shoot two metal strips from my uniform and aim them at Kuvira, she guides the strips away from herself, then metalbends out her cable at me. I duck under it, before it hits me and I grab it and wrap it around my wrist. Kuvira motions her hand upwards, so that the metal which is wrapped around me, launches me into the air. While I'm in air she tries to shoot several metal strips at me. But I evade the attack and fire my cable at her and it wraps around her ankle. As I land on the ground I metalbend my cable towards myself and Kuvira slides towards me, but seconds before she hits me, I undo the cable from her ankle and she skids to a stop, just inches from my feet. I look down at her and smirk. I help her up and give her a hug.

"Wow," says Su, her hanging open with shock. "Where did you learn that?"

"Kuvira taught me some of that." I say with a smile.

"I did? When?" Kuvira asks.

"Uh. Six years ago, while I was still working for you."

"Right." she says.

"But where did you learn the rest of it?" Both of them ask.

"The rest of it is self-taught." I say.

"That may explain why we've never seen anything like it." Su and Kuvira say.

"Yep," I say. "Alright let's take a break."

We walk back to the house side-by-side.

## Chapter 7

After the metalbending session me and Kuvira take a walk around the estate, instead of going back to the house. We walk into the city and walk to a restaurant, more specifically a noodle restaurant.

"You'll love this, Bolin and I went to one like this after Korra had visited Zaofu and now there's one here in Chicago." says Kuvira as we walk into the restaurant.

"Yum, noodles are my favorite." I say, with a light laugh.

"Well, if you love noodles you'll love this one even more." he walks up to the guy at the front desk and says. "I have a reservation for two"

"First names please." says the man without looking up.

"Kuvira and Christine." she says.

The man behind the desk looks up, when he hears both our names. He looks from Kuvira to me and back again. He just stands there for a few minutes before saying. "Yes. Right this way ladies."

We follow him to our table and we sit down. I look around the restaurant and don't see anyone else here. I look at Kuvira and say. "Where's everyone else?"

She looks at me and says. "I booked out the entire restaurant, for our first date, since we've never been on one."

"Aww, you didn't have to do that." I say smiling.

"Oh, but I wanted to," she says smiling back at me, then she adds. "There's something you should know about me... I always get what I want."

I let out a laugh and say. "Well thank you."

"Your welcome." she says.

I was just about to say something when the waiter comes over with two bowls of steaming, hot noodles and sets them down.

"I don't think you've have th s type of noodle, have you?" she asks.

"Nope." I say as I shovel a spoonful into my mouth.

"They're delicious, aren't they."

"Mmhmm."

By the time Kuvira has started hers, I'm already done mine.

"Whoa," she says. "I don't think I've ever seen you eat that fast."

"They're so good." I say and then I look at her bowl.

She looks at me and says. "Not a chance." Then she finishes her bowl.

---

When we're done eating, we walk back to the house and once we get there we sit down on couch.

I close my eyes for a moment, then I hear someone say. "Well it looks like you girls had fun."

I open my eyes and find Su standing by the couch.

"Yeah we did." I say as I look at Kuvira, who has fallen asleep.

"Well I'll let you two sleep." she says and then she walks away.

I close my eyes again and without meaning to I fall asleep.

Chapter 8

That morning I wake up on the couch  alone. I sit up and look around to see if I can find Kuvira, but I can't. So I get up and walk to my bedroom only to find her sleeping on my bed. I let out a quiet giggle as I walk over to my bed and give her a playful smack on the cheek, she wakes with a start and I start laughing. Once she realizes its only me, she gives me a playful shove and I stumble backwards, hit the wall and fall to the floor, which only makes me laugh harder. She gets up and runs over to me and picks me up off the floor.

"Are you okay?" she asks.

"I'm fine." I say still laughing.

"Oh thank goodness, I though that I had hurt you." she says.

"Nah. It takes a lot more than that to hurt me." I say with a smile, then I start to laugh again.

"What's going on in here?" says Su as she bursts through the door, eyes wide and alarmed.

"Nothing." I say.

She looks from me to Kuvira and narrows her eyes at her. "What are you doing?"

"Nothing." she says.

She looks back to me and I quit laughing.

"Are you okay?" Su asks me.

"Yeah, I'm fine." I say.

"Okay." she says and she walks out of the room.

"What was that all about?" Kuvira says.

I shrug and say. "I don't know, she's always been like that."

"Huh, well that's interesting. Do you know why?" she asks.

"Nope."

"Okay. Well we should go downstairs." she says.

"Okay."

---

When we get downstairs, we go to the living room and sit down on the couch. Then I look her and say. "Do you want to practice metalbending again?"

"Sure." she says.

---

When we get outside, we start to circle each and eventually Kuvira makes the first move. This time instead of firing her metal strips, she launches a meteor at me. I duck and it flies past me.

I laugh. "Okay, so this is how its going to be."

"Bring it on." she says.

I bend a piece of the meteor and shape it into a spear, then I bend it at her. When it get close to her she bends it back into its original form and throws it at me. I dodge the attack and run at her and tackle her into the ground and we start to wrestle. Then I look up, only to see, Baatar Sr, Su, Huan and the twins—Wing and Wei—all staring at us. They look at both of us in shock and Kuvira uses that as an advantage to throw me off. Then she tackles me to ground and I look at her and say. "Kuvira?"

"I've got you now." she says with a smile.

"Kuvira?" I say again.

I try to move, but she has me pinned to the ground. Then she says "Not now, I'm having fun wrestling with you."

"Kuvira!" I say more sternly this time.

"What?" she says finally.

"We're being watched." I say.

She turns around, only to see everyone staring at us.

"Oh," she says. Then she clears her throat. "Okay then."

Chapter 9

Kuvira gets up off the ground and then helps me up.

"Well, that was interesting." Wing and Wei say.

"Yeah, it was." says Huan.

"What were you guys doing?" Baatar Sr. and Su ask.

"Metalbending." Kuvira says.

"Oh okay, because I came out to get you guys for dinner and I found that all the meteors were lying on the ground and then the next thing I notice was you two tackling each other to the ground." Su says with a laugh.

"Well, we were metalbending, but then it turned into wrestling for some reason." I say.

"Well that makes more sense." Baatar Sr. says.

Su looks at both of us and says. "Come on, hurry up, we have a special guest joining us for dinner."

---

When we get to the dining hall and I see who's there, I stop in the middle of a step and Kuvira runs into me.

"Hey, watch where... you're... going." she says, as she looks at the person who's sitting at the table.

"Korra?" We both say.

"Hello," she says to Kuvira, then she looks at me and with a questioning look and says. "Christine?"

"Hi." I say.

"Wait. I thought you were dead." Korra says.

"Well, It's a long story. I'll tell you later."

"Okay," she says. "Where's Baatar Jr.?"

Me and Kuvira look at each other and then back at Korra and say. "He's dead."

"Okay. I assume you'll tell me all this later?" she asks.

Me and Kuvira nod and sit down at the dinner table next to Korra.

"Well this is awkward." Kuvira says.

"Yeah I wasn't expecting her to be here." I say.

"Me neither."

Kuvira turns to Korra and says. "So what brings you here?"

"Oh. Well I thought that I would come by and visit. Its been awhile since I've been here. You know besides from having to battle for a city."

"Oh I see." says Kuvira and her hands tighten into fists.

I look over at Korra and shoot her a dirty look, then I grab one of Kuvira's hands and she relaxes and links her fingers with mine. Then she looks at me and mouths the words "thank you." I nod, look back at Korra and say. "Hey did you want to practice metalbending with me later?"

"Sure," Korra says then she adds. "Wait you can metalbend?"

"Yep." I say with a smirk.

"Okay. let's do it." she says.

Chapter 10

After dinner Korra and I walk to the sparring area. Both Korra and I drop into our metalbending stances.

Kuvira walks up beside us and says. "Alright, start."

I raise an eyebrow at Korra, knowing that it always drives her nuts. Not even two seconds after I had done that, I was having metal sheets thrown at me. I quickly dart out of the way and bend some of the meteor at her. Korra guides it around herself and aims it back at me. I dodge the attack and shoot some metal strips at her. Korra deflects the attack and bends her metal rope at me. I wrap it around my wrist and before she knows what going on, I launch her into the air and as she falls I shoot some more of the meteor at her. It hits her in the stomach and she falls to the ground. After she gets up off the ground though, she puts a hand up signaling for me to stop.

"Wow," she says after a few minutes. "Your amazing at this Christine."

"Don't give me all the credit Kuvira taught me that." I say and I give Kuvira a smile.

Korra gives Kuvira a smile and then says. "You're a great teacher you know that?"

"Thank you." says Kuvira.

"So I don't mean to be a pain," Korra says. "But I'm still confused by how you're alive."

"No, its okay you're not being a pain." I say and I tell her what I had told everyone else.

"Huh. That's very interesting," Korra says, as I finish "So what you did, was pretty much what I did."

"Yeah," I sigh, then I say. "Oh did you know, that Su adopted Kuvira, and now she's a part of her family."

"No I didn't.," she says. "So how has it been for Kuvira?"

"Wonderful," I say. "You should've seen Kuvira, when she found out that I was alive."

"What did she do?" Korra asks.

"Oh you know, she ran up to me, gave me a really tight hug and then started to cry happily."

"Oh and you also told me that Baatar Jr. is dead, how did Kuvira handle that?" Korra asks.

"Well she wasn't really sad about that, I mean he did try to kill me after all." I say with a shrug.

"Oh, well that does seem like a reasonable reaction," she says. "Anyway we should get back to them, I bet they already miss us."

"Alright let's go." I say.

Chapter 11

Me and Korra walk back to the living room and sit down on the couch.

"Whew. I'm tired what about you?" Korra asks.

"Nope." I say, with a grin.

"How are you not tired? I mean we just spent two hours sparring with each other." she says.

"Well, if you spent three years working for Kuvira and always having to either protect her or having to defending yourself, then you end up being on alert all the time." I say.

"But I'm always on alert and having to protect the world, so ha!" Korra says with a smirk.

"Fine, you win."

Later that day, we walk to the dining hall and I sit down with Korra sitting on my left and Kuvira sitting on my right. I turn to Korra and ask. "So what brings you back here?"

Korra looks at me. "I already told you."

"I know, but you only told me half of the truth." I say.

"Huh, what do you mean I only told you half of the truth?"

"Christine can tell when you're keeping something from her." Kuvira says turning toward Korra.

"Oh. Well I'm—" Korra starts to say, but then the door to the dining hall opens, cutting off her words.

Everyone who is at the table looks over at the door only to see Lin walking in, with her usual scowl on her face. She looks from Korra to Kuvira. When she sees Kuvira though she walks over to her and grabs her by the collar of her shirt and shoves her against the wall, face first and yells. "Why in the world is Kuvira in here!?"

"What are you doing?" I ask Lin.

Lin ignores me and looks at Su and raises an eyebrow at her sister.

"Lin, what are you doing?" Su asks with a horrified look.

When Lin doesn't answer and doesn't let Kuvira go. Su gets up from the table and walks over to her sister and yells. "Let go of my daughter!"

Lin gives Su a shocked look as she lets go of Kuvira. Kuvira falls and I catch her before she hits the floor.

"Your daughter?" Lin asks.

"Yes. Kuvira is my daughter, I adopted her six years ago." Su says.

"Oh. Oops." Lin says and she shakes her head. Then both Lin and Su walk back to the table. A few seconds later Lin turns to Korra and says. "We need to get you out of here."

"Why?" Korra asks.

Lin sighs and looks at her sister, who nods. Lin looks back at Korra. "Its Zaheer."

Chapter 12

"What? I thought he was in prison." Korra says.

"Not anymore and he's coming for you again," Lin says. "We need to get you out of here now!"

"What? No! I'll be fine." Korra says.

"Yeah, she'll be fine." Kuvira insists.

"She has us." I say and I smile at Kuvira.

"I don't care!" Lin yells. "He'll be here soon!"

"What will happen when he gets here? Su asks. "As far as what you've told us he won't have a good enough reason, for Korra to turn herself over."

"Umm, yeah he kind of does," Lin says nervously. "he has the entire Air Nation held captive right now."

"Not again," Korra says as she drops to her knees. "This can't be happening again, when I had talked to him before, he said that he's changed."

"For all you know, he could have been lying the entire time, so that he could earn your trust." Lin says.

Korra just shakes her head.

Later that day, I pull Korra aside so that can talk to her.

"I have an idea Korra, you don't have to give yourself up." I say with a smile.

"What are you talking about? If I don't he'll wipe out the Air Nation." she says.

"I know," I say. "But I know you have the ability to give bending to other people."

"Yeah," she says. "Where are you going with this?"

"Well I was thinking that if you were able to give all your power, including The Avatar State to me. Then I could go and you could stay and you would still have all your power."

"What?" she says in shock. "What about Kuvira? You can't just leave her again."

"She won't be alone, she'll have you."

"No. I won't let you go!" Korra says.

"You have too! I can't just let Zaheer try to kill you again." I say, my voice more stern this time.

"Okay," she says. "Then meet me outside, just after dark."

"Okay." I say and Korra walks away, I wait until she's out of the room, before I feel the tears come.

Later that night after everyone but Korra and I are asleep. We walk outside and Korra tells me to get down on my knees and I do as I'm told. Korra took in a deep breath and closed her eyes, then reached forward to place one of her thumbs on my forehead. With her other hand she holds my shoulder. When her eyes opened again, they glowed bright, empowered by the Avatar State. Her points of contact on me soon glowed as well. Within a few brief seconds, the light faded, both from Korra's hands and her eyes. She takes a step back and allows me to stand.

"Did it work?" I ask.

"I should have," Korra says. "I definitely felt something happen. Give it a try."

I stand and take a deep breath and then shoot out two streams of water, one puff of air, three groups of rocks and four blasts of fire.

"Yes. It worked!" I turn back to Korra and give her a hug. "Thank you." I say as I hold back my tears.

"Alright, let's go tell everyone the news. Zaheer should be here by tomorrow." Korra says, with a sigh.

"Okay." I say and we walk back inside.


Chapter 13

When we get back inside, we expect to find everyone still asleep, but we don't. Instead we find everyone up and staring at us.

"What?" I say. "Why are you all staring at us?"

"What were you guys doing outside this late?" Su asks.

"We were...um." Korra starts, but I interrupt her. "Korra was just giving me access to all of the elements and the Avatar State, Why?"

Su was about to say something when Kuvira interrupts and says. "Why would Korra give you access to that unless you were planning on—" She stops mid-sentence and says. "Why Christine? We just became a family and now, you're going to disappear again." Then she starts to cry. "No! You can't leave me! You promised!"

"I'm sorry. But I can't let Zaheer kill Korra."

"But you promised." Kuvira repeats.

I walk up to her and hold onto her hands. "I know, but I have to do this, I'm sorry."

"Okay. But can you stay with me tonight? Since it will be our last night together." Kuvira says.

"Of course." I say.

Later that night I go back to my bedroom with Kuvira. We lie down on the bed next to each other.

"I don't want to lose you." Kuvira says.

"I know." I say.

"Then why are you going to leave me?" Kuvira asks as she tries to hold back her tears.

"I don't want to, but I can't let anyone else die because of me," I say. "I'm not worth it."

"You are worth it, you are worth it to me," Then she adds. "I love you."

"I love you too."

"Promise me that you're not going to leave, I want you to promise me that you won't go."

"I'm not going to make that promise, because you know that I will break it." I say.

"Well," Kuvira sighs. "Then I'll just have to let you go."

"No you don't, I'll always be with you. No matter what." I say.

"Okay. Well we should go to bed, you'll need your strength and energy for tomorrow." she says.

"Okay." I say and we both fall asleep.

Chapter 14

Me and Kuvira wake up, and walk downstairs, where we find Lin, Su, Baatar Sr. and Korra standing in the living room.

Zaheer and his team are standing just outside the door.

"Are you all ready to go?" Su asks me.

I nod. Kuvira walks up beside me and she rests her hand on my shoulder. I turn around and give her the tightest hug that I can muster and walk out the door. But once I'm outside I don't close the door. Instead I leave it open.

Zaheer walks towards me slowly and when he's inches from me, he stops, reaches for my hand and shakes it.

"Well, hello Christine," he says. Then he asks. "What are you doing here?"

I look at him and with a small smile I say. "You're here for the Avatar aren't you?"

"Yes," he says. "So if you could please hand her over, then that would be wonderful."

"Your looking at her." I say.

"Wait. I thought Korra was the Avatar." Zaheer says with a frown.

"Not anymore, I am," I say. "You don't believe me, just ask Korra herself."

"Yes. I would love proof." Zaheer says.

I nod towards Korra who steps outside and she tries to bend the elements and she also tries to enter The Avatar State but nothing works.

"Huh, that's interesting, now I would like to you to show me proof, that you are indeed the new Avatar."

"With pleasure." I say and I first let out a blast of air, then water, then earth and finally a blast of fire.

"Well then. You are the new Avatar, after all," he says with his unchanging smile. "Alright let's go."

"Can you please give me a minute, to say goodbye to my friends and family?" I say.

"Very well. Come board the airship when you're done." Zaheer says as his team retreat back to the airship.

I go back to the house, but I keep the door open. I walk up to Lin, Su, and Baatar Sr. and give them a hug. They all return the hug. Next I walk up to Korra and give her a super tight hug, she nearly squealed in pain from the force of the hug. She looks at me and whispers in my ear. "Good luck. We'll find the Airbenders and then get you out safely."

I nod and finally I turn towards Kuvira. Kuvira looks up from the ground and at me.

"Kuvira?" I say. But the words get stuck in my throat.

"Yes." she says.

"I want you to know, that no matter what happens I will always lov—"

I was about to finish the sentence when I had felt Kuvira press her lips against mine. I press a little closer and wrap my hands around the back of her neck.

When we break apart, she smiles and then blushes."Wow. I was not expecting that." she says.

"I love you," I say, then I give her another quick kiss. Then I turn towards the door, but before I walk out, I say with a smile. "I love you all and I'll see you soon."

Then I walk towards the airship and I get on, without looking back. Once the door is closed and the airship starts to take off, I sink to the floor and let the tears come. Its the only thing that will keep me calm, until we get to where we are going.

Chapter 15

I sit on the floor of the airship and try to move, but I always forget that my wrists and ankles are bound together with platinum chains and when I get up to move, I end up tripping and falling to the ground. So I just sit on the floor again and lean against the wall. I don't how long after I sat down, but at some point I close my eyes and fall asleep.

Su, Lin, Korra and Kuvira, all board their airship as they leave to find the Airbenders and save Christine from Zaheer, as she instructed before she left.

Kuvira let out a sad sigh as she looked out the window.

Korra walks up behind her and rested her hand on Kuvira's shoulder.

"I can't believe that Christine did this to save you and the Airbenders." says Kuvira as she starts to cry. She never cried in front of Korra, but she had too many emotions and thoughts going through her head at this moment to care.

"Don't worry, we'll get her and the Airbenders out safely." Korra says in a reassuring voice that seems to help Kuvira calm down a little.

"Thank you." Kuvira says, as she turned around and gives Korra a hug.

Korra freezed for a second, then relaxed into Kuvira's hug.

I wake with a start. Only to find that Zaheer has me slung over his shoulder.

"Oh hello," says Zaheer. "Did you have a good sleep?"

"Huh?" I say. Then I turn my head to side, and see Zaheer looking at me. "Zaheer!" I yell and try to move the rest of my body, but I find that I can't.

"If you're going to try to bend, then save it for later, right now I've got you chained and chi-blocked." Zaheer says with a smirk.

I sigh and close my eyes again. I know that I need to stay awake, but I'm too tired and weak to do so and once again I fall asleep.

---

      Kuvira, Korra, Lin and Su, walk out of their airship and look at their surroundings. They had just arrived at the Northern Air Temple, where Zaheer is holding the Airbenders. When they get to the entrance the lavabender—Ghazan—is standing there. Everyone stopped in their tracks and stand there, staring at him. Ghazan noddd towards the entrance, but everyone stayed still.

      Ghazan rolled his eyes. "Do you want the Airbenders or not?"

Everyone walked inside the temple and found Tenzin lying on the ground, Korra rushes forward and lifts him up off the ground. Tenzin mumbles something, but he has a cloth wrapped around his mouth. Korra takes the cloth from his mouth and then looked behind him, only to find that none of the other Airbenders are there.

      "Where are the Airbenders?" Korra asked him.

      "There not here, Zaheer never took them. He only took me." Tenzin says.

      "What!" Korra says in shock. "So he never took any of the Airbenders and he still has Christine held captive," She turns to the rest of the group and shouts. "We need to get out of here now!"

They get Tenzin off the ground and start to leave, but find that their path is blocked with lava and it starts to slowly move towards them. Kuvira blocks the path of the lava with some earth, but the lava burns through it.

      "Now what are we going to do?" Kuvira says.

      Tenzin looked over at the wall and then at Kuvira and says. "Kuvira can you get us through that wall?"

      "On it!" she says as she starts to bend through the wall.

      She bends through it until they get to a steep drop off. Everyone looks at the lava that's rushing towards them. Kuvira takes a deep breath, closes her eyes and runs towards the lava, she puts her hands up and presses them forward. The lava stops and turns solid.

      Korra look at her in shock and says. "You're a lavabender."

      Kuvira opens her eyes and stares at the now solid lava and says. "Huh, so I am."

Chapter 16

I wake up in a dark room, my wrists and ankles are still bound with the chains. I sigh and lean against the wall. Then I think *Maybe I can bend out of them.* So I take a deep breath and try to focus on the earth within the platinum. But I can't find any earth inside them. I lean against the wall again. Moments later the door to the room opens and Zaheer walks in with his team.

"Hello. It's nice to that you are awake." Zaheer says.

I scoff. "Since when does that matter to you? Didn't you want to rid the world of the Avatar?"

"If I wanted you dead I would've killed you already. But I know that Korra is still the old Avatar and that you had chi-blocked her just before we had arrived in Chicago and sadly for Korra she has been removed from power and soon you will be too." Zaheer says with a smirk.

"No!" I say and my heart breaks and I focus on the platinum itself. *Come on, come on.* I think. Zaheer turns towards Ghazan and nods. Ghazan starts the bend the lava and it slowly moves towards me.

I focus harder and the chains don't budge. I close my eyes and breathe in and out slowly, and ignore the lava that's coming towards me. I take another deep breath and *pop!*

I open my eyes only to find that I no longer have the chains linked together. I look down at the lava below my feet and quickly enter The Avatar State. I bend air at the lava and it turns to hard rock. Then I blast air at Ghazan and he flies backwards hitting the wall and he doesn't get up. Then I bend the chain at Zaheer and it wraps around him, then I bend the chain back towards myself and Zaheer flies towards me, but just before I can do anything else, Zaheer blasts me with air and I hit the wall. Then he tries to bend out the air from my lungs, but I don't let him get that far. I bend out a blast of fire at him and it hits the chain instead, setting him free. He takes that advantage to escape and flies out of the room with his airbending and I chase after him.

---

Korra and her team reach the place, where Christine is being held. When they reach the entrance however, Zaheer comes flying out in a panic, I follow him soon after. I bend the platinum chain at him again and it hits him this time.

Lin and Su stared at the platinum in shock, then at each other.

"Did Christine just bend platinum?" Korra asked.

"Yes she did," says Kuvira. "Come on we need to help her."

---

I finally catch up with Zaheer and when I do, I wrap the platinum chain around his ankle and slam him into the ground. As soon as I do that and land on the ground though, I suddenly can't breathe. Zaheer starts to take the air out of my lungs and I start to gasp, and he takes my final breath.
I fall to the ground and Zaheer starts to fly away, but Su stops him and traps him in rocks and earth. My vision starts to go blurry and then there is nothing.

Chapter 17

Kuvira ran over to Christine and grabbed her wrist to see if she can find a pulse, but there is nothing.
Kuvira, bends down and pressed her mouth to Christine's and breathes out, then she puts her palms on Christine's chest and presses down several times. Kuvira repeats the process several times, breathing air into Christine's lungs and then doing chest compressions. On the fifth time Kuvira tries this and Christine doesn't wake up, Kuvira drops to the ground and starts to cry. Seconds later I wake up and start to cough. Kuvira looks at me and gives me a kiss. My coughing stops as soon as she kisses me.

"Hey." I say weakly.

"I missed you, I thought you were going to die." Kuvira says through her crying.

"Well I'm not and I never will leave you." I say with a smile.

Kuvira laughs. "You are great at keeping that promise."

"Oh thank goodness you're okay." says Su, as she walks over to us.

"Hey Su." I say.

Then I look over to the left and see Korra standing there, her eyes full with tears.

"Korra." I say. She runs over and picks me up and gives me a hug.

Korra sets me down and we walk back to Lin who is standing in front of Zaheer to make sure that he stays put.

I walk up to Lin and give her a hug. Lin goes stiff for a moment and then relaxes and returns the hug. Zaheer looks at me and says. "No! How are you alive? I was sure that I had killed you."

I let go of Lin and look Zaheer in the eye and say. "I'm not sure if you've checked but as far as I know good always trumps evil."

Then I break apart the rocks and earth surrounding him, he stumbles forward and stands.

"Christine what are you doing?" Lin asks me.

I expect him to try to kill me again, but he stands there looking at me in confusion. I walk towards him and without warning, I punch him hard in the jaw. He falls backwards, hits the ground and doesn't get up. Everyone looks at me in shock for a few seconds, then both Korra and Kuvira walk up behind me and start laughing.

"Wow, that was awesome." Korra says to me.

"Yeah, that was awesome, *you* are awesome. Kuvira says.

"Thank you. You guys are awesome too." I say, still laughing.

"Alright let's go home." Su says.

---

When we get back to our house in Chicago, we walk to the living room and sit down on the couch. As soon as we sit down though I look at Korra and say. "I still need to give you back your bending."

"No you don't," Korra says. "I still have mine. You just had me chi-blocked before you left."

"Right," I say. "It will be interesting, having two Avatars help save the world."

"Well there's always a first time for everything, and no matter what we will always restore balance to the world." Kuvira says.

"Sounds perfect." I say.

## The Road To Redemption Is Hard Fought
### (Book 3)

Chapter 1

Christine

*Three months later…*

I walk around Chicago, It's night time now, but I am unable to sleep. Whenever I try to sleep, I keep having nightmares about Zaheer and how he tried to kill me. I know that it's only been three months, but I wish that I could just forget what had happened. I sigh and walk back to the house, when I get there though I see Kuvira standing in the living room.

I walk up beside her and say. "Hey."

She looks over her shoulder. "Hey."

I give her a hug.

"Can't sleep?" I ask.

She just shakes her head, then says. "No of course not."

"I'm still here, I'm not dead." I say.

"I know but, what if you had died? What if I was unable to save you? What if Zaheer had succeeded?"

"You do know that the "What ifs." never and didn't happen." I say.

"I know. But I don't know what I would've done if I had lost you." she says.

"You won't lose me. I promise."

She raises an eyebrow at me.

"I'm serious," I say. "You won't lose me."

"Okay." she says.

---

Later Kuvira and I sit on the couch and watch a movie. By the time we are done, Christine has already fallen asleep.

Kuvira looks down and smiles. Minutes later she falls asleep.

---

I wake up screaming. I look around and realize that I'm on the couch in my home and not with Zaheer as he tried to kill me. Korra comes running downstairs and with wide eyes she asks. "Are you okay? I just woke up to you screaming."

"I'm fine, I just had a bad dream." I say.

"What was it about?" Korra asks.

"It doesn't matter. It's over now." I say, still breathing heavily.

"Okay, but if you need anyone to talk to, then just call." she says.

"Okay."

Once Korra leaves though she sends Kuvira downstairs, Kuvira walks over to the couch and sits down next to me.

"Hey, what's up?" she asks me.

I shake my head. "Nothing."

"You're lying." she says.

"You metalbenders and your ability to tell if someone is lying." I mumble.

Kuvira laughs and then says. "Come on, what is it?"

"Well it's just…," I sigh. "It's just that I keep having dreams about Zaheer and how he tried to kill me."

"Okay, so do you know why you keep having them?" she asks.

"If I knew why, then I would be able to deal with them and I wouldn't be having them!" I snap.

"Okay, okay." Kuvira puts her hands up in defeat.

"I'm sorry." I say.

"It's okay." she says.

She leans over and gives me a kiss.

Chapter 2
Kuvira

The next morning me and Christine have breakfast, then take a drive around Chicago. Now that Christine is also an Avatar, she helps out Korra. I'm also part of their team. The radio in the car starts to make a static sound, I turn up the volume on the radio and we hear that there has been a robbery on Michigan Ave. We take a right at the next block only to find that, there is a car driving on the wrong side of the road. We chase after the car. Seconds later I bend my metal cable at the tire of the car and pull back. The tire pops off and the car skids to a stop. Three people run from the car and Korra bends a wall made of earth in front of them. Christine then bends water at the three people. Encasing them in ice. I walk to them and bend a few metal strips from my uniform and shape it into a pair of handcuffs.

"No. Wait. Don't!" says one of the bandits.

"Don't hurt us!" says another bandit.

"Why would I hurt you?" I say, confused and I drop my metal strips.

One of the other bandits opens her eyes and says. "Great Uniter Kuvira?"

I scowl at the girl and say. "What did you just call me?"

"I called you "The Great Uniter." says the female bandit with a smirk.

I let out a groan as I remember, what I did at the time I had earned the title. "The Great Uniter."

"Don't ever call me that again!" I yell.

"Kuvira? Are you okay?" Christine asks me.

"Oh okay," says the female bandit. "I won't call you that again. Great Uniter."

"Stop!" I yell. "Just stop!"

A dozen memories flood into my mind and I remember the time that I had taken over Zaofu, the time when I had chained the bandits to the train tracks and forced them to join me. When I had forced the states to join and the re education camps. The memories become to much and I break down. Christine rushes over to me and gives me a hug.

Then she turns back to the bandits and says. "What's wrong with you guys? First you rob a store and then you taunt Kuvira."

"I would expect that much, from someone who used to work for her. I mean as far as I know you were Kuvira's right-hand man." says the boy bandit with a laugh.

Christine lets out a yell, closes her eyes and blasts out a stream of water. She turns it into sharp ice spears and the bandits scream. Soon after the bandits start screaming, Christine opens her eyes and lets out a yelp before liquifying the ice. The water splashes onto the ground and so does the ice that was encasing the bandits. They take that advantage to run away.

"Are you okay?" I ask, as I walk up beside Christine.

"Yeah. I'm fine!" she says with a snap.

"Okay." I say unconvinced. Then I look in the direction of where the bandits took off.

"Well it looks like we lost this one." Korra says.

"We'll find them." I say.

"I hope so." says Christine with a growl.

"Hey, it's okay." I say.

"No. It's not okay." Christine spits back.

"You're right," I say as tears start to flow down my face. "It's not okay." I let out a yell of frustration.

"It's okay. It's okay." says Korra as she walks up beside me and gives me a hug. I relax for a moment before tensing up again.
I let out a sigh as I get back into the car, everyone follows soon afterwards.

"Alright, let's go get these guys." Korra says.
I rev the engine and then we take off.

Chapter 3
Christine
We drive through the city looking for the bandits and as Kuvira drives she lets out a frustrated sigh, and looks from me in the mirror to the road.

"Are you okay?" Korra asks Kuvira

"Oh yeah sure, I'm fine!" she snaps.

"No, you're not. I can tell." Korra says.

Kuvira revs the engine again and says. "I don't want to talk about it."

"Okay." Korra says. She looks at me and nods.

"Are you sure, you're okay?" I sigh. "If it's about me, then just spit it out."

Kuvira scoffs and says. "Of course, it's about you! I'm not sure what's going on inside your head, but you've been out of balance emotionally and mentally for three months."

"I haven't been out of balance, have I?" I turn towards Korra and she nods to confirm what Kuvira said.

"Come on what's going on with you?" Korra asks.
I shrug. "Nothing."

Kuvira slams on the brakes and the car comes to a sudden halt. "Get out!"

"What? No! Why?" I say.

"If you're not going to talk about what's going on with you then get out of the car!" Kuvira yells.

"Okay, fine!" I say and I get out of the car and close the door.
Kuvira starts to drive away, but I bend a giant metal wall in front of the car. Kuvira slams on the brakes to avoid hitting it.

"What are you doing?" Kuvira asks me, as she backs up the car.

"I'm not letting you go anyway until we've talked." I say with a glare.

"Uhh, why can't I bend this stupid wall?" Kuvira says as she tries to bend it away from the road.

"Because it's made of platinum, genius." I say with a smirk.

"Oh that's it!" Kuvira says as she gets out of the car. She drops into her metalbending stance. "I want you to bend away the wall or else."

"What are you going to do?" I say with a smirk.

Kuvira launches a rock at me and dodge the attack. I bend my metal cable at her and she jumps to the left to get out of the way.

"Come on guys. We shouldn't be fighting. We should be working." Korra says. But we ignore her. Kuvira was just about to fire two metal strips from her uniform, when I blast air at her. She flies backwards and hits the car.

I bend some water at her and she fires her metal cable at me.

After a round or two of fighting physically, I go into The Avatar State and launch a rock or two at Kuvira. She breaks the boulders apart with two metal strips from her uniform.

"I'm not going to let you win!" I say. My voice echoing, throughout the city.

After having watched this for too long, Korra decides to break it up. She ran up to Kuvira and grabbed her arms and yelled. "Stop!"

Kuvira stops instantly and relaxes, it takes Korra a little bit more time to calm me down though. By the time she has got me out of the Avatar State and calmed down. I had done a great deal of damage to the city.

"What happened?" I ask Korra.

"Um… you got into a fight with Kuvira and nearly destroyed the city."

I look around and my eyes go wide. "Uh oh."

"Now that you two are calm! We still need to go catch those bandits." Korra says.

"Right." I say.

We get back into the car and Korra says. "Um, Christine, you still need to bend away the the platinum wall so that we can drive."

I motion my hands to the left and the wall moves. We continue driving.

Chapter 4

Kuvira

After mine and Christine's fight. We decide to let Korra drive, Me and Christine sit in the back of the car, next to each other. We don't look at each other so i just stare at the buildings we pass.

Eventually I turn to Christine and say. "I'm sorry, that I got into the fight with you. I didn't mean to make so angry."

Christine turns towards me, with tears in her eyes and says. "That's okay. I should've just told you, rather than keeping my emotions bottled up."

She starts to cry and I give her a hug. Soon afterwards I start to cry too. My light crying turns in sobs and I lean into Christine and she leans into me.

---

I don't know how long we've been driving for, but it's dark now. Korra pulls the car over and says. "There's no sign of the bandits, I think we should stop for the night and rest."

"Okay." I say with a yawn.

"Yep, I agree." says Christine.

We turn off the car and fall asleep.

---

I wake with a start and look around, only to find that no one—other than me, Christine and Korra are still together. I woke up because I thought that I had heard something. I close my eyes, but moments later I feel something wrap around my hands. I open my eyes and find that there are metal cuffs on my wrists, I try to bend them away. But I can't, seconds later I fly backwards and I start to scream. But another metal cuff wraps around my mouth, cutting off my scream. I look down at the metal cuff and realize that it's one that I had used earlier.

"Well, well, well," says a voice. "Look who it is. I have to admit, I'm surprised that you continued looking for us. I thought that you guys would've given up on finding us."

The metal strip on my mouth comes off and I look up at the person who is talking. I recognize the person as one of the bandits that we had tried to arrest earlier today.

"Why are you doing this?" I ask as I try to bend the metal strip off my wrist.

"Hmm, I'm not sure. I guess because you deserve it and because of all the terrible things, you've done in the past." says the male bandit.

"That was in the past, I've changed." I say.

"Oh right you've changed, like that will ever happen," the women says with a laugh. "If you had changed then you wouldn't have taken over Chicago."

"That was six years ago!" I say. "Besides Chicago rules itself now."

"Once The Great Uniter, always The Great Uniter." says another bandit.

"I'm not The Great Uniter anymore!" I yell and tears start to roll down my face.

"Alright enough. Let's just tie her up and go." says a third bandit.

"What! No!" I say and I start to panic. "Christine! Korra! Someone please help!" I scream.

I feel a sharp pain in my neck and my vision starts to go black at the edges.

"The shirshu toxin should be kicking in by now." says one of the bandits.

I try to stay awake, but I can't. My body becomes weak and I close my eyes.

That is all.

Chapter 5

Christine

I yawn and stretch my arms above my head. I look over at Korra and start to giggle, she fell asleep with her seatbelt on and is hugging the seat. I start to laugh as she mumbles something,in her sleep. Something about her pet polar bear dog Naga. I laugh harder when she tells Naga to quit chewing on her shoes in her dream.

Then I quit laughing and lean over to Korra and say. "Good morning."

Korra pops one eye open and then the other and says. "Why are you staring at me?"

I start to laugh again.

"Why are you laughing at me?" Korra asks.

"You were talking in your sleep," I say. "You were talking about Naga and you were telling her to quit chewing on your shoes."

Korra's face turns red in embarrassment and that makes me laugh even harder. "Very funny." she says.

I quit laughing and look to my left and say "Hey Korra, have you seen Kuvira?"

"No. I haven't. Isn't she sitting back there with you?" she asks.

"Uh, no she isn't." I say.

"What!" Korra says and she turns around in her seat to look at me, she looks from me to where Kuvira was sitting.

"If she isn't sitting with you then where is she?" Korra asks.

"I don't know." I say.

We check the front of the car and in the trunk of the car.

"She's not here." I say.

"Where could she be?" Korra says.

---

Kuvira wakes up in a dark room, she tries to move, but she can't. She had been chained to the wall with platinum chains. She tries bend out of them, but she can't. The bandits walk into the room and turn on the light. Kuvira looks at them with her normal scowl and tries to bend out of the chains again. Then she leans against wall, feeling weak. She has always hated feeling weak.

"What do you guys want?" she says with a growl.

"We don't want anything, in fact if you cooperate, you will walk out of here unharmed." says one of the bandits.

"Alright what do you want?" Kuvira asks.

"We want the Avatar." one of them says.

"What, Why?" Kuvira asks, her heart racing.

"It doesn't matter why we want the Avatar, what matters is which Avatar we are asking for." the bandits say.

Kuvira's heart sank as she knew which one, they wanted. They wanted Christine, why else would they capture her and not anyone else.

"If you think that you can get away with this then you're wrong." Kuvira says, her voice shaking.

"Oh, but we already have." One of them says and they walk out of the room and lock the door.

---

I take a look around the car for any sign, of anything that might suggest Kuvira's whereabouts. I notice a sheet of paper on the windshield of the car and grab it, I read what's written on the paper and let let out a gasp.

"What is it?" Korra asks.

"This letter says that if we want to see Kuvira again, then we have to meet them in the lab in Erudite headquarters." I look at Korra with teary eyes and say. "Not again."

Korra walks over to me and says "You stay here and I'll go."

"No," I say. "I can't lose you too."

"I'll be alright." Korra insists, she gives me a hug and starts her way towards Erudite headquarters.

Chapter 6

Kuvira

I keep trying to bend out of the chains, but nothing works. *I need to get out of here, before they reach Christine, I have to.* I think. *But I also need to save my energy.* I quit struggling against the chains and lean against the wall. I let out a sigh, close my eyes and fall asleep.

Korra makes her way to the entrance of Erudite headquarters and finds that no one is there, she walks towards the lab and finds the door open, she looks inside, without actually walking inside though. Korra sees someone against the wall. She looks closer and realizes that it's Kuvira who is chained on the opposite wall. Korra runs over to me and tries to metalbend the chains off but they don't budge.

I try to say something, but there is a cloth wrapped around my mouth.

"Well, well, well," says a voice. "Avatar Korra what brings you here? I thought at least that Avatar Christine would've shown up herself."

Korra drops into her firebending stance and says "Well she didn't and you said that you wanted the Avatar, so here I am."

"You are very mistaken, when we sent you that letter, we wanted Christine not you, you're not relevant here anymore."

"You're wrong, both me and Christine are Avatars and I am going to stop you from hurting Kuvira and you can't stop me." Korra says with a smirk.

The bandits walk towards the door, close it and then lock it.

They all look at Korra and one of them says. "We're not going to hurt you or Kuvira, if you cooperate, then you'll walk out of here unharmed."

"Yeah sure, if you say so," Korra says and she rolls her eyes. "I'm going to get Kuvira out of here so, try to stop me."

Korra starts to freeze the chains with water. When suddenly her entire body, came to an abrupt stop. "What... is... going on?" Korra says as her body started to twist and bend out of place. Then the realization hit her like a freight train. "You're a *bloodbender*?"

"Exactly!" exclaimed one of the bandits then he adds. "You're not going anywhere, until you hand over Avatar Christine."

"I'm not telling you anything!" Korra says, weakly.

"Fine have it your way." says the bandit and he clenches his fingers together and Kuvira starts to scream as her body bends out of place.

"No, don't tell them!" I say through my screaming. "I'll be fine. Don't…"

The bloodbending bandit clenches his fingers tighter together, cutting off my words and says to me. "Will you quit talking for a few seconds." Then the bandit loosens his hold on me, enough so I quit screaming.

"Alright, alright, I'll tell you what you need to know. Just stop hurting Kuvira." Korra says her voice shaking.

"Excellent," says one of the bandits. "Now. Where is Avatar Christine?"

Chapter 7

Christine

I pace back and forth, Korra should have returned with Kuvira by now. I sigh and get back into the car, I hear static on the radio so I turn up the volume.

*"Avatar Christine, this is the leader of the bandits, speaking. I want you to listen carefully."*

Before I let him continue, I grab the radio and say. "Where is Korra and Kuvira?"

*"They're here and they're fine, for now."*

"I want to hear from them." I say, my voice shaking

*"No problem."* he says.

Seconds later he puts Korra on the radio *"Hey Christine."* Korra says, sounding weak.

"Are you okay?" I ask, my heart pounding.

*"Yeah, I'm fine."* Korra says, weakly.

"Oh, thank goodness. I'm glad you're okay." I say and my heart slows down for a second.

"Can I talk to Kuvira now?" I ask Korra.

*"Yeah just give me a sec."* Korra says.

The radio goes silent for a few minutes. Well long enough for me to start to panic. Seconds later I hear Kuvira speak on the radio. *"Hello Christine, how are you?"* she says.

"I'm fine." I say, then I ask. "How are you?"

*"I'm fine, thanks for asking."* Kuvira says and she starts to cough.

Seconds later one of the bandits comes back on the and says. *"Christine, you need to listen to me very carefully, unless you meet us in the lab in Erudite headquarters in the next ten minutes, you won't see your friends again. That is all."* Then the radio goes silent.

*In the next ten minutes. What are they insane?* I think as I hop in the car and I rev the engine and then drive off towards Erudite headquarters.

Korra and Kuvira let out a sigh as they look at the clock, if Christine doesn't make it here in the four minutes, then they are done for. They just look at each other. Kuvira tries to hold back her tears, but she is unable too and they flow freely down her face.

"Hey, it's okay," Korra said in a reassuring voice, trying to hold back her own tears. "Christine will make it here in time."

"Believe in whatever gives you comfort," says one of the bandits. "But it won't change the outcome."

Then the boy bandit glances at the clock and says. "Two minutes to go and Avatar Christine still hasn't shown up," He looked back at both Korra and Kuvira and said with a smirk. "Well that's too bad, it seems that she never cared about you two at all."

"What are talking about?" Kuvira says in confusion. "Of course she cares and she will get here and she will save us."

"Whatever you say." The bandit says and he walks over to the counter and pulls out something.

I finally reach Erudite headquarters, jump out of the car and run to the lab. When I get there though, the lights are off and the door is open, I walk inside and the door behind me closes and locks. Seconds later the lights come on, when my eyes adjust to the light. I see both Korra and Kuvira tied to two separate posts—well Kuvira is tied up with platinum chains and Korra is tied up with rope.

"Well, well, well. Look who's here, took you long enough to show up." says a voice.

I turn around and see the three bandits standing behind me.

Chapter 8
Christine
I drop into my firebending stance. "Let them go!"

"Listen to what I have to say and we just might." says another bandit.

I take a closer look at the third bandit and see that this bandit has black hair that has grown out a bit, a goatee and round shaped glasses.

"Why do I recognize you?" I ask the bandit with the black hair.

"Because we've meet before and you took something very important from me six years ago." he says.

I take a closer look at him and realize who it is.

"Baatar?" I say and I give him a confused look. "How are you alive? It's been six years and three months."

"There is a lot you don't know about me, like did you know that I'm the one who let Zaheer out of prison." Baatar Jr. says with a smirk.

"What?" I say in shock.

"Yep, that was me," he says, then he adds. "I knew that you would volunteer to give yourself up, instead of letting Korra go, so I told Zaheer that and I told him to just roll with it."

"Why?" I ask.

"I wanted you out of the way and to stay away from Kuvira, but now I see that won't happen." Baatar Jr. says.

"I'm going to kill you." I say.

"Careful Christine," Baatar takes a step back and motions to Korra and Kuvira. "Try something stupid, and you lose two more friends."

I shut my mouth and arms and hands relax. "What do you want?"

"I want you to make a choice."

"What are you talking about?" I mutter. "What kind of choice?"

"As you can see, we have two people very close to you here. Since I'm in a generous mood, I'll let one of them go," Baatar Jr, pauses, then darkens his gaze at me. "The other dies. You choose which."

I look at Baatar in disbelief and take a step backwards, wide-eyed *What? You can't be serious.*

Baatar smirks and says. "Oh, but I'm quite serious.

My hands ball into fists again. "If you think I'm going to choose between their lives, you're even crazier than last time."

"If you don't choose, then they both die," Baatar Jr. says. "Keep that in mind."

"Christine, don't listen to him!" Kuvira yells. "He's just trying to trick you. Don't worry about us, just worry about stopping him!"

Baatar straightened himself and moved off to the side, allowing me to have a clear look at my two choices. "I'll give you one minute to make up your mind. That's not a lot of time, so think carefully."

*"Baatar."* I hiss.

*There has to be something I can do to save both of them.* I think. I couldn't make this choice, not ever.

"Who's it going to be?" Baatar paced behind them, gesturing towards Korra "Avatar Korra?" I just glare at him. "No?" He continued on, moving behind Kuvira. "Then how about Dictator Kuvira?"

"Get *away* from her," I hiss. "Get away from *both* of them."

"Thirty seconds."

Kuvira took a deep breath and looks at me and says "It's okay... I think we both know how this needs to go."

"No!" I shout. "Kuvira don't!"

"I have to." she says, then she turns towards Baatar and says. "Let Korra go. You're going to keep trying to kill me anyway, so you might as well get it over with."

"Alright." Baatar says.

Chapter 9

Kuvira

I let out a sigh as Baatar Jr. thinks over the offer, seconds later he says. "Alright, I'll let Korra go, after I get rid of you once and for all." At that statement he turns to me and starts to bloodbend me. I let out a scream so loud that the windows shake.

"Stop! What are you doing?" I scream.

"I'm giving you, what you deserve." Baatar Jr. says with a shrug.

"Stop!" Christine yells "You said you wanted me and here I am."

"Hmm. I suppose you're right," Baatar says and he releases me from his bloodbending grip. I fall to the ground and shudder. Then a few moments later Baatar Jr. says to Christine "Today I'm going to rid the world of you forever."

Before Christine can react he raises his hand and she is under the control of his bloodbending grip.

"Christine!" I yell.

"I'll... be... fine." she says, between gasps.

"Baatar what are you doing!" I scream.

"I'm getting rid of the Avatar once and for all." Baatar says with an evil laugh.

While Baatar Jr. is distracted I grab my phone from my pocket. With a quaking hand I put in my mom's phone number.

---

Su, Lin and Baatar Sr. are sitting on the couch, watching a comedy movie with the rest of their family and during one scene they burst into laughter, when suddenly their phone rings.

"I've got it, Baatar Sr. says as he gets up to grab the phone, he looks at it and says. "Su look it's from Kuvira."

"Oh wonderful," says Su, then she adds. "We'll answer it."

Baatar Sr. answers the phone and says. "Oh hey Kuvira, What's up? I wasn't expecting a call from you so soon."

"I need to talk to Su like now!" I say my voice urgent.

"Oh sure," Baatar says. Then he hands the phone to Su and says. "Kuvira needs to talk to you."

"Can it wait?" Su asks.

"No it can't." Baatar Sr. says.

"Alright hand me the phone." Su says.

Baatar hands Su the phone and Su says. "Oh hey Kuvira. How is my daughter doing?"

"Not well," I say. "Me, Korra and Christine are in a sticky situation and when I say sticky. I mean life or death situation."

"Oh well, what's up?" Su asks.

"Well I can't tell you right now, all I need you to do is... Baatar what are you doing? Don't!" I yell.

"Wait did you just say "Baatar." Su asked.

"Yes. I did," I say. "Now listen carefully I need you and everyone to come to the lab in Erudite headquarters, like ASAP and then I need you to—" Then the phone line goes dead.

"Kuvira? Kuvira!" Su yelled, then she turned to everyone else and said. "We need to go!"

Everyone looks at her and says ."Why?"

"Kuvira, Korra and Christine are in trouble." Su said.

"What do you mean they're in trouble?" Lin asks.

"I'll explain it on the way, just get in the car. We're running out of time." Su says as she ran out of the house.

Everyone followed Su soon after.


Chapter 10

Christine

I struggle against Baatar Jr's bloodbending hold, but that only makes it worse. The more I move, the tighter his hold on me gets and the more painful it is.

"You're... not... getting away... with... this." I say, through the pain.

"Of course I am and I will." He says, with a sinister laugh.

Baatar rotated his wrist and my arms and legs bend near their breaking point. Finally I can't resist the pain any longer.

I scream.

---

Su and the rest of her family drive at full speed towards Erudite headquarters. On their way there Lin asked. "What happened?"

"I'm not sure, but whatever it is, it can't be good." Su said as she shifted gears, so the car will drive faster.

"Well, what did Kuvira say to you?" Baatar Sr. asked.

"She said that she needed us to come down to Erudite Headquarters and then she screamed something about Baatar." said Su

"What?" Opal said. "Do you mean Baatar Jr.?"

"I'm not sure," Su shook her head. "At any rate, she sounded like she was in trouble."

They reach Erudite jeadquarters and jump out of the car.

---

"Baatar stop!" I yell, as I try fight out of his bending grip.

"You want me to stop?" he smirks. Then he flicks his wrist to the left and I slam into the wall and fall to the ground and I don't get up.

"Christine!" Korra yells. She starts to bend a flame in her hand, hoping that the rope will burn and she will be able to break free. Finally the rope falls away and Korra makes a run at Baatar Jr. Before Baatar notices that Korra had escaped, she slams right into him and they both fall to the ground.

"You little... I'm going to get you." Baatar says.

"I'd like to see you try." Korra says as she gets up off the ground.

"Oh okay. Bring it." Baatar says with a smirk.

---

Su and her family run through the hallway and make it the lab. But the door is closed and locked. Su metalbends the door open and they walk inside. Once they're inside the door closes and locks. Su turns around and tries to open up the door but it doesn't budge.

"You're kidding me," Baatar Jr. says with a laugh. "That wasn't very smart of Kuvira to call you and put the rest of her family in danger."

"Baatar, why are you doing this?" Su asks.

"If I told you, would it even matter or change anything." Baatar Jr. says.

"Yes, it would." Su says.

"Well. I'm not telling you anything." he says with a scowl.

"Come on, Baatar, we don't want to hurt you." Opal as she drops into her airbending stance.

"If you guys think you can stop me, then go ahead and try." he says with a smirk.

---

I open my eyes and my vision is blurry, I try to sit up but I'm too dizzy. Once my vision is clear I look over towards the door and see Su and her family standing there. Baatar Jr. is standing in front of them. I look from from Baatar Jr. to Opal and Su. Opal looks at me but I press my fingers to my lips, telling her to be quiet.

I look across the room at Korra and Kuvira who are out cold on the ground. I try to move but I'm too weak and I collapse on the ground again.

Chapter 11

Kuvira

I wake with a start. I try to move but I'm still cuffed with the platinum chains, so I don't get far and I don't want to make noise, so I limit my movements. I look to my left and see that, Korra is still out cold. Then I look to my right and see that Christine is finally awake. I'm just about to say something when I realize that maybe I shouldn't. Christine looks at my platinum chains and then closes her eyes for a moment and motions her hands to the right. I'm about to ask her what she's doing when, the platinum cuffs on my wrists pop off. I give Christine a confused look and wonder how she got the cuffs off, but then I remember that she can bend platinum. I shake out my hands and then shoot some of metal strips from my uniform and aim them at Baatar Jr. before he can react, Christine gets up, runs at him and tackles him to the ground.

       She slams him into the ground face first and tries to cuff him with the metal strips that I had fired. But she doesn't get that far because Baatar Jr. starts to bloodbend her. Christine lets out a groan and she looks at Su and nods. Su runs at Baatar Jr. but doesn't get far. A second later she comes to a sudden stop and is unable to move do to Baatar Jr. bloodbending her.

       "Su!" I yell as I run towards Baatar Jr. but before I can even do anything, he starts to bloodbend me again. I squeal in pain, because I can't scream any louder.

       "Kuvira!" Opal yells and she starts to run towards me.

       "Opal, get out of here!" I say as evenly as I can. "I'll be fine!"

       Opal turns to Baatar Jr. and he says. "You heard Kuvira, get out of here!"

       "No!" Opal says. "I'm not going to leave you."

       "Alright, you asked for it." Baatar Jr. says with a smirk.

He starts to move his hand to bloodbend Opal, when suddenly he gets knocked to the ground with a blast of air. He loses his grip on all of us and we fall to the ground. We all turn around to see that Korra is awake.

       "Korra!" We all say.

       "Hey," she says, then she yells. "Duck!"

We all dive to the ground as Korra bends away a sharp piece ice that Baatar Jr. had tried throwing at us.

       "Thanks." I say.

Korra nods.

       "Baatar why are you doing this?" Christine asks.

       "Because you stole something that was very important to me!" Baatar Jr. shouts.

       "What did I take from you?" Christine yells.

       "Kuvira, you stole Kuvira from me!" he says.

       "What are you talking about?" I say.

       "Six years ago, when you were working for me and Kuvira. After you had saved Kuvira from being killed by Su and her family, you had become very protective of her and I don't know… I became jealous and that's why." Baatar Jr. explained.

       "I'm sorry, I never meant to make you feel that way." Christine says.

Baatar Jr. starts to cry and through tears he says "I'm sorry. I never meant to cause you any pain."

"Its okay, its okay." Christine says.

Chapter 12

Christine

"It's okay," I say. "Do you want a hug?"

Baatar Jr. nods and I walk over to him and give him a hug. A few minutes later Baatar Jr. looks at Kuvira and smirks. Kuvira gives him a confused look and then he pulls something out from his pocket. A needle.

"Baatar? What are you doing?" Kuvira asks.

"You'll see." he says.

It takes everyone a few minutes to realize what's going on and when they do they all yell. "Christine look out!"

I pull away from Baatar Jr. and he misses me with the needle by three inches.

"What are you doing?" I ask as he comes at me again.

"I'm going to get rid of you once and for all." he says with a growl.

"I thought we had an understanding. What happened?" I say.

"Yeah right, like that would ever happen." Baatar Jr. says with scoff.

I jump into the air and blast a stream of fire at him. He dives out of the way, dropping the needle in the process. The needle breaks and I stare at the color of the liquid, purple, death serum. I blasts him again this time with air. It hits him square in the chest and he flies backwards.

Then I quickly enter The Avatar State and blast air at him again. He hits the ground again.

"I will not allow you to win." My voice booms throughout the room.

---

"Should we help her?" Opal asks Su.

"I think Christine has got this one." Su says as she watches Christine strike Baatar Jr. with another blast of air.

---

I let out another blast of fire and Baatar dives out of the way. Eventually I become too tired to continue and I start to slow down. Once I'm on the ground though, I exit The Avatar State and stand there for a few moments and that is a mistake because Baatar uses that as an advantage to get more death serum.

"Christine look out!" Su yells.

I look to the right only to Baatar Jr. running at me with another needle full of death serum. I don't react fast enough because Baatar Jr. grabs my both my arms to keep me still, sticks the needle in my neck and presses down the plunger. I gasp, and start cough and finally I fall to the ground.

"I've got you now." Baatar Jr. says with an evil laugh.

Chapter 13

Kuvira

"Christine!" I yell and I run towards her fallen body, but Baatar Jr. stops me.

"You better stay back, unless you want to be next." he says.

I smirk at Baatar Jr. and say. "You seem to underestimate me, a lot."

"What are you talking about?" Baatar Jr. says and he gives me a puzzled look.

I don't say anything. I just stare at him for a few minutes and then instead of shooting my metal strips at him, I thrust my fist upwards and punch him hard in the jaw, he was not expecting that. Baatar stumbles backwards, but doesn't fall over. I punch him again, and he hits the wall.

"You killed Christine!" I yell.

"Yes I did." Baatar Jr. smirks. "What of it?"

"She was my girlfriend, she was part of our family, *my* family!" I shout.

"What?" Baatar Jr. says and he gives me a confused look. "She was?"

"Oh sure, act all innocent. You can fool everyone else but you can't fool me." I growl.

I punch him again and he puts his hands up in defeat. "Okay, okay. You got me."

---

Christine wakes with a start and sits straight up, and she starts to cough. She looks over at Kuvira and then at Su, Su just stares at her in shock.

Christine turns back to Kuvira and yells "Kuvira stop!"

---

Christine walks up behind Kuvira, but Kuvira doesn't notice her. Instead she keeps her focus on Baatar Jr.

Baatar Jr. looks past me and at Christine and says "Um Kuvira? Is Christine standing behind you or have you punched me way too many times."

"I think that I've punched you to many times." I say, my voice filled with rage.

"Um, I think that you're wrong. Christine is standing behind you." Baatar Jr. says.

"Yeah sure, whatever you say." I say.

"Kuvira?" Christine says, but I don't turn around.

"Kuvira?" Christine says again, but once again I don't turn around.

"Kuvira!" Christine yells and this time I turn around and when I look at the person behind me. I jump and let Baatar go and he tries to run out of the room but Su stops him and puts metal handcuffs on him.

"Christine? What? How are you alive?" I ask and I give her a hug.

"I'm alive because someone, never seems checks what serums he's using and he always ends up, using the wrong one."

"What are you talking about?" Baatar Jr. asks. "I used the death serum."

"You used a paralytic serum, that was dyed purple. Duh." Christine says.

"Huh? Wait what? I was sure that I had used the right one. Dang it!" Baatar Jr. says.

"You're never going to win. You know that." I say to Baatar.

"You're going to spend a long time in jail. With no chance of parole." Lin says as she escorts Baatar Jr. out of the room.

"Alright let's all go home." says Su.

Me and Christine walk out of the room, with the rest of our family.

## The Legend Of Korra Meets Insurgent
### (Book 4)

Chapter 1

*The following day…*

Baatar Jr. shuffled towards his cell, with Lin walking behind him. Since he is the first bloodbender to be put in prison, no one knew what to do at first. When Baatar got into his cell, he sat down at a small table. After Baatar sat down though, the door to his cell closed and locked and the shackles on his wrists were removed. Baatar let out a sigh and continued to look around his cell.

Baatar sat quietly on the lone chair in the middle of his cell. He stared out window, watching the clouds roll across the darkened sky. But then something caught his eye, and he moved to window and looked between the bars on the window the best he could. He turned his head to left only to see, the glow of lights in Erudite headquarters and even though it was on the other side of the city. Erudite headquarters… the sight of his defeat. The sight of his fall.

With a heavy sigh, Baatar shuffled over to the bed in the far corner and sat on the edge of it. He stared at the floor until his vision shifted out focus, he didn't move. He just… sat there. Silent. Still. Where had it all gone wrong? When had everything fallen to pieces? He had thought back over the course of the six years, trying to put it all together… what had been his point of no return? He didn't have to think about it for very long, of course. He knew what that moment had been. It hadn't been when he left home to work for Kuvira. It hadn't been when they had taken over Zaofu. It was when he had released the memory and death serum on Chicago, when he had let Zaheer out of prison and finally when he had tried to kill Christine those three times. He could still hear Christine's voice inside his head, telling him that she had never meant to make him feel jealous and that she was truly sorry. He believed Christine. But then he had tried to kill her with the death serum and he had bloodbended the rest of his family. Including Kuvira. Baatar dropped head into his hands and breathed in deeply… and then fell backwards onto the mattress. He needed to sleep.

Chapter 2

How long had Baatar been here now? Two weeks… maybe three. The first few of many, he knew. While his official sentence had yet to be handed, there was only so many ways that it could go; he could sit in this cell for a long, long time. Would it be the last place he ever lived? It seemed likely. It was what he had prepared for, at least.

"You have a visitor." The guard at the door said.
Baatar blinked, then slowly looked towards the door. He could see the guard's face peering through the slot, staring at him. The expression on the guard's face was not what he found surprising, but rather what the guard had said was surprising. A visitor? *Who*…

When the door opened, Baatar sat straight up and he felt a sick feeling in his stomach. The person who had come through that door was possibly that last he ever expected. "Su?"

The look Su gave him wasn't an angry look, but rather a calm look. But there was some caution in her eyes, uncertainty. "Hello Baatar."
Baatar clenched his jaw. He didn't know how to respond. Here was his mom and he had betrayed her. For the life of him, Baatar couldn't figure out why she would visit.

"What are you doing here?" Baatar asked calmly.
"I came to see you." was Su's gentle reply.
"But why?" he asked "After everything I did…"

Su left the doorway and walked farther into the room. The cell door closed and locked behind her. "I know what you did… and I know *why* you did it." Su let out a sigh and she turned her gaze away from him. There was so much pain in those, calm eyes. Pain that Baatar knew he had caused. "Its not something that is easy to swallow, or to move past. I don't need to tell you that." Su finally looked back at Baatar, with the ever so slight hint of a smile. "But there's no reason we can't try."

Baatar blinked, an odd mixture of confusion and surprise shifted through his head. He looked away. He couldn't bear to look Su in the eye or rather he felt he didn't deserve to. "Su, I tried to kill you. Our entire family. You only ever showed me love and kindness, and I betrayed you… all of you."

His mind suddenly flickered with a thought "*Christine! Kuvira!* How… how are they? Are they… I mean, did I…"

Su let out a sigh. She knew what he was asking. Are Christine and Kuvira alive? "Christine and Kuvira are okay. Heartbroken, but otherwise…" Su let the sentence hang in the air.

"I— I loved them and I almost killed them." Baatar could feel himself slipping and finally he fell apart. He fell forward, ever intent on letting himself drop to the floor and lose himself in his misery, but a pair of loving arms caught him. A pair of arms that hugged him tight.

"Shhh, shhh," Su whispered, holding him close. "Let it out. I've got you."

Baatar cried until his eyes went dry and he couldn't cry anymore. Slowly he pulled himself together. His breathing steadied. With a few deep breaths, he sat straighter and Su let him go.

Su smiled and said. "I'm here for you."

She checked her watch. "Its time from me to go, maybe you should try to find some peace."
Just like that Su was gone and Baatar sat there with a smile.

Chapter 3

*Thirty years.*

Baatar's sentence had finally been handed down; he would remain here in this cell for the next three decades. Well at least it wasn't a life sentence. He was lucky that Avatar Korra, had begged President Raiko not to give him a life sentence and he agreed. It left Baatar satisfied, at least he wouldn't be here for the rest of his life. He felt happy that he wouldn't be here for the rest of his life. But he also felt upset, he would be out of here, when he would be in his fifties. He let out a sigh. At least one day he would be free and he could start a new life again.

---

Baatar wasn't sure if it was morning or nighttime. He had fallen asleep. He looked out the window—sunset—nighttime then.

"Vistor."

Baatar sat up on the bed, looked down at the ground and he let out a sigh.

The door opened. But his gaze remained on the floor of his cell.

"Hey."

Baatar blinked. He *knew* that voice... he would never forget that voice. But what was *she* doing here? Baatar hesitated, but soon looked up at the entrance. "Avatar Christine?"

"Just Christine is fine." I say with a smile, then I walk forward; the cell door slammed shut behind me. I walk over to the table in the room and sit down. Baatar joined me soon after.

"So Christine...," Baatar couldn't think of anything else to say, at first. "What are you doing here?"

"Well I thought that you could use a visitor," I reply. "You know someone to talk to?"

"Christine, why are *you* visiting me?" he asked. "Of all people."

I shrug. "Like I said before: I just thought that would need someone to talk to. It must be lonely in here, I'm also supposed to show compassion to others. It's my job as the Avatar."

"But I've so many horrible things to you." he says, as tears start to flood into his eyes.

"I know, but Su told me that you really regret the things you did," I say. "That means you're not just some evil person and I don't believe you ever were. You're just a person who's made mistakes and now you're paying for those mistakes. That's the first step in bettering yourself."

Baatar let's out a sigh.

"Hey," I say. "We're family." I smile.

*"Family?"* Baatar shoots straight up and stares at me in confusion. "How... How can you say that? I tried to kill you Christine. We shouldn't be family, I don't deserve it."

"You do deserve it." I say.

"Why?" he asks. "After all that I've done?"

"Everyone deserves a second chance." I say with a smile.

Baatar looked at Christine, he couldn't figure whether if that smile, meant to be mocking or not.

"Well I should go, Kuvira would kill me if I'm late for dinner again. I promise I'll come visit again." I say and I give him a nod and walk towards the door.

"Hey Christine?" Baatar says.

"Yes?" I say and I turn around.

"Thank you, for having the time to visit me." he says, with a slight smile.

"You're welcome. I'll see you later."

I walk out of the room and the guard closes the door.

Chapter 4

The first year of Baatar's prison sentence went by relatively quickly. At least quicker than he would have thought. Had he been alone, it would have been slower. There were a few occasions where Su had come and she had brought the rest of the family. On one occasion Su had brought Wing and Wei, they stood in the doorway but said nothing. Su and Baatar had just talked the whole time. Even we he had tried to talk to them, to apologize for everything, they remained on guard. He could read them well enough, and knew how they felt even if they didn't speak… would they ever forgive him?

Aside from that Baatar Sr. had visited once, with Su. He didn't come into the cell though, he stayed outside and occasionally look through the little shot on the door. Up until this point there had been no Opal and certainly no sign of Kuvira. Baatar thought, even if she was busy. She wouldn't want to visit. Out of everyone, she had to hate him the most. Everytime he thought of Kuvira, he could still remember how hard she had punched him, until he started seeing stars.

Baatar wakes with a start, he thought he had heard someone talking. He turned towards the door, but no one was there. He rubbed his eyes, yawned and lied down on the bed again. He was just about to go back to sleep when the little slot on the door opened and the guard looked into his cell.

"Hey Baatar, you've got a couple of visitors."

*Visitors?* As far as Baatar knew, Su and her family were busy and Christine wasn't supposed to visit until next week. He sat up on the bed and waited for the door to open and when it did, Christine walked in. But instead of the prison door closing, it stayed open.

"Hi." I say as I sit next to him and give him a hug. Baatar tenses up.

"What are you doing here?" he asks.

"I came by to visit. I know that I was supposed to come in next week, but there's someone else here that wants to say hello."

We wait in silence for a few minutes. I tap my hand against my knee and wait for the special guest to arrive. After a few minutes, I roll my eyes, look at Baatar and say. "Hold on a sec."

I get up off the bed and walk out the door, it closes shut behind me.

Baatar walked over to the door and heard a second voice talking. "…don't think I can do this Christine."

"Of course you can," I say. "You don't have to stay long, you know that."

"I know," The other voice sighs. "But he did try to kill you three times."

"I know but he's family, we are family. As I said before: You don't have to stay long."

"Okay." says the other voice.

Baatar sits back down on the bed and waits. Seconds later the door opens and I walk in with someone else.

Baatar looks at the person behind me. It takes him a few seconds to realize who it is. When he does, his heart skips a beat and he has trouble breathing. Who he saw was was the last person he thought would visit.

"Kuvira?"

Chapter 5

Baatar tensed up at the sight of Kuvira.

"Hello Baatar." Kuvira says.

"What are you doing here?" Baatar asks, his heart racing.

"I came to visit you, duh." she says, rolling her eyes.

Baatar's muscles tensed up even more, he subsequently moved his hand across his jaw, even though its been over a year, he could feel the impact of Kuvira's fist connecting with his jaw.

"Why?" Baatar asks her.

"I came to visit because... we're family."

"How... can you say that?" he asks.

"Look, I know that you've done terrible things, but...," she sighs. "But everyone who has visited you is giving you a chance to be better."

"But. I don't deserve another chance. I deserve to be locked up." Baatar sighs.

"No. You don't. You don't deserve to be locked up, I mean for the time being yes, but not for thirty years."

An awkward silence lingered for a few minutes, then Kuvira ran up to Baatar and wrapped her arms around him, pulling him into a hug.

Baatar yelped in shock.

"You know I was never angry with you Baatar, I have forgiven you for your actions and so has Christine." Kuvira said.

"How can you forgive me so easily, after all I've done?" Baatar asked, as tears start to flow down his face.

"Because we're family, that's why." I say.

Kuvira let go of Baatar and with a sigh she walks back to me, then she nudges me in the side and hands me a bag full of clothes.

I look over at Kuvira and then walk over to Baatar and give him a hug. The tears start to flow faster and faster down Baatar's face, until he can't hold back the urge to cry anymore, he lets out a sob and collapsed against me. I hold him closer and whisper. "Its okay, its okay, I've got you, just let it out." I look back at Kuvira and nod.

She walks over and joins in, she wraps her arms around both of us.

Baatar sniffles, takes a deep breath and after a few minutes he says. "Okay, I'm good now."

We break away from each other. Me, Baatar and Kuvira stand in silence for a few seconds.

When Baatar looks back at me, I smile and say. "You know what someone once told me?"

"What?" he asks, taking deep breaths.

I smile a little more and say. "When we have done something wrong, we are open to change more easily."

"So... what you're saying is that, I'm open to change more and I'm going to get better?" Baatar asks.

"Me and Kuvira can help guide you through your healing process, but whether you get better or not is up to you." I say calmly.

"Yes, that's what I want more than anything." Baatar says.

"Okay." I say.

Chapter 6

I turn towards Kuvira and she nods.  turn back to Baatar, slide the bag over to his feet and say. "Get dressed."

"Get... dressed?" Baatar opened the bag and couldn't help but let out a gasp at what he saw inside—his old Zaofu clothes.

He looks up at us in confusion and says "What's going on?"

"You're coming with us, we're going to make an announcement." Kuvira says.

---

Baatar inhaled a deep breath and held it, trying to settle his nerves. He felt so strange to be standing in his Zaofu clothes again. Just fifteen minutes ago he had been wearing a Chicago prison uniform. Now, he standing inside the front entrance to Erudite headquarters, looking out the window at the hundreds of people gathered in front of the steps.

Atop the steps, a podium had been set up next to a line of seats. Asami sat in the first seat.

"Are you ready for this?"

Baatar jumped at the sound of the voice. He calmed himself a second later and turned away from the window. "No. Not even a little bit.  mean I should know what to say... what I *need* to say, but this is the last thing I expected to be doing today, I'm sure this is the last thing the people out expected, too. I'm nervous. That's probably an understatement, but yeah. Nervous."

"Hey, don't worry," I smile. I walk over to Baatar and give him a hug. "You'll do great. You've *earned* this... You're ready.

Baatar returned the smile and gives me a tighter hug "Thanks, Christine."

"Alright...," I glance out the window to see Lin arriving behind the podium. "Let's get out there. Looks like things are about to start."

We exit Erudite headquarters, coming out atop the steps with the others. I lead the way to the end of the row of seats, where me and Baatar sit in the two final empty ones, Kuvira sits on my left beside Korra. At first, no one seemed to notice us. Within a few moments, however, the reporters at the front of the crowd began whispering to each other, and pointing. Soon they all turned their cameras towards Baatar and started taking pictures. Baatar sat there, stiff as a board, keeping his attention focused on the podium and doing everything he could to ignore the growing murmurs from the crowd. Fortunately, Lin silenced them when her voice boomed out over the loudspeakers.

"People of Chicago," said the Chief of Police, leaning closer to the microphone. "You've been through alot in this past year. I don't need to tell you that. The good news is that because of the police, Avatar Christine, Avatar Korra and Kuvira, our city has been restored once again."

A round of cheers and applause erupted from the crowd. Once the cheering stopped, Lin continued, "The last thing to do is to announce the new president, as elected by the people of Chicago, during the last few months."

Lin looked over to Asami, "Without further ado, Miss Sato, would you please come forward?" Asami rose from her seat and approached Lin. Lin turned to her, moving slightly to the side to give her more room behind the podium.

"Asami Sato," Lin said. "You have been elected by the people of Chicago to serve as the president of the city of Chicago. Do you accept the responsibility this involves?"

Asami nods, leans into the microphone and says. "I do."

"Do you vow to uphold our laws, to always put the interests of your people, and guide this nation to the best of your ability?"

"I do."

"Then I present you with the presidential pin, in recognition of your position. May you wear it proudly." Lin moved closer to Asami and lifted a gold pin from the podium and she smiled as she attached it to Asami's shirt.

"Ladies and gentlemen, I give you your new president, President Asami Sato."

Again, the crowd burst into cheers. Asami stood in silence for a few minutes, then she started to wave. Finally she moved behind the podium. When the crowd died down, she looked out at the people and spoke. "Thank you all, it is an honor and a privilege to have been elected into office as your new president. I promise to all of you, I will do everything in my power to keep Chicago safe and to continue advancing our society to be the best it can possibly be."

Another round of applause broke out. "Now I would like to take a moment to recognize the brave men and women who helped restore peace and order to the city. To our very own Police Force, lead by Chief Beifong, and to both Avatar Korra and Avatar Christine, who helped take down Zaheer and his team almost year and a half ago, we thank you. We thank *all* of you."

Both me and Korra wave to the crowd, more cheering followed. When the crowd settled down again, their attention returned back to the president. Now though Asami's smile had disappeared. She had become stern, serious.

"There is one person in particular I would like to recognize now." That was when Asami glanced down the line of seats next to her, all the way down to the end. "Baatar Jr. Beifong."

Silence.

Baatar sat there, unable to bring himself to move a muscle. He couldn't even look out to the crowd. Instead, he just stared up at the podium, at Asami. All the while his heart thumped like mad in his chest.

"Even though Baatar did a lot of bad things in his past, he did do the right thing by surrendering to the police and he did serve a small amount of sentence in jail. All the while, he did show regret towards his actions that he made in the past, both Avatar Korra, Avatar Christine and even Kuvira have showed proof that he has indeed changed. That is why, in the light of his service to the world and to the people, I'm giving him a full pardon for his past crimes. From this day forward, he will be a free man, free to choose his own destiny, and free to help make this world a better place."

Baatar's jaw dropped at Asami's statement. The silence in the crowd also broke. A ripple of murmurs flooded through the crowd. Reporters scrambled over each other to get pictures, while some others shouted questions. He couldn't hear them, he still couldn't bring himself to look at any of them. I put my hand on Baatar's shoulder, he looks back at me and smiles.

It was time.

## Chapter 7

With a deep breath, Baatar rose from his seat and walked towards the podium. Asami moved off the side, giving him space. When he finally turned to look out to the crowd, his heart almost leaped up through his throat and out his mouth. He saw such mix of reactions and emotions among the people, confusion, caution, hesitation, anger, hate, fear… he used to it all.

Soon the crowd became quiet again. The stares though remained, countless eyes burning a hole through him as they watched, waiting for him to say something. He breathed in deep, but little did that do to settle his nerves.

"Greetings everyone. I uh…" Baatar's mind blanked. He swallowed, huffed out a breath and then turned a glance back down the line of seats, to me. I smile, and give him a thumbs up. It was then that his nerves calmed. With another sigh, he looked back out to the crowd.

This time he knew what to say.

"I know what many of you think of me, and I know that there is little I can do the change that." he says. "I did many terrible things to many people, even to people I know. I know that no amount of apologies will ever make that better. But… I'm going to try. I owe it all to all of you, to the world, to myself, to show you how I've changed, and to help the world however I can."

The tone of the crowd shifted somewhat. Most remained on edge, but few were looking at him now with intrigue, and speculation.

"I am touched to stand before you today a free man. It feels like a dream. I never thought that I would be given another chance at bettering myself and bettering the world." He swallowed, took in another deep breath and continued. "I may not make anyone forgive me, but I promise to do my best to help those who need it, and to keep peace in the world. I'll be working closely with Avatar Korra, Avatar Christine and Kuvira to make this happen," He turns towards us and smiled. "If there is anybody who can keep me in line, it's definitely them."

A few chuckles rippled throughout the crowd and it made Baatar smile, then he continues speaking. "That's okay if you hate me, then hate me. If you're still angry with me, then be angry and if you think that you can't forgive me, then don't. I'm not here to tell you how to feel about me. I'm only here to tell you that I will will do my best to right the things I've done wrong."

Another smile made its way onto his face. This one softer, distant… but also it was hopeful.

"Someday though, perhaps I can change a few of your minds."

---

"So Baatar Jr's alive, and out of jail?" Someone asks.

"Yes. Also Asami is now president of Chicago." Someone else says.

"Hmm, well… its bad that he's out of jail since he betrayed us, but its also no good that there is a president," The first person says, as he runs a hand across his jaw, its been hurting for the last little bit. Then with a hardened glare adds. "Well then, its time for payback."

Chapter 8

Me, Baatar Jr., Kuvira, Korra and Asami drive back to our house on the other end of the city. When we get there Baatar looks at the house, it was once his and Kuvira's house, when himself, me and of course Kuvira were uniting the Earth Empire. He shook his head, he couldn't think about that now, he should be grateful for them letting him out of jail.

I lead them inside and Su, Baatar Sr. and Lin stand in the living room with their arms crossed. Baatar Jr. comes to a stop and slams into me. We both let out a groan.

"Where have you guys been?" Su asks.

"We were with Asami, you should've been told this." Kuvira says, looking at Lin.

Su looks at Lin and asks. "What's going on Lin?"

Lin sighs and then looks at her sister. "Asami is now president and they attended her ceremony."

"Oh I see," Su says, then she looks behind me and says. "Hello, Baatar Jr."

Baatar tries to hide but its too late, he steps forward and says. "Hey mom."

Su looks from Baatar Jr. to Lin and back again and says. "Alright I'm confused, why is he out of jail?"

Asami steps forward and says. "I pardoned him from his crimes and let him out."

"Okay." Su says.

Both her and Baatar Sr. just nod

Seconds later someone says. "Uh, I'm trying to sleep, who's talking?"

Opal walks up behind Su following behind her is Huan, as well as Wing and Wei. They all come to a stop once they see Baatar Jr.

"Baatar what are you doing here?" They all ask.

"Asami let him out of jail." Korra says gently.

"Um... okay." They all say.

---

After Su, Lin and their family leave to go back to their house. Me, Kuvira, Korra, Baatar Jr. and Asami sit down on the couch. Asami looks at me and asks. "So where am I going to sleep?"

"There's a house next door, its empty. You could sleep there." I say.

"Thank you." she says. I nod.

Asami gets up to leave, but then I stop her and say. "Why don't you take Korra with you, I know you two are close. Plus its going to get crowded now that Baatar Jr. is here."

"What is supposed to mean?" Baatar asks, but we don't say anything, we just start to giggle.

"Oh, well thank you." she says, she looks over to Korra and starts laughing. We look over at Korra and laugh harder as her face turns as red as a tomato.

"Thanks for stating the obvious," Korra says quietly, then she adds. "You know what I think I'll stay here."

"No problem." I say and I smile.

I look back over at Korra and I swear if looks could kill, then I would be dead now.

Asami leaves the house. Korra looks back at me, smiles and shakes her head.

Baatar Jr. looks at us and says. "What did you mean when you said "Its going to get crowded now that I'm here."

Me and Kuvira look at each other, start to chuckle, then we say. "There's only one bedroom in this house and there are four of us."

Chapter 9

Baatar looks at us. "Oh… okay."

I roll my eyes and say "You can stay with Kuvira tonight, Korra and I will take the couch."

Korra's eyes get big. "Wait, what?"

I laugh and say. "Korra you knew what I meant, you sleep on the couch, I'll sleep on the floor. Kuvira and Baatar get the bedroom upstairs."

"Okay." Baatar says and he goes upstairs.

Just before Kuvira leaves, I stop her. "Me, you and Korra all need to work on building two other bedrooms, you know so things won't get awkward."

"Yep, I think you're right," she says, then she walks upstairs. "Goodnight Christine."

"Goodnight Kuvira."

I fall onto the floor and just before I fall asleep Korra says. "Great, now I have to sleep on the couch again."

I look at her and say. "Oh come on, its not that bad… unless you want to sleep on the floor."

Korra shuts her mouth. "That's what I thought."

"Alright I see your point, goodnight Christine."

"Goodnight Korra."

I close my eyes and fall asleep.

---

"Have you found her yet?" A voice asks.

"No, I haven't. For someone so young she's pretty hard to locate." Another voice comments.

"Has she tried to access The Spirit World yet?" the first voice asks.

"You know I haven't even thought to even check." the second voice replied.

---

I wake up to Korra staring at me. I stretch and yawn.

"Morning." she says.

"Morning." I say.

I sit up and Korra says "So… I have something planned for today."

"What is it?" I ask.

"I'm going to teach you how to connect to your spiritual side and show you how to enter The Spirit World." she says.

"Awesome." I say.

Chapter 10

Me and Korra stand in silence for a few minutes, then she says. "Well let's get started."

"So what am supposed to do?" I ask.

"Hmm, let me think." Korra says.

"Have you taught anyone this?" I ask her with a small chuckle.

"Yes I have actually… just hold on a sec, I'll be right back." Korra gets up and walks upstairs. I sit down down on the ground and wait. A few minutes later, Korra walks downstairs with Kuvira and Baatar.

Kuvira walks over to me and sits down. Then she asks. "What seems to be the problem?"

"I'm not sure…" I say "Korra is trying to show me how to get into the Spirit World, but she can't remember what to do."

"I see…" Kuvira says, after a few minutes she adds. "Get into your meditation position, we're going to try something."

I nod and get into position.

"Good, now I want you to think of all the good things in your life right now. Anything that makes you happy."

"Okay." I press my fists together and close my eyes, while taking in long deep breaths. There wasn't much to think about. I thought about Su, Baatar Sr, Kuvira, Korra, Both Wing and Wei, then there was Opal and finally Baatar Jr.

"You have it?" Kuvira asks.

"Yes." I say.

"Okay, now what I want you to do is push all those thoughts away, just forget about them, let them fade. All I want you to think about now are the negative thoughts."

I forget about everything else and focus on the negative ones. I think about how I nearly died the day Baatar Jr. released the memory and death serum, when Zaheer tried to kill me and finally once again when Baatar had tried to kill me.

"Sometimes, these negative thoughts can keep us from reaching peace with our spirits," Kuvira says "Whether we're thinking about them or not. When this happens, its important to acknowledge them, to stand up to them, face them head on. Even if you don't think you can get over them, or be free of them, you need to let them that they can't control you. Once you do that…"

Kuvira's voice faded.

I felt lighter, like I was floating. I open my eyes.

"What is this place?" I look around and see spirits flying around.

"Welcome to The Spirit World," Korra says. A moment later she appeared beside me, fading in from nothing until she took a solid form. "See I knew you could do it."

Then she looked to her side where Kuvira appeared a second later. "Thanks Kuvira."

"It was nothing. Just remember if you have trouble, just stand up to the negativity and you'll be fine." she says.

Chapter 11

I look around and see a tree in the far distance, then I look back at both Korra and Kuvira smiling. "Do you want to race?" I ask.

"Sure." Both of them say.

"I think…,"I look back at the tree and break into a sprint. "…I'll race you guys to that tree."

"Hey no fair!" They say and they chase after me. "Head start, much?"

I smirk and glance over my shoulder. "You guys are too slow!"

I get to the tree.

Korra and Kuvira reach me a few minutes later, breathing heavily. They both lean forward and put their hands on their knees.

"Okay…," Kuvira says. "You're fast."

I smile a little, then I curl my hands into fists briefly, before slowly releasing them "I noticed that I can't bend."

"Yeah, you can't bend in The Spirit World if you enter it through meditation. Only when you enter physically, though a spirit portal." Korra says.

"I guessed as much." I say.

---

I don't know how long we've been here. It must have been for a while though. Me, Korra and Kuvira all lay down on the grass, looking up at The Spirit World night sky. Kuvira lets out a sigh and says "Well this nice, isn't it?"

"Yes. It is." Both me and Korra say.

I close my eyes and say. "Well. I think that it's time to go back, what do you think Korra?"

"That sounds great." Korra says "What do you think Kuvira?"

"That sounds li— *argh!*" Kuvira stops mid-sentence and groans.

I bolt straight up, at the sound of her and look over at Kuvira. Korra stands beside her.

"What happened?" I ask.

"I don't know." Korra says.

"Kuvira?" I say as I walk over to her.

She doesn't respond.

"Kuvira!" I shout.

I still get no response.

I look over Korra shoulder and see two figures standing behind her.

"Korra look out!" I yell.

"What?" Korra dives out of the way.

She doesn't get out of the way in time, she gets knocked to the ground.

I stand in The Spirit World alone.

Chapter 12

I drop into my bending stance and wait for the attacks to continue, but they don't. In fact, The Spirit World became very quiet and still.

"Who's there?" I ask, trembling.

I receive no answer. I try to bend a flame in my hand, but then I remember that I can't bend unless I enter through a spirit portal.

"Who's there?!" I shout.

"Just relax Avatar Christine, Its just us." says a calm, soothing voice.

I shift out of my bending stance and relax my body, then I ask. "Where are Korra and Kuvira?"

"They're back in the physical world. But don't worry they will be safe." the voice responds.

"Okay," I say. "What do you want?"

"Nothing. Nothing at all. In fact all we need is a moment of your time, that's all." says a second voice.

"Alright, what is it that you want to talk to me about?" I say, my voice shaking.

The two figures step forward, I look from the first person to the second. I can't help it, I let out a gasp of shock. "President Raiko?"

"Hello Christine," His gaze darkens and with a more mocking tone he says "I'm sorry I meant *Avatar* Christine."

"What? I don't understand. How...," The words get stuck in my throat, but I push them out. "How are you alive?"

President Raiko smirked "Oh, there's a lot you don't know about me. Like did you know that, I'm actually the one who let Zaheer out prison. But I just framed Baatar Jr. and made him tell you that it was him, because I thought *"why not?"*

"But why?" I ask, still relaxed. *Why am I so relaxed?* I think. I push the thought away.

"I wanted you out of the way, I'm so sick and tired of you and Korra always taking my job of protecting the city of Chicago." The former president sighed.

"But me and Korra always maintain balance in the world." I say, confused.

"Yeah if you say so." A new voice says.

My eyes go wide, I instantly recognize the other voice. "Wait is that...? How...?" Zaheer walks up beside Raiko.

"Its nice to see you again." Zaheer says.

"What? No! This can't be right. You're dead, you're supposed to be dead." I say, backing up slowly.

"Well it seems, that I'm still alive," Zaheer goes quiet for a minute before continuing. "Now I think that we've stalled enough time, what do you think Raiko?"

Raiko nods and says. "Yes. I think our plan has worked. Korra, Kuvira, Asami, Baatar Jr and Christine should be captured by now." Then he disappears.

"See you in the physical world." Zaheer says before disappearing too.

"Zaheer! No!" I yell.

Chapter 13

Seconds later my spirit returns to my body and I open my eyes. I look over to my left and see Korra, Kuvira, Baatar Jr. and Asami.

"Oh thank goodness, you're okay." Korra says.

"Where are we?" I ask.

"I don't know." Kuvira says.

I sigh and lean against a wall. I try to sit down but I can't because I'm bound with chains… platinum chains.

I let out a small laugh.

"What are you laughing at?" Baatar asks.

"Well its just… I think Zaheer forgot that I could bend platinum."

I move my wrists to bend out of the chains.

"Um… I don't think that's a good idea." Korra says.

"Why not?" I ask and I stop trying to bend out of them.

"Well… I can't tell you." Korra says.

"Wait… why can't you tell…," I look at Korra and let out a disbelieving laugh as a thought occurs in my mind. "No. What you're trying to tell me is that…" I shake my head.

Korra sighs. "Yes I allied with Zaheer. I lured you into The Spirit World and got us all captured."

"What!?" Baatar, Kuvira and Asami say.

"I'm going to kill you." I say to Korra as I try again to bend out of the chains.

"Christine stop. Zaheer has already won." Korra says.

I still don't listen, finally the chains pop off. But my hands are still cuffed together. I clench my fists together to bend the cuffs, when suddenly I felt a searing pain jolt through my body, the shock was so sudden that I crumple to floor. I takes me a moment to realize that the cuffs are electrified.

"You… you electrified my handcuffs?" I ask Korra.

"Yes I did." Korra says with a smirk.

I look at Kuvira and say. "Kuvira, don't move. If my cuffs are electrified then so are yours."

"Yeah I know." she says. "I already tried to bend out of them earlier. So I found out the hard way."

"I can't believe you trust Zaheer after what he tried to do me!" I yell, my voice filled with rage.

"Christine, keep your voice down." Korra says.

"No! I won't. You need to listen to me Korra! I don't understand why you would stab me in the back like that. Even after I saved you from being killed by Zaheer!" I shout.

I feel a sharp pain in my neck and I become very tired and spots start to cloud my vision.

"I'm sorry." Korra says as I fall to the ground.

I close my eyes.

That is all.

Chapter 14

Something shakes me awake. I let out a yell and I bolt straight up. I open my eyes and see Kuvira standing over me.

"What is it?" I ask.

"Less talk, more running." Kuvira says, as she picks me up off the ground. We break into a run, we run through a hallway and down a flight of stairs. We exit through a door and run through a field. I take a look at our surroundings, we are near Erudite headquarters.

"How did we get back to Chicago?" I ask Kuvira.

"Does it matter?" Kuvira says as she runs.

"Uh yeah." I say.

"Well I'll tell you later, right now we need to focus on getting you out of Chicago." she says, as she runs faster.

I quit running and laugh. Kuvira comes to a halt and turns around. She runs back to me and tugges on my arm. "Come on, let's go."

"We can't go anywhere." I say.

Kuvira pulls on my arm, but I stay still.

"No. I'm not coming with you." I say.

"What are you talking about?" she asks.

"This isn't real," I say. "This is a sim."

"Christine, we're not in a sim, don't you think I know if I was in a sim." Kuvira says.

"Kuvira," I say, as tears start to roll down my face. "You're not in the sim. You are the sim."

I bend a blast a fire at her.

"Wait. What? Christine no!" she yells.

---

I wake with a start, breathing heavily.

"That was interesting." someone says.

I look over to my left and see Korra standing with President Raiko and Zaheer. I try to run at them, but I hit something hard and stumble backwards. I put my hand up and feel something hard and cool. Glass. I let out a heavy sigh.

"Alright I think that's enough for today." Korra says.

Zaheer raises an eyebrow at her.

"Just look at her, can't you tell she's on the brink of collapsing." she says.

Zaheer doesn't respond.

"You know we do need her alive for this work right." Korra adds.

"Alright. Shut it down." Zaheer says.

President Raiko nods and the lights turn off. I stand in darkness for a few seconds. As soon as my eyes adjust to the darkness, I see Korra standing in a doorway.

"Come on let's go." she says.

"Why would you do this?" I ask her.

"Let's go." she repeats.

"No." I say.

"Fine have it your way." she says.

I didn't even sense the electrified platinum handcuffs.

I fall.

Chapter 15

*"Christine."*

I wake with a start. I look around, I'm in my cell in Erudite headquarters. I look towards the door and see Korra standing there.

"Why did you do it?" I ask.

"Its not that simple, its more complicated than that. This situation is bigger than you can imagine." she says.

"Do you even hear what you're saying right now?" I say.

"Come on let's go." she says.

"No." I say.

Korra walks towards me with a pair of electrified platinum cuffs.

I chuckle and say. "You know that the more you put those things on me. The more resistant I will be to them."

She grabs my arms and wrenches me to my feet. The force of the pull popped my shoulder blade from its place. I groan. She puts both my arms behind my back and puts on the handcuffs. I was just about to tell Korra that I was right, when she turns up the intensity of shock on the handcuffs. I stand frozen for a minute and then she pushes me out of my cell. I look at the other cells as we pass them and see Kuvira in one of them.

"Kuvira?" I say.

"Christine! She shouts.

"Kuvira!" I shout back.

I struggle against Korra's hold.

"Christine!"

I struggle harder against Korra.

"Christine, stop." Korra says.

"No." I say. I keep my gaze on Kuvira.

"I don't want to do this." Korra says.

I almost don't hear the clicking of handcuffs being fired up. The shock was so powerful that I lurch forward on my knees.

"Christine!" Kuvira yells.

I fall to ground and blackout.

Chapter 16

*"Come on wake up!"*

I slowly come to my senses. I groan, pain shooting through every part of my body.

"Come on wake up!" The voice says again.

I open my eyes. Korra stands over me.

"Huh?" I say.

"We're late!" Korra says with growl.

I try to muster the strength to get up, but all I can do is put my arm up for Korra to grab it.

She wrenches me to my feet and then shoves me forward. I look into Kuvira's cell and notice that's she's not there.

"Where's Kuvira?" I ask Korra.

"I don't know." Korra says.

"How do you not know? You saw her, when you knocked me out earlier." I say.

"I don't know what your talking about." she says.

I try to turn around, but then my handcuffs start to make a beeping sound. I stop trying to move.

"I upgraded the settings on the handcuffs, so that if you try to resist them. They can shock you so much that your heart will stop beating." she says with a smirk.

"But don't you need me alive for this?" I ask.

"Not for much longer, Zaheer said to me that if you refuse to go along with this, I can kill you and then he will continue on with Kuvira." Korra says.

My heart skips a beat.

"So what will it be? You can refuse to go along with this and lose Kuvira or you can do this final test and save her life."

"Alright. I'll do it." I say, trying to hold back my tears.

"You'll do what?" she asks.

"I'll do this final test." I say.

"Excellent."

We continue walking forwards.

---

"Are you sure this is the right place?" Someone asks.

"Oh come on Asami of course it is." Someone else says.

"Okay, I'm only believing what you're saying because we need to save Christine and Kuvira. We need to focus on the task at hand, Baatar."

"Alright." Baatar says.

"Well we're almost there." Asami says.

They walk through the doors to Erudite headquarters and when they get inside they are greeted by Zaheer. "Welcome, you're just in time for the big finale." He shakes Asami's hand, then he turns towards Baatar.

"Baatar." he says and he nods.

"Zaheer." Baatar says with a nod of his own.

"Wait you two know each other." Asami says.

"Its complicated." Baatar says.

"Well come on, let's go." Zaheer says.

Chapter 17

Korra and I walk to the lab in Erudite headquarters, where we are greeted by Zaheer.

"Morning Christine." he says.

I just nod.

"Alright let's go." Korra says.

Zaheer starts to walk away.

"Knock me out first." I say.

Zaheer stops and turns around. "What?"

"There's no way you're going to get me where you need me to be, unless you knock me out first."

"Alright." Zaheer says, he nods towards Korra.

She walks towards me and turns up the settings on the handcuffs.

"Alright move." she says.

"But if I move, the cuffs will kill me and you need me alive." I say.

"Alright I get your point." she looks at Zaheer. "What am I supposed to do?"

"Hmm, let me think." he says.

---

Baatar Jr. and Asami pace back and forth.

"What's taking them so long?" Baatar says.

"I don't know." Asami says.

Seconds later Korra walks into the room with Christine slung across her shoulder. Christine's face is bruised and judging by the bruises on Korra's knuckles, it clearly had something to do with her.

"Whoa." Both Baatar and Asami say.

Baatar leans over to Asami and whispers. "Do you think Christine is alive?"

"I don't know, but I sure hope so." she says.

---

I wake with a start, still bound with the chains. I look around and see Baatar and Asami on the other side of glass. They give me a thumbs up and I nod. I know I can survive this. I think.

Korra walks over to me and says. "Are you ready?"

I let out a big sigh. "Yeah."

"Good." she says and undoes the chains and cuffs.

"You know you really did a number on my face." I say.

Korra laughs. "I think that was the point."

I chuckle and then cough.

"Alright, let's get this over with." I say.

"Good luck." Korra says.

Chapter 18

Korra walks back to Zaheer and is soon joined by President Raiko.

"Avatar Christine," Zaheer says. "Are you ready?"

"I'm ready!" I say.

"Alright." Zaheer says and he nods to Korra.

Korra takes a deep breath and then bends all the metal, away from the glass in front of me.

I take a deep breath and shake out my hands in an attempt to calm myself down. I look over President Raiko, but something seemed a little... off. He's not wearing his usual purple coat, the one he was wearing was blue instead, his hair color was off too, it was gray rather than black. Everyone in the room disappears. Suddenly someone grabs my shoulder, I flinch away from the touch.

"Christine." says a familiar voice.

I turn around "Su!"

"Hey." Su says.

"I miss you so much." I say and I give her a hug.

"I know you do, but I'm still with you," she says. "You can get through this, I know you can. Your brave."

"I'm not brave Su, I pretend that I am and I want people to think that I am. But I'm not. I'm really, really scared, that maybe we are what's wrong in this world…. Avatar's. Su I don't want to the Avatar anymore, I just want to feel safe again."

---

I wake with a start. It was all a simulation. My heart rate speeds up a little.

"Alright, she's done her practice test," Zaheer says. "Now let's give her a break."

"Alright." Korra says as she walks up to me. I put up my hands and she puts the handcuffs on me. Then she leans over and whispers. "Your handcuffs are turned off currently. But just act as if they're on okay?"

"Okay?" I say.

Me and Korra walk back to my cell together.

---

"I think we got caught." Baatar says.

"Gee, you don't say, is that why were sitting in a cell right. I wonder how you figured out that we got caught." Asami says, her voice filled with annoyance.

"I didn't know that Zaheer had heard us talking, about wanting to save Christine and Kuvira." Baatar says.

Asami sighs. "Well hopefully we're not in here for much longer. We really need to get out of here."

"I'll figure something out. I always do." Baatar says.

Chapter 19

Me and Korra arrive at my cell, she pushes me inside and closes the door. I stand there confused. *What is she doing? I still have my handcuffs on.* I think.

"Korra, you left my handcuffs on." I say.

"I know." she replies.

"Aren't you going to take them off?" I ask.

"I don't think so." she says with a smirk.

"Why?" I ask.

"If you want them off, then you have to bend them off." she says, with an evil grin.

"I don't think I like the look you're giving me."

"You shouldn't." she says.

"What are you thinking about?"

"You."

"Umm… okay?" I go silent for a moment. Then I ask. "Why are you thinking about me?"

Korra quits grinning and smiles. "I'm thinking about tomorrow and what's going to happen."

"What's going to happen?"

"Oops… I wasn't supposed to say anything." she says, covering her mouth.

"Korra, what's going to happen?" I ask.

"Nothing, just nothing." she replies.

"What's… going… to… happen… Korra?" I ask more sternly.

"Nothing." she smirks.

"Korra. Really? You can't tell me?" I say in annoyance.

"I'm not going to tell you unless, you bend your cuffs off." she says.

"Fine." I say. With a nervous breath, I close my eyes and clench my fists together and the cuffs don't budge. Platinum.

"What? Why aren't they coming off?" I ask. "I can bend platinum. I *know* that I can bend platinum."

"Really? Are you sure?" she asks.

"Yes, I was able to bend platinum the last time, I fought… Zaheer," I look at Korra. "No that's impossible."

"No, you're right. You're still with Zaheer. You were under simulation the last time too, the whole thing with Baatar was a simulation too."

*"What?"* I say.

"Yep. Just let that sink in." she says.

I fall onto the bed in my cell and let out a heavy sigh. "Wow."

"Alright, I'll see you in the morning." Korra says.

"Yeah okay," I say. "Oh, before you go can you take my handcuffs off."

"Yeah sure." she says, she walks into the room and undoes the handcuffs.

"Thank you." I say.

---

"Today was a long day today." Baatar says.

"Yeah it was." Asami says.

"Alright we should get some sleep." Baatar says.

Chapter 20

I wake to the sound of an alarm. I groan and sit up, then I look around and let out a sigh.

"Good morning." says a voice.

I look to my right and see Korra sitting on the bench in the corner of my cell, tapping her foot against the floor.

"Good morning." I say. I stare at her with a confused look.

"What?" she asks.

"What are you doing in my cell? Did Zaheer ask you to watch me?" I ask.

"No." she says.

"If he didn't send you, then why are you here?"

"I'm here to tell you…" Korra stops talking and swallows.

"You're here to tell me what?" I ask.

"I'm here to tell you that today is your final test. After today Zaheer won't need you." she says.

I sigh and say. "Yeah I know."

"Well let's go." Korra says.

I get up and we walk out of the room.

---

"We have to get out of here?" Asmai says as she bodychucks the door, trying to break it down.

"I know." Baatar says.

"Then why are you just sitting there?" The president asks him.

"Well, what do you want me to do?" Baatar asks.

"Uh break down this door." she says.

"How?" he asks.

"Dude, use your waterbending."

"Uh, right." Baatar bends the water from his water flask and freezes the lock on the door. The lock brakes and Asami slams into it. This time the door the opens.

Asami dusts herself on and says. "There we go."

She looks back only to see Baatar hiding in the corner.

"Come on let's go." she says.

Baatar clears his throat "Right."

Asami walks out of the room, with Baatar following behind.

---

Me and Korra walk towards the lab. When we get there. I walk behind the glass wall and Korra does up the chains.

"Korra?" I say.

"What?" she says.

"Thank you."

"For what?" she asks.

"As much as you're a pain. Thanks for being here."

"Oh," she stops talking for a few minutes, then she continues. "Thank you."

Minutes later Zaheer walks into the room

"Okay, let's get this over with," he says and he motions to Korra. "Bring the poison."

Chapter 21

I struggle against the platinum chains. But they don't budge.

*Shoot. I need to get out of here.* I think.

Zaheer walks forward with the poison and Korra bends it out of the container.

"Wait." Korra says and she bends it back into place.

"What's the problem?" Zaheer asks.

Korra leans over to Zaheer and whispers something. Zaheer nods and Korra leaves the room. I stand behind what used to be the glass wall. I try again to bend the cuffs and chains. But they still don't move. Korra returns moments with former President Raiko and Kuvira. Kuvira walks into the room with her hands cuffed together.

*Platinum.*

      *Wait, why am I suddenly sensing a connection to the platinum again?* I think.
My thoughts are interrupted a few seconds later though.

      "Christine." Korra says.

I look at her.

      "What?" I say, my voice sounding weak.

      "Zaheer wants to make a deal with you." she says.

      "What do *you* want?" I spit the question out like its venom.

      "Nothing actually." Zaheer says as he shoots Korra a dirty look.

I look back at Kuvira, she trying to fight her way towards me, but Raiko is holding her back.

      "Kuvira," I say. "Look at me.'

She stops and looks at me.

      I jerk my head towards Zaheer. She stares at me blankly and then without warning she shoots two metal strips at Raiko. He screams and lets her go. She takes that advantage to tackle Zaheer to the ground, she knocks him out before he can do anything. Kuvira then turns towards Korra. Korra drops into her waterbending stance.

      "Come on. You know you can't win against me Korra." Kuvira says.

      "Are you sure about that?" Korra asks.

      "Is that a challenge?" Kuvira asks.

      "Yes it is." Korra replies.

      "Alright. Bring it." Kuvira smirks.

Chapter 22

Asami and Baatar run through the hallway towards the lab. When they get inside though they see Christine chained against the wall and Kuvira shooting attacks at Korra.

      "Come on. We need to help them." Baatar says.

      Kuvira ducks as Korra bends a blast of fire at her. Kuvira shoots several metal strips at Korra. "Come on *Avatar*, show me what you got." Kuvira taunts.

      "Will you quit saying that." Korra growls.

      "Nope." Kuvira says with another smirk.

      "Will you quit smirking too."

      "Never."

"Really Kuvira?" Korra says as she bends a strip of metal at her. "You're going to use the "Never." line?"

"Maybe."

Korra smirks as she looks over Kuvira's shoulder at something or rather at *someone*.

"What are you looking at?" Kuvira says and she looks over her shoulder.

*"Baatar!"* she screams.

---

I struggle against the chains again. The chains break and my hands are still cuffed together. *Yeah. There's no way I'm falling for that again.* I think.

I bend the platinum around myself like armor. I jump down from behind the broken glass wall and run at Korra. I slam her into the ground.

"I'm going to get whoever just…" Korra growls as she turns around. I smirk at her.

"Christine? How?" she says.

"This is how." I say and bend some of the platinum off my armor. I shoot some of the platinum strips at Korra. She tries to bend the metal away from herself, but it doesn't work. It hits her in the chest and she screams.

"Impossible, you can't bend *platinum*." she says.

"Oh really?" I say. I shoot two more platinum strips at her and she gets hit two more times. I'm just about to kill Korra when I get knocked to the ground by a blast of air.

"Your welcome." Zaheer says.

Korra coughs out a mouthful of blood. "I had everything under control."

"Oh sure it *definitely* looked like it." he says.

"Zaheer look out!" Korra yells.

I slam him into the ground and freeze him there, so he can't get up again.

"I'm going to kill you." Korra says.

"I'd like to see you try." I say.

Chapter 23

Kuvira runs over to Baatar and gives him a shake. "Baatar wake up, please wake up." Baatar doesn't respond and Kuvira shakes him harder. "Baatar, come on. Wake up."

She checks for a pulse, but doesn't find one.

"No!" she shrieked. "Baatar no! You can't leave me or Christine!"

She instantly began doing chest compressions.

"Come on. Come on. Come on Baatar. Breathe!"

Kuvira continued doing compressions. Seconds later Baatar started to cough and Kuvira ceased the motion. Baatar opened his and tried to sit up. But he didn't have the energy to do so. He just laid there looking up at Kuvira

"Hey." Baatar says.

"Hey," Kuvira replied. "I'm glad you're alive."

Baatar lets out a chuckle. "Me too."

---

I kick out a blast of fire at Korra and she dives out of the way.

"Get back here!" I yell.

"You're going to have to catch me first." Korra teased.

"Fine." I say.

I start to run at Korra, but then she bends a piece of metal in front of me and I slam into it. I let out a cry of pain and stumble backwards. The impact from the metal makes me feel dizzy. I fall to my knees and the room starts to spin. Soon I pass out.

---

Kuvira helps Baatar up off the the ground. He gives her a hug. "Alright. Let's go, finish what we came here for."

"I agree." Kuvira says.

Kuvira shoots out some of her metal strips and Baatar starts to bloodbend Korra. Korra deflects the attacks and tries blast with air. But as soon as Baatar starts to bloodbend her, she goes into The Avatar State to avoid being hurt. She blasts Baatar with air, but he dives out of way.

Kuvira fires out her metal cable. It wraps around Korra's ankle, she metalbends the cable back and Korra exits The Avatar State.

"I can't let you win!" Kuvira shouts.

---

I wake with a start, I look around. I ease myself off the ground and see Korra, battling with Kuvira and Baatar. I run at Korra and slam her into the ground again.

"What the...?" she looks back at me. "You are really hard to kill." she says.

"That's the point. Isn't it?" I say with a smirk.

Chapter 24

I run at Korra to knock her out. When suddenly I feel a searing pain in my wrists and ankles. I let out a scream and collapse to the ground. I look at my wrists and notice a silver colored liquid slowly going into my body, it takes me a moment to realize what it is. *Poison.*

"No!" I scream.

"I've got you now." Korra says with an evil laugh.

I try to fight the urge to enter the Avatar State, though its very difficult.

"Christine! Hold on!" Baatar yells.

I groan and try to move but that only makes the pain even worse. I lift my head and look around, but my vision makes everything look blurry. I try to hold on, but after a few minutes I become very tired and weak. I could feel the poison coursing through my veins, through my muscles. It made my body feel like molasse. The deeper the poison went, the weaker my urge to stay out of the Avatar State becomes. I could feel my muscles twitching and jumping, my body starts to shudder.

I could just hear Korra's surprisingly soft voice through the ringing in my ears. "Come on, you know you can't fight. Just let go. Just give in."

"No!" I say, my voice weak.

---

Finally I can't stay in control. I enter The Avatar State and send a blast of fire towards Korra, she extinguishes it with a simple motion of her hands. Then she shoots a metal strip at me, I don't get out of the way fast enough. It wraps around my wrists and with a simple motion of her hands Korra sends me flying towards the other side of the lab. I crash into the wall and slam into the ground.

*"Christine!"* Baatar, Kuvira, and Asami, all yell.

I weakly get up.

"Its over, stop. Just stop." Korra says again.

"As long as I'm still breathing, its not over." I say.

"Oh really?" Korra smirks. "That gives me an idea."

"If you think you can win then you're...," I gasp as Korra drains the air from my lungs.

My vision starts to fade. I fall to the ground, but a pair of strong arms catch me. Through my fading vision I could see Kuvira and Baatar. I've never seen them so afraid before. I reach up and grab one of Baatar's hands. He clutches my wrist. When I look at them though, I then realize that if I let go. Then their lives will never be complete. I continue fighting to stay alive. For them. Only them. I fight against the poison. But it becomes too much. My eyes close.

"No!" Both Baatar and Kuvira scream.

Chapter 25

But I'm still breathing, not enough to completely restart my lungs. But enough, to still be alive. Somewhat. But the poison is too strong. I let out a final huff of air.

Kuvira let's Christine's hand go and gets up. She marches over to Korra. "You killed Christine!"

"So what?" Korra smirks.

Kuvira doesn't say anything, she just stares at Korra. Then without warning, she shoots her metal cable at Korra.

"I'm sick and tired of people trying to kill my girlfriend." Kuvira says as shoots several metal strips from her armguards.

Korra dodges all the attacks and tries to blast Kuvira with air. She shoots some more metal in Korra's path. Korra dodges and redirects the metal strips back at Kuvira.

"Come on Korra, you know you can't win." Kuvira teases.

---

Baatar Jr. gives Christine a shake, trying to wake her up.

"Come on wake up, *wake up*. Don't you *dare* leave us like this." Baatar says.

Baatar suddenly felt something click. It takes a moment but it finally hit him. *The poison is both metallic and water-like.*

His gaze shot back over to Kuvira, who was still dodging attacks.

---

Kuvira finally hits Korra with her metal strips. She clamps one on her left ankle, then her right ankle. Kuvira does the same thing with Korra's wrists. She pins Korra to opposite wall.

"You're too late. The Red Lotus has won." Korra declares

---

"Kuvira!" Baatar calls.

Kuvira snaps out of her daze and looks back at Baatar.

"The poison is metallic!" he yells.

Kuvira runs back over to Christine and closes her eyes to sense the metal. Once she can get a reading on it. She begins to bend through and out of Christine's body.

Chapter 26

My spirit floats in darkness. I'm not sure where I am, but it sure is nice. I start to faintly see the outline of The Spirit World. I let out a sigh. I'm ready to let go. I'm in a place where I feel free. I'm in a place, I feel safe. In a place where I can recover.

---

Kuvira and Baatar bend the last of the poison out of Christine's body. When suddenly Christine's eyes shot open, The Avatar State charging her with energy. She starts to cough and Baatar bends the poison away from her. I look at both of them.

"Hey." I say, weakly.

"Oh thank goodness. You're alive." Baatar says.

"Of course, don't you know it takes more than that to kill me." I say.

"Yeah, the world would probably have to end for that to happen." Kuvira says.

"Maybe not even then." I say with a chuckle.

"Yeah you're right." Baatar says.

---

I get up and walk over to Korra. She stares at me with stunned look.

"No! How are you alive?" she says.

"Are you really that hell bent on wanting me dead?" I ask.

"Well chaos is the natural order." Korra says.

"Ugh. Enough. Do you know how stupid that sounds? I mean you want to kill the Avatar, when you are the Avatar."

"I'm the old Avatar, you're the new Avatar." she says.

"It doesn't matter!" I say. "What am I saying is, that you're ideology is way out of balance."

"What are you talking about?" Korra says. "I'm perfectly balanced!"

"Alright I've had enough of you!" says a voice.

Suddenly Korra's body seized up instantly, bending and twitching under the control of bloodbending. We all turn around, only to see Baatar standing behind us.

"Baatar!" Me and Kuvira exclaim.

"Its nice to see you too." he says.

"Stop! Just stop!" Korra says, squealing in pain.

"I'm sorry, but I can't. You're just too dangerous." he says, hurt and guilt flashing in his eyes. He bloodbends her harder and Korra screams louder.

---

I look at Kuvira and she nods. I look at Baatar and nod. He snaps his fingers and Korra's screams come to a halt. Korra just hangs in the air for a few minutes, her body still, then Baatar lowers his hands and Korra's body slams into the floor.

Me and Kuvira walk up to Baatar—who is breathing heavily—and give him a hug. He returns the hug.

"Hey its alright." Kuvira says.

"Okay. Let's go home." Baatar says.

"Okay."

We walk out of Erudite headquarters together.

## The Legend Of Korra Meets Insurgent Part 2
### (Book 5)

Chapter 1

"For crimes against humanity, we find Avatar Christine, Baatar Jr. and Asami Sato guilty for the murder of Avatar Korra, President Raiko and The Red Lotus and sentence them all to death." The judge spoke.

I close my eyes, maybe I can escape the uproaring of the crowd.

---

*Two years earlier…*

*I get up and walk over to Korra. She stares at me with a stunned look.*

*"No! How are you alive?" she says.*

*"Are you really that hell bent on wanting me dead?" I ask.*

*"Well chaos is the natural order." Korra says.*

*"Ugh. Enough. Do you know how stupid that sounds? I mean you want to kill the Avatar, when you are the Avatar."*

*"I'm the old Avatar, you're the new Avatar." she says.*

*"It doesn't matter!" I say. "What am I saying is, that you're ideology is way out of balance."*

"What are you talking about?" Korra says. "I'm perfectly balanced!"

"Alright I've had enough of you!" says a voice.

Suddenly Korra's body seized up instantly, bending and twitching under the control of bloodbending. We all turn around, only to see Baatar standing behind us.

"Baatar!" Me and Kuvira exclaim.

"Its nice to see you too." he says.

"Stop! Just stop!" Korra says, squealing in pain.

"I'm sorry, but I can't. You're just too dangerous." he says, hurt and guilt flashing in his eyes. He bloodbends her harder and Korra screams louder.

---

I look at Baatar and nod. He snaps his fingers and Korra's screams come to a halt. Korra just hangs in the air for a few minutes, her body still, then Baatar lowers his hands and Korra's body slams into the floor.

Me and Kuvira walk up to Baatar—who is breathing heavily—and give him a hug. He returns the hug.

"Hey, its alright." Kuvira says.

"Okay. Let's go home." Baatar says.

"Okay."

We walk out of Erudite headquarters together.

Chapter 2

Present day…

I wake with a start. I look around my cell and let a sigh. I get rid of the most dangerous criminals in the world and this is how I'm treated. I think. I drop my head into my hands and take a deep breath. My trial was a complete disaster, my lawyer didn't defend me and neither did Baatar's lawyer or Asami's lawyer. Ours just sat there and when we were asked questions, the lawyers didn't let us answer. The judge falsely accused all of us for the murder of Avatar Korra. Now we are sitting in our cells, waiting for our executions to be carried out. Hopefully we can get out of here soon.

---

"You can't execute them, they're innocent." Lawyer Johanna says.

"They tried to wipe out Chicago, what do you want me to do? Let them go free?" Judge Evelyn asks.

"Yes." Johanna says.

"No. Avatar Christine, Baatar Jr. and Asami Sato are war criminals." Evelyn replies.

"They've been falsely accused, you need to let them go." Johanna shot back.

"No. How about I put them on trial again. How does that sound?"

"Fine." Johanna says.

---

Baatar paced back and forth in his cell. *One minute I'm free and then the next, I'm back in prison.* he thought.

Baatar sat down on his cell bed and looked down at floor. Memories of the event that happened with Zaheer almost over two years ago, was still fresh in his mind.

He dropped his head into his hands, took in a deep breath and without meaning too, he fell asleep.

---

Kuvira let out a sigh as she walked towards Erudite headquarters or rather Factionless headquarters. Right after the fall of Avatar Korra and The Red Lotus, Chicago's political system was transformed into a faction system. You know to keep the peace. Kuvira pushed open the doors and walked inside. She had so many terrible memories here. Like there was the time Baatar had tried to kill Christine... twice, or when Zaheer and Korra had tried to kill Christine. Kuvira pushed the thought from her mind. So she focused her thoughts on the Factionless symbol that she had on her shirt sleeve. Right after Christine, Baatar and Asami were tried for their "supposed" crimes, Evelyn wanted Kuvira to part of her "inner circle" and Kuvira agreed. So many things have happened in the last eight years. Kuvira only hoped things would get better. She pushed open another set of doors and walked into Evelyn's office. Evelyn sat at her desk looking over her documents.

"You wanted to see me?" Kuvira asked.

Evelyn looked up from her papers. "Uh y-yes, just pull up a chair."

Kuvira grabbed one of the chairs from the corner and sat down. Both women sat in an awkward silence for a few minutes, then Evelyn says. "I need your help with something."

"Alright," Kuvira says nervously. "What is it?"

---

## Chapter 3

Asami shuffled forward, her wrists and ankles shackled together with platinum cuffs. The room she was in, was silent. The lights were dim, so it was hard to see. She looked around, but her vision started to blur. Instead of seeing the people in front of her, she saw Korra and Zaheer. She remembered the fear and anger she felt, when she found out that Korra teamed up with President Raiko and Zaheer.

*Spirits, why am I thinking of this right now? I need to focus.* Asami thought.

Asami shook the thought from her mind. She took another look around the room, scanning the faces of the people in the room. Then she locked her gaze on someone, she had a feeling that she had seen that person before. She took a closer look, let out a gasp and fell to the floor. Dead.

---

Johanna paced back and forth outside the execution room, waiting for Asami's "trial" to be finished. She looked at her watch, it was quarter to eleven at night. She let out a sigh and continued to pace back and forth. When suddenly the doors burst open and a flood of people came out, two of which were carrying Asami Sato's body. Johanna stared at the lifelessness in Asami's eyes before looking away.

"I'm surprised you came, I thought you hated executions."

Johanna turned around and narrowed her eyes. "I thought it would make you happy, if at least I showed up."

Evelyn tried to ignore the threatening tone in Johanna's voice. "What has to be done, has to be done."

Johanna looked over Evelyn's shoulder at the people who still remained loyal to the factionless. "Tell me, how many of your people know about what you're truly planning?"

Evelyn tensed up temporarily, afraid that her people had heard what Johanna had said, but she soon relaxed.

Johanna smirked. "That's what I thought."

"Careful with the threats Johanna, you need to remember who you're dealing with." Evelyn whispered as she turned from Johanna and started to walk back to the group of factionless.

---

Baatar woke with a start, he could hear footsteps approaching. He looked around his cell, trying find a way to escape. He saw a window and instantly started to cut the metal away from the windows, with the water he had with him. He was getting out of here. He *had* to get out of here. Just as he cut the last of the metal away from the window, his cell door opened.

*Oh no.* Baatar thought.

"What on earth are you doing Baatar?!" A voice boomed.

Chapter 4

Baatar froze, unable to breathe or move for that matter.

*"What are on earth are you doing, Baatar?!"* The voice boomed again.

Baatar didn't turn around, he felt a strong hand on his shoulder. He tried to wrestle away from the grip. But then he was spun around and he squeezed his eyes shut.

*"Baatar, open your eyes."*

Baatar forced one eye open and gasped. "Kuvira?"

"Hey." Kuvira said, breathing heavily.

*She must have sprinted here.* Baatar thought.

"What are you doing here?" Baatar asked.

"I'm here to get you out of here." she replied.

*"What?!"* Baatar exclaimed.

"Come on let's go." Kuvira said, as she pulled on his arm.

Baatar and Kuvira ran out of the cell and down three? Four hallways? Baatar didn't know and frankly he didn't care, all that he cared about was getting out of this horrible place.

---

Johanna shuffled forward, her wrists and ankles shackled together with platinum cuffs. The room she was in, was silent. The lights were dim, so it was hard to see. She looked around, but her vision started to blur. *I need to focus.* Johanna thought.

Johanna shook the thought from her mind. She took another look around the room, scanning the faces of the people in the room. Then she locked her gaze on someone, she had a feeling that she had seen that person before. She took a closer look, let out a gasp and fell to the floor. Dead.

---

I pace back and forth inside my cell, I had just heard that Asami and Johanna were just executed. Now I'm making a desperate attempt to escape. I hear footsteps approaching and fear starts to coarse through my veins. I run over to the window and continue cutting through the metal, I've just cut through the last little bit of metal, when my cell door opened.

*Oh no.* I think.

"What on earth were you doing Christine?!" Two voices boom.

Chapter 5

I freeze, unable to breathe or move.

*"What on earth were you doing Christine?!"* The two voices boom again.

I don't turn around. Suddenly I feel two strong hands on my shoulders. I try to wrestle out of the grip. But then I'm spun around and I squeeze my eyes shut.

*"Christine, open your eyes."*

I force one eye open. "Kuvira! Baatar!"

"Hey." They say, breathing heavily.

"What are you guys doing here?" I ask.

"We're getting you out of here."

*"What?!"* I exclaim.

"Come on let's go." Kuvira and Baatar say.

Me, Kuvira, and Baatar get up and sprint out of the room. Kuvira, me and Baatar turn another corner and we all skid to a stop.

"Where do you think you're going?" Evelyn said.

---

"Where do you think you're going?" Evelyn said.

"Nowhere." We all say.

"Yeah sure. I'm pretty sure that both Christine and Baatar are supposed to be in their cells." Evelyn paused for a moment before locking her gaze onto Kuvira. "I would've expected more from you Kuvira, I thought that you trusted me."

"Yeah sure, like I would ever trust you." Kuvira mumbled under her breath.

"Careful Kuvira, I don't think you want to see what I'm capable of." Evelyn warned.

"Uh huh. Who's going to stop us, I've got the Avatar and I've got a bloodbender." Kuvira replied with a smirk.

"Oh yeah?" Evelyn challenged.

Kuvira was about to say something, when Baatar spoke up. "If you want to try and stop us, then by all means you can try. Now you can either let us pass or you can... "

"Or I can what?" Evelyn interrupted. "Face the wrath of your bloodbending, I don't think so."

Without warning Baatar bent the water from his hip flask and aimed it at Evelyn. She stepped off to the side to avoid the attack and then she just gave her fingers a simple twitch. Everything went silent for a moment, before a bone-chilling scream filled the air.

"What the...?" Baatar said and he started to turn around. *"Christine!"*

Kuvira turns around too only to see Christine's body bending and twisting in a way it never should.

"L-let me... go!" I squeal.

"I don't think so." Evelyn said.

*"Christine!"* Baatar yelled as he ran towards me.

"Baatar get out of here!" I say.

"But..." Baatar starts to say.

"Kuvira, get Baatar out of here. I'll be fine." I say through the pain.

Kuvira grabbed Baatar's arm and sprinted out of Erudite headquarters. Once they're gone, Evelyn loosens her grip on me.

"Now, we have a trial to finish."

Chapter 6

Kuvira and Baatar reach the outer edge of the city, and continue running.

"We're almost there!" Kuvira yells. "Just keep running!"

Suddenly Kuvira feels an odd metal attraction coming from the air and she stops, but Baatar keeps running.

"Baatar wait!" she calls.

"What?" he yells back.

Suddenly Baatar's body starts to shake violently and he drops to the ground. Unmoving.

*"Baatar!"* Kuvira screams.

---

I struggle again against Evelyn's bloodbending grip, but she tightens her grip even more and I start to scream again.

"Ah, ah, ah," Evelyn says. "What do you think, you were going to accomplish against me?"

"L-let m-me g-go." I squeal again.

"Try all you want, but you're not going anywhere." she says with a smirk.

I try to move, but she bloodbends me, until spots start to crowd my vision and I pass out

---

"Baatar wake up." Kuvira says, giving him a shake. But she receives no answer.

*"Baatar **wake up**."* Once again she receives no response.

"No, No, No. N-not ag-again." Kuvira stammers.

*"Baa-t-tar w-wake u-up."* Kuvira says again, her voice shaking.

Kuvira, then presses two fingers to the side of Baatar's neck and lets out a sob. "N-no Baa-t-tar p-please wake up."

She then bends down and starts doing chest compressions.

---

I slowly wake up as consciousness returns.

"Well, it seems that you're awake. How do you feel?" says a voice.

I groan, blink a few times and my vision starts to clear. When I can see properly, I look across the room and see Evelyn standing there.

"What a-are you doing h-here?" I ask, my voice hoarse.

"I just came to check on you. To see how you'll act during your final days." She says, with a small smile.

*"Kuvira! Baatar!"* I snap my gaze back at Evelyn. "What... what did you do to them?"

"Oh don't worry, they're alive for now."

"You're a *monster*." I say, through gritted teeth.

"Call me what you may, but that won't change the outcome. I will get rid of you once and for all."

Evelyn exits the room.

Chapter 7

Kuvira is still on the ground doing chest compressions, when suddenly Baatar starts to cough. Kuvira ceased the motion and Baatar opens his eyes.

"Hey." he whispered.

"Hey, sweetie. How do you feel?" Kuvira asked, in a soft voice.

"I feel like I got struck with a lighting bolt, that's for sure." Baatar replied flatly.

Kuvira let out a small chuckle. "I think you're partly right."

Baatar sat up slowly and leaned against Kuvira.

"What do you mean?" he asked in confusion.

Kuvira rested her hand on his shoulder. "I'm not sure how to say this but..." her voice trailed off.

"But what?" Baatar asked, fear rising in his chest.

"Well... you struck a magnetic force field and nearly died." Kuvira replied softly.

*"What?!"* Baatar nearly shouted.

"Hey, don't worry you'll be alright." Kuvira reassured him.

"No it won't be alright!" Baatar said, now yelling.

"Baatar—" Kuvira tried to say, but he cut her off.

"Did you know that the force field was there?" he asked in a stern voice.

"What! No!" Kuvira said.

"You're *lying!*" Baatar growled.

"I'm *not* lying!" Kuvira nearly yelled.

Baatar didn't answer.

Kuvira let out a sigh and finally gave in. "Yes. I knew that the force field was there. Evelyn installed it, right after she took over Chicago."

"Why?" Baatar asked.

"To make sure no one could get out. She wanted full control of the city." Kuvira told him.

Baatar just shook his head, before saying "Well, if we can't get out, then we should go back and save Christine."

"That sounds like a good idea," Kuvira agreed, then she added. "Hopefully we can get there before Christine's trial."

"Then we better start moving." Baatar says, as he starts his way back towards the city.

Together Kuvira and Baatar make their way back to the city.

---

I sit on my cell bed, staring at the floor. When my cell door opened.

*"Christine?"* a voice said.

I don't bother looking up, I know that Evelyn is in the room.

"Its time to go." she says.

I huff out a sigh and get off the bed. When I reach the door, Evelyn grabs my arm. I don't try to pull away.

"No funny business." she whispers.

"Got it." I say, with a defeated sigh.

Together we walk out of my cell.

Chapter 8

Evelyn and I walk towards the room where my trial will take place. Evelyn keeps her grip on my arm to keep me in place, but I'm not going to try and run... yet. We walk down a series of hallways and into a room. A dark room. We sit down and I put my hands on the table. Suddenly my hands, arms, legs and chest become restrained. The chair I'm sitting in is cold and frigid. *Frigid? Wait a minute.* My eyes widen as the thought hits me. *This isn't a chair... its a table! An execution table!* I start to thrash around, trying to break free of the bindings that hold me there. But nothing works. My heart rate begins climb and I feel a familiar sensation in my wrists, it takes me a minute to realize what it is... The handcuffs, the *electrified* platinum handcuffs. I look over at Evelyn.

"What are you *doing!?*" I scream as the jolts of electricity become stronger and stronger.

"I told you that you had a trial to finish, so that was the deal." she says with a smirk.

I start to breathe heavily as it gets stronger and stronger and stronger. Then there is nothing.

---

Kuvira and Baatar run up Michigan Ave, towards Factionless headquarters. When they get there, Kuvira and Baatar run up the hallway, and skid to a stop.

"Kuvira and Baatar Beifong, stop where you are!" one of the factionless soldiers shouts.

Both Kuvira and Baatar stop and put there hands up. One of the soldiers walks forward with a pair of handcuffs and puts them on, Baatar and Kuvira.

Kuvira takes a look at one of the soldiers and says "Take me to Evelyn."

"What?" the soldier says.

"You heard me, I said: Take me to Evelyn, I need to have a word with her."

"Alright." the soldier replies.

"No you can't leave!" Baatar yells. "I can't afford to lose you again!"

"I'll be alright." Kuvira smiles.

"Let's go!" The soldier shouts, as he starts to drag Kuvira down the hallway.

"Kuvira!" Baatar voice echoes until its barely more than a whisper.

Kuvira closed her eyes, hoping that this nightmare will be over soon.

---

Evelyn paced back and forth, outside Christine's cell. When suddenly, her radio started make a static noise. She picked it up.

"Yes, what is it?"

*"Uh there's someone here to see you."*

"Well send them in, you may want to hurry, because I'm in the middle of a trial."

*"Sorry ma'am. But—"*

Suddenly there was a loud crash on the other end of the line, followed by a few grunts and groans.

*"We're under attack! I repeat we're under attack! Evelyn you need to get out of there n—"* Then the radio goes silent.

Evelyn quickly runs over to the table that Christine is restrained to and starts tightening the straps that are holding her to the table and starts to move the table towards a storage room.

I groan and slowly come to my senses. I look over at Evelyn.

"What are you doing?" I ask, sluggishly.

"Be quiet!" Evelyn hisses as she opens up the door and pushes me inside, then closes and locks the door.

Then the main door bursts open and Kuvira runs inside.

Chapter 9

*"Evelyn, where's Christine?"* Kuvira roars.

"I— I don't know." Evelyn stammers.

"You're *lying!*" Kuvira yells. "I know she's in here. I'm not going to ask you again: Where's Christine?"

"Why would I tell you, *traitor!*" Evelyn spat.

"When I'm done with you, you will." Kuvira growled.

Without warning Kuvira shot out her metal cable and Evelyn dodged the attack. Then Kuvira shot out her metal cable and Evelyn froze it with the water she had. Once Kuvira realized that Evelyn had her. She metalbent her cable back and Evelyn flew towards her and the two women crashed into one another. They both let out a cry of pain upon impact, and stumbled backwards.

"You traitor!" Evelyn spat again, blood trailing out and down past her lips. She didn't bother wiping the blood off her chin.

"What you're doing isn't right!" Kuvira called. "You need to stop this now!"

"I'm not going to throw away, what I worked so hard to achieve!" Evelyn yelled back.

"I don't want to fight you!" Kuvira whispered to herself.

The other women let out a yell, as she bent the water she had with her at Kuvira.

"Is that all you got?" Kuvira challenged.

---

I struggle against the bonds holding me to the table.

"Somebody! Anybody! Please get me out of here!" I yell, hoping someone can hear me.

I close my eyes, I can sense another metalbender in the room. *Kuvira!*

"Kuvira! I'm in here! Please come quick!" I thrash again. My handcuffs though, automatically start to shock me, because of my movements.

---

Kuvira dodges another attack. Then she hears shouts coming from somewhere and she snaps her gaze towards the storage room door.

"Christine!" she tries to yell but it comes out, nothing more than a pale whisper.

"Ah, ah, ah. Pay attention Great Uniter, you should be worrying about me and not your precious little Christine." Evelyn says.

"Sorry, but I don't have time for you!" Kuvira says. Just as she was going to deliver a final blow, Evelyn rotates her wrist and Kuvira's movements stopped dead and just like that she fell helpless to Evelyn's bloodbending.

"Ah… no!" Kuvira groans.

Evelyn let's out a laugh. "I've got you now."

Kuvira struggles against the invisible hold on her body. Evelyn motions her hand to the left and Kuvira flies towards the opposite wall and crashes into it head first. She then falls to the ground and doesn't get up.

---

I struggle more and more against the bindings. Then I hear footsteps, the door to the storage room swings open and Evelyn marches in. She marches over to the table and stops a few inches away from me.

"Now that Kuvira has been taken care of, I can now finish you off." Evelyn says, as she undoes the straps.

"Let's go finish that trial."


Chapter 10

Baatar rushes through the hallway. Towards the lab. *I have to get there in time. I need to get there in time.* Baatar thought.

He continues running down the hallways, until he reaches the lab. But when he gets there, he sees that Christine and Evelyn are missing. He looks around and sees someone lying on the ground.

"Kuvira!" he screams.

He runs and kneels down beside her. He notices a big open gash on the top of her head, he bends the water around his hands and holds it to her head. It starts to glow a bright blue, and moments later, Kuvira starts to groan and move a little. Then she slowly opens her eyes.

"Baatar?" she says, sounding dazed.

"Don't worry, I've got you." Baatar says in a hushed voice.

Kuvira groans and slowly sits up. She brings a hand to her forehead and squeezed her eyes shut. "Ugh my head. What happened?"

"I don't know, I came in here and found you out cold on the ground."

Kuvira blinked and then shot straight up, ignoring the throbbing pain inside her skull. *"Christine!* Where, where is she?"

"I don't know where she could be." Baatar admitted.

"We need to find them!" Kuvira half shouted.

"Whoa, easy! You need to recover, just lay still." Baatar said, as he tried to lay Kuvira down again. Kuvira stood up, but her vision went blurry. She became really dizzy and she collapsed onto the ground again.

*"Kuvira!"* Baatar yelled.

---

"Ugh, where am I?" I blink and look around the room. The lights are dim and I can't see very well.

"You're in your trial room, that's where." says a voice.

"Ugh, Evelyn." I say.

"Its nice to see you too." she says with a smirk.

I try to move but I'm still strapped to the table.

*Oh, dang it.* I think.

"Come on, sit up." Evelyn says with a smirk.

I chuckle and say. "Yeah, no."

She glares at me. "Why?"

"I'm strapped to a table, duh." I roll my eyes.

"Hey, watch it, Christine." she says in threatening tone.

I roll my eyes and don't sit up. Suddenly my body lurched forward and started to bend and twitch, under the force of bloodbending. The pain is so powerful that I let out a small whimper.

"Now are you going to do what I say?" she asks.

"Y-yes n-now please let me go." I whimper again.

"Excellent." Evelyn responds.

Chapter 11

Baatar rushes over to Kuvira and lightly gives her a shake not wanting to injure her any further. She lets out a groan and once again she opens her eyes.

"Ow, my head." she says.

"You're still healing, you need to rest." Baatar whispers gently.

Kuvira looks up at him. "What about Christine? We can't just leave her."

Baatar bites his lip and says "We'll find her and get her out safely, I promise."

Kuvira lets out a sigh. Baatar sits down on the floor next to her. Kuvira rests her head onto his shoulder. They both sit in silence for a long time, occasionally sneaking looks at each other and linking their fingers together. They forget about the pain, anger, and fear that they've felt over the last eight? Ten years? she had lost count. But one thing she did know is that they finally feel at peace.

---

I let out a sigh. After mine and Evelyn's talk, she told me that my trial was going to be held at *exactly* 4:45 pm, I'm not sure what time it is now and frankly I don't care. I close my eyes and try to hold back my tears. But they leak out past my eyelids and stream down my cheeks. I just leave them there, its not like I can stop them anyway. I'm still laying on the table, still have the straps binding me to it. Making sure that I can't move or escape. So I just lie there. Silent and still. My eyes start to feel heavy, I yawn and close my eyes.

---

Evelyn walks through the hallways and into every room. Looking for Baatar Jr. and Kuvira.

*They've got to be in here somewhere.* Evelyn thought to herself. She continued her walk and suddenly she stopped.

---

Kuvira and Baatar are talking with one another, when the door to the room opened. They both froze and didn't move.

"Well hello, how are you guys doing?" Evelyn says.
Neither of them said anything at first, nor did they move.

"What do you *want?*" Baatar spat.

"I want to offer you something." Evelyn smiles.

"Yeah, like we would do anything for you." Kuvira says.

"Oh, but this is one you won t be able to refuse." Evelyn replied.

---

*"Oh Christine. Wake up."* says a soft voice.
I yawn and open my eyes, when I see who's standing there. I frown.

"Hey, how are you?" Evelyn says in a sweet tone.

"Why do you even care?" I say, my voice barely above a whisper.

Evelyn scoffs and says. "Of course I care," She stops for a moment and then says. "I have something to show you."

I sigh. "What is it?"
She steps off to the side and I see two people standing there.

*"Kuvira! Baatar!"* I yell.

*"Christine!"* They yell back, there voices muffled.
I slightly move my head to the side and notice a glass wall, separating me from them.

Evelyn glances back at me. "Let the trial begin!"

## Chapter 12

I start to struggle against the bonds holding me to the table, but nothing works. Evelyn walks towards me with a needle full of serum.

*What is that?* I think. Whatever it is, it can't be good.
Evelyn sticks the needle in my neck and I gasp. Seconds later my body goes limp and I can't move my arms or legs. My breathing becomes shallow. All I can do is move my eyes to the right, I see Kuvira and Baatar standing on the other side of the glass, crying, They must not know that I'm alive. I move my eyes back towards Evelyn.

"This wasn't the only thing, that I had planned." she smirks.

I try to speak and it comes out in a whisper. "What are you planning?"

"You'll see." Evelyn gives her fingers a slight twitch and I let out a scream louder than, I thought possible.

---

Kuvira's gaze snaps back at Christine. "Christine's alive and Evelyn's bloodbending her!"

"We need to help her!" Baatar yells.
Kuvira tries to bend the metal away from the wall, but it doesn't work. "Oh crap, its *platinum!"*

"We need to get over there! Keep trying!" Baatar urges.
Kuvira takes a deep breath and tries to bend away the platinum wall, but once again it doesn't work.

"I can't Baatar, I can't." Kuvira says.

"Just keep trying." Baatar says, more urgently.

"Baatar, listen to me. Christine is the only one who can bend platinum."
Something tugs at her mind. "But there is one thing I can do."

---

I keep screaming, the pain getting worse by the second. I start to breath heavily and spots start to crowd my vision.

I hear Evelyn's voice through the ringing in my ears. "We're almost there. Just a little more pressure..."

I can feel the bones in my legs reach their breaking point. *Pop!* My leg bone finally breaks and I scream even louder.

"There we go." Evelyn says.

I glare at her. "You're going to pay for this."

"Just keep thinking that." she says, with a smirk.

I start to feel light-headed and I pass out.

---

"You think this will actually work?" Baatar asks Kuvira.

"I'm very certain this will work." Kuvira says as they stack pieces of rocks in front of the platinum part of the wall.

"Okay, I think that will be enough." Baatar says.

Kuvira takes a deep breath and the rocks start to form into lava. Kuvira motions the lava towards the wall and it slowly burns a hole into the wall itself.

"Alright, let's save Christine." Kuvira declared.

Chapter 13

I wake with a start, I'm still strapped to the bed. I ignite a fire blade in my hand and start to burn the straps. I'm down to the very last one, when suddenly my body stops and starts to bend and twitch.

"What were you thinking?" Evelyn says as she bloodbends me.

My other leg nears its breaking point and the pain is too much. I just let out a squeal.

---

Kuvira bursts through the hole in the wall. "Evelyn!" she yells.

Evelyn turns around and loosens her grip on me. I quit screaming.

"Kuvira." Evelyn growls.

Kuvira drops into her lavabending stance. "Let Christine go!"

Evelyn starts to bloodbend me and I start screaming again.

"Take one more step and all snap her in half." Evelyn says and she clenches her fingers and...

*Snap!*

My other leg bone breaks, leaving me with two broken legs. Evelyn quits bloodbending me.

I scream louder than before. Then my legs go numb.

"Evelyn, what did you do?!" Kuvira yells.

Evelyn just shrugs. "I will give you one more chance to back down, or else... "

She twitches her fingers again and my arms start to bend and twitch out of place.

"Kuvira!" I yell. "You need to get out of here!"

"No! I'm not going to run from this!" she yells back.

Kuvira you don't... *agh!...* you don't have a choice! Get out of here!"

"Be quiet!" Evelyn says as she bloodbends me harder.

"You have three seconds, before I make this choice for you." Evelyn replies, with a smirk.

*I know I can figure something out I just know I can!* Kuvira thought.

"Time's up!"

*"Stop!"*

Kuvira spins around at the sound, it didn't come from her. When she looks behind her she sees someone standing behind her. She rubs her eyes to make sure, she's not seeing what she thinks she's seeing. But the truth is, what she was seeing *was* true.

"Baatar, you're here!" Kuvira exclaimed.

"Yes! Baatar replied.

"How?" Kuvira asked.

"I'll tell you later, but first let's get Christine out of here."

"Good idea... *agh!*"

*"Kuvira!"* Baatar yells.

"I'll be fine!" Kuvira yells.

Baatar tries to think of anything, to free Kuvira and Christine, but nothing comes to mind. *Come on, come on! Think of something Baatar! Come on think!*

Evelyn's voice, breaks through his thoughts. "I'll give you two seconds."

Baatar scrambled to think of something, *anything* to help.

"Two!" Evelyn says.

Baatar didn't know, what to do or what to say.

"One!"

*"Stop!"*

Kuvira and Baatar look at each other and then turn around.

"Impossible." Evelyn whispered to herself.

Chapter 14

Evelyn releases me and I slump back onto the bed, I let out a groan of pain. I try to move my legs, but they feel numb. I groan again and cough out a little bit of blood. I hear grunts and groans and through my blurry vision I see Evelyn, being bloodbent and she collapses onto the ground. Suddenly darkness surrounds me.

*"Christine."* a voice echoes.

I take a deep breath. My eyes flicker open, I feel light-headed.

*"Christine."* the voice echoes again.

I look around, my vision blurry. I rest my eyes on two? Three? Figures standing in front of me.

*"Christine, it's me."*

I take a closer look and there are three people standing in front of me. I look at the third person.

"What are you doing here?" I ask trying to sit up, letting out a groan of pain in the process.

"Whoa, whoa. Just take it easy." The women says.

"Wait I recognize your voice," I rub my eyes, take a closer look and tense up. "Korra?"

"Its nice to see you again Avatar Christine." Korra says with a smile.

"How are you alive?" I ask.

"Honestly, I don't even know." she says, with a shrug.

"I can't believe I'm saying this but... I'm glad to see you." I say.

"Never thought I would hear those words." Korra says with a chuckle.

"What about Evelyn? What happened?"

"Oh I took care of that problem." Korra smirks.

I try to remember what happened, all I can remember is Evelyn being bloodbent and then passing out. Then it hits me.

I look at Korra wide-eyed. "You're a bloodbender? How?"

"I don't know that either, but what I do know is that... I'm here for you." she smiles. She gets up off the bed and says. "Come on we're going home."

"I can't walk."

"Here." she says as she pushes a wheelchair towards me.

"But how can I protect the world, if i'm in a wheelchair?" I ask.

"Just trust me, because I've been there before, remember?"

"Right" I say. "I keep forgetting. Sorry."

"That's okay." she says.

She helps me into the wheelchair. Baatar and Kuvira push me forward. We exit Factionless headquarters and Korra stops.

"Wait." she says and she turns towards the building. She sends a blast of fire at the building and it burst into flames.

"Let's make sure, none of this ever happens again." she says.

"Agreed." I say.

"Alright, let's go home." Korra says.

Chapter 15

*Three years later...*

I sit in my wheelchair, staring at a mirror as Korra combs my hair. It's still as short as it was twelve years ago.

"How is your hair still so short?" Korra asks.

"How are you still so young?" I ask.

"Haha. You have a point," Korra says, with a roll of her eyes. "Alright your hair is done. Let's go."

---

Korra pushes the wheelchair out of the house and towards the car. Kuvira stands there with Baatar. We stop a few feet away from it.

"Are you all ready to go?" Kuvira asks.

I nod, Korra helps me into the car and does up my seatbelt. She sits next to me and I tense a little, before relaxing.

"I'm not going to hurt you, you know that right?" she says.

"I know," I reply. "Its just... I need to get used to you being here, that's all."

"Really? Its been five years, come on." she smirks.

"I know." I say.

I lean over and rest my head on her shoulder. She pats my head in return. We sit in silence for a few minutes.

Korra sucks in a deep breath, before saying. "Hey, where's Asami?"

I tense back up and move back to my seat, Baatar looks at Korra in his rearview mirror and Kuvira looks at her and then at me in confusion. "You didn't tell her?"

"What? You didn't tell me what?" Korra asks, sounding worried.

I let out a sigh and say. "I'm sorry Korra. Asami's... " my voice trails off and tears fill my eyes.

"Asami's what?" Korra asks, more forcefully now.

Kuvira looks from Korra to me and says. "You need to tell her sooner or later."

"Alright enough," Korra says. "Just tell me."

I let out another sigh and look back at Korra. "Asami's dead."

Korra let's out a sob, I lean back into her, and give her a hug. "I'm so sorry." I whisper.

She pulls away. "How did this happen?"

"Evelyn killed her." Baatar says.

"We're sorry, Korra." Kuvira says.

Korra leans her head onto my shoulder again and we both start to cry.

---

We sit there hugging each other and tears continue to flow down our faces. Korra cries until she feels tired and weak. She rests her head on my shoulder and closes her eyes. She takes in long deep breaths in attempt to calm down. I run my hand through her short brown hair and hold her close. Kuvira looks at me in the mirror and gives me a thumbs up. I just nod.

I huff out a sigh, look down at Korra and whisper. "I'm here for you. You know that."

I look back up at Baatar and Kuvira. "I can't believe, what we've been through. How did we ever survive it all?"

"I know right? I mean we have been through a lot in the last decade." Baatar says, as we pull up the driveway to our house. I shake Korra awake and tell her that we're home and its time to get up. We hop out of the car and Korra wheels me inside. She sets helps me out of the wheelchair and onto the couch.

"Alright, let's get started." Korra says.


Chapter 16

*"Korra!"* I yell.

I grit my teeth, about an hour ago I had found out that I still had some of the poison in my body. The news was devastating. Now she trying to bend the rest of it out, but it hurts so much.

"Korra! You're hurting me!" I say.

"I'm sorry, but... just hold onto something." she says.

I grab the closest things to me, which just happens to be Baatar's shirt collar.

"Hey!" Baatar says as he tries to pull away.

"Sorry Baatar!" I say through clenched teeth.

"It's okay." he says.

Baatar turns his head to the side, trying to avoid being choked. Kuvira is holding my other hand, trying her best to keep me calm.

"Almost there, Christine, almost there." Korra says.

She bends the last little bit out of my body. I lie on the couch, breathing heavily. I release Baatar and he rubs the back of his neck.

"Okay, you're strong." he says.

"Sorry." I say.

"That took a lot out of me." Kuvira says, plopping herself down onto the couch.

I look up at Korra and mouth the words "Thank you." because I can't speak any louder. Korra nods in return.

"When will I be able to walk?" I ask, once I'm able to speak.

"I'm not sure. The combination of the paralytic serum, the poison and the bloodbending, left you with severely damaged legs." Korra says.

"But will I be able to walk again?" I ask.

Korra shakes her head. "You will be able to walk once they're healed, but..." Korra let's her voice trail off.

"But there is permanent damage done to my legs." I whisper.

"Sadly, you are correct." she says, with a squeeze to my shoulder.

"Thank you for looking after me." I say.

"I wish I could do more."

"Its okay, you've done your part. It's up to us now." Kuvira says, with a nod.

---

That night, when I go to bed. Kuvira and Baatar help me get ready. I climb into bed and try to fall asleep, but everytime I try, I end up dreaming about Evelyn and how she tried to kill me. So I get out of bed, wheel myself to Kuvira and Korra's bedroom. I wake them up.

"Hey," Korra says. "Can't sleep?"

I shake my head.

"Come here." she says.

I hop onto the bed beside her and lay my head down on her shoulder. She puts her arm across my chest.

"Just close your eyes." she says.

I nod and minutes later I fall asleep.

Chapter 17

I open my eyes and bolt straight up. I look around the room and then take a deep breath.

"You okay?" someone asks.

I turn my head and find myself looking back at Kuvira. "Yeah I'm fine."

"Yeah, sure. I know you're not fine." she says.

"Okay you win. I just had a nightmare, that's all."

"About what?"

"Just about Evelyn." I say.

"I see." Kuvira nods.

"Uh, I'm trying to sleep." Korra mumbles into her pillow.

"Sorry, sleepy head. But Christine had a nightmare."

Korra rolls over and gives me a hug. I just sit there, relaxed. Kuvira just giggles.

"What?" Korra asks.

"You're funny." Kuvira says, starting to laugh harder.

"Why?" Korra asks.

"Well, one minute you're cranky and the next you're hugging Christine."

Korra's face turns red in embarrassment and she let's me go. We sit on the bed together. Korra gets off the bed.

"Well I'll go wake Baatar up and start to make breakfast." she says.

She walks out of the room and towards Baatar's new room, that me, Kuvira and Korra built. Me and Kuvira just sit on the bed and talk.

---

"Christine! Kuvira! Breakfast is ready!" Korra calls.

Kuvira walks downstairs and she wheels me over to the table with Baatar. But the table is set for ten people.

I look at Korra in confusion. "Why is the table set for ten people."

"You'll see in a minute, just sit down." Korra says, as she dries her hands with a towel.

I sit beside Kuvira and Baatar. Then the doorbell rings. Korra walks over to the door and opens it.

"Hey, Korra." a familiar voice says.

"Hey, Su. Long time, no see. Please come in." Korra replies.

"Yeah, it's been a while." Another voice says.

"Yes it has. How have you been Baatar Sr.?" Korra asks.

"I've been doing great actually," Baatar Sr. says. "Sorry that we didn't visit earlier, but it's so hard, since we live all the way over in Zaofu."

"Plus all the stuff that had happened with Evelyn." a third voice says.

"Yeah. How have you been Opal?" Korra asks.

"Meh, I've been okay." Opal replies.

Korra nods. "How about you Huan?"

"Okay." Huan says.

"Yeah, we've all been feeling great." two voices say.

"Hi Wing, Hello Wei." Korra says.

"Hey." The twins reply.

Everyone walks over to the table and sits down. Korra brings breakfast over and sets it down on the table.

Su gives me a concerned look. "What happened to you?"

"Um… my legs broke."

"What?! How?" Su asks.

"Its a long story." I say.


Chapter 18

Everyone stares at me in shock. I had just finished telling them what happened in the last two years.

"Can you walk?" Su asks me.

I shake my head. "No I can't. There is permanent damage to my legs."

Su gives me a hug. I close my eyes to try and stop myself from crying. I pull away and wipe my eyes.

"I can't believe she did that to you." Baatar Sr. says.

"I tried my best to heal her legs, but there's nothing more I can do." Korra says.

"At least we tried." I say.

"Yeah." Su sighs.

"What's wrong?" Kuvira asks.

"Well…," Su pauses, let's out another sigh and then continues. "I have something to tell Christine."

The look that Su gives me worries me. Everyone at table starts to stare again. I feel my heart in my throat and look at Su again.

"Okay. What is it?"

---

"Of course I'm staying here!" I say, my voice filled with anger and shock.

"Christine, you need to leave. You're not safe in Chicago anymore." Kuvira and Su say with a pleading look in their eyes.

"I'll be fine!" I insist.

"Sure, that's why everytime you're here, you always end up in a life-threatening situation, because that´s totally safe." Korra says.

"I'll be fine!" I say again.

"No you won't!" Kuvira says.

"Wait! I have an idea. Why don't we all go back to Zaofu, I'll be safe there."

"That might work," Baatar Sr. says. "What do you think Su?"

"Sure, why not." Su says.

---

Me, Kuvira, Korra and the rest of the family walk out of the house and hop on the train, I look out the window as we pass Chicago. This will be the last time, I will ever see it, so I enjoy the view.

Chapter 19

We arrive in Zaofu around 11:30 at night. We get off the train, walk to Su´s house and once we get inside, everyone but me walks to the living room and sits down. Su wheels me over and helps me onto the couch I let out a sigh and close my eyes. I need to take a quick nap.

"Tired, eh?" a voice says.

I open my eyes. "Oh Kuvira I didn't see you there."

She laughs. "Because you had your eyes closed, silly."

I roll my eyes. "Smart alec."

She sits down beside me, puts her arms around me and pulls me into a hug. I take a deep breath, the smell of her uniform wafts up my nose. The smell makes me feel safe. I close my eyes and rest my head on her shoulder.

Kuvira strokes my head and whispers. "You should get some sleep. I fight off the bad dreams if they try to get you."

"With what?" I ask.

"With my lavabending obviously." she says.

I laugh. "I don't that will be necessary."

Kuvira chuckles and says. "Shhh, just relax and go to sleep."

I snuggle my head into her shoulder. My mind goes blank and I drift off again.

---

I scream, pain ripping through my bones and muscles. My legs bend near their breaking point, only a hair away from breaking.

"Almost there," Evelyn says "Just a little more pressure and…"

*Snap!*

My other leg bone breaks, leaving me with two broken legs. I start to breath heavily spots start to crowd my vision. I scream louder than I thought possible.

"Now to finish you off." Evelyn says as she walks towards me, with a needle full of death serum. *Death serum? No! That can't be right it was all used up, like eight years ago!*

My mind starts to race and Evelyn sticks the needle in my neck, I start to gasp and cough. Black spots crowd my vision, my body starts to feel heavy. My heart stops. Darkness surrounds me.

---

I scream, and bolt straight up, eyes wide. My heart pounding so fast it hurts and breath heavily. I hear footsteps. I send a blast of fire towards the sound.

*"Whoa easy!"* a voice says. *"Christine, its me Korra."*

I rub my eyes and look at the person standing across from me. Korra stands by the couch, putting out the fire that I had started. Once she has put it out, I sit back down on the couch. I put my head in my hands and let out a shaking breath. Tears start to form in my eyes and I let them flow down my face freely. Korra sits down next to me. She leans over and gives me a hug. I hear more footsteps and tense up.

"Its okay. Its just Baatar and Kuvira." Korra whispers.

"What happened?" Baatar asks.

"I just had a nightmare, that's all." I say.

"About?" Kuvira asks.

I break away from Korra and look from Kuvira and Baatar. "The usual."

"I kinda figured that, it was the same dream." Korra says.

Baatar and Kuvira walk over and sit down beside me as well.

We sit together in silence for a long time.


Chapter 20

Later that day, we take a walk around the garden. Well I'm being wheeled around of course. I look up at the sky. Zaofu now leaves their metal domes open, to allow more people around The United Earth States to visit. After Evelyn was killed, the faction system was torn down and was replaced with a more structured political system. Free elections were held and Korra became the third president of Illinois and The United Earth States. Though some people were a bit on edge, about having an Avatar become president. Kuvira helped put the people's worries at ease. Now it doesn't seem to be much of an issue.

"The sky is beautiful, isn't it?" Korra says, snapping me back to reality.

"Yes it is." I say, still marveling at it.

Of course I had only been to Zaofu a couple of times, so I never really got a chance to see it all. Now I find myself wishing I could have seen more of it, earlier in my life.

"Just think, you'll be staying here." Korra says.

"What about you?" I ask her.

"I need to stay in Chicago to keep peace and order in the city." she says putting her hand on my shoulder.

"But aren't you going to stay and help me save the world?" I ask.

Korra puts her hand on my shoulder. "My time as the Avatar is over, its time for you, to help guide the world towards peace and balance."

"But I'm not ready, there are so many things that I need to learn." I say.

"Which is why you have us." Kuvira says.

She steps forward and so does Su and the rest of the family. "It is an honor to serve you Avatar Christine."

This is a challenge that I knew was coming and it is a challenge that I'm willing to face head on.

---

"I want you try something for me." Korra says, standing by my wheelchair.

"Okay." I say.

"I want you to try taking a step." she says.

Korra helps me out of my wheelchair and helps me stand. I struggle for a few minutes and then stand solid on my feet. Then I try taking a step and succeed at doing so.

"It worked!" I exclaim.

"Great job." she says, patting me on the back.

"Thank you." I say.

I throw my hands around her and pull her into a hug, she goes stiff for a moment before relaxing. She then returns the hug with a tight squeeze and then let's go.

"Thank you Korra." I say, with a bow.

"Its an honor Avatar." she says, with a bow of her own.

"I should get back to Chicago, it doesn't rule itself you know." Korra says as she walks to the door.

"Bye Korra." I say.

The last thing I hear Korra say, before she disappears is. "Goodbye, Avatar Christine."

Chapter 21

Kuvira looks down at me. I'm laying on the floor laughing, she bends down and picks me up off the floor, I continue laughing. Once I'm able to pull myself together, I look at Kuvira again. She holds her hand to her mouth trying not to laugh, but then she starts to laugh anyway.

"Why are we even laughing anyway?" I ask, holding back the urge to snort.

"I don't know. All I asked you was: "Do you want to go for a walk?" and you started to laugh." Kuvira says, now chuckling.

I smile and shake my head, but then I start to laugh again. I take a deep breath and calm myself down. We sit down on the couch again. I look at Kuvira again, over the last two years she has let her hair grow out, and it's still the same color, that it always has been. She's still is pretty young. Of course who am I kidding, we're the same age and my hair is still in a pixie cut and hasn't grown out at all. I'm still not sure how that's possible.

"So what do you want to do today?" Kuvira asks.

"Huh?" I say and I snap out of the daze I was in. "Oh uh, I'm not sure."

"How about we…"

"Before you finish that sentence, I will answer your question: yes I would love to go for a walk."

"Sounds perfect where do you want to go?"

"I want to go back to Chicago."

"That would be wonderful." Kuvira says.

"Don't forget me." Baatar says.

"Why would we?" I say.

Korra sits at her desk, looking over her paperwork, she huffs out a sigh and looks at the clock. It was only 2:30 in the afternoon. She had just signed a deal for Asami's company to be demolished. That was the hardest decision she needed to make. Well with Asami and her father dead, there was no one else to look after the company. Korra hadn't slept well the night prior, she way too many things she had to think about. She put her head down on her desk and closed her eyes, then the intercom in her office went off. Korra let out a groan.

"What is it?" she asked.

*"There's someone here to see you."*
Korra dropped her head into her hands. *I'm so tired. Why would Kuvira and Christine want to visit me now?*

"Alright send them in." Korra finally replied.
*"Yes ma'am."*

The door to her office opened and Korra let's out a tired sigh. "Seriously you guys couldn't wait until tomorrow?"

"No we couldn't."
*Wait, that's not Kuvira or Christine.* Korra thought.

Chapter 22

Everyone get's off the train and walks down the platform. "We finally made it to Chicago."
The train ride was a bit longer than expected, but we're in Chicago, so that's all that matters. The city looks a lot bigger than last time, but that tends to happen when more people move to a city. Since the last election things have been calmer in the city, I think.

I turn towards Baatar Jr. "Do you think we should stop and get something to eat, before we go visit Korra?"

"Sure, I don't see why not." he says.
"Alright, where do you want to go?" Su asks.
"I know the perfect place." Kuvira suggests.
I look at her and we both crack a smile, we continue walking together.

We arrive at the restaurant and sit down, lot's of people stare at us when we walk in. I'm not sure why.
We sit down at one of the table's and the waiter walks out and sets down our food. We look at the bowls, there's noodles inside.

"How does the the waiter always know, what we want to order." Kuvira asks.
"Because I own this restaurant, that's why." the waiter says.
We all look at him and I feel like I recognize him. I *do* recognize him. "Bolin!"
Bolin lets out a laugh and gives us all a hug. "Haha, It's so great to see you guys!"
"Same." I say, as I pull away from his hug.
"So, how you guys been?" Bolin asks.
"It could be better." Opal says.
Bolin looks over at Opal. "Opa , you're here too."
Opal get's up and gives Bolin a hug. "I missed you so much."
Bolin releases Opal. Suddenly everyone starts to hear a chittering sound. A fire ferret hops up on Bolin's shoulder.
"It's nice to see you too Pabu." Opal says.
Pubu squeaks in response. Opal let's out a giggle and we start to laugh.

"Do you guys mind if I hang out?" Bolin asks.

"No, not at all." Kuvira says.

Bolin sits down and we tell him everything, that has happened since we last saw each other. By the time we're done, we had received a very shocked look from him.

"Wow, you guys have been through a lot."

"Well, we should head over to city hall and go see Korra." I say.

"Can I come?" Bolin asks.

"Sure, why not?" Baatar Jr. says.

We walk out of the restaurant together.

Chapter 23

Korra stayed standing behind her desk, just in case if her intruders wanted to attack. The entire office went dead silent. The two intruders slowly walked towards her and she started to back up, until she was backed against the wall.

"Who are you guys?" Korra says.

She looked from the first person, to the second person. The first person though, Korra felt she knew. This person, had green eyes, long black hair and a red and black Future Industries jacket.

Korra mouth dropped open in shock and she dropped out of her bending stance. "Asami?"

Asami sat down on the couch, across from her. "Hello Korra."

"How…" Korra's words got stuck in her throat, but she pushed them out. "How are you alive?"

Asami let out a laugh and Korra let out a chuckle.

Asami finally spoke. "I'm not exactly sure how, but I would assume, that it was the same reason that you came back."

Korra walked over to Asami and gave her a hug, tears started to flow down her face. "I missed you so much."

Asami closed her eyes and returned Korra's hug. They both stood in silence, hugging each other.

Asami turned back to the other person standing at the door and mouthed the word. "Now."

The person by the door walked towards them, slowly.

Asami ran her hand through Korra's hair and whispered. "I missed you too, but I'm back now. So you have nothing to worry about."

The other person, stopped several inches from the other two were standing and handed Asami her shock glove. Asami continued to comfort Korra.

"I'm glad you're okay Korra, but I'm sorry that I have to do this." Asami whispered, as she slid her glove on.

Suddenly, Korra felt pain rip through her. She couldn't move and she slumped against Asami's chest. She let out a scream and then fell to the ground. She tried to keep her eyes open, but the pain was too much. Spots started to crowd her vision.

The last thing Korra heard was. "Alright, tie her up, and let's go."

Baatar, Kuvira and I arrive at City Hall, we walk inside and up to her secretary's desk.

The man behind the desk doesn't look up. "Can I help you?"

"We're here to see President Avatar Korra."

"Names please." The man says, now looking at his computer.

"Kuvira and Baatar Jr. Beifong, Avatar Christine, Bolin and Su Beifong and her family." Kuvira says.

The man looks up at us in confusion and says. "Wait, weren't you guys just here?"

"Uh no. We just came from a restaurant." Su says.

"I have it, in my computer that, you were just here." The secretary says.

"No."

"That's odd, I just let some people under your guys names in to see Korra."

He continues to look through the files on his computer. I give Kuvira a worried look and she shrugs.

"What time did I let them in?" Korra's secretary mutters to himself. "Ah ha, here we go."

He turns the screen towards us and shows us the time, we had supposedly checked in. "About an hour ago, someone else came by and checked in under your names. But go ahead, you guys can go in. "

"Thank you." I say.

We walk towards her office and when we get inside, we see that the room has been trashed and that Korra's not there.

"Where is she?"

Chapter 24

Korra slowly woke up and when she fully came too. She begins to look around, but everything was so dark.

"Ugh, where am I?" Her head throbbed and her ribs burned. She tried to sit up, but instead she let out groan and laid back down.

Once her eyes adjusted, she took in her surroundings. Aside from the room being dark, it was small. The room was about, six feet wide by six feet long. The only building in Chicago that had a room this size. *Erudite headquarters.* Korra's eyes widened.

*I thought the building burned down, I'm sure it did!*

Korra just shook her head, she tried to stay awake but she couldn't, she closed her eyes. That is all.

---

"Where could Korra be?" Su asks.

"I don't know." Baatar Jr. replies.

We're all in her office, looking through files and papers, trying to find anything about her whereabouts. But we can't find anything. Bolin looks at the door and inspects it for any sign of a break-in, there's nothing. He turns back to everyone and shakes his head.

"There's no sign of a break-in." he adds.

"Well, of course there would be no sign of a break-in, the people who kidnapped Korra wouldn't want anyone to know that they were here." Baatar Jr. says.

"We'll just have to keep looking," Baatar Sr. says. "Don't worry Bolin we'll find her."

Bolin just nods.

I plop down on the couch in Korra's office and exhale a sigh. I look down at the leather couch and notice a red and black colored piece of fabric. I pick it up and inspect it further. I'm not sure what it is.

Bolin looks over at me. "What is it Christine?"

I shake my head. "I'm not sure."

He walks over to me and I put the fabric in his hand. He takes a close look at it. "I know what this is."

"What?" I say.

"It's fabric from Asami's Future Industries jacket."

I snap my gaze back at him. "Did you just say *Asami?*"

"Yes, why?" Bolin asks.

"That's not possible," I whisper to myself. "She's supposed to be dead."

"There has to be some explanation for this." Su says.

While the other talk, I sit down on the couch again. I put my head in my hands and take a deep breath. My emotions take over and tears start to leak out of my eyelids. My next breath comes out shaky. Someone walks over and sits down next to me.

"What's wrong?"

I turn my head to the side and wipe my eyes. "Nothing."

"You're lying."

I lift my head "Really Kuvira, how is it that you know I'm lying. I mean, I—" My voice fades and I stop mid-sentence. "Sorry Baatar."

Baatar Jr. sits down next to me. "You don't need to apologize to anyone, including me. I know that me being around you is hard. But I can't go on acting and then being ignored all the time. You saved us, I know that."

I sniff and take another deep breath. "Thank you Baatar, I really needed someone to talk to."

"No problem."

I lean into him and he gives me a tight squeeze. I close my eyes and relax.

The last thing I hear Baatar say is. "We're going to get through this. I promise."

Chapter 25

*"Korra, wake up."*

Korra let's out a groan and slowly comes to. She rubs her eyes and blinks a few times. Once her vision clears, she looked across from her and at the other end of the room. There she saw Asami standing, shifting awkwardly on her feet.

"What are you doing here?" Korra asked.

At first Asami said nothing. She just stood there staring at Korra. She walked over and sat down in the chair by the bed. "Hey Korra."

Korra sat there in confusion, still trying to figure out how and why Asami is alive. She tried to think of something, *anything,* that made this make any sense. But nothing came to her.

"Korra…" Asami hesitated for a moment, then continued. "I know, that I may have hurt you, in more ways than I can imagine but..." Asami hesitated once more. Then she finally finished. "But can we at least be friends?"

The statement shocked Korra, she tried to say something, but then anger started to stir inside her and finally she snapped."You think that I would want to be friends with you, even after you kidnapped me! No! We are never going to be friends again! I never want see or hear from you again!"

Asami stood there speechless at first and then let out a sigh, she stood up and walked towards the small desk in the room. "Fine. You leave me no choice." She let out a yell and charged towards Korra with her shock glove and Korra let out a scream. Suddenly Asami's movement stopped dead and she let out a whimper.

"Don't move!" Baatar Jr. shouted as he bloodbent Asami.

Korra looked behind Baatar Jr. and sees Su and her family and Kuvira and Christine.

"Korra!" I yell as I run passed Asami.

"Christine!" she yells back.

I run up beside her and start to help her off the bed. She looks at me eyes wide. I scoop her up in my arms and start to run.

As I run out of the room with Korra, I turn back to Baatar and yell. "Finish her off!"

Baatar bloodbends Asami until her heart stops and she hangs lifeless in the air. He let's her go and runs out of the room, to catch up with us. Korra wraps her arms around my neck, so she doesn't fall.

She looks me square in the eye and says. "You're real?"

I smile down at her and say. "Yeah, I'm real. Now let's get you out of her."

We make it out of Erudite headquarters and keep running. Korra still hanging onto me tightly. We reach the train tracks and the train charges passed us. We start to run and I help Su, Kuvira and her family on. Korra is still running to catch up. I lean out the side of the train car.

"I got it!" she yells.

"I know you do." I lean over and with one arm grab onto her and pull her inside.

She stands once she's in the car and says. "Thank you."

"No problem." I say.

She leans into me and gives me a hug. I give her a squeeze. She leans her head into my shoulder and sniffles. Kuvira walks over and gives us a hug, before walking away.

"I lost everything today," Korra whispers. "I don't even know I am anymore."

"I know who you are." I whisper back.

"You sure about that?"

"Yeah."

Chicago is in pieces, we have no home, no place to live. But for now will ride the train to the end of the line... then we'll jump.

***Alternate ending***

Chapter 18

Everyone stares at me in shock. I had just finished telling them what happened in the last two years.

"Can you walk?" Su asks me.

I shake my head. "No I can't. There is permanent damage to my legs."

Su gives me a hug. I close my eyes to try and stop myself from crying. I pull away and wipe my eyes.

"I can't believe she did that to you." Baatar Sr. says.

"I tried my best to heal her legs, but there's nothing more I can do." Korra says.

"At least we tried." I say.

"Yeah." Su sighs.

"What's wrong?" Kuvira asks.

"Well..." Su pauses, let's out another sigh and then continues. "I have something to tell Christine." The look that Su gives me worries me. Everyone at table starts to stare again. I feel my heart in my throat and look at Su again.

"Okay. What is it?"

"I'm sorry... What now?" I say.

I just received news that Su got a message from someone in Cochrane, Alberta, Canada. The message said that someone, was looking for me. That someone is my family. I haven't seen them in over ten years, that I forgot about them.

"Is that true? Does you family live in Cochrane?" Su asks me.

I look over at Kuvira. Everyone else just stares. "Y-yes." I say.

Kuvira is first to speak "But... you told me... you didn't have a family."

"I know. I should've told you the truth from the beginning." I say.

"Tell me the truth now." she says.

"Well I ran away from Cochrane, because of too much family drama. I-I just needed a break. I'm sorry." Tears start to flood out from my eyes.

"But your family must be worried sick You've been gone for ten years." Baatar Jr. says.

"Christine, you need to go home." Korra says.

"But I want to stay here with you guys." I say, as I wipe tears from my eyes.

"Christine, listen to Korra. You need to go home please." Kuvira begs.

Everyone from Su to Kuvira try to convince me to go home, I refuse. Kuvira walks upstairs and starts to pack my stuff for me. She walks downstairs with a big suitcase and puts it by the door. By then I know I don't have a choice. I let out a sigh and wheel myself towards the door. Everyone follows us out and get's into the car. I get in and Kuvira sits beside me. I lean my head on her shoulder and start to cry. Kuvira runs her hand through my hair and hugs me.

"You'll be alright." Kuvira whispers.

I look up at her. "How do you know?"

"Because I just do." she says, with another hug.

I nod and close my eyes.

The last thing I hear is her saying. "I love you Christine and always will."

---

We reach my house, Kuvira wheels me out of the car we rented. We go inside the house and I see my mom sitting in her chair.

"Mom?" I say.

She turns around. "Christine!"

The Legend Of Korra Meets The Girl On The Train
(Book 6)

Chapter 1

I wake with a start and look around, but I'm on the train, it bumps over the rails. I look to my left, where Kuvira stands with Korra and Baatar, they're talking quietly to one another. But soon they notice that I'm awake.

"Hey." Korra says.

"Hey." I say back.

"How was your nap?"

"Not bad."

Korra looks over at Kuvira and they smile at each other. I stand confused, wondering what they're smiling at.

"What are you smiling at?" I finally ask.

Neither of them respond and Kuvira walks over to me and I give her a confused look. Kuvira is silent for awhile and she looks back at Korra. Korra nods and Kuvira turns back to me.

Finally she speaks "Christine will you... um," She stops and swallows hard, she get's down on one knee and pulls out something from her pocket. A box. She opens it up, revealing a beautiful emerald ring. She starts to speak again. "Christine will you marry me?"

I stand frozen for a moment. I was not expecting that. I try to say something but the words don't come. Finally I say. "Yes."

"Yes!" Kuvira exclaims.

She slides the ring onto my finger and we both kiss for a moment. When we break away from the kiss, Korra cheers.

Me and Kuvira kiss again and when we break away, I start to cry happily. "I love you Kuvira."

She responds with another kiss. "I love you too Christine."

---

We reach the edge of the city. Me and Kuvira lean out the side of the train car.

"Jump." I shout over the wind. We jump together out of the train car.

We all jump out and we land on our feet. We keep walking.

Chapter 2

*Three weeks later…*

I walk through the airport. I just came back from a trip. Now I'm heading home to see Kuvira. I reach the security checkpoint and show her my I.D. and she lets me through. Once my luggage is on the plane, I sit down and look out the window, as the plane takes off. Once we're in the air I pull out my phone and turn it on. I notice that I have one missed call and one voicemail.

I listen to the voicemail. *"Hey Christine. It's Su. I need you to call me back right away… its important."*

I save the message.

*Why does tone in Su's voice worry me?*

Once we get near Illinois, I pull out my phone and dial Su's number. It rings three times and then goes to voicemail. I try again and this time she picks up. "Hey Su," I say. "Why did you call me?"

*"I need to tell you something."* she says, with traces of worry in her voice.

"Okay. What is it?" I ask.

*"Well… I-It… ha… something… Kuvira."*

"Wait Su… I can't understand you, you're cutting in and out." I say.

*"I-Im tr-trying to say t-th… Kuvira…"* Then I lose her.

A dial tone replaces Su's voice and I hang up my phone and put it back in my bag. I look out the window and the view of Chicago's airport comes into view. We start to descend and once we touch down and get off the plane, we go get our bags. I rent a car.

We drive to the house that I used to live in. We go to the door and I knock on it. Su answers the door but doesn't open it fully. "Hey Su." I say.

"You can't come in." Su says and she slips outside and closes the door behind her.

"What do you mean "I can't come in?" I live in this house Su." I say.

I start to become worried again and try to push myself past Su, but she just blocks my way again. I just glare at her.

"You can't come in." she says again.

I suddenly become angry and I yell. "What do you mean I can't come in!"

Su tries to block my path again, but I break past her and walk into the house, giving her a glare, once I'm inside. I turn around to face the living room and stop dead in my tracks.

Chapter 3

The living room is a mess and I notice someone lying on the ground face down. I see metal shoulder pads, a forest green uniform and long black hair that's tangled in knots.

"Kuvira?" I say, my voice weak.

I run over to her and turn her over. I pull my hand away and it's sticky with blood, I look down at my pants and their soaked through blood. *Blood!* I look at Kuvira there's blood gushing from a wound on her head and a red patch stains her shirt, right over where her heart is. There's also a large gash in her ribcage and she's lying in a pool of blood. I reach down and press to fingers to the side of her throat and find that there's no pulse.

*"No!"* I scream.

---

I rise from Kuvira lifeless, bloodied body and turn back to Su. "How did this happen?" I ask in an angry tone.

Su doesn't answer and tilts her head down. She doesn't say anything for a while, but as soon as she tries to speak another voice interrupts her. "Christine, what are you doing here?" I turn around and stare wide-eyed at the person behind me. "Korra, what are you doing here?"

"I'm... uh... I came here to uh... visit. " Korra stammers.

She's lying of course. But I don't want to confront her right now. So I just stand there quietly. Staring her down. Korra raises her eyebrows at me and in a low tone asks. "Why did you do it Christine?"

"What are you talking about?" I ask.

"You killed Kuvira, Christine." Korra says.

"What, no I didn't." I say.

"You're lying Korra," I turn towards Su. "Korra's lying Su, you have to believe me."

Su sighs and says. "But I know Korra better than I know you. I mean how can I trust you, after you lied to me about your family?"

"I didn't kill Kuvira, I swear." I say.

"But you did kill her. You were seen in this area last night." Korra says.

"No," I say. "No, it's not true."

"Alright, enough," Korra says and she looks behind her. "Baatar I need you to take Christine to Erudite headquarters, where she'll be tried with Kuvira's murder."

Baatar steps forward and put handcuffs on me and pushed me forward and out the door. "You're making a mistake. I didn't do it Korra and you know it."

I struggle against Baatar and he turns up the settings on the handcuffs. I struggle again and the handcuffs power up and start to shock me. I lurch forwards on my knees and fall to the ground. Darkness surrounds me.

Chapter 4

My eyes flicker open, I look around. I'm back in my old cell. I stare at the ground and put my head in my hands, their trembling, I clench then into fists but that only it worse. So I relax them instead. Minutes later my cell door opens and I look up, but instead of seeing Baatar, I see Korra standing in the door.

"Christine it's time to go." she says.

"No." I say as everything comes together. "No I didn't kill Kuvira. You're... " Before I can finish my sentence, Korra wraps a metal strip around my mouth to stop me from talking.

"You killed Kuvira." Korra says.

I take the metal strip from my mouth and rise to my feet. "I didn't do it."

I deflect another one she throws at me. I run at her and tackle her to the ground. I wrap my hands around her throat and start to firebend against her throat. She thrashes and eventually throws me off. Before I can get to my feet, she starts to bloodbend me. I stop dead in my tracks.

"Come on." she says.

With a simple raise of her hands, I rise up off the ground. I struggle against the hold on my body. But its too strong. Spots crowd my vision. I can't keep fighting. I stop struggling. Korra lowers me to the ground and I collapse onto the ground. I cough out blood. I look up at Korra as she walks towards me. I'm too weak to say anything. She pulls her arm back and thrusts her fist forwards. It strikes me hard in the face. I hear ringing in my ears and I start to see stars. My vision go black. That is all.

I wake with start and look around, but all I see are pale lights, my vision clears and I see Korra standing on the other side of the room.

"Where are we?" I ask.

Korra just stands there, without speaking. Then she walks towards me slowly. I see something glimmer in her pocket. Handcuffs.

"Why are you doing this?" I ask.

"Because you killed Kuvira." was Korra's simple reply.

"No I didn't." I say sternly.

"Of course you did." she says.

I sigh. *How am I going to get out of here?*

Korra stops a few inches away from me and then smiles. She sits down next to me and gives me a long hard stare. I have to hold the bed I'm on to keep from shaking.

"Korra I didn't kill Kuvira. You have to believe me."

"I don't believe you." she says.

Finally she pulls out two photos and shows them to me. I look at them. Their photo's of me at the house.

"You were seen in the area when Kuvira was killed." Korra says.

"I wasn't at the house that night." I say.

Korra sighs. "Fine. Can you tell me where you were yesterday."

"I was at the airport, then I came to the house. That's when I found Kuvira dead."

"So... what you're saying is: You came to the house, but you didn't kill Kuvira."

"Yes. That's what I'm saying."

"Okay," Korra says. "We'll wrap it up here. But you need to stay away from the house. You don't live there anymore."

Chapter 5

I hop into my car and drive away from the police station. I need to get out of here. Korra asked me to stay in Chicago for the next few months, just in case she needed to ask me anymore questions. So I just stayed at a hotel and watched tv, went out for dinner at my favorite noodle restaurant, then drove around Chicago, avoiding my old house. I try to think of what I was doing that night, but I don't remember anything. So I try to mediate, but I can't. I can't even access The Spirit World. I sigh and lay back down on the bed again. I rest my hand on my forehead and close me eyes.

*One week earlier…*

I'm walking around Chicago, in the same street Kuvira found me in. It's nighttime now. I'm following someone, the person I'm following turns a corner and I jog to catch up to them. As I turn the corner, I realize where I am. The alleyway. I pick up the pace and then I'm in a dead sprint. The figure in front of me looks back at me and starts to run.

"Hey!" I yell.

Suddenly I'm shoved against a wall, something hard strikes my head making it bleed. I try to push the figure away, but then something grabs the back of my shirt collar and slams me face-first into the wall. I let out a cry of pain. I'm kicked to the ground and hit again. I breathe in, inhaling dust and start to cough. I look up at my attacker. But all I can make out is short brown hair. Something slams into my ribs and I let out a gasp. Then something colloids with my head again and my vision doubles.

"I told you to stay away." A voice says, but it sounds far away.

I hear footsteps receding, but it sounds like an echo. I look up again and see a car driving away. I try to get up but my vision blurs and all I see are dark spots.

I hear more footsteps and hear "Are you okay?"

I look up and see someone staring down at me.

"Yeah I'm fine." I say.

"You don't look fine."

"I said I'm fine! Now leave me alone!" I yell.

"Alright fine."

The person walks away and I stay there lying in the alleyway and eventually I black out.

*Present day…*

I wake from the nightmare with sweaty palms. I hold my hand to my head and pull it away. Its still tacky with blood. I groan as the throbbing in my head get's worse. Then I roll over and turn on my phone.

There's a voicemail. I listen to it. *"Hey Christine, it's Detective Avatar Korra. I need you to come down to the police station later today. Thanks."*

I get out of bed and make coffee and breakfast. I turn on the tv and watch the news. Police say that Kuvira died from blunt force trauma and several cuts.

Suddenly Korra is on screen. "I have ruled out any other suspects in this case and am investigating another suspect with Kuvira's murder. I am making a promise to the city of Chicago and the city of Zaofu, that Kuvira's killer will be brought to justice."

I turn off the TV and grab my keys, I'm going to the police station.

Chapter 6

I arrive and the police station and go inside. Once i'm inside though, I see Baatar Jr. sitting behind one of the desks.

"Baatar?" I say, as I walk up to his desk.

He looks up from his computer and jumps. "Christine, what are you doing here?"

"Can I talk to you?" I ask.

"Well I'm... uh." he trails off and looks behind me.

"Go back to work Baatar," a voice says. "I'll handle Christine."

I turn around and my heart leaps in my throat. Korra stands behind me.

"Hi detective." I say, my voice shaking.

"Why are you here?" she asks.

"I need to talk to you."

"Well let's go."

I follow her to her office and once we're inside I sit down. She sits down across from me, her hands folded on the table. She stares at me, but doesn't speak. I look at her and she smiles.

"What are you doing here?" Korra asks again.

"I..." I start to say. But then the words get caught in my throat. "Um..." My words fail me.

I take another look at her and I see a flash of the dream I had last night. All I remember is someone with brown hair striking me down, that's when it hits me. Detective Korra looks at me expectantly and I sit there unable to say anything.

Finally I get up from my chair. "I need to go." I say without looking at her.

I walk out of the office but Korra follows me into the lobby of the police station. As I near the exit I feel something grab onto my arm. I spin around and Korra stands there, holding me back. "I can't let you leave."

She wrenches me forwards. I grab her wrists and push as hard as I can. She loses her grip on me and stumbles backwards. I take that advantage to escape. I run out of the building, I hear shouts and running footsteps behind me. I hop into my car and drive away.

---

I drive towards my house and when I get there I knock on the door. Finally the door opens and Su is standing in the doorway. "What do you want?"

"Su you need to help me."

Chapter 7

Su is still standing in the doorway. She's standing in a in a defensive stance.

"Su," I say again. "I need your help."

"Why would I ever help you, after you killed Kuvira." she spits out the words.

"Listen. I didn't kill her," I hear police sirens in the distance. "Why would I kill someone that I love?"

Su considers her response. "Fine, but if Korra finds you here, you have to give yourself up."

I nod. "I understand. Thank you Su."

She just nods.

---

I stay hidden in Baatar's bedroom, I sit on his bed. Trying to mediate, trying to clear my mind. But i'm too worried and sad. I look around Baatar's room and see photos of Kuvira. I take a look at one of Baatar and Kuvira. They look so happy together. I see another photo, this one is of the whole Beifong family, me included. I'm so interested in the photos, that I lose myself in my thoughts and don't even hear the wail of sirens getting closer. I don't hear the doorbell and I don't hear Su calling my name. The door behind me swings open. I hear someone shout. "Christine, stop where you are and put your hands up!" I stop and put my hands up.

"Now turn around slowly."

With tears in my eyes, I turn around slowly.

"Now get onto the ground!" Korra yells.

I sink to my knees, while keeping my hands up. Korra walks towards me and I look up at her. She pulls out a pair of handcuffs. As I look at her I remember, what I had remembered at the police. She put's the handcuffs on and turns the settings up. She looks at me again and pulls back her arm, her hand clenched into a fist. I dive out of the way. She swings again and hits the wall instead. I run out of the bedroom and downstairs. Korra chases after me. Once I reach the livingroom, I try to bend out of the handcuffs, but they shock me. I let out scream. But then I feel something click. I take a deep breath, ignoring the pain shooting through my body. I try to bend out of the cuffs and... *pop!* The cuffs come off and I'm controlling the electricity from them. Korra looks me wide-eyed.

"Impossible." she says.

I stare at my hands "I can lightningbend? *I can lightningbend!*"

I send a lighting blast towards Korra, she dives out of the way. But my new skill tires me out and Korra runs towards me. She slams me to the ground and closes her hands around my throat. My lungs scream for oxygen. I start to thrash and I grab the first thing I can find which is the broken leg of a chair. I strike Korra hard in the head and she let's me go. I get up and grab the metal-plated sword from Kuvira's armor. I shove it in my pocket. I try to make a break for the door, but something wraps around my legs. A metal cable. I look back and see that Korra has wrapped it around my legs. She metalbends the cable back. It knocked my feet from under me. I slam face-first into the ground. She wraps the cable around my feet again and metalbends it back towards herself. We crash into each other. I punch down at her ribcage. She lets out a groan and shoves me off of her. She pins me to the ground and wraps her hand around my throat again. She starts to bend a steady stream of fire and I thrash again. At the same time she starts to draw the air out of my lungs. My lungs burn. My vision starts to go blurry. I gasp for air but don't get any. Finally I have enough strength to push her off. I run out of the house with Korra at my heels.

"You're not getting away." she says and it sounds like a growls.

I keep running, but I trip over my own feet and fall to the ground. I land on my back and start to crawl backwards. Korra keeps walking towards me. Her movements slow and deadly. I hit the neighbors house and then I'm trapped.

"Korra please don't do this." I whisper.

"But you'll just get in the way, I can't have anyone know that I killed Kuvira." she says, with a snarl.

I try to move but I'm still trapped. "Please, Korra please, don't do this." I whisper again.

Korra doesn't say anything, she just continues walking towards me. She grabs my arm and wrenches me to my feet. She punches me again and then tries to strangle me again.

"What am I going to do with you Chris?" Korra says as she tightens her hand around my throat even more.

I gasp. I start to feel light-headed and I pass out.

---

I wake light-headed, I look around the room. Well it would be a room if I was still inside. Instead I'm outside, still laying on the ground. Korra is still a few feet away from me. I jump to my feet and kick her feet from under her, she slams into the ground and I start to run. I'm almost to the house when she starts to bloodbend me. My body stops mid-step. I start to scream. Korra walks towards me and she stops a few paces from where I am.

"This time I'm going to kill you for good."

She twitches her fingers and I scream louder. My insides twisting and turning. My bones near their breaking point. My veins feel like they're on fire.

Then through the ringing in my ears I hear. "Christine hold on!"

Korra grip on me falters and I drop to the ground. Korra's body starts to bend and twitch. I turn around only to see Baatar Jr. standing behind me. He tries to hold his grip Korra, but she goes into the Avatar State, to avoid being hurt and blasts fire at Baatar, he stops it with his water, it creates a cloud of steam.

Baatar gives me a fearful look and yells. "Run!"

I break into a sprint as Baatar drops Korra to the ground. I run towards the house again, with Kuvira's metal sword in hand, when suddenly Korra bloodbends me again. I stop dead in my tracks. My body forcefully turns around. I metalbend the sword into my sleeve as Korra bloodbends my body towards her. My body moves and the next thing I know, I'm right in front of Korra. She grabs my throat and squeezes, I gasp. She pulls me forwards, so that our faces are just inches apart. I can see the murderous look in her eyes. I gasp for air and without thinking I thrust my arm upwards. The metal blade jams into Korra's throat. She gasps. Blood splatters across our faces and on our clothes. She releases me and stumbles backwards, clutching at her throat. She tries to bend the blade out, but it's made with platinum. So there's nothing she can do. I walk backwards away from Korra. Baatar runs forwards. He kneels down next to Korra and starts to move the metal blade. At first I think he's trying to save her, but then he shoves the blade further into Korra's throat. Korra is still laying there gasping for air. Baatar let's out a yell and shoves the blade down further. Soon Korra's gasps for air stops and Baatar rises, his clothes are drenched in her blood.

"Baatar." I say and it comes out in a whisper.

He walks over to me and gives me a hug, seconds later he starts to cry. The cries turn into sobs and for the longest time we just stand there holding each other.

Chapter 8

I'm sitting on a bench just outside the interview room, in the police station. Baatar is just being interviewed by Lin. I drop my head into my hands and huff out a sigh. Minutes or hours later. I can't tell, I hear the door to the interview room open. Baatar walks out, looking tired. He looks looks at me as he walks out of the station. Lin walks up to me and motions me to follow her. We walk into the room and we sit down across from each other. I put my hands on the table. Me and Lin just look at each other.

Finally she asks "Why did you kill Korra?"

"It was self-defense, she would've killed me."

"Okay," she says. She takes a breath and then continues. "So what did you do after you stabbed her?"

"I started to run back to the house." I say.

"So you left Korra to die painfully?"

"No," I say. "Baatar ran out of the house and ended her misery."

"Okay. I think that wraps up this investigation." Lin says, as she shows me out of the room. I walk out of the police station with Baatar.

---

We drive back to the house. When we get there, I follow Baatar inside. Su stands in the kitchen, when she sees us come in, she stares at us wide-eyed. I try to say something but my words fail me. Baatar walks over to Su, gives her a hug and whispers something to her. Su looks back at me, and with tears in her eyes, she walks over to me and gives me a hug.

"I'm sorry." she says.

"It's okay," I say. "Korra tricked all of us."

Su sniffles. "I'm sorry that I accused you."

"It's okay." I say again.

I release Su and walk over to Kuvira's body. I kneel down beside her and let out a sigh. I grab one of her hands and squeeze tightly, secretly hoping that I could bring her back to life. I know that isn't going to happen. Tears start to flow down my face. I sit there holding Kuvira's cold, lifeless hand, crying. Just when I think i'm done crying another sob racks my body. Su walks over and put's her hand on my shoulder. I turn around and press my face into her shoulder and continue to cry.

"Shh, it's okay." Su whispers

---

I cry for a long time. Su is still holding me tightly. Finally I quit crying and Su let's me go. I take a deep breath and turn towards Baatar "Are you sure, you can't bring Kuvira back?"

"No. Its far beyond my healing abilities," he says. "I'm so sorry."

I nod. I turn back to Su. She tries to hold back tears of her own. "It's okay." I pull her into another hug.

We hold each for a long time.

Chapter 9

I kneel beside Kuvira's body, I look back over to Baatar. He nods. I let out a sigh. But then I decide on something else. I turn back to Baatar and say. "Get me some water."

He gives me a puzzled look, but doesn't object. He get's up and return's moments later with a jug of water. "Here you go."

He get's up to walk away, but I stop him. "Wait," I say "This will only work if both of us do it at the same time."

He nods, then asks. "What are we doing?"

I look at him. "Just do what your told and you'll see in a minute."

He nods.

"Alright," I say. "We're both going to heal her at the same time, so when I start to bend the water over the cuts, you need to do the same."

He nods again.

"Ready?" I say. "One, two, three."

At three, we bend the water over Kuvira's injuries. The water glows a bright blue for a moment and I struggle to keep it going. The blue light fades moments later.

"What happened?" Baatar asks.

"I don't know," I say. "Let's try again.

We try again and as I struggle to keep the blue glow of the water going, I take a deep breath and enter The Avatar State. This time, when we try again the water's glow is so bright, that Su and Baatar have to shield their eyes for a moment. I exit The Avatar State and the water's glow disappears. The injuries on Kuvira's body disappears. But she lies on the floor, motionless.

"No!" I yell. "It should've worked, It should've!"

I collapse onto Kuvira's chest and start to cry. Baatar get's up and walks away from Kuvira's body, wiping tears from his eyes in the process.

"Christine?"

"Not now Baatar," I say. "Can't you see I'm crying?"

"Christine?"

I look up "Didn't you hear me Baatar? I said not n—" I stop mid sentence. I'm unable to say anything.

Finally I speak. "K-Kuvira?"

Chapter 10

I stand speechless, I just stare at Kuvira wide-eyed. She's alive. She's *alive!* Kuvira coughs for a bit before opening her eyes. She rests her eyes on me and tears start to form there.

"Christine?"

I don't say anything, I just hold her there close and start to cry. I bury my face into her neck and let the tears roll down my face.

She gives me a puzzled looked "What happened?"

"You were dead, I thought I would lose you." I say, as I cry.

"What?!" she says, as she bolts right up off the floor.

"Careful!" I say.

"How did I...?" her voice trails off.

I look her in the eye and say. "It was Korra."

Kuvira sits down on the floor again. She puts her head in her hands, her hands trembling. I give her a hug and she relaxes a little bit. She's still shaking. We sit on the floor together. I hold onto Kuvira as tightly as she holds onto me.

Finally she asks. "Where's Korra?"

I sigh and point outside. "Over there."

Kuvira and I walk outside and over to Korra's body. The metal sword still lodged in her throat. Kuvira looks at me with a shocked look. She walks over to Korra and tries to bend the sword out. But she can't. She looks back at me.

"Its platinum." I say.

Kuvira gives me another look.

"I'll take it out." I say.

I take a deep breath and bend the platinum sword out from Korra's neck. I wipe the blood off and give it back to Kuvira. She attaches it back onto her uniform.

After a few long minutes of silence, I say. "She would've killed me. It was self-defence."

Kuvira walks over to me and gives me a hug. "It's okay."

We walk back to the house, where we see: Su and Baatar Jr. Everyone looks shocked.

Baatar walks over to Kuvira and gives her a hug. "I missed you so much."

"Me too." Kuvira says.

---

"So... how long was I gone for?" Kuvira asks me. We're walking around the house, trying to clear our heads.

"'Bout a week." I say.

She stops walking. "A week? How did you bring me back?"

I stop walking and turn back to her. "Well Baatar used his water and I just used The Avatar State. Why?"

"Just wondering." she says, with a shrug.

I walk over and wrap my arms around her. She return's the hug.

"I missed you." I whisper.

"I know," she says. "I know."

Chapter 11

"So what do we have planned today?" I ask.

Kuvira mumbles an answer, but I can't hear her. She laying on the couch, with her face pressed into the pillow. I laugh and she mumbles something else. Whatever it was, it didn't sound pleasant. An awkward silence follows. But it breaks, when I hear Kuvira start to laugh into her pillow.

"What?"

"Nothing." she says.

"Okay."

She sits up and I give her a hug. She leans into my shoulder. She let's out a content sigh and we look at each other. She stares into my eyes and I'm not sure why. Then I remember that I was supposed to tell her about the meeting I had today with Baatar Jr. at the police station. At first I don't what to say. We just sit there staring at each other, waiting for each other to speak.

Kuvira is the first to speak "So how was the meeting?"

"It was fine. The meeting was fine."

"So... what... did Baatar say?"

"He said that I made it onto the police force. I'm starting tomorrow."

"That's wonderful! I'm sure you'll have so much fun." she says.

"Yeah I'm excited." I say.

I breath in deeply and look out the window. Storm clouds start to roll in and it starts to rain. The raindrops make a pit pat sound when they hit the roof. I look out onto the lawn. But instead of seeing the lawn, all I see is Korra standing on the lawn and I'm backed up against the neighbors house. Her movements slow and deadly and I hear her voice. *I can't let you get in the way.*

"Christine, are you okay?"

Kuvira's voice snaps me out of the daze I was in. "What? Oh... uh... I... I'm fine."

"You sure?"

"Yeah... everything's fine."

"Okay. But if you need someone to talk to, you can talk to me." she says.

Kuvira gets up and goes to the kitchen, to make dinner. I stay on the couch and stare down at the floor.

*What am I going to do?*

Chapter 12

"Christine, dinner is ready!" Kuvira calls from the kitchen. Whatever dinner is, it smells delicious.

I walk to the kitchen, and look at the food. Kuvira made a seared Elephant Koi, with a fruit salad. I smile and give her a hug. She turns around and slides her arms around my side and pulls me in close. I wrap my arms tighter around her and she tries not to squeal in pain. I laugh into her shoulder and then release her. We sit down at the table and start to eat dinner. After we're done, we watch the news. Baatar is still on the news, he's talking about the new recruits for the police force. I had completely forgotten it was today.

---

After we watch the news, we go for a walk around Chicago. We walk to a familiar area, though it takes me a little bit to recognize the place. We are near the alleyway. I have a flashback about the night when Korra attacked me. I stop in my tracks and my heart pounds faster and harder against my chest.

Kuvira looks back at me. "Are you okay?"

I don't hear her, all I hear is Korra's voice and the sound of rain. I can still feel the pain, when Korra had slammed me into the tunnel wall.

Kuvira shouts something at me but her voice is muffled.

Suddenly I get shoved into the wall, I'm too shocked from the impact to say anything. I fall to the ground and my head hits something hard.

My vision goes black.

---

*"What am I going to do with you Chris?"* The words echo in my head. No. They echo in my dream. Moments later the dream fades and I open my eyes. Once my vision clears, I realize where I am. I'm in my house.

Something hard strikes me in the side, I wheeze and cough. I lie there on the floor. Unable to move do to the pain in my ribs. I move my head to the side and see Kuvira laying on the couch, her body limp. "Kuvira?"

Seconds later I hear another voice. "Well, well, well. If it isn't Christine. You know, I'm surprised that you're alive, considering how weak you've become."

I look around the room again and I see someone standing across from me, I blink a few times and I see Korra standing a few feet away. I'm too shocked to say anything. I blink again and I see a streak of red on Korra's neck. It takes me a few minutes to realize that its from where I had shoved the metal blade in. I stare at her and don't say anything. Korra just smirks at me.

Then she walks over and stops a few inches from me. "I need your help with something."

"What?!" I say.

"Oh Christine. You have no idea what's coming for you. Now you can either help me or you can say goodbye to Kuvira. Which will it be?"

She walks over to a now awake Kuvira and holds another metal blade to her throat. The she looks back at me and says. "Oh, Christine, we are going to have so much fun."

Chapter 13

I look at Kuvira and then at Korra. Kuvira whimpers and tears start to fill her eyes.

"It's okay." I say.

Kuvira just stares at me and I look from her to Korra and back again. Korra raises her eyebrows expectantly at me. I drop to my knees with my hands in the air.

"Good girl." Korra says.

"You're not getting away with this." I say.

"Oh but I already have." she says.

Korra let's Kuvira go and walks over to me. She stops several inches from me and I look up at her. She smirks at me again. I look over at Kuvira. She's trying not cry. I give her a nod, reassuring her that everything will be alright.

I look back at Korra again. "Please, don't let Kuvira pay for my mistakes. Please just let her go."

Korra smiles at me and says. "Oh, don't worry. Kuvira won't pay for your mistakes," I let out a relieved sigh. Korra leans over to my ear and whispers. "She'll suffer from them."

I stare at her wide-eyed. "What? No!"

Korra pulls her arm back and her fist smashes into my face. I let out a yell. I start to see stars and I hear ringing in my ears. I crash into the ground and I stay there. Then I black out.

*"Christine!"* Kuvira screams.

---

I'm walking around Chicago, once again I'm near the alleyway. This time instead of following Kuvira or Korra. I'm running from someone. Though I'm not sure who I'm running from. I can hear footsteps and it makes me run faster. But the footsteps get louder and it takes me a moment to realize that I'm running from my own footsteps.

I hear someone shout. "Hey."

I turn around and see someone shove someone else into a wall. I start to back away slowly and I trip on something. I take a closer look at the person against the wall and realize that it's me. The person standing above me is Korra.

"Stop!" I yell.

Korra stops and turns around, and instead of the other me against the wall, I'm now against the wall. Korra's face is tightened into a scowl, she strikes me hard and I inhale dust. I hear her footsteps receding. I black out.

---

My eyes flicker open. I'm laying on the floor in my house. I see Korra sitting on the couch, staring at me. "You're like a polar bear dog. One of those unwanted polar bear dogs. The one's that come back to you, no matter how many times you kick them away."

"You're nuts!"

Korra just smiles. "Well, if you think I'm crazy, that's your opinion."

I jump up and kick her feet from under her, she slams into the floor.

I look back at Kuvira. "Now we can get rid of her."

Chapter 14

Me and Kuvira walk over to Korra's body and we give each other a quick glance. Then we both pick her up and start to haul her body out of the house. We get to the car and we put Korra in the backseat. I put platinum handcuffs on her just in case she wakes up. I get into the backseat as well. Kuvira gets into the driver's seat.

"Are you sure you want to sit back there with her?" she asks.

"Yeah, I'm sure," I say. "Someone has to watch her and make sure that she won't hurt anybody."

Kuvira nods. "But what about you?"

I sigh and look over at Korra. "I'll be fine back here, she's handcuffed with platinum handcuffs, what could go wrong?"

"Alright, I see your point." she says.

We start to drive, I keep an eye on Korra. She's still out cold. I let out a sigh and look out the window. We are near the train station. Kuvira stops the car and we hop out, dragging Korra behind us. We walk up to the train platform. We get on the tra n and sit down with Korra seated across from us. Me and Kuvira look at each other and let out a sigh.

---

I look out the window as we pass Chicago. The sun is about to set. The city passes by us in a blur. In the distance I see the glow cf Erudite headquarters. I turn away from the window. I get out of my seat, but just as I'm leaving, I hear Kuvira say. "Where are you going?"

I turn back to face her. "For as much as a walk, this train allows."

She nods. I turn away from her and Korra. I start my way down the aisle, pushing past people that are in the way. I walk to one of the other cars and sit down. I look out the train window again, we are almost near Zaofu.

*Good.* I think. *I can get away from Korra after this.*

My thoughts are interrupted though when the train comes to a sudden halt. I fall off my seat and hit the ground. People start to rush past me and I see one of the train conductors run passed me as well. I get up and grab him.

"What happened?" I ask.

"I don't know," he says. "There aren't any scheduled stops along here."

"Did that feel like a scheduled stop to you?" I say.

"Well… um." he starts to say.

"No of course not!" I say.

"Well, I don't know what happened." he says.

"Well, I can think of only one reason why we've—"

I take off towards my train car.

Chapter 15

I sprint through the train, elbowing through the crowd of people who are crammed in the aisle. Some people give me a dirty look and some elbow me back. I'm almost back to my seat. That's when I see a polar-bear dog—Naga—lying on the train tracks. I get off the train and run to the front. The conductor looks up at me.

"I thought I said that this train never stops."

"I'm sorry ma'am, but there is animal on the tracks."

I'm about to say something when I heard another voice speak up. "Sorry, I'm late I came as quick as I could."

I spin around only to see Lin, Su and Baatar Jr. standing there.

"What are you doing here?" I say.

"We came to help." They say.

"Alright." I say.

We start towards the animal on the tracks, but then I stop. I look up at everyone. Then the thought hits me.

"Wait," I say. "Why are you all standing here? And who's watching Korra?"

"Well, Kuvira is." Baatar says.

"Kuvira. Alone?"

"Yes." Baatar says.

"Do I need to remind you who we are transporting?"

"No." He says.

"Go back to your stations," I say. "Now!"

Baatar, Lin and Su begin to walk away, but then the conductor says. "Wait, we need three people to move this animal."

"Alright," I say. "Lin, wanna give us a hand?"

She nods and walks over to help us.

Kuvira is sitting quietly across from Korra, staring out the window. Then something tightened around her arm and she doesn't have any time to react. She's pulled to the ground and something crashes into her head. Her vision goes black.

Chapter 16

After we have moved Naga off the train tracks, we get back onto the train, I walk back to my seat. But when I get there I stop dead in my track. I see Kuvira with a sword against her throat and Korra holding it there.

"Korra," I say. "What are you doing? How did you get your cuffs out from behind you?"

"You see, I got them out in front of me in less than two seconds. Impressive isn't it?" She smirks at me.

"Korra, you have no idea what you're doing."

I start towards her, ready to strike if I need to. But the moment I start to walk towards her, she presses the metal blade closer to Kuvira's neck. It starts to leave a mark on her skin. Kuvira stiffness. I come to a halt and stand there frozen.

"You take one more step and I'll cut her throat." She presses the blade closer and the skin on Kuvira's neck starts to turn red.

I freeze again and put my hands up. "Korra, please don't."

Korra pulls the blade away from Kuvira's neck and I relax a bit. "Good girl."

"What do you want from me Korra?" I say, my voice trembling.

"I want you to tell the conductor to stop this train."

I scoff. "Not a chance."

"Oh okay." She presses the blade closer and Kuvira stiffens.

My mind starts to race and I look from Korra to Kuvira and back again.

Korra laughs. "I know what you're thinking: How fast can you get to her. At what point does the risk of losing Kuvira matter less, than taking me down?"

I stop and look at Korra.

She smirks again. "Good girl."

"If you hurt her." I say, as I get down on the ground.

Korra sighs and then smiles. "Oh Christine, you made a terrible choice."

She let's Kuvira go, but without warning she stabs her in the chest with the metal sword and pushes her forwards. Kuvira screams and falls onto the floor of the train. Korra runs towards the engine and I follow behind her. But before I chase her, I turn back to Lin, Su and Baatar and say. "Don't just stand there, heal Kuvira! I'll go after Korra."

They nod and I run to the engine, I jump out of the train and land onto the ground. I look up and see Korra running away from the train, I run and catch up to her. I slam her into the train tracks and punch her once, twice, three times.

I pull my arm back for another swing and she puts her hands up. "Alright! Alright! You got me. Now stop hitting me."

I stop and push her down to the tracks again.

"This is it," she says. "This is the final chapter, won't you miss me?"

I shake my head. "No."

"Not even a little?"

"No." I say, as I relax.

That was a mistake, because Korra pushes me off of her and shoves me to the ground, she starts to run again. This time towards the bridge again. She runs to the edge and looks down at the water.

"Stop! The water's too shallow, you will be killed."

She looks back at me and says. "Well, I've got nothing to lose."

Before I can do anything she jumps off the bridge. "No!" I yell.

I run to the edge of the bridge and prepare to jump off when I hear someone say. "Christine no!" I look back and see Baatar standing there, he just shakes her head. I don't think, I just jump.

*"No!"* Baatar yells.

Chapter 17

I wake with pain shooting through every part of my body, I try to move but I realize that I'm hung up on a tree. I struggle to get off of it. My shirt digs into my neck and I gag. I hear a creak and the branch snaps, I crash into the ground. I cough and gasp for air. I try to get up but I'm too dizzy and I have to stay on my knees so I don't pass out. I crawl across the ground, I look up and see the bridge. My head spins at the sight of it. I try to keep walking. But my ribs and chest are burning. I breathe in and I feels like someone has stabbed me in the side. I let out a cry of pain, but continue walking.

I walk for what seems like a long time. My breathing is shallow and I need to find everyone. "Su! Lin! Baatar! Where are you?!"

I cough and blood comes out past my lips. I call for them again. "Su! Baatar!"

My vision starts to go blurry and I fall to the ground. In the distance I hear. *"Christine!"* Then I pass out.

---

Something shakes me awake and I jolt right up, wincing at the pain in my ribs and chest. I hear a voice. "Christine!"

My vision becomes clear and I see Lin, Su, Kuvira and Baatar Jr. standing in front of me. "Kuvira?" I say.

"Oh thank goodness you're alive." she says.

I let out a weak chuckle. "Yeah."

Baatar and Kuvira help me up, but I groan at the pain and they lay me back down again. I let out a wheezed breath.

Baatar lifts my shirt. My sides and stomach are covered in black, purple and blue bruises. "Okay," he says. "That needs to be treated."

"I'm fine." I croak.

"No you're not."

I try to push Baatar away, but it only makes the burning sensation worse and I lay back down again. I cough again and Baatar raises his eyebrows at me. I sigh and nod. Baatar lifts my shirt and bends a blob of water around the dark patches. I wince as the pain becomes worse for one second and then I relax. I take a deep breath and the pain becomes bearable for a moment.

---

After Baatar has healed the bruises as best as he can. I stand up and face Kuvira.

"Why did you jump?" she asks.

"She was getting away. What would you have done?"

Kuvira doesn't say anything, then I hear a voice behind me. "There's no sign of her."

"Are you sure?"

"Christine, the water get's deep and fast. If she was still handcuffed… "

"You didn't see her?"

Baatar just shakes his head.

"Baatar!"

"Don't worry, we'll find her. I promise." Baatar says and he walks away.

Kuvira walks up to me. "It's over Christine. We have to believe that."

I shake my head.

"Come on." she says, as she leads me and everyone else away from the water.

Chapter 18

I wince as pain shoots across my body, but I continue walking. We are trying to make our way to the nearest train station. I huff out a breath.

"How far until we're at the train station?"

"Shouldn't be far." Kuvira says.

"Okay." I say.

---

We reach the train station and board the train. This time we're going back to Zaofu. We go back to the house and sit down on the couch. I sigh and lean against Kuvira's shoulder. She runs a hand over my shoulder and I smile.

"So what do we do now?" I ask.

"I don't know," Kuvira says. "I guess we just try and forget everything that has happened."

I nod.

---

"No stop!" I yell. "The waters too shallow you will be killed."

"Well then I've got nothing to lose."

Korra smiles and then jumps off the bridge.

"*No!*" I scream.

I run to the edge of the bridge and jump. I keep falling. Then I hit the water. I gasp when I come up for air, but I swallow water instead. I sputter and cough as the water goes into my lungs. The water gets faster and faster by the minute. I crash into a few rocks on the way before being caught up onto the a tree branch. I start to panic, but my shirt starts to choke me.

I pass out.

---

I wake with a racing heart. I look around the room wide-eyed. Kuvira is having a nap on the couch. I walk out of the house and towards the train. I get on and travel to the bridge that I jumped off and just stand there. I look down at the water and jump again. I hit the water and then get onto dry land. There I see someone, standing by the water facing in the opposite direction. "Hey!" I yell.

The figure turns around and I stand frozen for a moment. "Christine. I'm surprised you came after me, you're not very smart."

"I came to finish this Korra. Who's going to win, you? Or me?"

She let's out a laugh. "Do you really think you can win against me?"

"Maybe, maybe not," I say. "Let's finish this right here, right now."

I bend out my platinum plated sword and Korra prepares to bloodbend me. I let out a yell and charge towards her. She tries to bloodbend me and I punch her hard in the face. I press the blade against her throat and she pushes me back and grabs my sword. She runs at me and I take a deep breath as I remember something. Our moment on the bridge. I remember when she asked me.

"Won't you miss me?" she asks again.

"No!" I say, but my heart isn't in it. The truth is I will miss her. I'll miss our fights. I'll miss fighting together, when she was still a good person.

I charge at her again and she grabs my wrists and pushes as hard as she can. "If I go down, you go down with me!" I yell.

I run at her again and kick her feet from under her, she slams into the ground and I pin her there. I then turn to leave, thinking the fight is over when she shoots the metal strip at me. It covers my eyes so I can't see. I struggle to get it off. The next thing I know, I can't breathe. I struggle for air as Korra starts to suffocate me. I fall to my knees, my vision blurry. I put a hand to my head as she takes more air. But at the last second before I faint. I somehow kick her feet from under her. She hits the ground again. I pull out the sword and point it at her throat. She freezes in place. I smirk at her. But suddenly the platinum sword is pointing towards my throat. I stare at Korra wide-eyed. "How? You can't bend *platinum*."

"Maybe you're not as smart as you think you are." she says, as she presses it closer.

Its now just millimeters from my neck. I swallow hard and stare into her eyes. I don't anything in them, they just look emotionless. I sink to my knees and look up at her. She smiles and presses the blade closer, just so that its just touching my throat. I swallow hard again.

"You're never going to win." I say, my voice weak.

"Oh really?" she taunts. "Well, I challenge you to a duel."

"Alright fine."

I get to my feet and we stand a few paces away from each other, Korra makes the first move. She always does. I evade her attack and start firing out attacks of my own. One of my metal strips covers her eyes and I wrap my metal cable around her. I metalbend the cable back and she comes towards me. She starts to bloodbend me and I go into The Avatar State, so I don't get hurt. She let's out a frustrated yell and runs at me. She swings at me and I duck out of the way. She steps forwards and I step back. She runs at me again and I push her back. She flies back, but sends a blast of air at me. I don't get out of the way in time. The blast of air hits me and I fly back and slam onto the ground. The impact knocked the wind out of me and I see stars. She walks over to me and looks down. I don't get out of the way fast enough. Her foot slams into my face and I black out.

Kuvira wakes with a start, she looks around wide-eyed. She looks around for Christine and doesn't find her. She looks over at the table by the couch and sees a envelope tucked under a glass of water. She opens the envelope and finds a sheet of paper inside. The paper reads:

*Dear Kuvira,*

*I left last night to find some answers on whether Korra was alive or not. My guess is that she is and if that is true then I'm going to take her down. I love you Kuvira, no matter what. If I'm not back by the time you read this. Then assume the worst. I may or may not see you again. But just know that I love you.*

*Sincerely,*
*Christine.*

Kuvira clutched the letter in her hands and held it against her chest. She could feel the tears start to leak from her eyes and she let them flow freely. But then worry started to take over and she grabbed her car keys and bolted straight out of the house. She was going to the police station.

Chapter 19

Kuvira arrives at the police station and runs inside. She runs up to Baatar's desk and yells. "Baatar!"

Baatar jumps out of his seat. "Oh Kuvira you scared me. What is it?"

"Christine's missing. She wrote me a letter saying that Korra was alive and that she went to confront her, but we need to find her fast."

Baatar's eyes widened. "Korra?! I thought she was dead."

"So did I Baatar, but if Christine went looking for her, then that must mean that she's alive. We need to find her ASAP, before something bad happens."

Baatar nodded. "Alright, I'll send out a search party maybe we can find her."

"Thank you Baatar."

My eyes open, I try to sit up, but I'm too dizzy, so I just stay on my hands and knees. I sense something coming and dive to my right. Just in time before the metal blade hits me in the side. I hear a loud snap, which can only signify metal cracking bone. A few moments later, I scream. The pain in my already damaged ribs is getting worse. Something collides with my ribs again. I let out a groan of pain. I look up and my vision doubles. Korra stands above me with the metal sword and I roll to the side just as she hits the ground with it.

"Korra, why are you doing this?"

She swings at me again. "Because you always cause trouble."

She swings a third time and the end of the sword slams into my side. My ribs feel like I'm on fire. I cough and my next breath rattles on the way out. I try to get up but my muscles feel like lead. I collapse onto the ground. My vision starts to fade.

In the distance I hear. *"Christine!"* But really its just my imagination.

I black out.

---

Kuvira and Baatar are sitting at the desk, monitoring where Korra is. But the setting is so dark, that they can't tell where it is. Baatar yawns and says. "I don't think we will get there in time."

Kuvira looks at Baatar and the slaps him in the face. "Wake up! This is not the time to rest."

Baatar looked to shocked to object about getting hit and went back to monitoring. He blinks and then it hits him. "I know where they are."

"What?! Where?!" Kuvira asks.

He points at his screen. "You see this bridge? That's the one Korra and Christine jumped off of."

"Really?! Well let's go." Kuvira says, as she drags Baatar out of the police station.

They take off towards the train station.

Chapter 20

I open my eyes. My body aches, but my ribs hurt the most. I crawl to my knees and clutch my ribs, but when I touch my ribs, I feel something cool and hard there. I wrap my hands around it and pull really hard. The pain in my ribs gets worse and out of the corner of my eye I see the sword jammed into my side. I wince. I wrap my hand around it again and pull as hard as I can. The blade comes out and my ribs start to bleed. I clutch my side again. I breath in and the pain is so bad that I scream.

I hear someone laugh. "Wow. How stupid can you be?"

I turn around. "Korra." I say, trying to hide the pain that I'm in.

She smirks and walks towards me and I start to take a step back, but the pain gets worse. I cry out. I collapse again. Korra just smiles and shakes her head at me. All the while she's laughing, taunting me. She bends down and yanks me to my feet. I scream, it feels like someone has stabbed me in the side with a hot poker. I swing at her, she ducks and pushes me backwards. I trip on the tracks and my head slams in the metal. But before I start to feel dizzy, I jump to my feet and shove her backwards. She stumbles backwards but doesn't fall.

"You little... I'm going to get you."

She runs at me and I step out of the way, I grab her arm and yank her to the side. She stumbles and then regains her footing. She sends a blast of fire at me and I send a blast of lightning in her direction. She drops into a lightingbending stance and tries to re-direct it back at me. I dive out of the way and land on the ground. I hit my head on the tracks again. Korra wrenches me to my feet on puts one hand one hand on the back of my head and presses her arm against my throat.

"Now what are you going to do?" she taunts.

---

Kuvira and Baatar arrive at the train station and get on the train. Kuvira walks up to the conductor and says. "I need you to get us to the bridge."

The conductor looks at her and says. "I'm afraid I can't make an unscheduled stop."

Kuvira yanks him forwards and says. "If you don't do what I say, then you'll find yourself hanging onto the train for dear life and hoping that you won't fall off. Do I make myself clear?"
He swallows hard and nods. He runs to the engine and the train starts to move. It moves slow at first and then gets faster. Kuvira looks out the window, watching for the bridge. Baatar sits down beside her and wraps his arms around her.

"Don't worry," he says. "We'll get there in time."

"I hope so." she whispers.

---

The train slows down and comes to a halt. The conductor comes out and says. "Alright, we're by the bridge."
Both Kuvira and Baatar nod and run off the train.

Chapter 21
I stand still, trying not to move, Korra still has me in a chokehold. I breathe shallow breaths. Korra leans in and whispers. "You my as well give up no one's coming to rescue you."
I don't say anything, one movement and she'll kill me. I close my eyes and try not to focus on Korra. I take a deep breath and Korra increases the pressure on my neck a little more and I stand frozen again.

---

Kuvira and Baatar keep running. Then skid to a stop. Both of them look at each other with panic.

---

I stare at Kuvira and Baatar with wide-eyes. Korra now has the platinum sword pressed to my throat. I shake my head a little and Kuvira stops in the middle of a step as Korra presses the blade a little bit closer.

"Take one more step and I'll slice her throat!" Korra yells.
Kuvira freezes and Korra releases me a little. Kuvira looks at me with tears in her eyes. I just stare at her. We stand a stalemate and Korra still doesn't release me fully. Without warning Korra starts to drag me near the edge of the bridge. I struggle away from her, she stops when she get's to the edge. She looks back at me and smiles. My eyes go wide as she jumps off the bridge. I scream, but I catch the edge of the

tracks. I'm just holding on by my fingertips. Korra still has the platinum sword in her hand. I feel something sharp stab into my ribcage. I scream again and I let go of the tracks. I fall.

"*No!*" I scream.

"*Christine!*" Kuvira and Baatar yell.

---

Baatar looks at Kuvira and grabs onto her arm. Together they jump off the bridge. They let out a scream as they fall, they hit soft ground and they let out a laugh. "How did that happen?"

Kuvira looked around. "Ugh… we landed in mud."

"Oh come on. It's not that bad." Baatar says, as he splashed some at her.

Kuvira shook her head. "Well, let's go."

Chapter 22

I let out a groan, and roll to the side. I fall. "Ow!"

I landed on something hard I look up and realize that I'm upside down in a tree. I try to move and realize I'm handcuffed to Korra. I take a look at her she's staring at me blankly. I let out a yelp and slap her hard in the face. She doesn't move. I shove her to the side and we fall out of the tree. We slam into the ground. I bend out of the handcuffs and give Korra a shake. She doesn't move or speak.

"Korra?" I say.

She doesn't answer. I press to finger to the side of her throat. There is a pulse, but a very weak one. Part of me wants to leave her to die, but the other part of me wants to save her. But before I can think about what I want. I find myself pulling her out of the tree and laying her down on the ground. I look around and see that we landed near the water. I bend the water from the lake and start to heal Korra. I know that she should die. But not like this. I wouldn't be able to live with myself if she did. I check the pulse again and its getting weaker by the second. I start doing chest compressions.

"Come on, come on!" I say.

I know this is crazy. But my life would never be complete without her. No one's would. I start on my third attempt to bring her back.

---

"Christine, where are you?! Baatar call out.

Both him and Kuvira landed not far from the water. They keep walking. They need to find Christine. They *had* to find her.

"Where could she be?" Kuvira says.

---

"Korra please come back." I say. Tears start to roll down my face. I've been performing chest compressions for the last forty minutes. I check her pulse, I can't feel anything. I let out a frustrated yell. "Wake up! Don't do this! Wake up!"

Korra still doesn't move.

*"No!"* I yell.

---

Baatar runs through the trees and bushes that are in his path. Kuvira is close behind him. They're closing in on Christine's location. "We're almost there!"

---

I sit on the ground, with Korra at my side. I've done everything I can. But I can't bring her back. "Please Korra, come back." I whisper.

I collapse onto her chest and start to cry. I feel something move, but I don't pay any attention to it. At least not until I feel something wrap around me and pull me close. I jerk to attention and look up. I can't believe what I'm seeing.

"Korra?" I say.

"Hey." she says.

Chapter 23

"We're almost there!" Baatar yells.

They still keep running, until they see something that they thought that they would never see. They look at each other with shock and stop running.

---

"Korra?" I say again.

"Hey." she says.

I help her to her feet and give her a hug. She hangs onto me tightly. I wipe tears from my eyes and sniff. I start to laugh. I laugh into Korra's shoulder. I let her go and control my laughter. She gives me a confused look.

"What happened?" she asks.

A breath hitches in my throat and I just stare at her, unsure of how I can tell her what happened. We stand in silence, just staring at each other.

"Alright," I say. "I'll tell you what happened. It all started back, when I came back to Chicago. Su had called me. Telling me not to come over to the house. I went anyway. When I got there. Kuvira had been killed and I was set up for the murder."

"What?!" Korra exclaims.

I put my hands up. "I'm not done yet. As I was saying: I was set up and you had arrested me for the murder. In the end I found out that it was you. After that you tried to kill me... a few time actually. After me, Kuvira and Baatar arrested you. We took you to your prison. Unfortunately you escaped and took me with you. Hoping that I would let you go," I take a deep breath, before I continue. "Then you jumped off the bridge, dragging me with you. I survived the fall, but you died and I brought you back to life."

Korra gives me a shocked look. "That doesn't sound like me."

"I know, but it was."

"Well, if I did all of that stuff then why did you bring me back?" she asks.

"I brought you back, because I couldn't live with myself. If you had died. I know you did a lot of bad things to me in the past. But I'm willing to forgive you for them."

I give her a hug and she tries to hold back her tears.

---

I'm still holding Korra, when I hear a voice. "Christine?"

I turn around and my heart stops. Kuvira and Baatar stand behind me. Their eyes wide with shock. "What are you doing?"

"I can explain." I say.

"Christine, get away from Korra." Baatar says.

"No. Listen to me you guys. She's not evil anymore." I say.

"I'm not going to ask you again Christine. Get away from her."

"No!" I say.

"Christine," Kuvira says. "Listen to Baatar please, I don't want to have to fight you."

"No." I say again.

"Alright you asked for it." Kuvira says.

She drops into her metalbending stance and I drop into mine. Baatar does the same, dropping into his waterbending stance. I look back at Korra. She just stares at me with tears in her eyes.

I turn back to Kuvira and Baatar. "You want Korra, you'll have to get through me first."

Chapter 24

I look back at Korra again. "You don't have to do this." she says. She pleading with me. Telling me that my life is not worth risking for hers.

"Of course I'll fight for you. You've changed. I can see it. It's worth it." I say.

I turn back to Kuvira and Baatar and just shake my head. I can't believe that I'm fighting them. The people that I love. The ones who looked after me, when I had nowhere else to go. But now that I can see that they're willing to fight me just to take down Korra. Potentially to the death even. I take a deep breath and wipe away the tears that are forming in my eyes.

"I'll give you one more chance to step away from Korra. We don't have to fight Christine." Kuvira says.

"If that's how its going to be, then so be it." I can feel my heart break as I say the words.

I don't want to fight them but if they want to choose this path, then there's nothing I can do to stop them.

"Korra you need to stay out of this one," I say. "I don't want to see you get hurt."

"Alright." Korra says with a defeated sigh.

I turn back to Kuvira and Baatar. "Let's finish this right here, right now."

---

I step forward, Baatar and Kuvira do the same. We stand at a distance. Korra stands a few feet behind me. This is not how I wanted it to end. We stand in silence for a few seconds. Without warning a giant pillar of earth shot up beneath my feet. I jump out of the way and shoot out a metal strip. Kuvira deflects the attack. I dive out of the way and shoot another strip at her. Kuvira tries to bend it away. But by the time she realized that it was made of platinum it was too late it strikes her in the arm, making it bleed. She screams and fires out her metal cable, I don't get out of the way in time. It wraps around my ankle and she launches me into the air. I crash into the ground and let out a groan. I quickly get my to feet and just in time, because Baatar had started to attack too. He bends out the water from his hip flask and I don't get out of the way fast enough. The water hits me and knocks me to the ground, he takes that advantage to freeze me there. I lay there helpless. Kuvira walks over to me and Baatar unfreezes the water. Kuvira bends down and yanks me to my feet, she swings and I duck, her fist just skimming the top of my head. The movement was so sudden that I become dazed. I don't see Kuvira swing her arm forward. Her fist connects with my jaw and I cripple to the ground. My body shudders in agony. Kuvira almost smiles at the sight.

---

"What's the one thing you will always promise me?" I ask, leaning into Kuvira.
"I'll promise you everything." Kuvira whispered, looking back at me.
"But what's one thing—no matter what happens—you'll hold onto?" I ask, giving Kuvira a hug.
"One thing above all… I'll always care about you."
We sit in silence for a few minutes. I had a wide smile on my face from Kuvira's promise. I breathe out happily and lean back into Kuvira.
"What about you?" she asked.
"What?"
"What's something you'll always promise me?"
I lift my head to look at her.
"I promise I'll never leave you."

Chapter 25
I refuse to let Kuvira beat me. Even though the pain was agonizing, I won't quit. There's no way I'm letting this end now. I try my best to go into The Avatar State. I know that's the only way I can defeat her. However I'm too weak to do so and I try to use what little strength I have left. I lunge at her and punch her hard in the nose. Kuvira cried out in pain. I pin her to the ground and slam my fist into her face again, this time her jaw. Blood poured freely from her nose and the pain was a non-stop throb in Kuvira's face. But Kuvira refused to quit, even if my strength was a little bit alarming to her. I wrap my hands around her throat. I start bend a steady stream of fire against her skin. Kuvira starts to thrash from the pain and she let out a scream. Kuvira wasn't going to lose and she regained enough strength and pushed her way off the ground, crashing through me. I don't even let out a squeal as the metal blade drove through my stomach. A wicked smile creeped its way across Kuvira's face as she did. I quit bending the fire against her skin. Kuvira pushes me back onto my knees, further wedging the blade in. Soon I'm clutching at the blade and I run my hand along one of Kuvira's, which was the one that the blade was still attached to. That small contact was enough to snap Kuvira out of her murderous daze.
"Christine… " she whispered, and she looked down to see my hand resting loosely on my hand that was still holding the blade.
I fall forward, collapsing against her chest. I start to grip at the fabric of Kuvira's uniform as a small trickle of blood began to leak from the side of my mouth.
I didn't want to let go.
Kuvira rests her free hand on my back and gently lays me back and she held me close, as she looks down at me.

I look up and that's when everything hits me.

"K-Kuvira?" I got out, and I bring a shaking hand to rest on her cheek.

"Christine… what did I do? I-I'm so sorry." Kuvira whispered as she looked down at the metal blade again and the realization hits her like a freight train.

I let my hand drop, leaving a streak of blood on her cheek. But neither one of us cared. I remember when we first met; in the tunnel in Chicago.

"I… love you… Kuvira." I rasp out, my voice getting weaker and softer by the second.

Kuvira felt the tears coming to her eyes. She knew she'd never forgive herself for this. She had let her anger and pain overtake her… and it cost her the most important person in her life.

Kuvira could see the life draining from Christine's eyes. She could feel her breathing getting shallow, with every intake of air. She knew it was soon.

For a rare moment in Kuvira's life, she felt helpless.

"I love you too Christine. I always will. I'm s-so sorry. I-I didn't mean for th-this to h-happen," Kuvira got out in between her deep breaths as she tried to hold back her cries.

"It's okay." I say.

I smile softly.

Then my eyes close.

"Christine?" Kuvira shook her slightly. "Christine no!" she shouted and tears flowed freely down her face, confirming for her what she didn't want to accept.

She pulled the blade from Christine's stomach, not looking down as she didn't want to see what she did.

Kuvira was about to end her own life when she heard Baatar and Korra yell. *"No!"*

The next thing she knew was that she no longer had her metal blade. She spun around only to see that Korra was the who took it. "Korra give it to me."

"No." Korra says.

Kuvira was about to run towards Korra when something strikes her hard in the head.

She blacks out.


Chapter 26

I step back from Kuvira, she stares at me in disbelief. Korra is still standing safely behind me.

"Now you know, that's your's and my future. Unless you decide that killing Korra isn't worth it. Would you really risk my death so you can kill Korra?"

Kuvira doesn't say anything she just hang her head low and I hear her start to sniffle, as if she was about to cry. She sighs and moments later she lifts her head again, her face is tear-streaked. She looks from Korra to me and back again. She just shakes her head and sniffles again. She takes a deep breath. I wait for her to say something. But she remains silent.

After a while she finally speaks. "No. Its not worth risking your life, Christine. We won't fight."

I step forward again and place my hand on her shoulder. "Korra is no longer a threat. You need to believe that. You need to believe *me*."

"I do believe you." She takes a deep breath to calm herself down.

She gives me a hug and turns towards Korra and starts to walk towards her, Korra starts to back up slowly, but she stopped when her back hit the railing behind her. Kuvira stopped a few feet away from her and then suddenly lunged forwards. Korra screamed and closed her eyes. She was expecting Kuvira to throw her over the railing. But that moment never came. Instead she felt something wrap around her and she tensed up. She opened her eyes and realized that Kuvira was hugging her. She soon relaxed.

"I'm so sorry," she heard Kuvira say. "I'm sorry that I've treated you terribly. Korra will you ever forgive me?"

Korra took a deep breath and after a few seconds replied. "Yes, Kuvira I can forgive you."

Kuvira released Korra and they stood there looking into each other's eyes. They both smiled and then started to laugh. They laughed for a while. When they're done, I clear my throat. They both turn around.

"What?" Kuvira asks me.

"I hate to break this to you but… we're still standing on the tracks and there's a train coming."

"Run!" Baatar yells.

The tracks start to rumble and we hear the train horn and start to run. I look behind us, the train is catching up to us. I look around and notice a tree near the tracks, I pull Kuvira and Korra with me.

"What are we doing?" Kuvira asks.

"Jump!" I say and I give her a shove. She lands in the tree.

Korra is the next to go.

"Jump!" I say again.

She jumps and makes it onto the tree. The train is getting closer, I don't think I just jump. But I miss the tree and fall. I scream.

*"Christine!"* Everyone yells.

---

I continue to fall and I look around, the tree runs parallel to the bridge beside me. I smile as I bend out my metal cables, one wraps around the bridge and the other wraps around the tree trunk. I jump to the tree and the bridge and back again.

I'm not falling today.

Chapter 27

Kuvira, Korra and Baatar are still in the tree. When suddenly something shot up beside them. "What was that?"

"Over here!" They hear someone shout.

They all turn around and gasp in shock. *"Christine?!"*

"Hello everyone." I say.

Everyone runs over and gives me a big hug. They release me. We stand in the tree. I sigh. At least we're safe… sort of.

---

"So…" Korra says. "How are we going to get back?"

"I don't know." I say.

Suddenly, we hear the train horn, it blasts in our ears. We turn around and the train charges past us on the tracks.

"Let's go!" I shout over the train.

I run and metal bend my cable it wraps around one of the handles on the train. "Hang on!" I yell to the others.

"Hang on to what?" Baatar asks.

I grab onto him and drag him with me, I jump out of the tree and Baatar starts to scream. We land on the train and Korra and Kuvira follow suit. They jump and land on the train. We hold onto the side of the train and ride it to the train station. Once we get there we hop off the train and get onto another one. We all sit down and look out the window.

---

The land between Chicago and Zaofu is much different. Chicago's land is hot and dry, while Zaofu's land is green and fresh. The dry land that belongs to Chicago comes into view. We look at each other and smile. I pull out my phone and turn it on. I have one voicemail.

I listen to it. Its from Su. *"Hey, Christine. Hope all is going well with you and everyone else. Talk to you later. Bye."*

I smile and look at everyone else again. I get up and give everyone a hug. Then we look out the window again. We near the train station and when we get there we get off the train and go home. When we get there we sit down on the couch and cuddle with each other. We've had a long ride and we've had a lot of ups and downs. But I have learned that life is one big, long, bumpy ride. But for now we will live our lives. Not alone, but together, as friends and as family...

The Legend Of Korra Meets The Girl On The Train Part 2
(Book 7)

Chapter 1

We step down onto the platform, when we get to the train station. "Ah, we finally made it to Chicago." Korra says.

I walk over to her and give her a hug. "Of course we made it to Chicago. What did you think? That we'd be stuck on that train forever and that I wouldn't want for us to get off?"

Korra chuckles. "Yeah. That's what I was thinking."

I give her a playful shove to the side and she starts to laugh. Then she runs at me and gives me a noogie. "Ow." I say, as I shoot out a metal strip.

She deflects it away from herself and she starts to laugh. She splashes some water at me, I splash some back at her, but this time with mud in it. She glares at me, but then starts to laugh. We just stand there. Firing the elements at each other.

Kuvira just shakes her head. "Guys... stop."

We don't listen we just keep throwing earth, fire, air, water, metal and platinum at each other. At one point Korra throws a metal strip at me and it covers my eyes.

I drop dramatically to my knees. "Ah! My eyes!"

I take the metal strip from my eyes and Korra helps me to my feet and then fires another metal strip at me. I laugh and shove Korra to the side again. Kuvira just stares at us, with her arms crossed and she's tapping her foot impatiently against the ground. Finally she clears her throat.

"What?" I say.

She looks at her watch. "Can we go now?"

"Why?" I say. "Is someone not in the mood to play?"

I walk over to her and tackle her to the ground. She grunts as she pushes me off and helps me to my feets. We then walk together away from the train. Unaware that a certain someone was watching us go...

---

We walk to our car and my phone buzzes in my coat, I pull it out. Su is calling me. I look at everyone. "Does everyone want to say hi to Su?"

"Sure." everyone replies.

I put my phone on speaker. "Hello Su!" We all say.

*"Hello!"* she replies.

I then take my phone off speaker and talk to her. Though a few seconds after she starts talking, I drop my phone.

"What is it?" Kuvira asks.

"One minute." I say.

I pick up my phone again and start to talk to Su again. "Hello Su."

*"Hi."*

"So, you left me a message."

*"Yes."*

"Why did you want me to call you back?"

Silence.

"So what is it?"

*"You need to stay out of Chicago."*

"What? Why?"

*"It's for your own safety, that you stay away from the house."*

"But why?"

*"Because—"*

Then the phone line goes dead.

## Chapter 2

With a shaking breath I put my phone back into my pocket. I stare at everyone wide-eyed. "What is it?" Kuvira asks.

I shake my head. "Nothing."

"Alright." she says.

We get in the car and start to drive towards the house. I call Su again and by the time it goes to voicemail a third time, we are at the house. We hop out of the car and walk to the door. I knock on the door and wait. After a few minutes I knock again. Still no answer. I try the door and find it locked.

I turn back to everyone. "The doors locked."

"Don't you have a key?" Baatar says.

"Oh yeah."

I pull out the key and unlock the door. Just as I turn the doorknob, I hear something on the other side. I turn around and touch my finger to my lips, telling everyone to be quiet. Slowly, I turn the doorknob and push the door open. We walk inside and don't find anyone there. We walk through the kitchen and no one is there and everything has now become eerily quiet. We walk towards the living room and the doors are closed. I push the doors to the living room open and stop walking.

"*Su!*" I yell.

Su is in her chair with duct tape around her mouth and her hands are bound behind her back with platinum chains. She stares at us wide-eyed and mumbles something. She has an alarmed look in her eyes. She struggles out of the chains. I step towards her and she mumbles again and shakes her head. I take another step, She shakes her head again. "Its okay, Su. We're going to get you out of here."

I take the duct tape from her mouth and she yells. "Watch out!"

I look around but don't see anything, something strikes me in the back, I let out a grunt and fall to the ground with a crash. I cough and roll to the side, I look up and my vision blurs, through my blurry vision I see two figures standing over me. But before I have any time to react something sharpe goes into my neck. A drop of whatever was inside falls and I recognize it as the shirshu toxin. I try to move but my muscles feel like lead and my eyes close.

*"Christine!"* Everyone yells.

---

Kuvira whips around to see where the attack came from, but before she can do anything she's struck in the neck with something sharp and she crashes into the ground and passes out.

*"Kuvira!"* Baatar yells.

Baatar looks around. Not able to see anything. He turns back to Su, but by then it was too late. Su still sitting in her chair, was slumped forwards, her head rested on her chest. Baatar rushed over to her and gives her a shake, but she doesn't say anything.

"Mom?" he says and he gives her another shake.

Still he receives no answer. He shakes her again.

"Mom?" he says again.

Nothing.

He checks her pulse. "No!" He coughs out a sob. "No mom!"

He just sits there with Su in his arms, crying. Then he hears a crash and his head snaps up at the sound. Kuvira's and Christine's bodies were no longer in the house and he hears the roar of an engine in the distance.

He rests Su back in her chair and with a shaking breath, whispers. "I love you, mom." Before running out of the house.

He was going to track down whoever kidnapped his family and murdered his mother.

Chapter 3

My eyes flicker open and I let let out a groan. My head hurts so much. I try to move but I'm paralyzed. I look to the right and see Kuvira laying next to me on a table. I try to move again but then I realize that I'm not paralyzed but strapped to a table and my wrists and ankles are shackled together. I look back at Kuvira again.

"Kuvira?" I say, my voice weak.

She has a cut on her face and her arms are bruised. Like she tried to get away, but someone was holding her back. I lift my head and my vision goes blurry so I lie back down. I shake my head.

*Not again.* I think. *This can't be happening again.*

I hear a faint creak and my head snaps towards the door. Its open just a crack. I don't remember it being open just a minute ago. I look back towards Kuvira, she's now wide awake and staring towards the door. I look from Kuvira to the door, then back again. But there's no one here or so I thought...

---

Baatar drives through the city, he *needs* to find everyone. He needs to find his mom's killers. He pulls up to the police station and runs inside where he finds Lin sitting at her desk. She looks up from her computer when he comes close to her desk. "Hey Baatar! What are you doing here?"

Baatar bites the inside of his cheek and says "I need one of the computers."

Lin leans back in her chair. "But you don't have any shifts today."

"I know," he sighs, then looks back at Lin. Tears start to collect in his eyes. "But…"

"But what?" Lin asks, now sounding worried.

Baatar hangs his head and finally says. "She's dead."

Lin just blinks at him. "What?"

Baatar walks up to her and says. "I'm sorry, she's… Su's gone Lin. I… I'm sorry. I'm so sorry."

Lin's eyes started to fill with tears. "My sister's dead?"

Baatar just nods.

Lin shook her head. "How did this happen?"

"I don't know. But Christine and Kuvira have disappeared too. We need to find them."

Lin nods then calls him over to her computer. The screen is full of surveillance footage. "Okay," she says. "Where did you see them last?"

---

"Kuvira?" I say.

She doesn't answer.

"Kuvira!" I say again.

Still no answer.

I sigh and lean my head back on the table. I close my eyes for a moment, but then I hear another voice, this one is soft. "Don't worry, Kuvira is safe... for now."

My eyes snap open and go wide when I see the woman standing in front of me. "Impossible," I say. "Evelyn?"

Evelyn smirks at me. "It's nice to see you again, Christine. Did you miss me?"

Chapter 4

Baatar and Lin are still at the police station, looking through computer files and photo's trying to find stuff that can help them with the other's location. Baatar wipes tears from his eyes and continues to look.

Lin looks over at him and says. "Don't worry, we'll find your mother's killers."

Baatar wipes his eyes and laughs. "I'm more concerned with Kuvira and Christine really. I know that must sound horrible but..." His voice trails off and he just shakes his head.

"It doesn't sound horrible, Baatar. You're concerned with everyone's safety, I understand, don't worry."

Baatar takes a deep breath and he shakes out his hands. He will get through this, he will find his family.

---

The sight of Evelyn makes my heart pound against my chest so hard that it hurts. *No, this can't be right! She's dead! I saw her die!*

She steps forwards towards me and I start to panic. She's holding a pair of handcuffs. The electrified ones no doubt. I take a deep breath. *Calm down.* I tell myself. *Control your breathing.* When close enough, she cuts the straps that are holding my hands together. I wait until she's close enough to my hands and then I jerk forwards. I wrap my hands around her throat, and pull my feet free from their bindings. I push myself forwards, wrapping my hands tighter around her throat. She gasps and I push her back even further. She goes still and her eyes close. A smile creeps its way across my face and release her. *Finally.* I sigh. *Its finally over.*

---

"Where are they?" Baatar mumbles under his breath as he scrolls through the camera footage of Chicago. "Where could they be?"

He sighs, turns away from the computer and drops his head into his hands. Tears leak from his eyes and he sniffles. He takes a deep breath and it shakes on the way out. Why couldn't he just have a normal life? Without violence and without pain.

"Taking a break?" Lin asks.

Baatar lifts his head. "Yeah."

She sits down next to him and pulls him into a hug. "We'll get through this, I promise."

Chapter 5

I sigh and walk away from Evelyn's body, I shudder and shake out my hands. I turn back to Kuvira and she stares at me wide-eyed. I smile and walk over to her, I cut away the straps binding her to the bed and give her a hug. She laughs into my ear. "You did it!"

I laugh and scoop her into my arms. I start to walk away, when I hear a mocking laugh. I stop and turn around, another figure stands five paces away from me. I sigh and put Kuvira down. "Come on, really?"

Evelyn rubs the back of her neck and smiles at me. "Are you ready for round two?"

I chuckle and shake my head. "Of course, I am. I'm always ready."

She laughs. "Good."

I run at her and she steps out of the way, I skid to a stop and turn around. She smiles at me. I let out a low growl and send out a blast of water. Evelyn re-directs it back at me and I try to move but then I realize that I can't move. My body starts to twitch. Hot white pain races through my veins. I groan and try to move but then the pain becomes unbearable and I scream.

"Christine!" Kuvira yells.

She runs towards me. "Kuvira! Get out of here!" I say.

"No!" she says. "I'm not going to leave you again! I can't!"

"You don't have a choice! Go!"

She nods and runs out of the room. Then she skids to a stop. "No! President Raiko!"

He smiles. "Hello Kuvira, It's nice to see you again."

---

"No! President Raiko!"

"Hello Kuvira. Long time, no see." he says.

Kuvira's mind started to race and she started to panic. She shoots out a metal strip and it hits him in the arm, and Raiko screams. She takes that advantage to run out of the room. But she doesn't get far, because then she felt something wrap around the back of her neck and she's yanked back. She tries to wrestle out of his grip. But he increases the pressure on her neck. Kuvira stops trying to escape. The president drags her back into the room and handcuffs her to the table.

"Kuvira!" I shout.

"I'll be fine!" she says.

Evelyn clears her throat and says. "Now that we are all here. We can get started."

She pulls out a vial of serum. My eyes go wide as I realize what it is. The simulation serum.

*Where on earth did Evelyn find simulation serum?* I think.

---

Baatar is looking over Lin's shoulder at the security footage, Lin scrolls past the footage of Erudite headquarters and then his eyes go wide. "Wait go back!"

Lin scrolls back to Erudite headquarters and he bolts out of the police station.

"Where are you going?" Lin calls to him.

"I know where they are!" he calls back.

He runs out of the building and crashes into someone. "Ow!" he says.

"Oops, sorry Baatar."

He rubs his head and looks up. "How did you not see me I mean I... Oh sorry Korra."

Korra helps him up off the ground and says. "What are you doing?"

"I'm going to find Christine and Kuvira. They're gone."

"Oh... I know where they are. I was just on my way there." she says.

"Well let's go!" Baatar says.

They both take off towards Erudite headquarters.

Chapter 6

Evelyn still has her hold on me, I struggle against it. She steps closer and when she's close enough I kick out a fire blast. Her hold on me falters and I slam into the ground. Moments later I hear a scream. I smile, thinking that I hit Evelyn with it. But then I hear an evil laugh, I look over at Evelyn and find that she's unburned. Another scream fills the room and I turn towards Raiko, he just smiles at me. I look beside him, where I see Kuvira on the floor clutching at her face. That's when the realization hits me. I run over towards her and lift her up. "Kuvira!" I say. "Look at me!"

She lifts her head to look at me, but she's covering her eye with her hand. I take her hand from her eye and there's a burn mark.

I hear a laugh, this one not coming from Evelyn or Raiko. I hear someone say. "That's why you don't play with fire Christine. Someone could get hurt."

Still holding Kuvira, I turn towards the voice. "No! Zaheer!"

Zaheer starts to walk towards me and I start to back up slowly, but I back right into Evelyn. She grabs my arms and holds me back, as Zaheer steps closer. I try to break free and she tightens her hold on me. Her fingers dig into my arms and I cry out in pain. I stop struggling. Zaheer smirks at me and then reaches for me. I start to thrash. But instead of grabbing me, he grabs Kuvira and chains her to the table. Then he starts his way towards me again. I thrust my elbow back, it hits Evelyn square in the nose. She let's out a cry of pain and let's me go. I start to run and Evelyn bloodbends me. I groan as my limbs starts to bend and twitch.

Through the ringing in my ears I hear. "Christine hold on!"

I drop to the ground as the hold loosens. I look up and gasp. "Korra!"

She runs over to me and picks me up off the ground. "I've got you!"

She starts to run when she stops dead in her tracks, she drops me and I land on the ground with a sickening thud. I hear a scream. "No!"

My head snap up and I see Korra being bloodbent. Her limbs bending in an inhuman way, she tries to break free and her legs bend near their breaking point, she tries to move and her body twitches even more. I get up but something strikes me down. I look up and see Raiko standing over me, his mouth is set in a smirk. He handcuffs me to the table. I stain forwards but the cuffs shock me and I collapse onto the ground. I look over at Kuvira and she tries to break free.

Evelyn walks towards Korra, who had collapsed onto the ground and pulls out the simulation serum. She yanks her to her feet. Korra struggles for a moment. Then without warning Evelyn sticks the needle into Korra's neck. Korra collapses onto the ground again and she shudders.

"Korra!" I yell.

I strain forward and break out of the handcuffs. I send out a lightning blast and Evelyn steps out of the way. I charge at her and she sends out a blast of water, I re-direct it back and I wrap my hands around her throat. I shove her against the opposite wall and start to bend a stream of fire against her throat, she flinches but doesn't make any big movements.

"What did you do!?" I growl.

Evelyn just smiles at me. I start to tighten my hand around her throat even more and she starts to gasp. Suddenly, something wraps around the back of my neck and wrenches me backwards. I let Evelyn go and she clutches at her throat and starts to breathe heavily. I try to break free from the grip. I'm slammed into the ground and I look up. There I see Korra standing over me, her eyes hold a murderous daze. I jump to my feet and she runs at me. I duck and her fist skims the top of my head. She swings and I grab her arm. She thrusts her arm back and it hits me in the nose. I put my hands up to block her next blow. Her fist hits me in the stomach and I gasp. "Korra," I say. "You're in a sim."

"She can't hear you." Evelyn says.

Korra wraps her hand around my throat and I gasp. She squeezes my throat, black spots start to crowd my vision. I start to feel lightheaded and I gasp for air again. My lungs scream for oxygen. I black out.

Chapter 7

Kuvira struggles against the shackles that hold her to the table. She takes a deep breath and clenches her hands, but the handcuffs shock her. She does everything she can not to scream. She slumps back against the table. She sees Korra standing over Christine's body. She picks Christine up and shoves her against the wall. Christine jerks awake and cries out in pain. Kuvira wished she could do *something*, to help her. So she struggles against the handcuffs again and she get's shocked again and she passes out.

---

Korra has me pinned against the opposite wall. I struggle and she shoves me up the wall. I choke and I start to gag. "Korra," I say, my voice weak. "Please."

She tightens her grip and I can feel my windpipe being squished. My vision blurs and I start to get lightheaded again. My head pounds. I pass out.

---

Baatar runs through Erudite headquarters and into the lab. But Christine nor Kuvira were there. He looks on the ground and sees a trail of blood, so he decides to follow it. He follows it to a room. This room had rows of tables with computers on them. He walks through the room and looks at the computers. They have surveillance footage on them. He takes a closer at the footage on one of the screens, there's footage of the prison, of the city, there's footage of Zaofu and of their house. He stares at the screen wide-eyed. They were being watched. He hears a loud bang and then a ear-splitting scream. He bolts off in the direction of the scream. He runs, until he reaches a large room, larger than the lab. He stops dead in his tracks.

---

I let out a loud groan. I clutch at my side, the stitches in my ribcage are torn. My side starts to bleed. Blood soaks the side of my green uniform, creating a dark patch. Korra yanks me to my feet, I let out a scream. The stitches tear even more, the dark patch on my shirt gets bigger. Each breath I take only makes the pain worse. Korra swings at me and I duck out of the way and my ribs throb with pain. I cripple to my knees. I cry out in pain. Korra stands over me. A metal blade in hand. I roll out of the way and the blade misses me. I jump to my feet and look over in Kuvira's direction. I stop in my tracks. Zaheer and Raiko are holding Kuvira back. Evelyn is holding a needle full of death serum.

"Christine," she says. "If you don't stop fighting, then I'll use this needle full of death serum and stick Kuvira with it. Do you understand?"

"Christine," Kuvira says. "Don't listen to her, I'll be fine!"

Evelyn presses the needle so close to her neck that Kuvira flinches. "Don't!" I yell. "Stop."

She stops. "You'll do as I say?"

I let out a shaking breath. "Yes."

"Good."

I nod. "Can I just say goodbye to Kuvira first?"

"Alright."

She nods to Raiko and Zaheer. They let her go, she runs up to me and gives me a hug. Tears run down my face.

"I love you." I say and I let her go.

I turn back to Evelyn. "Alright."

She runs at me and I close my eyes. But then something hard strikes me in the head.

I black out.


Chapter 8

Baatar is still standing where he was before, he tries not to breathe to loudly. He's just outside the room that the others are in. Inside the room he sees Evelyn, Former President Raiko, Zaheer, Korra, Kuvira and Christine.

Kuvira is being held back by Raiko and Zaheer. Evelyn is standing with them also. Christine is on the ground unmoving and Korra is standing above her, with a smirk on her face and she's holding something. It looks like a needle.

My eyes flicker open I let out a cry of pain. My side is burning. My head is pounding and my heart is racing. My nose twitches, something smells like smoke and spice. I roll to the side and Korra stands above me, with a needle. I let out a deep breath and look Korra in the eye. She's stuck under the simulation still. The smoke and spice smell gets stronger and I recognize it as death serum. I close my eyes and wait for the worst to come. Korra yanks me to my feet and shoves me against the wall a few feet away. I hear footsteps getting closer. They are loud, thundering against the floor. But then I hear a squeak and a yell, accompanied by the sounds of grunts and groans. I hear a loud crash and then a scream. But I keep my eyes closed. I feel dizzy and fall to the ground. My head hits the tiles and I black out.

"Is she still alive?" a voice says.

I open my eyes and see several people standing in front of me, or rather above me. Once my vision clears, I see them standing there. Evelyn, Raiko and Korra. Korra still hasn't gotten any better. I jump to my feet and start to run. But Raiko grabs my arm and pulls me back. He shoves me towards Korra, who instantly comes after me. She tries to hit me, but I put my arms up to block the blow. I look over my shoulder and see that Zaheer is laying on the ground. Dead. It brings a smile to my face. Korra tries to hit me again and she misses, I grab her arm and pull her close. I thrust my knee up into her stomach and her elbow connects with the side of my head. I see stars, but keep moving. I punch her and my fist hits her in the jaw. I turn and run, but she grabs my arm and yanks me backwards. I thrust my free elbow backward and hit her square in the nose. "Korra. It's me!"

She punches me to the ground and I start to crawl backwards, I look around and see a syringe lying on the the ground. I grab it, just as she yanks me to my feet. I point it towards her throat. "Please stop!" I say. Then I turn it towards myself and she lurches forward and grabs it. I put my hand on her chest and feel her heartbeat. Its beating fast. "Its okay, its okay. I forgive you Korra. Its okay."

She starts to look away as she presses the needle closer. I put my hand on her cheek and turn her head so she's looking at me. "Its me," I say. "Its me."

I look into her eyes, they no longer look stimulation-bound and she whispers. "Christine?" I nod my head and put my hand back on her chest. Her heartbeat has slowed down to almost normal. She picks me up and gives me a hug. I let out a sigh of relief. I turn towards Evelyn and Raiko. They stare at us wide-eyed. I look at Korra and nod. She sprints towards Raiko and plunges the needle into his neck. He collapses onto the floor. Dead.

Evelyn starts to look panicked and she starts to run. But I run after her. I catch up to her and slam her into the wall. She stares at me wide-eyed. I look into her eyes. "You killed Su!"

She looks over my shoulder and then smirks. "Of course, I did. I couldn't stand her anymore. She hasn't done anything to help anyone in this city. So I thought I would take of the problem."
I don't say anything I just stare in her eyes as I stick the needle in. She starts to gasp and cough. I watch the life drain from her eyes and then let her go. She falls to the ground with a loud and sickening thud. I sigh and look down at her body.
It was over.

*"Baatar!"* Kuvira screams.


Chapter 9
I jerk up at the sound of Baatar's name and look back at Kuvira and Korra. I run over to them and look down on the ground. There Baatar lies, his skin pale and his body motionless. Korra presses to fingers to the side of his throat and looks up at us, she just shakes her head.

Kuvira coughs out a sob. "No, Baatar. Please wake up."

"Kuvira…" Korra starts to say, but she cuts her off. "No Korra. He's not dead, he… he can't be. No its not true. It *can't* be true."

"I'm sorry Kuvira, but its true. Baatar's dead."

I wrap my arms around her and pull her into a hug. "I'm sorry," I say. "I'm so sorry."
She cries into my shoulder. We just stand there and I let her cry. Korra comes over and joins the hug. Kuvira is still crying. I wipe away the tears that are forming in my eyes.

After a while, when we finally break apart. Kuvira bends down and picks Baatar up. She hugs him. "I l-love you B-Baatar."
Another round of sobs rack her body and she sits there on the floor, holding him close. I put my hand on Kuvira's shoulder and give her a hug.

"Kuvira? Its time to go."

"No! I can't just leave him here."

"You don't have too."
We pick Baatar up and walk out of Erudite headquarters. We walk all to the other end of the city and back to the house, where we find, Lin, Baatar Sr., Opal, Huan and Wing and Wei. I walk up to Baatar Sr. and give him a hug.

Then I walk up to Lin and give her a hug. "What happened to you guys? Where's Baatar…" She stops mid-sentence. Junior! What… what happened?"

"He was killed by Evelyn." I say.

"What happened to Su?" Baatar Sr. asks.

I sigh. "Evelyn killed her."

"No," he says. "No… this can't be true. No!"

"I'm sorry," I say. "I am truly sorry."

I look around at everyone, they all have their heads hung low and are crying. Tears come to my eyes and run down face.

Its one thing to lose one family member, but is too much to lose a second one. I start to cry and I cry until I feel sick.

Kuvira gives me a hug and comforts me. "Shh. Its okay. Its okay."

I look up at her and give her a tighter hug. She holds me close. "I'm sorry," I say. "I'm so sorry."

"Its okay." she says.

"I-I need to take a walk." I say, as I pull away and start to walk passed her.

"Christine wait." she says.

But I ignore her and keep walking. She calls after me.

I keep running.

Chapter 10

I keep running through the city. I run until I get to the alleyway and I stop. I lean against the wall and tears run down my face. I slide down the wall and sit on the ground, I put my head in my hands and cry. I sit there in the alleyway and eventually I stop crying. I just sit there and think about everything that has happened. It makes me feel guilty about what has happened. So I take a deep breath and start to meditate. I start to feel the world fade away and when I open them I'm in The Spirit World. I get up off the ground and walk through the tall spirit grass and past a giant glowing spirit mushroom. I keep walking, until the sky becomes dark. I see a tree in the far distance, I walk up to it and sit down, I lean against it, stretch my arms above my head, yawn, close my eyes and fall asleep.

*"Christine!"* Kuvira calls out. "Christine where are *you?!"*

She walks towards Erudite headquarters and goes inside. She checks every room, including the lab. But she's not there. She checks all the cells and all the other rooms, but Christine isn't there. She walks out of Erudite headquarters and around the city some more.

"Christine. Where are you?" she calls out again.

She walks past the road that leads to the alleyway and then she stops. She turns towards the road and runs up it. She reaches the alleyway and she sees her. Christine is sitting on the ground. Her eyes closed. Kuvira runs over to her and shakes her.

No response.

She shakes her again. "Christine! Can you hear me? Christine!"

She checks her pulse, its a steady rhythm. Kuvira felt relieved, at least she was alive.

But why wasn't Christine responding?

That's when the thought hit her. *She's in The Spirit World!*

Kuvira hugged Christine and sat down in front of her. She started to mediate and soon she felt the world fade away.

My eyes slowly open and my mind is foggy. I hear a voice. *"Psst! Hey you! Wake up!"*

I stretch my hands above my head and let out a yawn. I blink and then frown. Where was I? Oh yeah, The Spirit World.

*"Psst! up here!"*

I look up at the tree and see a spirit inside.

*Wait what's a spirit doing in a tree?* I think.

The spirit inside the tree calls me over. *"Yeah, you. Can you help me? I'm trapped."*

"Yeah sure." I say. I walk over to the tree and start to climb up to open it.

I'm about to let the spirit free, when I hear another voice, its so hushed that I don't notice it at first. *"Christine don't let this spirit free."*

"What was that?" I say, and I stop for a moment.

I look back at the spirit in the tree. He just shrugs. Well it would've been a shrug if he had a physical body. I continue to climb the tree. I stand in front of what seems to be a barrier that's keeping him back.

I hear the voice again. *"Christine, this spirit is evil don't let him out."*

I shrug off the voice and walk closer to the barrier.

"Who are you?" I ask, as I look up at him.

*"I'm just a spirit that's trapped in a tree."* was his simply reply.

*"Get away from the tree, Christine and don't let him out!"* The voice inside me says.

"Raava," I say. "Why do you have a problem with me letting help this spirit. I mean he's..." My voice fades. "Wait *Raava?*"

*"Yes. Its me Raava,"* Raava says. *"The spirit in the Tree Of Time is—"*

"Vaatu."

Chapter 11

Kuvira walks around The Spirit World. Looking everywhere for Christine. "Christine! Where are you?"

*What if something happened to her? What if she was killed?* Kuvira shook the thought out of her mind.

She starts to run, she runs past a glowing spirit mushroom and then skids to a stop, she turns around and runs back to the mushroom.

"Hello!" The spirit mushroom says.

"Umm... Hi." Kuvira says and she scratches her head. She didn't know how to ask the spirit the question that had been itching in the back her mind.

"Was there something you needed?" The spirit finally asked.

"Uh... yes actually," Kuvira says, she paused for a moment. "This might be a crazy question," she pauses and lets out a awkward laugh "But have you seen another human come through here? She has short brown hair that's in a pixie cut and she's about my height."

"Hmm," The spirit says. "Actually yes. She went down the path that leads to the Tree Of Time, I believe."

"Thank you!" Kuvira exclaimed.

"No problem." The spirit says.

Kuvira starts to walk toward the Tree Of Time and that's when the thought hit her. *The Tree Of Time! Wasn't Vaatu imprisoned there?*

She breaks into a sprint she needed to get there and she needed to get there quickly.

---

I slowly back away from the tree. "Vaatu?" I say. "How? Korra defeated you during the last Harmonic Convergence."

Vaatu let's out a deep laugh and says. *"Korra never really got rid of me."*

"What do you mean?"

*"Well, as Raava once said: Peace and Chaos cannot exist without one another."*

I open my mouth to speak when Raava interrupts. *"How dare you use that against me! You only want out so you can reak havoc on the world. There's no way I'm letting that happen!"*

I turn away from the tree and soon I feel The Spirit World slip away.

Kuvira runs up the path. There she sees Christine and she calls out for her. But seconds later, her spirit disappears. Kuvira stops by the tree and soon she felt herself and The Spirit World slip away.

---

I wake from the nightmare with a start. I start to breathe heavily, I look around. I'm in the house sitting on the couch. "Christine?" A voice says.

I look to my left. "Kuvira!" I say.

"Christine!"

She gives me a hug and tears roll down her face.

"What happened?" I ask.

"You fell asleep. You've been asleep for a couple days now."

"A couple?" I say.

"You told everyone that you were tired and that you weren't feeling very good. So you went to take a nap and then you fell asleep."

All I can say is. "Oh."

We sit beside each other and watch TV.

## Chapter 12

We walk around the city, the sun is about to set, it glows a bright red-orange against the sky. I'm enjoying the the sky, when my phone rings. I take it out of my pocket. I've been dreading this moment. I take a deep breath and answer it. "Hello?"

*"Hi Christine. Its Lin."*

My heart breaks.

"Oh, hi Lin," I say. "What did you need?"

Lin keeps talking. I look over at Kuvira. She knows what's coming.

I sigh. "Alright. We'll be right there."

I put my phone back into my pocket and let out a sigh. I turn toward Kuvira and give her a hug, tears leak from my eyelids and I bury my face into her shirt and my next breath shakes on the way out. I feel Kuvira's arms wrap around me and when I pull away she stares at me.

"What is it?" she asks.

"Lin called me… Um," I take a deep breath and continue. "She… um… she called me and wanted for us to come back for… uh… for Su's and Baatar's funerals. They're having them tomorrow, but… she wants us back tonight, so we can say our last goodbyes."

Kuvira tries to hold back her tears. "Right… so let's go."

---

I stand in front of a mirror in mine and Kuvira's house. Kuvira stands behind me, she's just doing up the back the dress that I'm wearing. We're both dressed in funeral attire. Mine is a simple Zaofu dress and so is Kuvira's. I let out a sigh and look at Kuvira in the mirror. Her eyes meet mine and I look away. She lets out a sigh. We stay in silence. She puts her hand on my shoulder. I turn around and she pulls me into a hug. I clutch her shirt as I start to cry. Moments later we hear a knock on the door. Just a simple. *Tap, tap, tap.*

Kuvira looks into my eyes. "Are you ready?" she asks.

I nod. "Yeah."

We walk out of our bedroom and Baatar Sr. stands in the hallway. He looks tired and he looks like he's been crying. I suck in a deep breath and we start to walk.

---

I stand on the balcony that overlooks Zaofu. I haven't been here in so long. The last time I was here, it was to help Kuvira conquer it and reunite the Earth Empire. Since then we've been in Chicago.

Now I'm here for the funerals of two people that I loved dearly. I sigh and Kuvira walks up beside me. "Hey, its alright."

I let out a half laugh, half sob. "No, nothing is alright. Su and Baatar are both dead."

"Its not your fault, none of this is your fault." she says.

"I know," I say. "I know."

She looks down at the town square. "Well, we should get down there."

"Yeah."

## Chapter 13

The square is packed with people from Zaofu and Chicago. A portrait of Su and Baatar Jr. had been set up at the front of the square and flowers littered the ground near them and a statue of them both had been placed there as well. A podium had been set up too. One by one the people that were close to Su went up to say a few words, and finally it was my turn. With shaking legs, I walk up to the podium. I stare out at everyone. I take a deep breath and after a few silent moments, start to speak. "I just wanted to say that Su and Baatar meant everything to me. They meant a lot of things to a lot of people. They both had loving hearts. They loved their city, their people and their family. I know that they still would love us all now. I…" My breath catch on the way out and I collapse onto the podium. Tears erupt from my eyes. "I-if, I had been on time that one day. None of this would've happened and I… I'm sor… ry. I was t… too I…ate. I was t… too late. I'm sor… ry." I'm unable to control myself any longer, I cry.

I lean onto the railing of the balcony. I watch as the people in the square leave. Though the portraits of Su and Baatar are still there, the chairs have all been cleaned up and put away. I let out a sigh and put my head in my hands. I let out a shaking out and start to sniffle. Tears leak from my eyes and I wipe them away. I look down at the square again. Everyone has left. I shake out my hands and lean on the railing again. I close my eyes. I feel something wrap around me. I hear her voice. "Shh, its okay, just let it out. I've got you. Its alright."

I jerk out of the embrace and turn around, only to see Kuvira standing there. "Oh, Kuvira you scared me."

Kuvira walks up and stands beside me and looks down at town square. "Sorry, I didn't mean too." I nod and look back down at the square. I let out a sigh and close my eyes again. I can still see Baatar's lifeless body laying on the floor and I open my eyes. I turn and walk away from Kuvira. I walk out of the house and start my way towards the train station.

I get on the train and make my way back to Chicago. I sit down in my seat and lean my head against the window. I close my eyes. Moments later the train comes to a sudden halt and I jerk awake. I look out the window and see smoke in the distance. It takes me a moment to realize that the smoke is coming from Chicago. My eyes widen and I run off the train.

The smoke makes my eyes water as I get closer. I stop near the edge of the city and look up. My eyes widen. I hear a deep, mocking laugh. Though the smoke I see him, towering above the city. His mocking laugh becomes louder as he comes closer. He just stops inches away from me. Vaatu's voice booms throughout the city. *"How are you feeling Raava? This time I will get rid of you once and for all!"*

## Chapter 14

Vaatu towers over me. I have to crane my neck to look at him. His laughter shakes the ground. I drop into a bending stance. He snickers. "No human can stand against me!"

"Are you sure about that?" I say.

I send out a blast of lightning and is strikes him, making him smaller.Vattu shoots out an energy beam and I jump out of the way. I launch out a few rocks and they hit him. He blasts out another beam. I jump out of the way but it strikes me. I fly backwards and slam into the ground with a sickening thud. He towers over me and he starts to get ready for another attack. I get hit again and fall to the ground. I cough and roll to the side.

He towers over me again. *"To hate me is to give me breath, to fight me is to give me strength, now prepare to face your demise!"*

Vaatu charges his energy beam and I lie there helpless. I hear a loud blare and the ground below me gives away. I fall and then scream. The vines in the ground though stop me from falling to my death. I hear a shout and see several blasts of fire and a barrade of rocks. Vaatu's form becomes smaller and smaller by the minute.

I hear a familiar voice. "Christine! Where are you!?"

"Down here!" I yell.

Moments later the vines are replaced with earth and rocks. I jump from one side to the next until I'm out of the trench. Someone pulls me to my feet. I blink and see two familiar faces. Kuvira and Baatar Sr. I give them a hug.

"Let's get out of here!" Baatar Sr. shouts.

I nod and we start to run. I look back and see Korra launching rocks and fire at Vaatu. He shoots out his energy beam and Korra jumps out of the way. I pull Baatar and Kuvira to a stop. "We can't just leave her here."

We turn back to Korra and start to run towards her, she looks back at us. "What are you doing? Get out of here." she shouts.

"I can't just leave you here!" I shout back.

She jumps out of the way to avoid another one of Vaatu's blasts. "You don't have a choice! Go! Before its too late!"

I just stand there unable to move. Korra struggles to keep Vaatu at bay, he pins her to the ground and she struggles out of the grip. I look back at Baatar Sr. He knows what I'm thinking. He just shakes his head. I don't think, I just run.

"Christine no!"

I send out several attacks and hit Vaatu. He just brushes them off and continues to attack Korra. I send out more attacks.

"Let her go!" I yell.

Vaatu groans as I let out more attacks and let's Korra go. Korra stares at me wide-eyed. I continue my attacks. Vaatu grows smaller and smaller, with each new attack. I send out a blast of lightning and the electricity makes him shrink more. Now he's small enough to fit in a teapot. Vaatu lies on the ground, getting smaller and smaller. I bend up a rock from the ground and hover it over him.

Just as I plan to finish him off, he speaks. "There's one thing, that's most important to you. That I could give back."

"Yeah, sure," I growl. "What could you *possibly* give to me?"

"Your family," he says. "I can bring back your family."

Chapter 15

I stare at Vaatu wide-eyed. Surely this was a trick, wasn't it?

Vaatu looks up at me and says. "Now if you want your family back, here's what you need to do…"

"So… what will it be?" Vaatu asks. "You or your family?"

I stand speechless. I look back at Baatar Sr. and Korra. They stare at me wide-eyed. I turn back towards Vaatu. I let out a sigh and hang my head low.

*"Christine,"* Raava says. *"Don't. He's just trying to trick you."*

I ignore her.

"Alright. I give in." I look back at Korra and Baatar Sr.

There was a sudden flash of light and there stood Baatar Jr. and Su, looking dazed but unharmed. I walk over to Su and give her a hug. She gives me a hug back. I walk up to Baatar Jr. and give him a hug too.

"Christine?" Baatar Jr. says. "Don't do it."

I don't say anything I just turn back towards Vaatu. He was now back to his full size and he laughs as he comes towards me. Without warning I send out several attacks and they hit him. He becomes smaller and smaller. He blasts me with with his energy beam, I fly back and slam into the ground. He towers over me again and stops inches from my face. I stare at him wide-eyed. I jump to my feet and send out a blast of air. He doesn't move. Suddenly I feel a pull deep from inside, not just my body, but in my soul, it felt as if something was being torn away. The feeling grew stronger and stronger and more painful in the following seconds. Soon my vision goes black. I can't see or hear anything in the outside world. Instead I hear a shrill scream coming from the inside. My vision becomes clear and I look over at Korra she's has collapsed onto the ground as well. The scream becomes louder and I realize who it is and where it came from.

*Raava!*

I get up and I see Raava disappear. Vaatu shoots out an energy beam and it hits her. I collapse onto the ground as my past life and only past life disappears. Korra does the same collapsing onto the ground with a grunt.

*"No!"* We yell.

I lie on the ground, staring up at the sky. My body unable to move. Vaatu towers over my and I just lie there. He laughs a mocking laugh. "The era of Raava is over!"
I summon enough strength to try to bend fire at Vaatu. But nothing happens.
"What! Why… why can't I bend?" My eyes go wide as the revelation hits me. "I can't *bend!*"
Vaatu laughs. "Foolish human. You should know that Raava provided the ability to control all the elements and use of The Avatar State. Now you are nothing but powerless."
"No!" I say, trembling. "This can't be happening. No!"
Korra jumps to her feet and drops into an earthbending stance. "You cannot win Vaatu!" She tries to bend a piece of earth and nothing happens. "What no! Not again!"
Korra stares at me with wide eyes. We turn back to Vaatu. He laughs again. "The era of Raava is over."

## Chapter 16

Vaatu hovers over me and Korra. I start to crawl backwards. I get to my feet and turn to run when I see a flash of light out of the corner of my eye. I turn around and let out an audible gasp. Three people stand by Vaatu. A smile creeping across their faces. "No," I say. "Not again."
Former President Raiko, Evelyn and Zaheer stand there. They all drop into a bending stance—with the exception of Raiko of course—I start to back up instinctively. Evelyn makes the first move and she sends out a stream of water. I try to redirect it but it hits me and I slam into the ground. I jump to my feet before Evelyn can freeze me there. Zaheer blasts me with air and I slam into the ground again. My vision doubles and my muscles start to bend and twitch. I let out a cry of pain and collapse onto the ground. I breath in and find that I can't get oxygen. I become light-headed. Through my vision I see Zaheer and the other two. I gasp and suddenly I can breathe again. I look over Korra. She launches water attacks at Zaheer and Evelyn. Raiko lies on the ground. Dead.
Vaatu laughs. "Oh come on is that all you can do?"
"Well I can do this." I say and I shoot out several metal strips. They strike him. He becomes smaller. I start to prepare another attack when I'm blasted back with air. I shoot out several earthen pillars and one hits Zaheer. He slams into the ground. Unmoving.
Evelyn's eyes widen as she realizes that she no longer has protection. She turns and runs. Vaatu lets out a growl. "Where do you think your going?"
He starts his way towards her and she runs away. He catches up to her and moments later she collapses onto the ground. Dead. Vaatu starts his way towards me and I turn and run. He pins me to the ground. I thrash. But moments later his grip on me loosens. I look up, he starts to glow a bright yellow and I recognize it as spiritbending. Vaatu starts to disappear completely and I see a white light escape from him. It darts away and hides behind a building. Soon the last of Vaatu disappears completely, back to The Spirit World.
The light that hid behind the building comes closer to us. I let out a gasp. "Raava!"
"Hello." she replies.
"Well. I'm glad that's over." Korra sighs.
"So am I." I say.
I walk up to Baatar Jr. and Su and give them a hug.
"I missed you guys so much." I say.
They sigh. "We missed you too."

I look over at Kuvira and motion her over. She walks up Baatar Jr. and gives him a hug, then she walks over to Su and gives her a hug.

Su recoils back for a moment. "Kuvira!"

They stay in the embrace for a while and when they break apart. They smile.

"I can't believe we won." I say.

"Yeah," Korra says and she turns back to Raava. "So now what?"

"Well…" Raava says. "We can connect with each other again."

"Awesome!" We say.

There was a sudden flash of light and I feel Raava's presence again. Me and Korra let out a sigh.

"Well," I say. "Should we all go home?"

Everyone nods and we make our way back to the train station. We board the train and soon arrive in Zaofu. We go back to the house and sit down on the couch together.

I lean against Kuvira and she gives me a hug.

No matter what happens… no matter how crazy things get. We will always restore balance to the world.


The Legend Of Korra Meets The Girl On The Train Part 3
(Book 8)

Chapter 1

Christine

We sit on the couch, watching TV. I lean against Kuvira and she gives me a kiss. I giggle and sit up. Its been almost two weeks since Vaatu's attack and the city has gone back to somewhat normal.

Kuvira let's out a sigh. "So… how are you feeling?" she asks.

I takes me a minute to realize that she's talking to me. I put a hand over my ribcage. "Oh." I say. The gauze has stopped it from bleeding and with Baatar's and Korra's help, is almost healed. "I'm feeling fine. I mean my ribs still hurt but I'm fine."

"Oh…," she says. "That's great, but that's not what I meant."

I knew that's not she meant. There's no backing out now.

"I'm fine," I say. "I'm doing fine just… the nightmares haven't stopped."

"Oh," she says. "Well that's not good."

I shake my head. "No its not."

---

*Vaatu hovers over me and Korra. I start to crawl backwards. I get to my feet and turn to run when I see a flash of light out of the corner of my eye. I turn around and let out an audible gasp. Three people stand by Vaatu. A smile creeping across their faces. "No," I say. "Not again."*

*Former President Raiko, Evelyn and Zaheer stand there. They all drop into a bending stance—with the exception of Raiko of course—I start to back up instinctively. Evelyn makes the first move and she sends out a stream of water. I try to redirect it but it hits me and I slam into the ground. I jump to my feet before Evelyn can freeze me there. Zaheer blasts me with air and I slam into the ground again. My vision doubles and my muscles start to bend and twitch. I let out a cry of pain and collapse onto the ground. I breath in and find that I can't get oxygen. I become light-headed. Through my blurry vision I see Zaheer, Raiko and Evelyn. I drop to the ground and my eyes close.*

---

I scream and bolt right up. I breathe heavily and open my eyes. I see Kuvira staring at me wide-eyed. "What is it?" she asks.

"Nothing," I say. "Just another nightmare."

"The same one?" Korra asks.

"Yeah."

She pulls out a pad of paper and a pen and put's a tally mark down. "That makes it thirteen of the same nightmare in the last two weeks."

My heart is pounding. Sweat collects on my palms and face. I put my head in my hands. I'm shaking.

Kuvira hugs me. "Hey, Its okay, we'll get through it. I promise."

I sniff and bury my face into her uniform. She runs a hand through my hair. Korra joins in on the hug and we just sit there holding each other.

## Chapter 2

The next day Korra, Christine, Baatar and I take a walk around Chicago. Some people who were affected by Vaatu's attack are still recovering. Most of the city was destroyed, leaving hundreds of people without a place to stay. The streets are crawling with people. Most have injuries from his attack and some people have lost their loved ones. The realization hits me like a freight train and it makes my heart ache. I look around and see children, some with parents who have abandoned them or some whose parents were killed. It brings tears to my eyes and I wipe them away before they fall. Of course I know the feeling. My parents cast me aside when I was six and I spent two years on my own, just barely staying alive. When I was eight, Su found me in the streets of Zaofu and took me in and gave me a place to stay. I never felt part of the family though, I'm not sure if Su ever knew that.

"What are you thinking?" Christine's voice snaps me back to reality.

I shake my head and look at her. "Nothing."

"You have to be thinking about something." Christine tilts her head to the side.

I look away. "I don't want to talk about it."

"Why?" she asks.

"I said I don't want to talk about it okay!" I snap.

My sudden anger shocked both me and Christine. I look away and Christine let's out a sigh. I look over at Baatar and Korra they are talking to each other in low voices. I look back at Christine and she is looking down at the ground. I continue to look around the city and the more I look, the more abandoned kids I see and my heart shatters into a million pieces.

---

"Wait here sweetie, okay?"

Perhaps it was because I was too young, or because I was too excited over the day's events that I did not recognize the sad look in my mother's eyes when she said that. It was rare when my parents were able to take time off from their jobs, and even rarer that they would spend that day at a festival in a totally different city with their daughter. My family was not rich, or even working class for that matter. In fact, even in their poor neighbourhood, they were among the least fortunate. Families of nonbenders always had a harder time making ends meet than benders. It was the sad truth of this world – nonbenders simply were poorer and had fewer opportunities in life than their bending counterparts. My parents had hoped that I would show the capabilities that neither of them had, but she was already eight and showed no such promise.

To my mother's suggestion, I nodded enthusiastically, still not fully recognizing that sorrow in my parents expressions. Maybe they were a little sad because they had to go back to work tomorrow, and they couldn't have fun like this again today? That must be it. Kuvira was sad about that too, honestly. She wanted nothing more than to be able to have fun with her parents every single day like how today was.

"We'll be right back, alright? We love you very much." This time, it was my dad who spoke, since my mother had turned around so I wouldn't see the tears beginning to form in her eyes. Again, I just nodded.

My father hugged her tightly and then gestured for me to sit on the nearby bench. After a heartfelt yet goofy salute to him, I skipped over and sat down. My feet didn't quite reach the ground, so I swung them happily while humming a soft tune that my mother would sing to me at night.
I watched my parents walk away until they were no longer visible. Then I waited and waited.
By the time I decided to finally get off the bench, it was dark, and the street was deserted.

"Mom...? Dad...?" I whispered softly, and soon I began shouting for my parents. Though it was as if no one heard me; this was more of a city than I was used to... maybe no one could hear me because of everything else going on? Not that it mattered... I wanted my parents.

My little legs began to run as fast as they could in the direction I had seen my parents disappear hours ago. My mother had told me to wait, but now I was scared, and all I wanted was to run back into my parent's warm embrace.
So I ran, and ran, and ran until I couldn't run any longer.

I collapse on the ground, finally realizing that they weren't coming back. Something must have happened... surely they did not leave her there all alone on purpose? They love me! I was their little girl and they love me, they said so every night.
But they never came back.
They promised they would come back.
*Why...?*

With that realization, I began to cry and I remained slouched on the ground, which began to shake around me. Small pebbles began to float in the air, but I didn't recognize or care about them. Only when a piece of thrown away scrap metal floated in front of my eyes, did my sobs begin to calm, partially giving away to a sense of wonder.
I was an earthbender.
Not only that... I was a *metalbender.*

I hold my hands up to guide the piece of metal towards me. I keep it suspended in the air; it felt almost as if it was a part of me. Much more a part of me than the earth underneath my body, anyway. I stare at it, as if it would give my some answers as to why my parents would just leave me here. If only I had discovered my bending hours earlier.
Perhaps then I wouldn't be alone.

---

"Kuvira?" Christine's voice snaps me back to reality.
"Yeah?" I say and I wipe my eyes. My hand comes away wet with tears.
"Are you okay?"
I sniff and wipe my eyes again. "Yeah I'm fine."
Christine tilts her head to the side and looks at me expectantly. I just shake my head and she turns away.
I look back around and see the children standing in the street. My eyes fill with tears again and I grab Christine's arm and we start to walk towards the train station.

---

We arrive in Zaofu and me and Christine, start to walk towards the Beifong estate. After Vaatu's attack on Chicago, Su moved the rest of the family back here, because she was afraid that something would happen to her and her family and she didn't want to risk anything happening to them. She asked me if I wanted to come live with her back in Zaofu. We walk into the house and to the livingroom. We walk inside and I see Tenzin sitting across from Su. I stop in my tracks. I look from Su to Tenzin and back again. "What's going on here?"

Chapter 3

Su gets up from her chair and walks over to me. "A slight problem has occurred. But don't worry we have it under control."

I frown. "A problem? What kind of problem."

Tenzin get's up and walks over beside Su. "The Earth Kingdom is in chaos again, the nation is broken. There's no one running it."

"What do you mean 'there's no one running it'?"

"Well… after Vaatu's attack all the leaders were killed and now there are riots and looters in the streets and bandits are stealing supplies from the towns."

"Okay. So what do we do?"

Tenzin turns towards Su. "I came here to talk to Su about her possibly helping with the situation in The Earth Kingdom, but she has… declined to help."

I turn towards Su. "Su I think you should step up and help."

"I'm sorry, but i'm not interested in imposing my ideals on a whole nation. I'm afraid I can't help you."

"Su, you of all people should know that Zaofu is a beacon of modern progress and now you can share that with everyone."

"I'm sorry but my answer is no."

Anger bubbles up inside me and I turn toward Christine. I motion my hand towards the door and start to walk. Christine follows suit behind me.

---

We return to Chicago and go to the house. We walk inside and sit down on the couch. "I can't believe that Su won't help," I turn toward Christine. "You would help me restore order to The Earth Kingdom, wouldn't you?"

"Of course." she says.

Baatar walks downstairs. "What's going on?"

"I met with Su and Tenzin. The Earth Kingdom is in chaos and Su won't help. Christine has agreed to help me. What about you Baatar?"

He sighs. "My mother always makes bad decisions, of course I'll help."

"Great," I say. "Now there's one more person that could help."

---

"Of course! I love helping people." Bolin exclaims.

We are sitting at a table in his noodle restaurant, Pabu is sitting on Bolin's shoulder. He chatters in agreement.

"Good," I say. "We'll leave first thing tomorrow morning."

Chapter 4

The next morning Christine stands in front of the mirror, she puts on her Earth Empire uniform, this one is no different from the last, aside from the three chevrons on the right arm. Mainly because Christine's rank is now Sergeant.

I sit at the table wearing my commander uniform. Christine sits down beside me and I'm soon joined by Bolin and Baatar. We eat breakfast and then we make our to the train station. We get on the train and make our way towards all the other cities and towns that were affected by Vaatu's attack. We help town after town. Most people are happy to see us, but others are very timid. Afraid that we might hurt them. Once as soon as they see that we are only there to help, they relax.

After the day is over we head back to the train, and go to our bedrooms. I lie down and Christine lies down next to me. We snuggle up to each other and eventually I fall asleep.

Its morning when I wake. I look around the train has come to a stop. I look around and see Zaofu in the distance. I walk to the engine of the train.

"Hello Great Uniter." The engineer says.

"We don't need to stop at Zaofu."

"Bu—" The engineer protests.

"But nothing. You'll do as I say."

"Yes Great Uniter."

I walk back to the bedroom and look out the window as the train pulls away from Zaofu. Once its out of sight I lay back done on the bed again.

Christine rolls over and gives me a hug. "What's wrong?"

"Nothing."

"Are you sure?"

"Yes I'm fine."

She sighs. "Okay."

We walk out to the meeting room and sit down on the couch. A map of The Earth Empire hangs on the opposite wall, ten percent of the empire has been reunited in less than two weeks. I look out the window, at the cities I have reunited. The Earth Empire banner hangs on buildings, showing that I have brought them back together. I look back at the map, there are so many places that need help. I look back at everyone, Bolin and Christine are talking quietly and Baatar is staring at the floor. I turn and look out the window as we pass more towns. We stop at the state of Yi and the people are very happy to see us, though the governor isn't. "Hello governor, I need to speak with you privately."

I give the governor the contract; which reads: *"The Yi State shall be dissolved under this contract; and under the appointment of the international community, shall come under the protection and the regulations of the Great Interim President of the Earth Nation, Kuvira of the Metal Clan."*

"Well," I say. "Are you going to sign our deal?"

He nods and I pass him a pen. He signs the contract, passes it back to me, I sign it and he exits the train with his head hung low. Later we come back with food and supplies, everyone cheers and The Earth Empire banner is hung on the main building in the town. The governor turns back to me and the cold, non trusting look he gave me earlier is gone, this time he smiles. "Thank you Great Uniter." Maybe reuniting The Earth Empire won't be as hard as I thought.

## Chapter 5

We get back to the train and sit down on the couch. I let out a content sigh and Christine sits down next to me. I close my eyes. I'm just about to drift off when I hear her say. "Wow, what a long day."

I open my eyes and look over at her. "Yeah, but at least the governor signed the contract."

"Yeah," she says. "It wouldn't have been a good outcome if he didn't."

I frown. "What do you mean?"

She laughs. "I mean that if he hadn't signed our deal we would've had to take the town by force and that if anyone stood in our way they would be crushed."

"Um—" The words get stuck in my throat.

"That's what you told me and everyone else."

My heart skips a beat. "Oh, um, y-yeah. That's what would've happened."

She nods. "Well, I'm going to take a nap, we have a long day tomorrow."

She get's up from the couch and walks to the bedroom and closes the door. I look around the train. Bolin and Baatar are still talking with each other. I look over at the map, now twenty percent of the empire has been reunited. I look at the states that aren't united and Zaofu is one of them. I put my head in my hands. *What am I going to do about Zaofu? I can't just attack them for no reason. But Christine is already planning to take over it.*

"Are you okay Kuvira?"

I look up and Baatar is sitting on the couch beside me. "Yeah I'm fine."

"Are you sure?" he asks.

"Yes."

He gives me a hug. "You know its okay not to be happy."

I sigh. "Yeah I know."

He hugs me again. "Well I'll give you some space."

He get's up and him and Bolin walk to another part of the train. I sit there alone.

---

Later that day, I take a walk around the train. All my soldiers are sleeping right now, so I don't want to wake them. I look out the window just as it slows to a stop. We are near a mountain side. I walk to the engine. "Why have we stopped?" I ask the engineer.

"Apologies, there are rocks on the tracks, it's most likely bandits. We're sending troops to handle the situation."

"Call them off, I'll handle the bandits myself." I say.

He nods and calls them back. I climb to the top of train and see bandits on the mountain side. They bend rocks at me and I guide them away from the train. I shoot out my metal strips and cover their eyes with them. Once I've contained them, I chain them to the tracks. I take the the metal stips from their eyes and one stares at me in shock.

"You're Kuvira." she says.

I nod. "You're the bandits that are causing chaos, where I am trying to establish order aren't y—"

"I'm sorry, we didn't know this was your train an—" The bandit interrupts.

I silence the bandit with a metal strip. "Don't talk over me!"

She looks down at the tracks. I smile.

"Now I'll give you two options you can either join me or I can leave you here and hopefully someone saves you before the next train speeds through. But I don't count on it."

"No don't leave us here!" says one bandit.

"We pledge our loyalty to you Great Uniter."

Chapter 6

After I've made a deal with the bandits, I let them go. I walk back onto the train and find Christine sitting with Baatar and Bolin, they are playing a card game. She looks up at me when I walk over to her.

"Hey." she says.

"Hi." I say.

Christine, Bolin and Baatar all flip a card over and Christine starts laughing. She takes Baatar's and Bolin's cards and puts them in her pile. Both Baatar and Bolin shake their heads.

I lean over to her. "I need to talk to you."

She nods. "Alright."

She get's up and follows me to our bedroom. I close the door and we sit on the bed. I hold her hand and she gives me a hug. I hold her close and she hugs me tighter. "Well its about Zaofu." I say.

She looks at me in confusion. "What about Zaofu?"

I bite my lip.

"What about Zaofu?" She asks more forcefully this time.

I sigh and say. "Maybe we should leave Zaofu alone. They can rule themselves, it won't hurt the empire."

She laughs. "You're joking. Tell me this is a joke."

"Well…" I start to say, but she interrupts. "If it isn't, then I'm going to have to send you to a reeducation camp and I don't want have to do that."

My mouth snaps shut.

"Well?" she says, raising an eyebrow at me.

I let out a nervous laugh. "Uh, y-yeah, it was a joke, I was… uh… joking."

She claps me on the back and gives me another hug. "Good," she says. "Was there anything else you wanted to say?"

"No," I say. "Nothing at all."

"Great," she says. "Well I'm going to go find us some dinner, so you can do whatever you want."

I nod.

She get's up and walks to the door, but before she leaves, she says. "If you want to talk to me about anything else just let me know."

I nod again and she walks out and closes the door. I look down at the floor.

*What am I going to do?*

I walk out of the bedroom around dinner time and sit down next to Christine. We eat and talk, and after that we sit back down on the couch I look back over at the map, now fifty percent of the empire is ours, but Zaofu has been left untouched. The closer we get to uniting the empire the more nervous I become.

That night I lie in bed and stare at the ceiling, Christine is snuggled up beside me. I try to sleep, but I'm too nervous to, so I get out of bed and I take my metal armor off and put it in my dresser. I grab my coat. I put my hand on the doorknob and look back at Christine, she's out cold. I turn the doorknob and walk out of the bedroom.

I know what I need to do.

Chapter 7

I make the long trek from the train to where I need to go. It's almost daytime. That means that if I want to get there before Christine wakes up then I'm going to need to get there fast. I break into a sprint, the world around me becomes a blur as I run. I only stop when my heart feels like it is going burst out of my chest. I look up at the horizon, I see a sliver of sunlight. But ahead of me I see it. Zaofu.

I walk towards my old house and open up the door, though when I get inside I'm stopped by a guard. "What are you doing here?" he asks.

"I'm here with news for Su." I say.

I start to walk forwards but he stops me. "I'm sorry but I can't let you see her."

I sigh.

"Now," he says. "I'm going to have to place you under arrest for treason."

I pace back and forth in my cell, my mind and heart is racing. What just happened? I continue pacing back and forth. I hear the door to the prison open and I see her run inside. She runs up to the cell. "Kuvira!" she yells.

"Su!" I yell back.

She reaches into the cell and places her hand on my cheek. I close my eyes and tears leak from my eyelids. I hold onto her hand.

"What happened?" she asks.

"I'm sorry, I couldn't stop her." I say, as more tears run down my face.

"What are you talking about? You couldn't stop who?" Su asks.

Before I have time to speak, we hear a loud bang and the sound of metal creaking, my eyes go wide and I give Su a fearful look. The creaking becomes louder and the cell starts to shake.

Su snaps her gaze back to the prison door. One of the guards is running towards her. "What's going on?"

"The domes…" he pants.

Su furrows her eyebrows. "What about the domes?"

"They…" he pants again. "They're… gone."

Su's eyes go wide. "Gone? What do you mean they're gone?"

"Su," I say. "You need to get out of here. Christine is going to take over Zaofu, you need to keep everyone safe."

"What? No! I can't just leave you here."

"You have to leave me here, if Christine takes over the city, and finds that i'm gone then she'll hunt you down. I need to keep you safe."

Su hesitates for a moment. Then she closes her eyes. "I don't care if she hunts me down, you're my daughter and you're coming with me."

Before I have time to object she opens the cell door and pulls me into hug. When we pull apart we break into a sprint. We run through the prison and out of the house. We skid to a stop and my eyes go wide.

"Where do you think you guys are going?"

## Chapter 8

I stare at Christine wide-eyed. She smirks at me. I back up slowly and she steps towards me. My heart races and my head pounds. "Christine," I say. "How?"

"I followed you here, that's how. It seems that you broke your promise of leaving Zaofu to me to deal with. Do you really think that I would let you protect Zaofu? You of all people should understand it's part of the Earth Empire and you are interfering with my progress of reuniting it. By betraying me you have committed treason to the empire. You know the punishment."

"I…" I start to say.

"I don't want to hear what you have to say." Christine spits.

I hang my head low and look down at the ground. Christine steps towards me and I just stand there unable to move.

I turn towards Su. "You need to get out of here. You need to go somewhere safe. I'll be fine, I promise. I love you."

Su finally nods. "Okay," She hugs me and tears run down my face. "I love you too, Kuvira."

"Go now!"

She nods and starts to run away from Zaofu, I look back at Christine. "You're a traitor to the entire empire!"

She stops a few inches from me. "No Kuvira, you're the traitor. All I want is a United Earth Empire and you're in my way of achieving that goal. Now you get to pay the ultimate price."

I take a deep breath and send out a chunk of earth, it strikes Christine in the chest she let's out a cry of pain and she sends out a blast of fire, I dive out of the way. I shoot out more earth and she deflects it away. Christine enters The Avatar State and I send a giant boulder at her. She strikes me back and I don't dive out of the way fast enough, I get blasted with air. I go flying across the field. I land with a sickening thud. I hear a loud crack and pain shoots across my entire body. I try to move but white hot pain shoots across my ribs and chest.

*That's got to be, broken ribs.* I think.

I try to move but the pain is too much. Christine hovers above me with a giant boulder. I just lay there helpless. Christine launches the boulder toward me and I take a deep breath. I hear a loud crash and the world fades away.

---

Christine let's out a sigh. *It was hers. The Earth Empire was finally hers.*

She turns back to the city of Zaofu. She walks to town square and announces the news. Everyone then kneels before their new leader.

Chapter 9

Christine sits at her desk on the train, she put's a checkmark beside Zaofu on the map. The empire was finally reunited. She let out a sigh. *Its too bad that Kuvira didn't want to be part of it, there was so much that we could've accomplished together. Oh well.* She thought.

There was a knock at the door. "Come in." she says.

The door opened and Christine smiled. "Ah Baatar, please come in, I'm just doing the paperwork for the cities and towns that are under the empire's contract."

Baatar walks in and sits down in a chair across from her. They both stay in silence for a little bit, Baatar just sat there. He felt nervous, if he said one wrong thing, that was the end for him. He looked around for a moment before resting his eyes back on Christine. His heart beat faster and faster. He started to sweat and he wiped it off his face.

"What is it that you need?" Christine asked.

Baatar swallowed hard and finally he spoke. "I… its about Kuvira."

Christine narrowed her eyes. "Oh? What about Kuvira?"

He swallowed hard. "Well…"

---

Su runs over to the boulder that landed on Kuvira, she bends it away and gasps. Kuvira is sprawled on the ground, blood is pouring freely from her nose and mouth. She coughs and Su bends down and picks her up and holds her in her arms. "Hang on Kuvira there's a healer on the way, just hold on please."

Kuvira looks up at Su and coughs. Blood trickles from her mouth and she tries to focus her eyes on her mother. "You came back." Kuvira says, weakly.

"Of course I did," Su says. "I'm your mother now just hang on."

She tries to hang on but her breathing becomes shallow and her vision blurs. Kuvira becomes weak and her eyes close.

---

Baatar let's out a nervous laugh. Christine gives him a long, cold stare. Finally she speaks. "So… you want me to pull *all* my troops from Zaofu? Is that correct?"

"I didn't say that you should pull *all* your troops from Zaofu, its just… that I think you should… rethink about what you're doing. I know that Zaofu means a lot to the empire, but I think that you're being…" Baatar's voice trails off.

"Being what?" Christine asks, raising an eyebrow at him.

"I just think that you're being a bit… unreasonable."

Christine get's up from her desk and starts to pace back and forth. "You think that I'm being unreasonable? What makes you think that?"

Baatar bites his lip. "Well you challenged Kuvira to a duel and you well… you took her out."

Christine stops pacing and shrugs. "Well she turned her back on me and she committed treason to the empire, what else was I supposed to do?"

"Well…" Baatar starts to say, but Christine interrupts him. "You do realize that by defending Kuvira's actions that you too, are committing treason towards the empire?"

Baatar remains quiet.

"You do realize the penalty for treason is death right?"

"Uh… yes, yes I do." Baatar stammers.

"Good," Christine says. "Now was there anything else that you wanted to tell me?"

"No."

"Good, now it's time for you to go."

"Yes. Thank you commander."

Chapter 10

My eyes flicker open. I'm so sore. Wait why was I sore? Where was I? I blink a few times and then I hear a voice. "Oh thank goodness you're awake."

Confused, I look to my right and see Su sitting near me. I clutch my ribs and I try to sit up, searing pain shoots across my chest, I wince and lie back down. My next breath wheezes on the way out. I look over at her.

"Su? What... what are you doing here?"

Su lays me back down and whispers. "Its okay, you're safe now."

I furrow my eyebrows. "What do you mean 'you're safe now'?"

Su purses her lips and a moment later she speaks again. "Well after you came to warn us about Christine's attack on Zaofu, you tried to stop her. But..." Her voice trails off.

"But what?"

"But Christine attacked you and you nearly died."

Fear pulses through me and my heat races. Christine nearly killed me? No that can't be right, can it? She cares about me doesn't she? I stare at Su wide-eyed.

"So..." I finally say. "How bad are my injuries?"

"Pretty bad, you had a dislocated shoulder blade, a broken nose, your jaw was fractured and several of your ribs were broken."

My heart skips a beat. I didn't know that Christine was capable of doing so much damage. I shake my head and look bad over at Su. "Are we home?" I ask.

Su shakes her head. "No..."

"Then where are we?"

Su takes a deep breath. "In a reeducation camp."

---

Christine clasps her hands behind her back as she paces back and forth in front of her soldiers.

"So..." Christine says. "What do you think? Do you think that we could accomplish this goal?!"

All the soldiers cheer.

"Are you guys with me?!" Christine yells.

"Yes!" Everyone yells.

Everyone starts to cheer and Christine cheers with them. Everyone's loyalty makes her feel like nothing could stop her.

"No."

Christine stops and everyone turns towards the back of the room. "No? Who said that?"

Baatar stood there with a scowl on his face. "That would be me."

Christine let's out a chuckle. "Why not?"

"Well," Baatar scoffs. "You just threw our family into a reeducation camp, what make you think that I would want to help you after that."

Christine slowly steps towards him. "Our family betrayed the empire and refused to join. They knew the punishment and so that's what they received," She takes a deep breath. "Now do you wish to be with me? Or do you wish to join them?"

"Why would I ever want to work for you, after everything you've done. You're a *monster!*"

"Very well," Christine says and she snaps her fingers. "Grab him!"

Baatar eyes go wide and the soldiers start towards him. One grabs his arms and starts to drag him away, he struggles out of the soldiers grip, but its no use. But then he remembered something. He clenches his fingers and the soldiers movement stop dead. Christine is unable to move as well. Her body bends and twitches. She starts to scream. Just as Baatar was about to finish Christine off, something hard connects with his temple.

His vision goes black.

Chapter 11

Baatar lets out a groan of pain as consciousness returns to him, he opens his eyes and he looked around but his vision is blurred. He blinks a few times and his vision starts clear. Then he realized that he was lying on the floor in a cell, he jumps to his feet and runs towards his cell door. When he is millimeters away from the door though something jerks him back. His shoulders start to ache, he tries to move his hands and finds that they are covered in metal shackles. He tries to freeze them off, but it doesn't work. Moments later though he hears a voice. "Baatar? Is that you?"

He turns towards the voice and when he sees them, he let's out a gasp. "Mom! Kuvira!"

"Baatar!" Me and Su yell.

---

"So that state is ours and that one still hasn't joined us and that one…" Christine looks over her contracts for the states that are part and aren't part of The Earth Empire, her thoughts are interrupted when she hears a knock at the door. "Come in." she says.

The door to her office opened and one of her soldiers walks in. "Hello commander." he says.

"Ah, Bolin, please come in." she says.

Christine motioned for Bolin to sit down and he did what he was told. He sat down in front of her and she looked at him expectantly. They both remained quiet for quite some time, after a few moments Christine finally spoke. "So Bolin… I need your help with something."

"Okay," he says nervously. "What is it?"

---

I grab onto the platinum bars that form a cage to hold me in. I take a deep breath and clench my hands together on the bars. But nothing happens. *No… no… no… I need to get everyone out of here.* I try again and still nothing happens. On my third attempt, I stand in a metalbending stance, I take a deep breath and push my hands forward. My cell door opens. "Haha. I did it, I opened the cell door."

"Oh sorry, I don't mean to burst you bubble but you didn't open the door, I did." a voice says.

My eyes go wide as I realize who is in front of me. "What?! No! Christine!"

Christine yanks me forward by the collar of my shirt. "Did you really think that you could bend platinum? You know very well that I'm the only one who can bend it."

I struggle out of Christine's grip, but she doesn't let go. Her hand closes around my throat and she squeezes, I gasp for air. Christine slams me against the back wall, the impact broke more of my ribs. My vision starts to go black and I thrust my fist upwards it hits Christine square in the jaw and she yanks me to the side, I slam into the wall again.

*Snap!*

The impact splintered three more of my ribs. I scream louder that I ever thought possible. I punch Christine hard in jaw again and she let's me go and she stumbles backwards, but doesn't fall.

"Christine," I whisper. "Stop… please."

She starts her way towards me again and slams me into the wall again. I fall. My head hits the hard platinum floor.

Then there is nothing.

Chapter 12

Baatar takes a deep breath and the shackles around his hands start to freeze, he takes another deep breath and… *pop!* Baatar's shackles come off, next he freezes the platinum door and kicks it down. He runs over to Christine and before she knows what hit her, he knocks her out and freezes her to the wall. He then runs over to Kuvira's cell and blasts down the door. There Kuvira lies, motionless on the cell floor. Baatar kneels down beside her and ever so gently he lifts her head.

"You're okay… you'll be fine… everything will be alright…"

---

I breathe in deeply, pain shoots through every part of my body and everything hurt much more than before. I open my eyes and I hear a gasp. "Kuvira? You're alright!"

My vision clears and that's when I see him. "Baatar! You're… you're alright!"

"Meh. More or less," he says. "What's more important is that you're alright."

I cough. "Well I feel horrible."

Baatar chuckles. "Well that does tend to happen when you're not wearing armor."

I cough again. "What do you…" I look down at my shirt. "Oh my god! Wh-where… is my armor!?"

Baatar just shakes his head. "I don't know."

I look over my shoulder. "Su!"

"Kuvira!" she hollers.

"Su look out!" I call out.

But Su doesn't get out of the way in time and Christine knocks her to the ground, she then knocks Baatar to the floor. I jump to my feet and start to run at her. Christine pulls out her platinum sword and points it towards Su and Baatar. "You come any closer and it'll be the end for both of them!"

I skid to a stop.

Christine let's out an evil, mocking laugh. "Now what are you going to do?

---

"Christine don't hurt them!" I yell.

She raises her eyebrows at me."Don't hurt your family? Why are earth would I do that?"

My heart leaps into my throat. "Then let them go."

"No. They're all traitors. You should leave."

Tears start to fill my eyes and I say. "Can you let me say goodbye to Baatar and Su first?"

"Alright, fine."

She opens Baatar's and Su's cells and they run up to me and give me a hug. They both start to cry and tears leak from my eyes. I let them go. I give Su another hug, I lean over and whisper into her ear. "I will escape I promise."

I pull away and Su's and Baatar's eyes go wide as I push them out of the cell.

Christine gives me a shocked look. "You traded your life for theirs?"

"Their *our* family, it's what you do."

Christine's demeanor doesn't change. "Their both fools."

She starts to drag Baatar and Su away and my heart shatters.

"Kuvira!" They both yell.

"I'll be fine!" I yell back.

The prison becomes quiet.

Chapter 13

I try to move around the cell, but my ribs burn, so I slow my movements to a minimum. My cell doesn't have windows, so its hard to tell what's going on outside. I sit down on the cell floor, trying to think when everything had gone wrong. When I think about it though, I instantly have my answer. It was when Christine had stolen away her trust and gone behind her back to take over Zaofu. That was it. *I thought I could trust her!* I put my head into my hands.

Moments later I hear my cell door opens and I hear. "Kuvira its time go."

I lift my head, Christine stands in the doorway, scowling. "What are you doing here?" I ask. Christine's expression doesn't change and she walks towards me slowly. She stops inches from me and yanks me to my feet. My ribs burn and I let out a cry of pain. I try to push her away, but she shoves me against the wall. I let out a grunt from the impact. My ribs burn even more and I hear a loud *crack!* I let out a loud gasp, because I can't make a sound any louder than that. I fall, but I catch myself before I hit the ground. I roll onto my back and cough. I blink and Christine stands over me. I jump to my feet and kick her feet from under her. She falls but doesn't hit the ground. She get's to her feet again and runs at me. I punch her hard in side, near the stitches. Her side starts to bleed and she let's out scream and I duck as she swings at me again. I grab onto her wrist and push her back again. She shoots out a metal strip. I try to redirect it, but it's made of platinum. I jump out of the way at the last minute. I grab Christine's arm and yank her to the side. She loses her balance and falls. I run and jump out of the cell door, just before it closes. It slams shut. Christine scowls at me. I run out of the prison. I need to find the others.

---

"We have to get out of here." Baatar says, as he tries to break out of the cell. Su is in the cell next to him, trying to bend the metal.

"Its no use." Su says. "Its made of platinum."

"Well we have to keep trying." Baatar says.

---

I run through the camp, I need to find everyone. I run past one section of the cells and skid to a stop. I turn and run up to the cells and that's when I see them. "Su! Baatar!"

They turn towards me. "Kuvira!"

"Hold on!" I stop in front of their cells. "Stand back!"

Both of them step back and I take a deep breath. Lava starts to form and it starts to melt through the platinum. But just as I create more lava and something wraps around my mouth, I try to bend it off, but it's made of platinum. *Platinum!* I hear a evil laugh. I turn around and that's when I see her, I let out a gasp. *"Christine?!"*

"Ah, ah, ah," she says. "You wouldn't want your family hurt now would you?"

"What do you mean?" I say.

Christine is about to speak when that's when I hear the screams. *"Kuvira! Help!"*

---

I whip around at the sound. The lava is burning through the platinum and both Su and Baatar are screaming. The lava get's closer and closer to them. I run towards the cell, but something is holding me back. "No! Let me go!"

Christine snickers. "No. You made your mistake, you need to witness the consequences." I thrust my elbow back and it hits Christine in the nose, she flies back and hits the wall, she cries out in pain and let's me go. I take a deep breath and clench my hands into fists, the lava forms into solid rock. I let out a sigh and walk over to the cells, both Su and Baatar Jr. crawl out of the cells and give me a hug. "I'm sorry." I say.

Baatar and Su look at me. "Hey. Its alright you saved us."

We start to walk away and that's when I hear the voice. "Kuvira?"

Chapter 14

I whip around at the sound of my name and let out a gasp. There I see Christine slumped against the wall, her hand pressing against the back of her head. She looks dazed. I run over to her. I pull her hand away from her head and it comes away sticky with blood. She looks from the blood back to me. The color in her cheeks starts to drain. "Kuvira!" she rasps out.

I squeeze her hand. "Hold on! You need to hold on!"

"Kuvira, what did I do? Baatar was right, I am a monster. Just leave me." Christine rasps out again.

Tears form in my eyes. "Don't talk like that, you'll be alright. Just hold on!" Christine coughs, her breathing becomes shallow and her heart is beating slower and slower by the second.

"Baatar!" I yell. "Get over here!" Baatar rushes over and kneels down beside me. He looks at me expectantly. "We need to bring her back." I say, urgently.

*"What!?"* he exclaims. "But why? She tried to kill you and she threw you, me and Su in prison. Why on earth would I bring her back?"

"Because… I love her that's why. So unless if you want me to spend the rest of your days feeling guilty about not bringing my only love back, then I suggest you do as I say."

"Alright." he says.

He takes a deep breath and motions his hands over Christine's body. The force of the bloodbending causes all of Christine's bones to realign and the wound in her side is healed and is no longer bleeding. Soon after I start to feel her heart beating again. Moments later she starts to gasp for air and she opens her eyes. She looks at me and tears start to form in her eyes. I pick her up and she wraps her hand around the back of my neck and pulls me in for a kiss. We only pull away when we need to breathe.

"I love you." she whispers.

"I love you too." I whisper back.

We kiss again and Su and Baatar both clear their throats. We turn to look at them. "What?"

"Well," Su says. "Maybe we should do this in a place a little more private. You know like at your guys house or at a restaurant, you know anywhere then here."

I look back at Christine and she blushes. "Yeah, I think that would be a good idea."

---

We make our back to Chicago and Christine walks up to city hall. "People of Chicago," she says. "I'm glad to announce that the states are allowed to run themselves and that there will be no more interference with any of the people or their respective leaders. I have learnt that people who seek power often misuse it for there own selfish needs. So that's why I'm handing it back to the people that it's trust upon. The Earth Empire is no more. You are now free to choose your own paths and your own destiny." The crowd cheers and Christine takes a bow. Then she turns back to me and gives me another kiss. The crowd cheers ever louder.

When we break apart, I smile at Christine. "Let's go home."

"Yes," she says. "Let's go home."

Chapter 15

We walk towards the car and Christine gets into the driver's side. I sit in the back seat and she starts to drive, I look out the window. The city passes by in a blur. I close my eyes and breathe in deeply. My mind starts to relax. I listen to the roar of the engine, the chirp of birds and the sound of the train on the tracks. The car comes to a halt and I open my eyes. Christine looks back at me. "Where are we?" I ask.

"At the train station." she says.

"Why are we at the train station?" I ask. "Aren't we going home?"

"Yes, we are going home, but first I want to show you something."

"Really?" I say. "What do you want to show me?"

"Shhh," she says. "It's a surprise."

I give her a concerned look, but she just takes my hand and helps me out of the car. We walk up to the platform and get onto the train and sit down. The train starts to move and I look at Christine she smiles at me. I'm about to say something when her phone rings. She smiles at me again and she get's up and answers her phone.

"I'll be right back."

I nod and she leaves. I look back out the window, the city of Chicago passes by in a blur.

Moments later Christine returns and sits down again. She let's out a sigh. "What?" I ask.

She looks at me. "I can't tell you."

"Why? Is it part of the surprise?"

She nods.

"Okay." I say.

---

I look out the window again and the train starts to slow down. This time we are near Zaofu, the train stops and we get off. We drive towards Su's house. When we get there Christine knocks on the door and it opens. There Su stands smiling at us. "Come in." she says.

We go inside and Su leads us to the living room.

"What's going on?" I ask.

"You'll see." Christine says.

We stop at the doors and I look back at Su and Christine. "Are you guys coming?"

"No, this is something you need to face on your own." Christine says. "We'll be right here when you're done."

I nod and breathe in deeply, I shake out my hands and slowly I open up the doors to the living room.

---

I step inside and close the door behind me. I turn around and two figures stand in the livingroom. One is a middle-aged man and the other a middle-aged women. I look at the man and notice something that he has the same hair color as me and that the women has the exact same eyebrows as me.

The woman steps forward. "Kuvira? Is that you?"

I furrow my eyebrows. "How do you know my name?"

"Well, you wouldn't remember, but the last time we were together, you were eight and I told you to—"

"'Wait here.'" I finish the sentence and the realization hits me.

"What?" The woman says.

"Oh my god, the last thing you told me was to 'Wait here,'" I let out a shaking breath. "This can't be true. Mom? Is that you?"

My mom runs over to me and gives me a hug and tears leak out of my eyelids. "Kuvira. I missed you so much. I'm sorry that I left you. I should've never left you."

My mother let's me go and my father walks over and gives me a hug. "Hello sweetie." he says.

I give my father a really tight hug. "I love you so much."

Chapter 16

I let my father go and wipe away tears, I give my mother another hug. Moments later the door to the living room opens and Su and Christine walk in. Christine walks up to me and gives me a small kiss. I hear my parents gasp behind me and I blush. Christine turns towards my parents. "Forgive me, I forgot to introduce myself. My name is Christine, I am Kuvira's friend and well um… crush for that matter."

My face turns red with embarrassment and I turn towards her. "Well… you didn't have to show yourself up just yet."

Christine laughs. "You certainly know how to charm your girlfriend."

She gives me a hug and my parents start to laugh. I can feel my face get redder and redder by the minute. I clear my throat and everyone becomes quiet. I pull away from Christine and lean over to her ear. "You know, you didn't have to introduce yourself like that." I whisper.

"I know, but I love making your face turn red."

I give her a playful shove back and she stumbles backwards, she starts to laugh and she runs at me and tackles me to the ground. My ribs burn. I let out a groan of pain. "Well," Christine says. "It looks like someone has relaxed a bit."

"Christine," I say. "My ribs."

"Oh right."

Christine get's off and helps me up. Moments later we stand again and I turn back to my parents again. We stand in silence for a few minutes. Then I turn towards my parents. "I want to show you something."

"Okay, What is it?" They ask.

I smile. "You'll see."

---

I let out a grunt as I dive out of Christine's line of fire. The metal cable just missing me. I shoot out some metal strips and Christine guides them away from her body. She then shoots out several chunks of earth and I melt them into lava. Christine sends out a blast of air, the lava turns solid. Next she sends out more metal strips. I try to bend them away only to find that they are made of platinum. One strikes me and I let out groan.

"Come on Christine," I say and I wince. "A platinum strip?"

"Sorry."

We both stop our attacks. Christine walks over to me and starts to heal the the wound on my arm from where the platinum struck me. The wound disappears moments later. We stand back up and turn towards my parents they stare at me wide-eyed. My mother let's out laugh. "Oh my god! You can bend!"

I let out a chuckle. "Yeah."

My mother runs up to me and gives me a hug. "When did you figure that out?"

I sigh. "When I was eight, on the same day you guys left me."

"Well at least you figured it out." My father says.

"Yeah."

My mother turns towards Christine and nods. "Kuvira you forgot to mention that Christine is the Avatar."

"Hmm?" I say. "Oh yeah, she is."

"That's amazing!" My mother eclaims.

"Well…," Christine says. "I can't take all the credit. Kuvira did teach me what I needed to learn."

"Kuvira." my mother says. "You're an amazing daughter."

"You guys are amazing parents." I say.

"Well," Christine says. "Do you want to head back to the house?"

"Sure." I say.

We walk back to the house together.

Chapter 17

We all sit down on the couch. I sit with my mother and father on my left and Christine on my right. My mother and father are talking quietly with each other and Christine is talking quietly with Su and Baatar Sr. Christine nods and get's up. They walk out of the living room. I snuggle up to my parents. Moments later Christine return's, she walks over to my parents. "I'm sorry to interrupt, but we have some guests coming over for dinner tonight."

"Oh that's wonderful!" My mother says.

"When are they coming over?" My father asks.

"In about an hour." Christine says.

---

We sit down at the table and Christine puts the food down on the table. Just as Christine is setting the rest of the food down, the doorbell rings. Christine walks over to the door and answers it. "Hello, Korra how are you?"

"I'm doing okay, as usual." Korra replies.

"That's good." Christine says.

Korra walks into the house and over to the table, where she greets my parents and after everyone has been introduced, we have dinner.

---

After dinner Christine has another talk with Su and the rest of the family. When Christine comes back this time she motions for me and my parents to follow her. We walk to Su's office and Christine closes the door. "What's going on?" I finally ask.

"Well." Christine says. "We were thinking that it would be best if you went home with your parents. We finally found them, so I think that it would be best."

"What? But what about you Christine?" I ask.

"I need to go home." she says. "I've spent the last decade avoiding it and i've only gone back there once."

"But—" I start to say.

"Kuvira," Christine says. "You're not the eight year old girl Su found on the street anymore. You're grown up. You need to do what's best. You need to go home."

"Alright." I say.

Christine gives me a hug. "You can always come visit me you know. Its not like your cut off from me entirely."

"Right." I say.

Chapter 18

Later that day I walk around the house and pack my things, when I'm done I put my stuff by the door. Christine puts her stuff by the door soon after. We go outside and put our stuff into the car. Then we wave goodbye to everyone. Christine starts the engine and drives towards the train station. When we get there we get onto the train. I look out the window and watch as the train passes by all the cities and towns. The train comes to a stop and I look out the window. We stopped at the state of Yi. We get off the train and I turn towards my mother and Christine. "Was I born here?" I ask.

"Yes," my mother says. "That's why the governor trusted you so much when you first set out to reunite The Earth Kingdom and created The Earth Empire."

"Wow," I say. "I always thought he hated me."

"No, of course not. I mean he was upset that you wanted power and that you changed a lot, but he knew that one day you would realize your mistakes and set out on a better path. Which is what you've done."

Moments later the governor comes running out of his office. "You guys made it. I wondered when you would show up."

"Don't worry Governor we're alright." My father says.

"Yes I can see that." he says.

"Well you guys should get settled," Christine says. "I'll be back later to say my goodbyes to everyone."

I give Christine a quick kiss before she leaves and then she is gone.

Later I sit down and have lunch with my parents and afterwards we watch TV. I look over at the clock. It's five in the afternoon. That means that Christine will be back soon to say goodbye. I give my mom and dad a hug and we just sit there waiting for Christine's return.

The doorbell rings and I get up to open the door. Christine stands in the doorway. "Hey." she says.

"Hi." I say.

"I brought you something." she says and she hands me some flowers.

"Thank you." I say.

"No problem."

I put the flowers on the counter and Christine walks over beside me.

I turn towards her. "So I guess that means your off then?"

"I'm afraid so." she says.

"Why do you have to leave?" I ask.

"You know why." Christine says.

"I know."

"You know, you can always text and call me. I mean you some how got my number." Christine says.

I chuckle. "Yeah."

I give her a hug and she gives me a tighter one and when she pulls away she hands me something, a locket. "What is it?" I ask.

"Open it." she says.

I open the locket. Mine, Su's and Christine's photo's are inside.

"Now you'll always have a way to remember what I look like." she says.

"I like it." I say and I give her another hug.

When we break apart, she walks toward the door. "I'll see you later Kuvira."

"Goodbye, Christine." I say.

Just like that she is gone.

Epilogue
Christine
I let out a pleasent sigh as I walk through security in the airport. I show the security guard my badge and he let's me through. I put my luggage on the plane and then sit down. I look out the plane window. The plane starts to move and soon we are in the air. I pull out my phone. Kuvira sent me a million text's.

*Dear Christine,*
*Thank you for all you have done for me, I know that we have had a long and tough road. But one thing I have always known is that you care very deeply for me and you would never do anything to hurt me. So I have a great day and text me when you get home.*
*Love,*
*Kuvira*

I smile and turn off my phone. I look out the window and see that the airport is coming into view and when I get there. I get my luggage and get my car. I sit inside my car for a moment while I send Kuvira a text:

*Dear Kuvira,*
*I'm glad that you aren't mad at me for anything and I'm glad that you're doing well. I just thought that I would let you know that I landed safely and that I'm on my way home. Have a wonderful time with your family and if you ever need to, you can call me.*
*Love,*
*Christine*

I drive to my house and when I get there my mom is waiting for me at the door. I walk up to her and give her a hug. "I missed you."
She hugs me back tighter. "I missed you too."
"Well," I say. "Should we go inside?"
"Gladly."
We walk inside and sit down on the couch. "Where can I start?"
My mother smiles. "Tell me everything."
I smile back. "With pleasure."

(Book 9)

Chapter 1

*Four years later…*

I walk out of the house with my luggage, which includes my uniform. I get into my car and my mom runs outside, she leans inside the car and hugs me. "Have a safe trip!"

"I will!" I say.

I wave her goodbye and start to drive, I get to the airport and show the security guard my badge he nods and let's me through. I get onto the plane and look out the window. Moments later I close my eyes and drift off to sleep.

When I get to Chicago, I get my stuff and hop onto the train. I get off at the state of Yi and walk towards Kuvira's house. When I get there I knock on the door. Moments later the door opens and Kuvira pulls me in for a kiss. When we break apart, we walk into the house.

"Where are your parents?" I ask.

"At work." Kuvira says.

"So they're working again?"

"Yes."

"That's wonderful!"

Kuvira nods and pulls me in for another kiss. When we pull away I blush.

"What?" she asks.

"I love you." I say.

"I love you too."

We sit down at the dinner table and have dinner. Afterward, we spar with each other. I fire out my metal cable and Kuvira jumps out of way. She sends out a metal meteor, I deflect her attack. I fire out a platinum strip and she stops it with her lavabending. The lava starts it way towards me and I blast the lava with air. It becomes solid. I send out a chunk of earth and Kuvira sends it back at me. We continue to fire attacks at each other and after two hours of sparring we stop. We walk back to the house and when we get there, we sit down on the couch.

"Why are you here?" Kuvira asks.

"Well I thought that I would come back for a little bit." I say.

"I think that it's a great idea." Kuvira says with another kiss.

I blush and Kuvira starts to laugh. My face turns red and she laughs harder. I just shake my head.

"So," I finally say. "What do we have planned today?"

"I don't know, what do you want to do?" Kuvira asks.

"I don't know. Have you talked to Baatar lately?"

"Not really." she says.

"Well maybe we should go visit him."

"Yeah that would great."

We get onto the train and make our way to Chicago. On our way there Kuvira tells me that Su and the family moved back to Chicago.

"Do you know why?" I ask.

"Nope. They just decided to move here."

"Okay."

Chapter 2

We get our car and Kuvira starts to drive. We pass Erudite Headquarters and I shutter. All the memories of what happened there are still fresh in my mind. I shake my head and breathe in deeply. I look out the window again. We drive down Michigan Ave and my phone rings. It pull it out and answer it. "Hello?"

*"Hi."*

"Who is this?" I ask.

*"It's Su."*

"Oh! Hello Su!"

*"I need to talk to you."* she says, sounding urgent.

"Okay."

"You need to stay away from the house."

But before I can ask why, I lose her.

I hang up my phone and look back at Kuvira. She raises her eyebrows at me and I shrug. Kuvira looks back at the road.

---

We get to the house and I knock on the door. Moments later it opens and Su appears in the doorway. "What are you doing here?" she asks.

"Coming to visit Baatar," Kuvira says. "Why do you ask?"

"I don't know." she sighs.

"Why did you say that I needed to stay away from the house?" I ask.

"Because... Well... I don't know," she says. "I guess its a habit, since I used to say it to you all the time."

"Okay."

We walk inside and the entire family is there. When they see us they run up us and they all hug us.

"We missed you!" Opal says.

"We missed you too." Both me and Kuvira say.

---

We all sit on the couch and talk. Kuvira gives me a kiss and I return it. We start to watch the news. There are reports that there has been some suspicious activity in Chicago area and that the police force are investigating the incident. I turn toward Kuvira and notice that she is staring blankly at the screen.

"Kuvira?" I say.

"Huh?" she says.

"Are you okay?"

"Yeah I'm fine."

---

Baatar coughed and dove out of the way. A siren blared in his ears. The air became cloudy and he started another round of coughing. His lungs gasped for air and he started to feel lightheaded. His vision went blurry. "Shut it off!" he croaked. "Shut it off now!"

"I can't!" someone yelled. "The emergency lever is broken!"

Baatar stumbled forwards and clenched his fists, the cloudy air formed into icicles and the blare of the siren stopped. He continued to cough and he gasped for air. He looked down at the ground and he saw vials of liquid. He picked one up and put it in his pocket. He opened the window to air out the room. Soon the air cleared and Baatar could finally breathe.

Chapter 3

Kuvira and I sit together with Su and the rest of the family. We talk with one another, next we watch the news and there are more reports about the mysterious activity going on in downtown Chicago. The police force are having a hard time with investigating the problem in the downtown area. I look over at Su. She looks puzzled. Next I look over at Opal, she's scratching her head in confusion and lastly I look over at Baatar Sr. he's looking over at Su, his eyebrows lifted in concern. I take a deep breath and look back at the TV. Police have released a statement advising that everyone stay away from the downtown area. I take another deep breath.

Finally after many long minutes I finally speak. "What do you think is going on?"

Kuvira just shakes her head. "I don't know. But whatever it is, hopefully it ends soon."

I nod and get up from the couch.

"Where are you going?" Kuvira asks.

"I'm going for a walk." I say without looking at her.

I walk to the door and open it. I go walk out but there's someone blocking my path.

"Lin?" I say.

"Can I come in?" she asks.

"Sure." I say and I step off to the side to let her pass.

We walk to the living room and sit down. Lin is quiet for a little bit.

Finally she starts to speak. "I have some important information to tell you guys."

"What is it?" Su asks.

Lin takes a deep breath. "My police force is having a hard time with investigating the activity going on in downtown Chicago. Some of my men are coming back to the station with damage to their lungs and others are mysteriously dropping dead."

"What?!" Su exclaims.

Lin nods. "There also have been reports that some of the civilians in Chicago are unable to remember anything."

"We need to do something." I say.

Lin nods. "We do. That's why I came here. I need your help with finding the suspects before something bad happens."

"I'm in." I say.

"Me too." Kuvira says.

"So am I." Su says.

---

We stand beside Lin at the police station. We look at the footage of Chicago, but we can't see anything. I bite my lip. "I know this isn't the right place to say this right now. But has anyone heard anything from Baatar Jr. lately?"

Everyone turns toward me and I smile. Lin raises her eyebrows at me and Kuvira gives me a look. Su puts her hand on her chin. "Now that I think of it I haven't seen him in a while."

"Where is he?" Kuvira asks.

"I don't know," Lin says. "Let me try to call him."

She pulls out her phone and dials his number. I sit down at one of the computers and start to look through surveillance footage.

Chapter 4

I scroll through footage after footage. But still no sign of Baatar. *Come on Baatar, where are you?* I continue looking and after a few minutes I put my head down on the desk. Someone sits down next to me and gives me a hug. I lift my head and see Kuvira, I try to smile but it doesn't work.

"What's wrong?" Kuvira asks.

"Well... its just that we can't find Baatar and I'm worried for him."

"I know," she says. "So am I."

"What if something happened to him?"

"We'll find him don't worry."

"I hope so."

---

"Come on," Baatar says as he tries to fix machine that he was using earlier. "This has to work it just has to."

He turned towards one of his workers. "How's it going on your end?"

"Not so good," The worker says. "The generator is broken and some of the panels are damaged from the previous fires in this building."

"Well keep working," Baatar says. "We need to get this fixed before our time runs out."

---

I continue to look through the footage, but still nothing. I sigh. "Come on Baatar where are you?" I mumble. I put my head in my hands again and close my eyes. But something pokes in the back of my mind and I bolt right up. I scroll through the footage and find that the cameras in Erudite headquarters are not working. "Um... guys you might want to come take a look at this."

"What is it?" Lin asks.

"Aren't the cameras in Erudite headquarters usually on?"

"There supposed to be. Why?"

"Because they aren't on now. Someone must have manually shut them off."

"Well who would to that?" Kuvira asks.

"I don't know." I say.

---

Baatar wiped the sweat off his eyebrows as he tightened the screws and bolts on the generator and then he took a step back. "All right let's fire it up again!"

His worker nodded and Baatar stepped back. The worker pressed a button and the air became cloudy. Moments later Baatar nodded at the worker again and he hit the button again and the air began to clear. When the air was finally clear, Baatar walked over to the young worker and clapped him on the back.

"Great job," Baatar says. "Now we just need the right timing and the right person."

"Who's that?" his worker asked.

Baatar glanced at him. "I can't say now. But you will know soon enough."

"Okay."

Baatar put his hand on his chin. "Now here's what we need to do..."

Chapter 5

I sit back in my chair and try to think about where Baatar might be, but nothing comes to mind. I stare at the screen, its completely black. I look around the desk and around the computer and I notice that some of the cords have been pulled. I pick them up and see that the wires have been cut. I look over at Kuvira and Su. "Hey, I got something!"

They both come running over to me. "What is it?"

"You see these wires. They've been cut."

"So that's why we're not getting any footage in that area." Kuvira says.

"So who cut the power?" Su asks.

"I... don't... kn-... wait a minute! I just figured out where this camera is and where Baatar might be."

"Where!?" They both exclaim.

I turn towards them. "Erudite headquarters."

"What!" Su exclaims. "Why would he be there?"

"I don't know, but whatever the reason it can't be good."

"Well what should we do?" she asks.

"You need to get everyone out here. If he's in Erudite headquarters, then... well he has access to some bad stuff." I say.

"Like what?" They ask.

"I'm not sure... as far as I know all the serum was used up four years ago. So we can rule that one out."

"So what do we do?" Kuvira asks.

"You guys need evacuate Chicago." I say.

Kuvira nods. "Okay, let's go."

We go door to door and tell everyone to evacuate quickly and then we walk to the edge of the city but when we get to the edge of the city. I look over at Kuvira and take a deep breath. "I'll stop him." I say.

"What?" Kuvira says.

"I'm going to stop Baatar once and for all." I say and I start to leave. But Kuvira grabs my arm.

"I can't let you leave!" she exclaims. "I've lost you too many times and it's not going to happen again."

"You need to evacuate Chicago, you don't have a choice."

I start to walk out but she grabs my arm and holds me back I turn towards her. "Please..." she says, with tears forming in her eyes. "You can't leave me again."

"I'm not going to leave you," I say, but her grip doesn't loosen. "I promise."

"Are you sure?"

I don't say anything I just look into her eyes and put my hand on her cheek. With tears in my eyes I lean in close and give her a kiss. With tears in my eyes, I pull away and look into her eyes.

"Now I'm never going to let you go." she says.

"You don't have a choice. I need to stop Baatar you need to trust me." I say.

She sighs. "Okay."

"I'll see you soon." I say.

Kuvira nods and I turn towards the city and start my way toward Erudite headquarters.

Chapter 6

As I walk into the city. I notice that the city has been completely evacuated. *Good.* I think.

I continue walking. When I get close I have a hard time breathing, so I breath in shallow breaths. Soon I'm standing in front of Erudite headquarters and I don't hesitate. I just push the doors open and walk inside.

---

As soon as I am inside, I look around to make sure that there are no guards around. But all that matters is stopping Baatar. I walk through the building and toward the lab. I take a deep breath and walk inside. When I get inside though the door closes behind me and locks. I let out a sigh and drop into a bending stance. My heart is pounding. "Nice try, I know you're in here. Now come out."

"Why would I do that?" A voice says. "Then you'll be afraid."

I laugh. "No I won't."

The voice scoffs and the figure walks forward. I let out a shaky breath. "Baatar?"

"Hello Christine." he says.

"What are you doing Baatar?" I ask.

He scoffs. "Well as you probably remember that you were in this same situation sixteen years ago and now it seems that you are in it again."

I furrow my eyebrows. "What are you talking about?"

Baatar walks over to the centre of the room and pulls something out. He walks over to me. "Remember these?" he says. He holds up a vial of serum and my heart skips a beat.

"Impossible," I say. "How did get a hold of death serum? That stuff was all used up last year when me and Korra defeated Zaheer and his team."

"No it wasn't," Baatar says. "You only used two vials of death serum on them. The stuff that I released on Chicago was actually the paralytic serum dyed purple and the red stuff was actually the memory serum, because at that time I never wanted to kill you."

*"What?!"* I say, my voice filled with shock.

Baatar smirks. "But the stuff that I'm holding now *is* death serum and your time is up."

I start to back away slowly, but I back into someone. I turn around. *"Bolin?!"*

Bolin grabs my arms to keep me in place. "Christine, I'm sorry I have to do this."

I struggle out of his grip, but something hard connects with my temple and I black out.

---

I start to breathe heavily and my eyes flicker open. I jump to my feet and shoot out a metal strip at Baatar and he screams. I run forward and try tackle him to the ground, but before I get anywhere, my body comes to an abrupt halt and I start to bend and twitch. I let out a groan. I struggle out of his grip but it's no use.

Baatar looks over at Bolin. "Do it now!"

Bolin nods and runs over to the serum machine and presses a button. Death serum fills the air and I gasp, my lungs are straining for air. I struggle again and this time Baatar loosens his grip on me completely and I smash into the ground. Through my semi-blurry vision, I look back towards Baatar and Bolin and find that they aren't in the room and that the window is open. They must have escaped through it. I drag myself to the door and with trembling hands I open the door and crawl my way into the hallway. Once I can breathe in clean air, I get to my feet and run through the hallway and out of the building. I gasp and suck in as much clean air as possible. Seconds later the air fills with the death serum, making it smell like smoke and spice. I run through the city trying to avoid the airborne serum.

I know what I need to do, I need to find Kuvira, Su and her family before its too late.

I keep running.

Chapter 7

I run through the city, the airborne serum is moving quickly through the air, making it harder and harder to focus. *I might not make it in time.* I think. *No, I can't think that, come on Christine focus. You need to find everyone.*

"Su, Kuvira where are you?" I call out. I start to cough, and my next breath wheezes on the way out. "Su! Kuvira! Where are you?"

Finally I get a response. "Over here!"

I turn towards the voice and see Kuvira and Su. I run towards them and put my hands on my knees. I breathe in shallow breaths.

"Are you okay?"Su asks.

"I'm fine." I say and I cough even more.

"Did you stop Baatar?" Su asks.

I shake my head. "No, I'm sorry."

"That's okay. At least you tried." she says.

"'Tried' Isn't good enough." I say and I stand up straighter, my lungs feel better.

I look back at Kuvira, she's now crying. "What is it Kuvira?!"

"My parents. Their still in the city." she says.

"It's okay. I'll get them out." I say and I give her a kiss.

Before she has time to react, I'm running back to the city.

"Christine, wait!" Kuvira calls.

I keep running.

---

I run through the city. I run up one of the streets and that's when I see them. I run over to them. "What are you guys doing!? We need to get out of the city!"

"We wanted to help." Kuvira's dad says.

"We need to go now!?" I say and I start to drag them with me, we run through the cloud of death serum and I cough.

We get to the edge of the city and Kuvira's mom turns to me. But then I hear coughing. "What was that?" Kuvira's dad asks.

"Someone's still in the city." Kuvira's mom says.

I stop and turn towards the city, I close my eyes and turn towards Kuvira's parents. "You guys get out of here. I'll go save whoever it is."

"But—" they say.

"Go!" I say, urgently. "We're running out of time."

They nod and start to run away from the city. I take a deep breath and run towards the city again. When I get there I see a figure slumped against a building. "Korra!" I yell.

I run over to her and swing her arm over my shoulder and start to walk. My lungs start to burn from lack of oxygen, but I push forward. Korra starts to cough and she lifts her head to look at me. "Christine?"

"Just hang on. We're almost there."

Korra gets enough strength and she stands. I start to bend an air bubble around us and we start to walk. When we get to the edge of the city, I collapse onto the ground.

*"Christine!"* Kuvira screams.

She picks me up. I try to focus my eyes on her. "I'm sorry," I say. My voice weak. "I promised that I wouldn't leave you," I use my remaining strength to pull Kuvira in for a final kiss. "I love you."

"I love you too, Christine and I always will." Kuvira says.

Christine smiles softly and her eyes close.

"Christine?" Kuvira says. "No! Please don't leave me. Please, wake up."

Christine's heart stops and her body goes limp in Kuvira's arms.

The Legend Of Korra Meets The Fate Of The Furious

(Book 10)

Chapter 1

Something shakes me awake and I bolt right up. I look around the room wildly. Finally my eyes settle on my target. My heart slows down and I take a deep breath. I look at the figure in front of me, it motions for me to follow. I jump out of bed and look down at my clothes; I'm wearing my commander uniform. I follow the figure downstairs and through the kitchen. We walk out of my house. I look up at the sky. The stars aren't visible tonight. I follow the figure up Michigan Ave. and around a corner. We arrive at a building and walk inside. We go to a room. I hear a metal door slam shut behind me and a deadbolt sliding into place with a thud. Soon I'm engulfed in darkness. My heart pounds hard against my chest. My eyes adjust to the darkness and I blink a few times. I feel the presence of someone standing behind me and I stiffen. I hear a click and feel cool metal on my wrists. I try to move my hands but their shackled together. I clench my fists, as I try to bend them off. But they shock me and I jerk forward. I slam into the ground. My head pounds and my wrists sting. The room becomes bright as the lights flicker on. I squeeze my eyes shut, shielding my eyes from the light. I'm yanked to my feet and I open my eyes. My eyes widen when I see the person in front of me. But before I have anytime to react I'm struck in the neck with something. I gasp and fall to the ground. I try to move but my body is paralyzed. My eyes feel heavy and they close.

I scream and bolt right up. Someone grabs hold of me and I panic. I thrust my fist forward and it strikes something hard.

"Ow!"

I open my eyes and look in front of me. I let out a gasp. *"Kuvira!?* I… I'm sorry. I didn't mean to hit you."

Kuvira straightens her jaw and smiles at me. "It's okay, Christine."

I smile and pull her in for a kiss. When we break apart, I sigh.

"What is it?" Kuvira asks.

"Another nightmare," I say. "This one much worse than the last."

"Oh. I'm sorry to hear that."

I nod. She pulls me into her arms and hugs me. I take a deep breath and it shakes on the way out.

"You're safe with me." she whispers in my ear.

I nod again and kiss her cheek. She smiles and kisses me back.

Eventually when we break apart again, we go downstairs and sit down at the table and have breakfast.

The sun is shining when we step outside. I smile and look at Kuvira, she grabs my hand and I lace my fingers with hers. We walk through Chicago, passing the alleyway and away from Erudite headquarters—the building that has caused so much trouble—and through a broken down section of the city. The buildings are slowly crumbling to dust. We walk to a park.

A sign near the entrance reads: *Millennium Park.*

"I've always wanted to bring you here," Kuvira says, as she guides me to a bench so we can sit down. "But we've never really had the time to do so."

The bench is made of steel and it makes me feel cool when I sit down. Kuvira sits down as well. Our fingers still laced together.

I look around, there are metal bars that do a criss-cross above us. "Well you pick the most amazing place in Chicago. I wouldn't have wanted to be anywhere else."

She looks down at me. "I love you."

I look up at her. "Say it again."

"Christine, I love you."

I smile and snuggle my head into her chest. "I love you too."

Chapter 2

Kuvira and I walk hand-in-hand back to the house and when we get there we sit down at the table. Kuvira leans into me and I lean into her. I close my eyes and take a deep breath. I'm just about to drift off when I feel someone sit next to me, on the left. I open my eyes and see Baatar Jr. I smile at him. Baatar just looks at me from the corner of his eye. I look to my right and notice that Kuvira has moved to the very end of table. Confused, I look back at Baatar, who has moved his seat closer to me. I shift my chair to right just a bit and find that it won't budge. I try to move my feet and find that they are bound to the chair. My hands are in the same scenario, bound by chains. I try my best to break free from the restraints and they don't budge. I start to struggle out of them, but my body comes to an abrupt halt. I start to feel a deep ache run through my muscles and veins. I gasp and the pain becomes worse by the second.

I look at Baatar from the corner of my eye, he's sitting calmly at the table. My breathing becomes faster and I start to feel light-headed. I feel something on my shoulder. I try to turn around, but the restraints start to shock me and I let out a groan. I look around again and see that Baatar and Kuvira have disappeared. I'm all alone. I look at my shoulder, but there is nothing there. I struggle against the restraints again and this time I break out of them. I jump from my seat and start shooting out metal strips. They just hit air, even though I can feel the presence of someone else in the room. Something hard strikes me in the side and I gasp. I fall but catch myself before I hit the ground. My vision doubles but I keep moving. I run to the door and open it. I run out of the house... or what I thought was the house. What I ran out of was Erudite headquarters. I continue to run, but something stops me. I look down and let out a scream, the ground is beginning to sink. I try to move but that only makes it worse. Soon the ground is up to my chest. I take one last breath before the ground swallows me.

I gasp and sit up. My heart pounding and my body aches. I put my head in my hands and take deep breathes, as I try to calm my nerves. I calm down a little and look around. But I'm not surrounded by the usual walls of my house. Instead I'm surrounded by white, pale-lit walls. I look down at the floor and notice that isn't the normal hardwood floor that's in my house. I struggle against the restraints holding me to the bed, but its no use. I'm trapped. I hear a creak and turn my head towards the cell door, its open just a crack. I frown. It wasn't open before. Someone steps inside and starts to walk towards me. The person stops meters away from me. My heart pounds. She pulls up a chair and sits down by the bed. She then leans over and turns on a lamp.

"Hello Christine."

My eyes widen. *"Kuvira!?"*

I sit there speechless. A few seconds later my cell door opens again and someone else walks in. She's tall and thin and she has long brunette hair.

My heart skips a beat. "Evelyn?"

She smirks at me. "Hello Christine. Did you miss me?"

"How?" I croak, unable to form words. I take a deep breath and push the words out. "How are you alive?"

Evelyn just shrugs, looks over at Kuvira and says. "I have my ways and thanks to Kuvira here, I have full control over the city again."

I look over at Kuvira. "How could you do this to me? How could you betray me like that? I thought you loved me!"

"It's not that simple... I—" she starts.

"It is that simple!" I yell. "You either love me or you don't. So which is it?"

"I..." Kuvira stammers. "I do love you, but..." Kuvira looks over at Evelyn who nods. "But I obey my orders."

"Very good," Evelyn says. She turns towards me. "Let's begin."

Before I can protest, I'm struck in the neck with something. My body becomes heavy. I have one last thought before I hit the ground.

*I'm going to die.*

Chapter 3
*Beep. Pssssssssh. Beep. Pssssssssh.*
I let out a groan and try to move but my body felt heavy and too weak to move my own muscles. I was lying down.

*Beep. Pssssssssh. Beep. Pssssssssh.*

There was a noise, it was rhythmic and soft, somewhere near my head. Wherever I was, the noise was nearby. I try to move my head, but my neck wouldn't turn. I try to open my eyes, but they wouldn't open.

*Beep. Pssssssssh.*

I can hear something else, but I can't make out what it is. Something pokes at the back of my mind. Waking up in Erudite headquarters, Kuvira betraying me, Evelyn injecting me with something. I make an effort to move my hand. Dragging it across the table. It hits a barrier, a leather restraint; I could feel one on my other hand as well. I was tied down.

I hear voices. "She moved. Didn't you sedate her?"

I open one eye and then shut it quickly. The pale lights too much of a shock for my eyes. I hear a rustle and a metal crash.

"Get those out of her face, she's waking up." Kuvira's voice.

I cough and crack my eye open just a fraction.

Kuvira is standing over me.

"You," I cough, "traitor."

"We have to begin." a voice says.

"Stop!" Kuvira says, urgently. "She's awake!"

"Then we have to sedate her again. With a bigger dose this time."

"You,"-I cough again- "traitor."

I can see better now, my eyes are adjusting to the pale lights. Two women stand near me. I'm in the lab. The walls glowed bright, with computer screens, alive with graphs and charts. I see my own heartbeat, the thin line in perfect unison with the pounding in my chest. I panic and my breathing starts to accelerate; my heart pumped. I see my own face on the screen as well. My eyes alive with fear.

"I'm sorry," Kuvira says. "I tried to tell her that you came willingly—"

"That's right!" Evelyn says and she steps forward, her eyes are cold and unfeeling. "You have succeeded, what I myself had failed to achieve."

Kuvira nods and turns back to me. "She asked me to be here, to talk to you, so you'd have someone you trusted—"

"I don't trust you!" I shout. My voice echoed throughout the room. "I helped you all your life! I rescued you when you were in trouble! I believed everything you told me! Every word about how we would always be together and how we would always love each other—and it was all a lie?"

"I was telling the truth," Kuvira says. "When we went to Millennium Park, I was trying to keep you away from Evelyn until I could explain things."

"Then let me go!" I sob and I try to break out of the restraints holding me down. "Get me out of here!"

"I…" Kuvira says, stopping herself for a moment. "I can't," She let out a breath and she relaxed. "I can't," she repeated and her expression darkened. "I obey my orders."

"Very good." Evelyn says.

She walks towards me with a needle full of serum. I start to protest but Evelyn sticks the needle into my neck. I gasp, my heart rate increases and my eyes close.

Evelyn looks over at Kuvira. "Let's begin."

Kuvira nods and walks over to Christine and gives her one last hug, tears start to run down her face. "I love you Christine."

## Chapter 4

I gasp and open my eyes. I'm standing by my bed in my cell. I look over at the door and frown, it was open. *Nice try.* I think. *I'm not falling for it.* I sit down on the bed and put my head in my hands.

No sooner then I did that I hear a voice. *"Christine?"*

My head snaps up at the sound of my name and I stand, confused. I walk towards the door, I peer out into the hallway, but there's no one there. I start to walk and then I hear my name again. *"Christine, where are you?"*
I continue to walk, I turn a corner and walk towards a room. the door to the room is open, I peer inside the room but there is no one there. I shrug and start to walk away. I walk down a couple more hallways and I hear my name again—this time sounding closer than before—and walk towards the sound. I walk towards the room again and I go inside. I take a deep breath and look around the room, but I don't see anything. I turn to leave and find that the door is locked. I try to metalbend it open but before I have the chance, a metal cable wraps around my wrist. I gasp and jerk my arm back. I hear a crackle and feel sharp bursts of pain shoot across my body. I clench my teeth to keep from screaming and collapse onto the ground. I pass out.

I open my eyes but its too dark to see anything. Though my eyes eventually adjust to the darkness. I stand and let out a groan of pain. My ribs burn. I put my hand on my ribcage and when I pull it away its sticky with blood. The stitches in my side tore again. I lean against a wall and try to breathe in, but it hitches in my throat. I hear a creak and turn towards the sound there's a door at my right, its open just a crack. I start to walk towards it when I hear voices. I turn towards the sound and the lights in the room turn on, blinding me for a moment. When my eyes adjust to the light and I can see. My eyes widen and my heart skips a beat as soon as I realize where I am. I hear another creak and look back towards the door. I see a figure standing in the doorway and my heart pounds in my chest. The figure steps forward and I step back, hoping to put as much distance as I can from them. I take another step back and trip over something. I slam into the ground and the figure continues walking towards me and soon its towering above me. I squeeze my eyes shut and wait for the worst to come. But it never happens. Instead I feel something wrap around my arms lightly. I flinch, then I hear a voice. "Its okay, Christine. It's only me, I'm here to get you out."
I crack one eye open and gasp. "Korra?"
Korra smiles at me and helps me to my feet. The movement hurts my ribs and I gasp. Korra's smile fades. "What's wrong?"
"My ribs," I say, with a sharp breath. "Their still damaged."
"Okay," she says. "But I need you to move, their are soldiers patrolling the entire building, so we need to be quick and quiet."
I nod and put my arm across her shoulder and together we make our way out of the lab.

We make down one or two hallways and turn a corner. I take another step and collapse onto the ground again.
"Christine!" Korra nearly shouts.
She runs towards me and kneels down beside me. Soon the hallway is packed with soldiers. Kuvira and Evelyn are with them.
I cough and look up at her. "Korra you need to get out of here. If you try to save me, they will kill you. I'll be fine, just go."
With tears in her eyes, Korra leans in and presses her lips to mine and when she pulls away she whispers. "I'll be back, I promise."
Korra gets up and runs out of the building. Evelyn walks over to me and motions Kuvira over as well. Evelyn kneels down beside me and sticks a needle into my neck and my eyes close.
Chapter 5
*"Christine?"*
I jerk awake and blink a few times. I'm back in my cell. I turn my head and see Kuvira standing next to me. Her body tense, sweat forms on her forehead and she's shaking, as if she was trying to hold back from carrying out an order. She takes a step forward, but I'm too scared to move, so I lie there, helpless.

She stops inches from me and sits down on the bed. She let's out a long sigh and looks over at me, her eyes not quite meeting mine.

Kuvira takes a deep breath and looks over at the door and then back at me. "There's, um…" she stops and swallows, glances at the door one more time before finally looking back at me. "There's something I need to tell you." She pauses again. I just stare at her not wanting to say anything. She begins speaking again. "I know that you may not want to have anything to do with me right now, but I want you to know that I still love you Christine, no matter what happens, I will always love you."

I put my hand on my head. "Do you even hear what you're saying right now?"

"Christine—" she starts to say, but I cut her off. "Why did you betray me? After all the things we've been through?"

Kuvira says nothing and I look up at the ceiling. I hear a click and a side. The cell door opens and Evelyn walks in. She stops in front of us. "Its time to go." she says.

Kuvira nods and turns to me. "Christine?"

I just look at her. "If you think I'm coming with you, you're insane."

Kuvira sighs and looks back at Evelyn. "Can we have a moment?"

Evelyn nods. "Alright, come out when you're done."

Evelyn leaves the room and its just me and Kuvira. Kuvira grabs my hands and laces our fingers together. I look over at the far wall.

"Christine," Kuvira says. "I'm sorry that I have to do this."

Before I have anytime to react, she grabs my arms and starts to drag me out of the room. I thrash, but its no use. She drags me out into the hallway and then lets me go. I jump to my feet and try to run, but she blocks my path. I see something glimmer in her pocket. The handcuffs. I reach for them, but she's too quick. She grabs them from her pocket and puts them on my wrists. She turns up the intensity and I freeze. She starts to drag me down the hallway again and I don't dare to try to escape. At least not until I realize where we're headed. The lab. We arrive at the main doors and I start to struggle. The handcuffs start to shock me and I scream. Kuvira continues to drags me into the room. She drops me and I slam into the ground. The impact knocked the wind out of me. I hear another click and the handcuff are gone. The door has closed and Kuvira is gone. I breathe in deeply and get to my feet. I see Kuvira in front of me and run toward her. But I hit a glass barrier. Kuvira is on the other side of it. The lights come on, in her side of the room and three people walk in.
I try to break the glass but it's no use.

I hear the door to room open and I see Zaheer walk towards me. "No!" I say. I start to back up, but I back right into someone. I turn around. "No! Raiko!"

"Hello Christine," They both say. "It's nice to see you again."

Chapter 6

Baatar let's out a groan as he tries to move. He opens his eyes and it takes them a minute to adjust to the darkness. *Where was he?* He tried to sit up, but pain shot across his body and remembered something. He remembered being knocked unconscious, but nothing else after that. Baatar scanned the room, trying to find clues to where he might be. But instead he found nothing.

I jerk awake and let out a groan of pain. I was lying on the floor. The handcuffs had long been taken off, but my body was still sore from the last shock that the handcuffs had given. I try to sit up, ignoring the pain. I slowly get to my feet and look out at the four people on the other side of the glass. I remember, Kuvira dragging me out of my cell and ending up here, as well as Raiko and Zaheer being in the room. But that's all I can remember. My thoughts are interrupted though, when I hear the door to my left open. I look at it and I see Kuvira walking towards me. A pair of handcuffs in hand. Her movements slow and deadly. I start to back away slowly, but I back into a wall. Kuvira continues walking towards me, all the while slowly turning up the settings on the handcuffs. When she reaches me, she stops. I know better than to fight with her, not only that but I'm too weak to try anyway, whatever they did to me while I was unconscious made me very tired. I put my hands out in front of me. The handcuff go on with a click and Kuvira slips behind me. She starts to push me forward and I start to walk. We walk out of the room and when we get into the hallway, I stop abruptly and Kuvira runs into me.

"Come on let's go." she says.

I don't move, instead I take a deep breath and spin around and shoot out a blast of lightning, the handcuffs no longer on my wrists. Kuvira dives out of the way. The lighting strikes the wall and soon the hallway is packed with soldiers, including Evelyn, Zaheer and Raiko. I send out another lightning blast and Raiko screams. But not for long, it soon turns into a sinister laughter. I look over at him wide-eyed. He's controlling the lightning. Raiko redirects the lightning back at me and I catch it. I feel it course through my body and I motion for it through. I groan in pain as I feel it shoot across my chest and it explodes against the opposite wall. I fall to the ground, my body trying to recover from the misdirected lightning. My vision starts to blur. I know that I'm going to black out any minute now. My breathing becomes shallow and I struggle to keep my eyes open. Through my blurry vision, I see Raiko walk over to me. He's holding something. I feel a needle plunge into my neck. My body starts to feel heavy. "You can't put me under again." I say, as I struggle to stay awake.

Raiko smirks. "Oh, but I can."

He holds out another needle and sticks it in. I struggle again. But the serum is too strong. My body relaxes and my eyes close.

Baatar continued to look around the room for any clues, but still he found nothing. He walked around, trying to find an exit. But he couldn't, he was boxed in, or so he thought. He leaned against the wall and reached down. He felt a lever on the door. Baatar grabbed it and took a deep breath. The handle started to freeze and soon it fell off and hit the ground it a *clink!*

Baatar started to do the same with the hinges on the door. When the hinges were frozen, he kicked the door down. He ran out of the room and turned a corner. This one much like the last hallway, filled with pale lights and pale walls. He continued to run and he turned another corner. This hallway was different, but he continued to run. He only stopped when he felt like his heart was going to burst out of his chest. He leaned forward and put his hands on his knees.

Once he caught his breath, he looked up. He was in the lobby of Erudite headquarters. He'd never seen the lobby lit up before. He'd ever only seen it when the lights were off and it was dark. He shook the thought from his head and turned away from the lobby. He started to run deeper into the building.

He needed to find everyone.

Chapter 7

Something hard pokes me in the side. I groan and open my eyes. I try to sit up, but my muscles ache and I lie back down again. Someone scoops me up in their arms and starts to jog. My heart starts to beat faster. Soon I start to panic. But the person carrying me doesn't stop running. My vision clears a breath hitches in my throat. I try to speak but I can't say anything. Korra smiles down at me.

I cough. "K-Korra?"

"Let's get out of here." she says.

She continues to carry me through the hallway and I see Baatar leaning against a wall and peering around a corner. He put his hand in the air. Telling us to be quiet. We try to be as quiet as possible. Soon Baatar motions his hand again. Telling us to slowly start walking. Baatar takes the first step and nods. Korra takes a deep breath and starts to walk. I'm still cradled in her arms. Korra picks up her pace, she's almost sprinting.

I look up at her. "You came back."

She smiles at me again. "Of course I did. You're my friend. I would never leave you behind."

I smile at her again. "Thank you."

She nods and continues to sprint. Baatar is still close behind us. We turn a couple of corners and reach the lobby. To my surprise there are no soldiers patrolling the area.

Korra sets me down and I give her a hug and let out a sigh of relief. We were finally getting out of here.

Me, Korra and Baatar walk towards the exit. I let out another sigh of relief. But that moment doesn't last very long, because as soon as we push the doors open an alarm sounds and the lobby becomes crowded with soldiers, Evelyn and Kuvira are among them.

"Stop right there!" Kuvira yells.

I stop and put up my hands. Korra and Baatar drop into a bending stance, ready to strike at any moment. I look over at Kuvira and Evelyn. Then I look back at Korra and Baatar. I just shake my head. "Don't fight them," I whisper. "They'll kill you if you do. Let me take care of this."

They nod. I turn back back to Evelyn and Kuvira. I take a step forward and Evelyn gets into a bending stance. I stop. "I give up," I say, loud enough for Baatar and Korra to hear. "No more hiding and no more running. It's time to do what I should've done a while ago. I surrender."

"I…" Evelyn's voice trails off and she looks at me very closely. "That's not what I expecting at all."

"Me neither," I say and I clench my jaw, trying not to cry. "Let's go," I say softly. "Now before I lose my nerve."

"Alright." Evelyn says and she turns away from us.

*I have have to go with them.* I think. *I have to take a step, and then another one and go to… to I don't even know where. The end.* I shake my head to get the thought out.

"Christine," Korra says, and I feel a tear in the corner of my eye.

"Korra," I say. "I… I'm sorry, I don't know…" I turn to face her, trying to find the right words to tell her what I felt, I didn't even know it myself, and suddenly Korra was holding me. She pulls me in for a kiss. I kiss her back. I hold onto for as long as I could and when she pulls away to breathe, I press my face against her chest.

"I'm sorry for bringing us here, for everything I've done," I say. "I'm so sorry."

"I choose to follow you," she says, her voice is sweet and calming. "And I'll find you again."

We kiss one more time, and then Evelyn's soldiers started to pull me away from Korra. I turn my head to look at her. But before we start to walk, Kuvira wraps her hand around the back of my neck and pulls me in for a kiss and I can't move or speak. She pulls away and laces her fingers with mine. "Let's go." she says. We start to walk. I turn and look at Korra from the end of the hallway, and she stares back, motionless. We turn a corner and I lose sight of her. I take a deep breath and we continue walking.

Chapter 8

We get onto the train and I sit down, as far away as I can get from Kuvira. I look out the window, watching Erudite headquarters disappear from view. I take a deep breath and shake out my hands. I look down at my uniform, it's been striped of any metal—even platinum—and has been instead replaced with a black, crisp business suit. I sigh and close my eyes. Maybe I can pretend that I'm not here and that none of this has happened. I'm about to drift off, when someone sits down in the seat in front of me. I open my eyes and see Kuvira sitting there. I glance at her and then look out the train window. Kuvira sighs and gets up to sit in the seat beside from me. I sigh again and look at her.

"Something on your mind?" Kuvira asks.

I go back to looking out the window, watching the clouds roll across the nearly darkened sky. I get up and for a few minutes, I pace back and forth. Then I sit down again.

"Look," Kuvira says. "If you have something to tell me say it."

I snort and look at her. "I have nothing to say to you…" I pause, for a moment. "But, I have one question."

Kuvira sits up straighter. "Oh, and what's that?"

"It's about when we were in the lobby in Erudite headquarters, when you kissed me in front of Korra. Was that for her? For you? For me? Or was it even necessary?"

"Well, everything is a choice, you could've stopped me, but instead you didn't. So there's your answer."

I look out the window again.

Kuvira gets up. "I think you need a reminder as to why you're here."

We walk through the train cars and stop at one, we walk inside and Kuvira motions for me to walk forward. I take a step forward and see my reflection. I put my hand on it and feel something hard and cool. Glass. A lamp in the room on the other side of glass turns on and I see someone lying on a bed. She gets up and walks over to the glass. "Christine?" she says.

My heart skips a beat, I would recognize that voice anywhere. "Su?"

"Hi." she says, her voice muffled by the glass.

She looks pale and tired, like she hasn't slept in weeks.

Kuvira walks forward and Su takes a step back, disappearing into the room. I turn toward Kuvira. Unable to form words.

"Now," Kuvira says. "Are you going to do as I say? Because I would hate for something bad to happen to her."

I swallow hard and breathe in deep, when I breathe out it shakes. "Alright. What do you want me to do?"

Kuvira smiles. "Work for me. I want you to work for me."

Chapter 9

I stare at her wide-eyed, I was not expecting that. I breathe in deeply.

"You want me to work for you? Why?"

She laughs. "I want you to work for me because I give you the one thing that's important to you." She pauses for a moment and smiles. "Family."

I swallow hard, my heart is pounding. Its not the first time that I have heard this threat, but I don't want to risk Su's life, so I nod.

Kuvira nods. "Excellent."

I turn away from Su's cell and follow Kuvira through the train again. I wipe the tears from my eyes. We walk to the engine of the train and sit down. Kuvira looks out the window. I breathe out shakily and wipe my hands on my pant legs. I'm shaking. I clench my fists to stop them from shaking.

Finally I turn to Kuvira and ask. "Why did you do this?"

She looks at me. "Why did I do what?"

I chuckle and get up. "Why did you take me and Su captive?"

She shakes her head. "Well, for starters you chose to come with me, you could've run away, but you didn't. Second of all, I thought that if you did come, that it would be nice to have to two of you around."

"That's not what you told me." I say.

She gets up. "You're right, that's not what I told you. But you made you choice, so here you are."

I sigh. "Look, I'm not here to play games. You're going to let Su walk out of here, unharmed. If you don't, then I won't do as you ask."

Kuvira chuckles. "I think that you've forgotten that you're the reason Su is in this mess to begin with, is if hadn't tried to escape with Korra then you wouldn't be in the situation. Plus I want to see the old Christine."

I clench my hands into fists, but I relax them moments later. I take a deep breath to calm myself.

I turn away from her. "You want to see the old Christine. Watch."

---

"Come on Baatar, we need to make it to the train station before the next train leaves." Korra and Baatar run through Chicago, as they run they look over their shoulders to make sure no was following them. The cost was clear. They continued to run.

*Tzzzztttchhh!*

There was a flash and the building next to them had a charred hole in it. They looked over their shoulders again and saw that they were now being pursued by Evelyn and her soldiers, as well as Raiko and Zaheer. Korra saw that Raiko was preparing to strike again. "Baatar!" she yelled. "Duck!"

"Huh?" Baatar said, as he turned around.

Raiko shot out the lightning. There was a flash and Baatar dropped to the ground. Motionless.

*"Baatar!"* Korra screamed.

Raiko sent out another blast and Korra redirected it back to Raiko. It struck him in the chest and he slumped to the ground, but didn't die. Zaheer stopped and so did Evelyn, they stayed by Raiko's side.

Korra dropped to her knees beside Baatar and began to do chest compressions. "Come on Baatar," she whispered. "Don't you *dare* die on me."

Chapter 10

*"Come on Baatar!"*

Korra continued the chest compressions and then check his pulse. Nothing. Korra continued to revive him, but it was no use. There was just no way. Korra collapsed onto his chest and started to cry. He had to wake up, he *just* had to. Korra wiped away her tears and started on another round of chest compressions and she prayed that he would be alright.

---

"So, this area has no defence so that would be a good place to strike." Kuvira says, pointing to a spot on the map.

I shake my head and point to an area near it. "Actually this area here is crawling with soldiers, and they would outnumber us like a lot. Besides we wouldn't be able to get anything in there, the pathway would be too small."

"So we take out their defence system, that will leave them vulnerable to an attack." Evelyn says. "Besides, we've got metal, earth and lava benders, plus we have you," Evelyn points at me. "You're the Avatar, you'd have enough power to take them out."

"Alright," I say, with a nod. "I see your point."

"So now all we need is a date and time to carry this out." Kuvira says.

I smile. "Now, that I can take care of."

"What do we need to do?" Evelyn asks.

I put my hand on my chin. "Well…"

---

"Come on, come on. Wake up Baatar." Korra says, she'd been trying to bring Baatar back for the last hour. Once again she had no result. Tears began to leak from her eyes and she rested her head on his chest. "Please…" she whispered.

She closed her eyes and layed there crying. She checked Baatar's pulse again and then she put her head on his chest and cried. "Come on Baatar," She put her hand on his cheek. "Please don't die on me."

Chapter 11

The train slows to a halt, the wheels screeching against the metal tracks. The door opens and I step onto the platform. The air smelt fresh and green, with a mix of copper. Buildings loom in the darkness and I soon recognize them as the metal domes in Zaofu. Evelyn steps down onto the platform beside me, Kuvira following right behind her. Both of them start to walk and I'm right behind them. We walk through town square and to the Beifong estate. When we get there Kuvira motions for us to be quiet. Everyone falls silent. Evelyn walks to the door and knocks on it, moments later she breaks it down. We file inside and I see the rest of the Beifong family, including Bolin, Opal, Baatar Sr. and Lin.

"What are you doing here?" Lin asks, narrowing her eyes at Kuvira.

"We're here for something that Su stole from us a long time ago." Kuvira says.

"Oh," Baatar Sr. says. "What's that?"

"That is none of your business." Evelyn retorts.

Kuvira clears her throat. "As long as you guys cooperate, no one will be hurt."

She starts to walk forward and everyone backs away slowly. Kuvira walks to a table, pulls out a briefcase from one of the drawers and opens it. Inside it are several maps showing highly populated areas. Kuvira shuts the case and starts to walk toward the door. We all follow her. When we get outside, she hands the case to me. We start to walk and we turn a corner. I hear footsteps behind us. I stop and turn around. My jaw drops in shock. Korra stands behind me. I no longer feel the weight of the briefcase in my hand and see that she now has it. She turns and runs toward an alleyway I chase after her. "Korra, stop!" I yell.

She continues to run and I launch a boulder at the wall beside her. She stops dead and turns around. "I don't know what you're doing," Korra says. "But I do know one thing, you love me and you're not going to hurt me." She looks at me one more time and then she turns to walk away. She walks around a corner and I follow her. When I turn the corner though, I see Evelyn drop into a bloodbending stance, she tries to take the case from Korra.

"Give it to me." Evelyn says.

"Over my dead body." Korra replies.

Evelyn chuckles. "Oh, okay."

She's just about to kill Korra when I shove her against the wall. Korra still stands in front of her and the three of us are holding the case.

"I don't think it would be a good idea to try and kill her." I say to Evelyn.

I turn towards Korra and yank on the case. She doesn't let go and I give it another yank. This time she let's go.

Evelyn brushes the dirt off her shirt and says. "Let's go."

She starts to walk away and I give Korra one last glance, before following Evelyn back to the train station.

Chapter 12

Evelyn and I walk up to the glass barrier and look into Su's cell. My heart leaps into my throat. I can't see her.

Moments later I hear a voice. "Well, well, well. It seems that you failed to get the maps and you almost let Korra get away with them."

I see Kuvira on the other side of the glass. She steps forward, just so that it's the glass separating us.

"But I did get the maps!" I say, urgently.

"Evelyn got the maps," she says. "You chose to let Korra go."

"I doesn't matter! You got what you needed, now let Su go!"

My heart is pounding in my chest.

Kuvira just shakes her head. "I don't want to do this but, I guess I have to."

She pulls out a platinum sword and I pound on the glass. "No, don't do it!" I scream.

"You've left me no other option." Kuvira says.

She thrusts the blade forward. Su gasps. Blood trickles past her lips and she collapses onto the floor. Her body lifeless.

*"No!"* I scream.

I start to cry and Evelyn holds me in her arms.

---

I put my head in my hands and take a deep breath. I stare down at the floor, trying to ignore the aching feeling in my chest. I also wipe away any tears that were forming in my eyes. I hear footsteps and don't even bother looking up to see who it is. I already know. Kuvira sits down next to me and I get up. I walk over to the window and stare at the land beyond it. In the window I see Kuvira's reflection, her eyes meet mine and for a moment I feel like I can see the old Kuvira, the one that always cared about me. But then that moment is over. I just stand there staring out the window. Thinking that Kuvira isn't going to say anything, but a few moments later she speaks. "I think I know what your thinking."

I keep looking at her from the window and say. "Really? What is it then?"

"Well, right now you're feeling angry, at the world, at me., she sighs. "I know that what I did may have hurt you a lot, but you have to understand that I only did that for the greater good. If I hadn't killed her she would've caused a lot of trouble. But I do understand why it hurts you. I mean she was *our* family after all."

I scoff. "If she was really family to you, you wouldn't have done it."

She gets up and walks over to me. "Well, I think your family, plus I haven't tried to kill you yet. Have I?

"Well, no," I say. "But I think that I—" Kuvira stops me mid-sentence with a kiss and I push her away. I turn and start to walk.

I walk slowly at first and it turns into a jog, I run through the train and and to the engine. When I get there I lean against the wall, I take a deep breath and then another one and another one. I stare up at the ceiling, hoping that will distract me from all the pain and grief and betrayal that I'm feeling.

Chapter 13

Korra sighed as she made her way back to the Beifong house. She walked through the gate leading up to the front door and pushed the door open. As she made her way back into the house, she couldn't help but think about what had transpired yesterday and she pushed the thought out of her head. She didn't want to think about it right now. Korra pushed the doors to the living room open and walked inside. There she saw Baatar Sr., Opal, Huan as well as Wing and Wei. Korra walked up to Baatar Sr. and gave him a hug.

"I'm sorry." she says.

"For what?" he asks.

"They got away with the maps, I couldn't stop them."

Baatar takes a step back and shakes his head. "No," he says."No this can't be happening." He turns towards Korra, his eyes wide. "Do you have any idea what they could do with those maps."

"Is it bad?" she asks.

He nods. "With those maps, they can wreak havoc on the world."

"Uh oh."

Baatar runs to the door and Korra chases after him. "We need to stop them and we need to do it fast," he says. "We're running out of time."

---

I walk through the train cars and towards my personal apartment. When I get there I close the door and lock it. There's a mirror on top of the dresser. I look at my reflection. I look pale and tired. My eyes are red from sleepless nights and crying. I try to smile but it's falters. I look away from the mirror and open the top drawer of the dresser. Inside are photos of me, Baatar Jr., Korra, Kuvira and Su. I pull them out and look at them. I look at the one of me and Kuvira. It was from one of the first times we went out together. When we went to the noodle restaurant, it was our first date. Next, I pull out the family photo. The one with the entire family. That photo had been taken after we had gotten Baatar Jr. out prison. My eyes start to well up with tears and I wipe them away. This is all I have left of Su. I hear a knock at the door and the doorknob rattles. I jump and put the photos back into the drawer and walk to the door. I open it and my eyes go wide.

"Hello, Christine."

---

I stare, wide-eyed. *"Kuvira?"*

"May I come in?" she asks.

"Sure." I say. I step off to the side and she steps in and looks around. I breathe in deeply, trying to calm my nerves. She walks over to the dresser and my heart pounds. She opens the top dresser, she scowls and closes the dresser.

"Is everything alright?" I ask.

She turns toward me again and this time she smiles. "Of course, everything's fine."

She walks to the door, but before she leaves she turns toward me and says. "You wanna walk with me?"

*This can't be good.* I think.

I nod and together we walk out of the apartment.

Chapter 14

Me and Kuvira walk to the engine of the train and she tells me to sit down. I obey, and sit down. She opens the door to the engine room and tells the engineer something. She then sits down beside me. I look at her. She's no longer scowling. Instead she smiles at me and I look away. I stare out the window and at the passing cities.

After a long moment of silence, Kuvira speaks. "We have one last job to do."

I look at her again. "What job is that?"

"You'll see," she says and she pauses for a moment and then begins speaking again. "If you get it done right, I'll let you go."

"What if I don't do it right?" I ask.

She opens her mouth to speak and then decides against it. Instead of telling me, she just smiles. I get a nervous feeling in my stomach and I just nod. Whatever it is, it can't be good.

She get's up and starts to leave, but when she reaches he door, she turns and says. "One thing that I can tell you is that no one will be ready for this."

I nod and she leaves the room.

I follow her into the hallway. "Kuvira?" I say.

"Yes?" she says.

I walk up to her and look her in the eyes. "I want you to be careful about what you do next."

She raises her eyebrows. "Why's that?"

I smile. "Because if you don't, you'll have a big problem afterward."

"What kind of problem?" she asks.

"Well let's just say that the only problem with putting your foot on a tiger seal's neck, is that you can never let it up."

I turn and walk away from her.

---

"Can you see it?" Korra asks.

"Yeah, I can," Baatar Sr. says. "The train is about to stop."

"At which station?" Korra asks.

"At a station just north of here. I can see the train starting to slow down."

Korra puts down her binoculars and looks over at Baatar. She motions her hand and they both start to jog.

---

I lie on my bed and stare up at the ceiling. I'm unable to sleep. I end up tossing and turning and eventually I get out of bed. I walk around. I look out the window and see lights in the distance. My heart leaps into my throat and I run to the engine. "We have a problem." I say.

"What kind of problem?" the engineer asks.

"Someone's following the train."

"Shoot." he says.

He picks up the speed of the train and the lights fade into the distance.

Chapter 15

We arrive at the state of Yi and get off the train. Evelyn looks at one of the maps that we stole from Su. "According to the map, the governor lives somewhere in this state and the stuff we need is in one of his top secret buildings."

"Well let's go." Kuvira says.

We break into a run and I look around, making sure that no one sees us. We duck into an ally and continue to run. We make it to the building and we knock out the security guards that are standing outside the door. We walk inside and to one of the offices. Kuvira looks at me and nods. I take a deep breath and metalbend the door off its hinges. We walk inside and Kuvira stops at the governor's desk.

"Hello Governor." she says.

The Governor looks up and stares at wide-eyed. "Kuvira?" he says. "What are you doing here?"

"I'm here for those." she says, pointing at the blueprints on his desk.

"Why do you need those?" he asks.

"I don't see a reason to provide you with that information," she says. "Now we can either do this the easy way or the hard way. Its up to you."

The Governor starts to speak, but then we hear another voice. "Kuvira? Christine? Is that you?" We turn towards the voice and see Kuvira's parents.

"What do you want?" Kuvira says and it sounds like a growl.

"We want you to stop," her father says. "You know better than this."

"How would you know?" she snarls. "You left me when I was eight."

"Kuvira, please," her mother says. "You know that we feel bad about leaving you. But we're here now and maybe you should forget the past and focus on the the future."

Kuvira looks away from her parents, and I see tears gleam in her eyes. She drops to her knees and the tears run freely down her face. She looks up at me and I nod. She takes a deep breath and gets up. She turns to her parents. "I'm sorry."

She let's out a yell and shoots out several metal strips, they strike both her parents and they collapse to the ground, but don't die. The Governor stares at Kuvira wide-eyed. Kuvira starts her way towards him and he tries to back away, but he's against the wall.

"Give me the blueprints and I won't hurt you." Kuvira says,

"Not a chance." he says.

"Fine, have it your way."

She fires out two metal strips and they pin the Governor to the wall. He struggles against them, but its no use, he was as good as stuck. She walks over to the table and takes the blueprints.

"Come on." she says.

We turn away from the Governor and start to walk.

---

"Come on hurry up." Korra says as she runs.

Baatar was right behind her. They ran silently, trying not to attract attention to themselves. They made it to the next trainstation and hid behind a bush. After a long silence Baatar asks. "Where do you think they are?"

"I don't know," Korra says. "but I'm certain that they are here somewhere."

"Even if they are here," Baatar Sr. says. "Don't you think that you should stop chasing them, I don't think anything good can come out of this."

"We don't know that." she says. "There's a reason Christine's doing this and if we find out why, then maybe we can figure out how to stop her."

Baatar sighs. "For the world's sake, I hope so."

Chapter 16

I sigh and put my head in my hands. I'm sitting on my bed in my apartment, with one thought swirling in my head. *I don't know how much longer I can deal with this.* I stare at the floor. I hear the door to my apartment open and I don't even bother looking up. I know exactly who it is.

"How are you feeling?"

I scoff. "Why would you care?"

Evelyn scoffs. "I do care, its just... I care about our mission more."

"Our mission," I laugh. "You mean *your* mission to start a war? To kill innocent people?" I look at her. "The only reason I came with you guys is so that I could save Su, but now she's dead and I have no other reason to work for you guys."

"What about Kuvira? I thought you still loved her."

"Not anymore, she betrayed me, Su and all of the Earth States." I say.

"She didn't betray you or anyone else. You have to understand Kuvira's only doing what's best for the world. She's only doing what's best for you."

I glare at her. "If she was doing what's best for me, than she would've let me out by now."

Evelyn sighs. "Look, we can sit here and dwell on the past or we can focus on the future. Which do you choose?"

"Fine" I say. "I'll focus on the future."

"That's good," she says and she get's up. "Well, I gotta go. It was nice talking to you."

I give her a small smile. "Yes it was."

---

I jerk awake, at some point after Evelyn left, I fell asleep. I hear my bedroom door squeak and it opens a crack. I see a figure step in and my heart starts to race. The figure walks toward me and stops just inches from me. Then I hear a soft voice. "Christine?"

I swallow hard. "How do you know my name? Who are you?"

"Its me Korra." the voice says.

"Uh huh," I say. "How do I really know that its you and not one of Kuvira's spies?"

"Could one of Kuvira's spies do this?"

Suddenly I feel a connection that I can only feel when Raava's spirit is around. I turn on the lamp beside my bed and gasp. "Korra it is you."

"Hey." she says.

"What are you doing here?" I ask.

"I'm here to get you out and we don't have much time so we need to move fast." she says.

I nod and get out of bed. We run out the apartment and to the engine of the train. I look out the window. The train has stopped. We get off the train and start to run. I look over Korra. "You came back."

She smiles at me. "Of course I did. I told you I would find you."

I smile and stop running. Korra does the same and give her a quick hug. "I missed you."

"I missed you too." she says. Korra smiles again and pulls me in for a kiss. When we break apart, I smile. "What is it?" she asks.

"I love you." I say.

"I love you too."

We're just about to start running when something wraps around my wrists. Its a metal cable. I'm jerked back and I land onto the ground with a heavy thud. There was only one other person I know that could metalbend, aside from me and Korra. Kuvira. She walks up to me and I can see a scowl on her face.

"Kuvira, let me go." I say.

"No." she says and she launches me into the air.

I shoot out a platinum strip and it strikes her in the arm. She groans and shoots out her own metal strip and I feel a searing pain in my leg. I land onto the ground. I look at my leg. It's bleeding. Kuvira bends out her metal sword and I blast her with air. She ducks and runs at me with her metal sword. When she gets close I grab the sword and push it backward. Kuvira gasps and clutches at her chest. The sword is lodged there. She collapses onto the ground and blood sprays on her uniform. There she lies gasping for air. Within moments her gasps for air stops and she's gone.

I sigh and turn toward Korra. "I guess that's it."

She looks down at Kuvira's body. "Yeah I guess it is."

"Well, should we go home."

"Sure." she says.

Together we make our way back to the train station.

---

When we get back to the house I tell her the news about Su and she tells me the news about Baatar Jr.

I nod and we lean into each other. We will be waiting for the next adventure to find us. But for now we'll wait.

The Legend Of Korra Meets The Fate Of The Furious Part 2

(Book 11)

Chapter 1

*One year later…*

I lay in bed, Korra lies next to me. I roll over and look at Korra, she's still sleeping. I smile and get out bed. I walk down to the kitchen and start to make breakfast. Once breakfast is made I put it on the table.

"Smells delicious."

I turn around and see Korra standing behind me. "Thanks." I say.

She walks up to me, pulls me close and presses her lips to mine. I wrap my arm around her and press in closer. We break apart and stand in the kitchen. "I love you." she says.

"I love you too." I say.

We sit down and have breakfast and after we're done, we sit down on the couch. We turn on the TV and watch the news. Though there's nothing of interest on today. After that, we go for a walk around Chicago. We arrive at the noodle restaurant, we take our seats and open our menus, moments later the waiter stops at our table and sets down two bowls of noodles.

We start to to eat and I look around and then say. "I'm guessing you booked out the whole restaurant?"

Korra smiles. "Of coarse."

"Let me guess," I say. "This is also a date."

Korra puts down her chopsticks and smiles again. "Wow, you really pick things up quick."
I laugh. "Probably because I've been in so many bad situations that its become a habit."
"Yeah, probably." she says.
When we finish eating, we walk to Millennium Park and we sit down on the bench. I sigh and lean into Korra. She puts her head down on mine. Moments later I drift off to sleep.

I let out a yawn and open my eyes. I roll over and see Korra laying beside me, her hair is covering her eyes and I brush it away, trying my best not to disturb her sleep. Sometime after I feel asleep at Millennium Park, she must've carried me back to the house. I watch her chest rise and fall as she breathes deeply. I smile and lay back down, I take a deep breathe and stare at the ceiling. I sigh and get of bed, still trying my best not to wake Korra. I slip into my shoes, grab my coat and I leave the bedroom, closing the door quietly. I walk downstairs and walk to the front door, I open it carefully and walk outside. I close the door behind me. I start to walk and it turns into jog. I continue jogging and soon I arrive at the the train station. I get on the train, sit down and look out the window. I watch Chicago until it disappears in the distance.

I arrive at Zaofu and get off the train. I walk to the cemetery and stop by Su's and Baatar Jr.'s graves. I kneel down and tears start to run down my face. "I'm sorry," I say. "I'm sorry I couldn't protect you and Baatar."

I take a deep breath and get up, I walk to the Beifong estate and knock on the front door, moments later it opens and Lin motions for me to come inside. We walk to the living room and sit down. "What are you doing here?" Lin asks.

"I just needed a break from being in Chicago and I needed to be around someone else other than Korra and plus we haven't talked to each other in a while."

"I completely understand," she says. "There were days when I needed to get away from Korra sometimes as well."
I laugh.

Lin laughs too and then get's up. "Well, you should get some sleep."
I nod and lay down on the couch and moments later I drift off to sleep.
Chapter 2
The next morning I get up and walk to the front door and I open it. I take a step outside and start to walk. As I make my way to the train station, I look around to make sure no one is following me. I get to the station successfully without being spotted. I get onto the train as make my way to Chicago. I look out the window and watch the landscape go by. It's still early in the morning, so the sky is still dark. Though when I get back to Chicago, the sun has risen. I step down onto the platform and start my way back to the house. When I get there, I open the door carefully and step inside, close the door and when I turn around, I see Korra standing in the kitchen with her arms crossed and she's tapping her foot against the floor. I give her a half smile, then start to walk to the living room and Korra follows me. I sit down on the couch and she sits down next to me. I don't look at her, I just stare at the TV in front of me.

"Where did you go last night?"
"What?" I ask and I turn to look at Korra.
"Where did you go last night?" she asks again.
"Oh, uh, I went to Zaofu, why?"
"Just wondering." she says. She get's up and starts to walk away, but then she stops and turns around. She then continues to speak. "I find it interesting that you leave in the middle of the night to go to Zaofu and not leave me a note, I mean how hard is it for you to leave me one?"
I shake my head. "I don't know. But I'm sorry next time I'll be sure to leave you one."
"Alright." she says and she leaves the room. I stare at the ground and moments later Korra walks back in. "Wanna walk with me?" she asks.

"Sure." I say and together we make our way out of the house.

---

Korra and I walk to the station and get on the train, we ride all the way to Zaofu and then get off. As we walk through the city Korra asks. "Are you sure that you stayed here last night?"

"Of course," I say. "Where else would I go?"

Korra nods. "Show me exactly where you went."

"Alright." I say and we walk to the cemetery.

We stop and I kneel beside Su's and Baatar's graves again. Korra rasies her eyebrows at me. "Just look at the trail of tracks that I left here last night."

She looks around. "Alright, I see your footprints."

I nod and get up off the ground. "Why are you so concerned as to where I was last night?" I ask.

Korra sighs. "Well its just that with what happened last year…" she pauses for a moment, then continues again. "I just don't want to lose you, I want to make sure that you're safe and when you disappear in the middle of night like that, it makes me worried."

I sigh and turn to look at her. "You won't lose me, I'll be alright. Honestly Korra, why are you so overprotective suddenly?"

Korra starts to walk and I walk with her. "I…" she says, struggling for words. "I don't know. I guess its because I've lost you so many times that I can't afford to lose you again."

I stop mid-step. "What did you say?"

"What?" Korra asks.

I shake my head. "Never mind."

"Okay?" she says and I could hear the uncertainty in her voice.

I laugh. "Let's just go for our walk." I grab onto her arm and we start to make our way away from the cemetery.

There was something oddly familiar with that sentence and I was certain that I had heard it before. Though I can't quite place my my finger on it.


Chapter 3

We arrive at the Beifong estate and knock on the door. The door opens as soon as I knock.

"Hello." Baatar Sr. says.

"May we come in?" I ask.

"Yeah, sure." he says and he steps off to the side to let us in.

We walk to the living room and sit down. Baatar joins us a moment later. He sits down beside us and I give him a hug.

"Are you guys hungry?" he asks.

I look over at Korra and she nods. I turn back to him. "Actually, yes, we are."

"Alright," he says and he get's up. "I'll go put dinner on."

Baatar get's up and walks to the kitchen. I turn and start to talk to Korra, but then I see someone out of the corner of my eye. I turn to look and the figure disappears around the the corner. I get up and walk from the living room to the hallway. "Opal?"

She peers around the corner. "Christine?"

"Hey." I say.

Opal runs up to me and gives me a hug. I gasp as she squeezes me really tightly. I wrap my arms around her tightly as well.

"It's been so long since I've seen you." she says.

"I know," I say. "I missed you."

"I missed you too."

When we let go of each other, I smile and say. "Hey. Do you want to say 'hi' to Korra?"

"Well of course I would love to say 'hi'"

We walk to the living room and Opal runs up to Korra and hugs her. I smile and sit down on the couch again. We start to talk and we talk until dinner's ready and then we make our way to the table. We sit down and soon everybody's sitting at the table.

"So how have you guys been?" I ask Wing and Wei.

"We've been okay." They both shrug and look down at the table. "I mean its still hard not having Su or Junior around and some days it gets really lonely around here, but I'm sure we'll manage."

"Oh," I say and I look down at the table. "I'm sorry to hear that."

"It's okay." Wing says and he sniffles.

"Hey," I say and I give him a hug. "It's alright."

He sighs and we break apart, he sniffs and then says. "I'm sorry. I just that we've all been stressed lately."

"There's nothing to be sorry for," I say. "I've been stressed lately as well."

This time it's Wei that speaks. "Really?" he says.

"Yeah." I lean over to him. "Do you want to hear something funny?"

"What?" They both ask.

"The reason that I'm stressed is because, well, no offence to Korra or anything, but some days she can be like an elbow leech."

Wing and Wei cover their mouths to try and stop from laughing.

I smile and say. "What's even more funny is that there are some days where I'm like 'wow, and she really stuck on there too.'"

The three of us burst into laughter and everybody at the table looks at us.

"What's so funny?" Korra asks, which makes the twins laugh even harder.

"Nothing." I say and I cover my mouth to keep from bursting into laughter again.

After the three of us have calmed down, we continue to talk for the rest of dinner.


Chapter 4

The sun is about to set by the time we leave Zaofu and make our way back to Chicago. On the train ride back me and Korra talk quietly. When we arrive in Chicago, we descend from the train. I start to make my way back to the house.

"Hey Christine?" Korra says.

"Yes?" I say and I turn around.

"Can you take a walk with me?"

"Sure."

She turns and starts to walk away from the train station. We walk through Chicago and as we walk, I notice that Korra's posture is a bit rigid and that her breathing is a little bit heavier than normal. We arrive in a broken down part of the city and we stop walking. Korra leans against a brick wall and takes a deep breath.

"What is it?" I say.

"Well..." she says, then pauses.

"Well what?" I say.

She let's out a long sigh and continues. "Well... what if I am not who you think I am? What would your reaction be?"

"I'm sorry," I say. "I'm confused."

"I mean..." Korra sighs. "I mean what if I'm not really Korra?"

I laugh. "Well of course you're Korra."

"That's not what I—" she starts to say, but I stop her with a kiss.

"Look. I don't care who you are., I say. "All I care about is that we're together."

"But—" she starts.

"Korra, do you not hear what I—"

"I'm Kuvira!" she yells.

I laugh. "Very funny."

"No, I'm being serious." she says.

"Haha."

"No…" Korra sighs and then says. "This is going to seem a bit weird, but I'm wearing a mask. I'm not Korra."

"Haha." I say, again.

"Christine I…" Korra sighs and then says. "The mask I'm wearing is made of latex rubber."

"You're funny," I say. "Kuvira's dead."

Korra takes a deep breath and says. "Close your eyes for a moment."

"Why do I—"

"Just do it!"

I sigh and close my eyes.

"Okay. Now you can open them."

I open my eyes and my jaw drops. *"Kuvira?!"*

"Hi." she says.

"Wait a minute," I say. "If you're Kuvira and you were dressed like Korra… then who betrayed me a year ago?"

Kuvira sighs. "Korra."

My jaw drops again. *"What?"*

"When you thought that it was Korra who saved you, it was actually me."

"So… Korra teamed up with Evelyn, Raiko and Zaheer?"

Kuvira sighs again. "Yes."

I put my head in my hands and lean against the brick wall.

*What is going on?*

Chapter 5

I shake my head and take another deep breath. My heart is thumping hard against my chest. I let out a shaky breath. Kuvira puts her hand on my shoulder. "You okay?"

I lift my head. "Yeah, I'm fine. It's just… wow."

"I know," she says. "Its a lot to take in."

I let out a weak chuckle. "Yeah."

I let out another shaky breath.

"You sure you're okay."

I nod. "Yeah, I'm sure."

"Okay." Kuvira says.

I look up at her. "Let's go home."

Kuvira nods and we start to make our way back to the house

---

We arrive at the house and stand about ten feet away from our house. Kuvira breathes out nervously.

"What?"

"There's something else that I have to tell you." she says.

"What's that?"

Kuvira sighs again. "They're coming back."

"Who?" I ask.

Kuvira starts to say something, but her response is cut off by a loud boom. I spin around only to find that part of our house is on fire.

"No," I say, as I run toward it. "No!"

"Christine, wait! Don't go toward—"

I hear another boom, but I'm too close to the house and the explosion sends me backwards. I slam into the ground with a sickening thud. The last thing I see are three figures walking towards us, then I black out.

---

I breathe in deeply and then start coughing. I roll onto my side and continue coughing. When I'm done. I breathe in shallow breaths this time and let out a groan of pain. My eyes flicker open and I realize that I'm lying on the ground. I get up and notice that I'm on a train. I try to run, but something jerks me back. I groan at the pain in my shoulders and look at my wrists, their shackled together. I take a deep breath and clench my fists to bend them off. I hear a crackle and I jerk forward as the cuffs shock me. I scream and collapse onto the ground.

*Where was I?*

## Chapter 6

I pace back and forth in my cell. I still have no idea where I am. All I know is that I'm on a train but that's about it. I take a deep breath and shake out my hands, which only causes the handcuffs to shock me even more. I grunt and then take another deep breath, trying to absorb the pain rather than feeling it. I clench my fists again, but end up with another painful shock. Sweat starts to gather on my face, but I can't wipe it away. I end up just sitting down on the floor again. I take another look around and see someone walking toward the glass and I yell. "Help!"

Moments later I get a response. "Wow, you must really be weak if you're asking me for help."

"Look," I say. "I don't care who you are, but can you let me out of here."

"Oh, don't worry I'll let you out, but not yet." says the voice.

"Please," I say. "Just let me out."

"I don't know if we should. What do you think Zaheer? Should we let her out."

"Wait a minute… Zaheer?" I say.

Zaheer steps forward and someone else steps forward with him.

"I don't know, what do you think, Evelyn?"

Evelyn looks at me and then back at Zaheer. "I don't know. I think we should leave her for now and see how she adjusts, after all we never completed the jobs that we had her captured for in the first place. Now did we?"

Zaheer nods. "I think you're right, how about we come back in a while and see how she's doing then?"

"Sounds great."

Both of them start to walk away and I could hear their laughter echo throughout the train.

I pace back and forth inside my cell. It has been a whole week since I was put in here and no one has told me anything. Though its really not that surprising. I yank on the metal cuffs again, but receive another powerful shock of electricity. I gasp and try my best to absorb the shock, but instead I jerk forward. I then collapse onto the floor and breathe heavily.

Through the ringing in my ears I hear a voice. "So... how's life working out for you?"

"Why would even care?" I growl.

"Really?" Evelyn says. "We're going to go through that again?"

I get up and walk as close to the glass as the chains will let me. "I have no reason to talk to you. So you can save your crap for someone else who cares."

She frowns. "But you're talking to me right now."

I growl and turn away from the glass. "Why are you really here?"

"I'm here because we have one last job to do and you're going to help me with it."

"What makes you think that I would want to help *you?*"

"Alright, so you want this to be the hard way." she says and she whispers something to Zaheer. He nods and leaves the room. Moments later he returns and my heart sinks.

"No." I say.

Kuvira lifts her head, she looks dazed, but soon she focuses her eyes on me. "Christine?"

"No," I say again. "No!"

Tears form in my eyes and I look over at Zaheer and Evelyn.

"Fine." I say.

"Fine what?" Evelyn asks.

"I'll help you with this one last job."

"Wonderful," she says. "I'll let you know more when I receive the details."

Both her and Zaheer turn and walk away, taking Kuvira with them and leaving me in the cell, alone.

Chapter 7

I pace back and forth, trying not to trip over the chains that hold me back. I'm more nervous now than I've ever been.

*What am I going to do?* I think. *Now they have Kuvira. I have to get her out of here.*

I sit down on the floor and begin to meditate. I take a deep breath, trying to contact Korra's spirit. Then I remember that I can't contact my past lives. I sigh and get up. I stare out at the rest of the train. I'm still waiting for Evelyn to tell me what their plans are, but she hasn't shown up yet.

*What is going on?*

Another week has past and still no answer. I'm starting to think that Evelyn isn't going to tell me what her plans are and I haven't seen Kuvira either. I look down at my clothes, I'm wearing a gray prison uniform. I look up from my clothes and out at the train. I start to feel very tired and my vision starts to blur a little. I've eaten very little in the last two weeks. I sway a little and I lean against the wall for support. My head pounds and I collapse onto the ground. I pass out.

*"Christine?"*

I slap my hand onto the ground and grunt as I push myself to my knees. I blink a couple of times. My vision clears and I see Evelyn standing over me.

"What do you want?" I say, my voice hoarse.

"Get up."

I try to stand, but my legs feel weak and I collapse onto the ground again. I put my arm up, she grabs onto it and pulls me to my feet. I lean against wall.

"What do you want?" I ask again.

"I'm here to tell you what our plans are."

I nod.

"So," she says. "You know how a year ago we received the maps and blueprints?"

"Of coarse. We got the maps from Su's place in Zaofu and the blueprints from the Governor at the state of Yi. Why?"

"Well, if we can combine the two plans together, we could be the most powerful people in the whole world. Also if you do this I'll let Kuvira go. What do you think?"

"I think…" I pause for a moment and then continue speaking. "I think that I want in. But I have have one question."

"What's that?"

"Who's Kuvira?"

"Uh, well she's… um… your girlfriend."

"I have a girlfriend?"

Evelyn nods. "You what to see her?"

"Sure." I say.

She leaves the room and returns moments later with a woman about my age. I assume she's my girlfriend. She lifts her head to look at me. "Christine!" she says. She runs up to me and gives me a hug. I push her away.

She frowns. "Christine?"

"I'm sorry, but who are you?"

"It's me, Kuvira." I shake my head and start to walk away from her and toward Evelyn.

We walk out of the cell and Kuvira follows us. She grabs onto my arm. "Christine wait."

"Don't touch me!" I say. "I… I don't know who you are."

She let's go, I turn away. Evelyn shoves Kuvira into the cell and locks the door. We walk to our destination.

Chapter 8

We arrive at The Earth State capital of Ba Sing Se and get off the train. We walk to what used to The Royal Palace and go inside. We walk to the throne room and and I break down the door. We walk inside, but there's no one there. Me and Evelyn stand guard while Zaheer searches for the final piece that we need to begin our plan.

Moments later we hear him say. "I got it!"

We walk out of the room and make our way back to the train station.

---

We get back onto the train and I sit down on the couch, near the engine of the train. Evelyn sits down beside me. "Are you excited about tonight?"

"Of coarse."

"Good, 'cause no one is going to be expecting this."

I nod. "You're right, no one will be expecting this."

"Alright, next stop Zaofu."

---

We arrive at Zaofu and get off the train. I look over at Evelyn and she nods. I take a deep breath and start to bend the platinum domes away from the city. They creak and groan as they come apart. I strain as I struggle to bend them off.

"Come on Christine," Evelyn says. "Just a little more. Come on."

---

"Baatar!" One of the guards yelled. "You have to come see this."

"What's going on?" he says.

"The domes are gone. Someone bent them off."

"What!" he exclaimed. "Alright, grab the remaining guards, we're going after whoever did this."

"Uh, why?" the guard asked.

"Whoever did this, also killed my wife." Baatar Sr. says. "Now get to it!"
The guard nodded and ran off to tell the others of the news.

"Wing! Wei! Opal! Get down here!" Baatar yelled.

The twins rushed downstairs with Opal following behind them. "What's going on?"

"Grab your stuff. We're going to find whoever killed your mother and brother."
The twins grabbed their spools of metal cable and Opal grabbed her wingsuit. They returned downstairs with their gear.

Baatar Sr. nodded. "Let's go hunting!"

Chapter 9

We return to the train with the pieces of the platinum domes that we "received" from Zaofu and put them in a storage room. That's part two of our plan that's complete. I walk towards the prison cell and walk inside. The light inside turns on and Kuvira wakes with a start. When she sees me, she jumps to her feet and runs toward me. I smirk as the chains yank her back and she strains to bend the chains off. She collapses onto the ground and her body jerks as the electricity courses through her. She groans and rolls onto her back. The platinum armor she's wearing, causes the electricity to shock her even more. I watch as it shoots across her chest and she let's out a scream.

"Just stop," I say. "Don't move."

Kuvira looks up at me and in a hoarse voice asks. "Why?"

"Why, what?" I say.

She coughs and another electric shocks runs through her. When she recovers from the shock, she asks. "Why did you put me in here?"
I don't say anything.

She sits up gently. "Don't you love me?"

I just shake my head. "How can I love you if I don't know you?"

"You do know me. But you just don't remember., she gets up and walks over to me. I take a step back, but Kuvira holds me in place. "Do you remember this?"
She presses her lips to mine and I jerk my head back and before I know what I'm doing I bring my hand back and curl it into a fist. It crashes into her face. She yelps and jumps backwards, covering her face with her hands. I lock the door. I turn and run away from the prison cell.

I run to the meeting area on the train. I put my hand on my forehead and lean forward. Someone walks up behind me and says. "Are you okay?"
I nod.

"Are you sure?"

"Yeah." I say.

"Positive?"

"Yeah."

"Well are you really—"

"Yes! I'm fine! Stop asking."

Evelyn sighs. "I was just asking."

"I'm sorry," I say. "Its just... well, I have no memory of who Kuvira is and she just kissed me."

"I see. That must've been rough."

"It was." I say, as tears flow down my face.

"Come here." she says.

I walk over to her and she gives me a hug. I bury my face into her shoulder and for a moment we just stand there hugging each other.

But a voice interrupts us a moment later. "Hey, I just got done finalizing our plans, so we can go whenever we—" Zaheer stops for a moment. "Oh, did I catch you guys at a bad time?"

"No," I say and I pull away from Evelyn. "I'm fine. Now, what were you saying?"

"Oh, I was just saying that we can leave whenever we're ready."

I nod. "Let's go now."

"Alright," he says. "Next stop, Chicago."

Chapter 10

Baatar Sr. looked through his binoculars, trying to locate where the train is. He looks for the train and when we sees it, he mumbles something under his breath, then he says. "We have to go. Now."

"Why?" Everyone asks.

"Because, we have to stop them," Baatar says. "I don't know what their plans are, but whatever it is, it can't be good."

"How are we going to stop them?"

"Well," he says. "We have to find out what they're doing first."

"How do we do that?" Opal asks.

"I actually have a plan for that." Baatar says.

"What's that?" Wing and Wei ask.

Baatar starts to run. "We'll discuss it on the way, but we have to hurry."

---

I open up the door to Kuvira's cell and walk inside. I close the door behind me and lock it. Just to make sure that anyone who follows me can't get in. "Kuvira?" I say.

She doesn't say anything.

"Are you okay?" I ask.

She doesn't say anything and she has her back turned to me so I can't see her face. "Are you okay?" I ask again.

"Go away." she says.

"What happened?"

"It doesn't matter." she says.

I reach out to put my hand on her shoulder and jump back when she says. "Don't touch me!"

"Fine," I say. I walk to the door, but before I leave I say. "Are you sure yo—"

"Get out!" she yells, cutting off my words.

I sigh and walk out the door. I take one last look at Kuvira before closing the door quietly. I start to make my way to the meeting room.

"Are we all good to go?" I ask Evelyn as I walk into the room.

"Yes, we are," she says. "Everything is going as planned."

"Good," I say. "When we arrive in Chicago, we can begin phase two."

"Of course." she says.

"Now," I say. "Go get Zaheer, we have a plan to carry out."

Chapter 11

I walk toward Kuvira's cell. I walk inside and close the door. Kuvira's still facing the wall. I try to say something, but nothing comes to mind and I end up leaving the room again. I look out one of the windows and notice that it's nighttime. That means that we're still a while from arriving in Chicago.

I walk back to Evelyn and say. "So when are we going to use the materials that we got and how are we going to use them?"

Evelyn smiles at me. "You'll find out. We just have to get to Chicago first."

"Okay," I say. "Next stop, Chicago."

I let out a yawn as I walk to my bedroom, on the train. I walk past Kuvira's cell on the way there— She's sleeping on the floor—and to my bedroom. I know that we'll be in Chicago later, but I need a quick nap. I lay down on the bed. I close my eyes.

*Finally.* I think. *I'm finally going to get some—*

"Get out of bed! Now!"

I let out a yelp and fall off my bed. I groan and look up. "Why?"

Evelyn stares down at me. "We're only two hours away from Chicago, that's why."

"Okay." I say and get up off the ground.

We walk to the meeting room and Evelyn offers me a cup of coffee. I chug the entire thing and set it down on the counter. I look out the window and watch as the city of Chicago comes into view.

The train slows to halt when we arrive at the train station. But as I step down onto the platform, Evelyn stops me. "I think you should try talking to Kuvira one last time."

"Why?" I ask. "She wants nothing to do with me."

"Just try one more time, we'll get the stuff set up."

"Okay." I say.

I turn and walk back onto the train, I walk to Kuvira's cell and go inside. I close the door behind me. "Kuvira?" I say.

"Go away."

"Evelyn told me that I should come talk to you."

"I said: Go away!"

I sigh and start to make my way around so I can look at her while I'm talking. She looks down at the floor when I stand in front of her.

"Kuvira?"

"Go away!" she says more forcefully this time.

"No!" I say. "Now look at me."

Kuvira sighs and lifts her head. I recoil at the sight of her face. She has scars criss-crossing all across her face, a cut lip and a black eye.

"Oh my god!" I say, my voice barely above a whisper.

Chapter 12

"What happened!?" I say, in a shocked tone. "Are you okay?"

"I'm fine," she says. "But you need to get out of here."

"No!" I say. "I'm not going to leave you."

Kuvira looks around the room nervously, like she's afraid that someone is going to attack us at any moment. She sighs and looks back at me. I see tears forming in her eyes. I shake my head and walk behind her. I start to fiddle with the chains, holding her back.

"What are you doing?" she asks.

"I'm letting you go," I say. "If what you said about us being together is true, than I'm letting you go."

I continue to fiddle with the chains and just as I'm starting on the last one. She yells. "Get out of the way!"

I don't react fast enough and something plunges into my neck. My vision blurs and I collapse onto the ground. The heavy feeling of sleep overwhelms me and my eyes close.

---

*"Christine!"* A voice echo's. *"Help me!"*

*"Kuvira!"* I yell. *"Where are you!?"*

*"Christine!"* she yells again.

I try to locate her voice, but the closer I get, the farther away it sounds. I follow her voice, even though I'm unable to find her. I turn a corner and that's when I see her. I run up to Kuvira, but I can't reach her. Something is holding me back. "Kuvira!" I yell.

She looks over at me and I see blood spilling out from her mouth and down her chin. *"Christine, help!"*

Moments later Kuvira collapses onto the ground and blood sprays on her uniform.

*"Kuvira!"* I scream.

---

I groan and open my eyes slowly. I have to blink a couple of times before my vision clears. When it does, I see Zaheer carrying me. I groan and try to move, but I can't. Zaheer put's me down. I put my hand on my head. "W-what happened?"

"You'd been knocked out." he says. "I found you out cold, on the floor inside of Kuvira's cell. I had to knock Kuvira out. "

"Why?"

"She would've killed you."

"Thank you," I say. "For saving my life."

"No problem," he says. "Now, we have a job to finish."

I blink a couple more times and that's when I realize where we are.

Erudite headquarters.

Chapter 13

"Alright, let's get this party started!" Evelyn exclaims.

I look around and notice that the platinum pieces that we got from the domes in Zaofu have already been constructed into something. Though I'm not sure what exactly.

"So what are we doing?" I ask.

"You'll see in a second." Evelyn says and she winks at me.

I nod.

Raiko walks into the room, with a bag slung over his shoulder and with Kuvira in chains behind him. He sets down the bag and it makes a *clink* sound.

"Kuvira?" I say.

"Don't worry," Raiko says. "She's fine."

I nod and then ask. "What's inside the bag?"

"The last of the equipment that we need." he says.

He opens the bag and pulls out a vial of clear serum. He walks over to me with a syringe and a needle.

"What is that?" I ask.

"It's a serum to help inoculate you from the effect of other serums."

"Okay." I say.

Just as Raiko is about to insert the needle, I hear a voice. "Christine!" Raiko stops and we both look up, Kuvira has woken up and staring at me wide-eyed. "Don't do it!"

"Don't do what?"

"Don't let him inject you with the serum!" she says urgently.

"I'll be fine," I say. "Its just an inoculation serum."

I nod to Raiko and he poises the needle over top a vein on the side of my neck. He plunges the needle in and presses down the plunger slowly. I feel the effect of the serum almost immediately. My mind starts to feel hazy and that's when I realize that its not an inoculation serum. *Its simulation serum!*

*"Christine!"* Kuvira yells.

My mind starts to race. *I can't fight it!* I think. *Its too strong!*

My thoughts are interrupted though when Evelyn says. "Christine?"

I turn to look at her. She beckons me forward and I walk towards her. She pulls out a needle and hands it to me. I look down at the liquid inside. Its purple. Death serum.

"I want you to finish the job." she says.

With the needle in hand, I turn towards Kuvira and start to walk towards her slowly. Kuvira starts to back away slowly. I pick up the pace. Kuvira hits the wall and I lunge at her. She ducks out of the way and I lunge again. She grabs onto my arm and pushes me backward. I crash into a table, but I quickly regain my footing. I drop the needle and it shatters when it hits the ground. I bend the liquid into a frozen spear and throw it. Kuvira dives out of the way. The ice spear shatters against the wall and I let out a yell. I run at Kuvira and tackle her to the ground. She tries to throw me off, but I hold onto to her. She let's out a yelp of pain and tries to throw me off again. But I keep my grip on her as tight as possible. I bend the death serum back into a frozen spear. I jerk my arm upward and Kuvira jumps up to avoid being hit. I jump to my feet and bend out platinum strips. One strikes Kuvira and she collapses onto the ground.

"Christine," Kuvira says. "Please."

## Chapter 14

I charge at Kuvira, death serum ice spear in hand. She jumps out of the way and I let out a low growl. I run at her a third time and she grabs onto my arm, she yanks me to the side and I lose my footing. She brings her knee up and it slams into my chest. I fly backward and hit the ground.

Through the ringing in my ears I hear Evelyn yell. "Finish the job!"

I close my eyes and then jump to my feet. Kuvira charges at me and I try to blast her back with air but she evades the attack quite easily. She grabs both my arms to hold me in place. "Christine, it's me Kuvira!"

I try to break out of her grip and she grips onto my arm even more. "Christine!" she yells. She releases me and shoves me backwards. I stumble and fall. I jump back to my feet and I swing at Kuvira, she ducks and dives towards one of tables. I dive after her. I grab onto her and she turns and shoves a syringe into my neck. I gasp and as she pulls the plunger up, extracting the serum from my bloodstream. I scream, but soon my head doesn't feel as clouded. I drop to my knees and breath in deeply. I remember everything. When we met. I was fourteen, I had run away from home and Kuvira took me in. We became friends and soon after that I had helped her and Korra defeat Zaheer. I remember asking her out on a date. I remember everything.

"Kuvira?" I say.

---

"Finish her off now!" Evelyn orders.

I turn away from Kuvira and towards Evelyn. I take another deep breath and charge at her. Evelyn's eyes go wide as I slam into her. She crashes into the ground with a thud. I look over at Kuvira and she tosses me a needle. I look back at Evelyn. "You messed with the wrong couple." I say. I shove the needle of death serum into her neck and she slumps to the ground.

I turn towards Raiko and charge at him. I slam him into the ground. I shove another needle of death serum into his neck and he slumps to the ground. Lastly I turn towards Zaheer. He drops into a bending stance and I drop into one of my own. He runs at me and I blast him with fire. He avoids the attacks and suddenly I can't breathe. I gasp and through my blurry vision I see him. I drop to the ground. I'm about to pass out. But then I'm able to breathe again. My vision clears and I see Zaheer clutching at his neck. There's a metal sword lodged there. He collapses onto the ground and blood sprays onto his face. I turn away from Zaheer and toward Kuvira.

I give her a hug. "Thank you for saving me."

She hugs me back. I bury my face into her chest and sigh. Though a few seconds later I feel cold metal on my neck. I recoil from her and look down. I gasp and Kuvira smirks. She presses her metal sword closer to my neck. "Don't move." she whispers.

Chapter 15

I stand frozen and wide-eyed. I try to turn my head so I can look at Kuvira, but she presses the blade closer. My body stiffens and I take shallow, slow breaths to make sure that I don't move as much. Finally I have enough courage to speak. "What are you doing?"

"Be quiet!" she hisses.

"What's going on?"

"I said be quiet," Kuvira pauses for a moment. "Do you hear that?"

"Hear what?"

There was low rumbling and the ground began shake. Kuvira dove behind a desk, dragging me with her. The rumbling became louder for a moment and then stopped. Everything was silent. "It stopped." Kuvira whispered.

Kuvira stands up, talking me with her. I look around. I thought I could hear something else, like a creaking sound. I look over at the lab door. It almost looked like it was expanding and it was almost ready to burst. The creaking becomes louder. My eyes widen and I yell. "Get down!"

The door burst open. There was a powerful gust of wind and it knocks us off our feet. We slam into the ground. I look up and let out a gasp.

"Korra?"

She looks over at me and when she sees me, she yells. "Christine!"

"Korra!" I yell.

She starts to run over to me. But when she sees Kuvira she drops into a bending stance. "Kuvira, let her go!"

"Korra?" Kuvira says, confused. "Is that you?"

"Yes, it is," Korra says. "Now let Christine go!"

"What?" Kuvira says, and she looks down. I look up at her. She gasps and lets me go, jumping back in fear.

Korra runs over to me and grabs onto my arm, pulling me in close. "What on earth is going on? Why did you try to kill Christine?"

"Wha—" Kuvira stammers. "I… I don't know what you're talking about."

Korra motions to Evelyn, Raiko and Zaheer who are lying on the ground. Dead. "I didn't kill them, if that's what you're thinking." Kuvira says.

Korra glares at her. "Are you sure?"

"Yes!" Kuvira says.

Korra let's me go and starts to walk over to Kuvira. She almost trips on the bag full of serum in the process. When she recovers, she looks down at the bag. "What's this?" she asks, opening the bag. She looks inside. Moments later she looks up again and you could see the anger in her eyes.

"Its not what it looks like." Kuvira says.

"Why do you have simulation and death serum?" Korra asks and I could feel her anger turn into rage.

"Its not what it looks like." Kuvira says.

## Chapter 16

Korra drops the bag and starts to walk over to Kuvira. "What were you going to do?"

"Nothing, I swear!" Kuvira insists, and she starts to back away.

Korra takes another step towards Kuvira, making her back into a wall. I try to step forward, but Korra holds me back. I stop moving and stand there. All I can do is watch as Korra walks over to Kuvira with slow and deadly movements. I can see the fear on Kuvira's face. At the last minute Korra turns and swings her arm, her fist crashes into Kuvira's face. Kuvira reels backward.

I run forward. "Korra stop! She did nothing wrong!"

Korra pushes me back and I stumble but catch myself before I fall. I stand there, unable to move. I take a deep breath and force myself to take a step. But as I start to walk, I feel something wrap around my ankle. I look down and let out a quiet gasp. Evelyn staring up at me. She let's go of my ankle. "Help me up."

I stare at her, shocked. "*What!?* Why?"

"'Cause, you won't want to be here when those two really start to fight and I want to talk to you outside."

"Okay." I put out my hand and she grabs it. I pull her up and look over at Korra and Kuvira, they're too busy fighting each other. We walk toward a window and I open it up. I look at Evelyn and nod, I give her a boost and she jumps out the window. I grab onto the window sill and jump up, pulling myself through the window. I jump down and land on my feet.

"So, what do you want to talk to me about?" I ask.

"Well, I've been thinking that maybe you could work for me."

I laugh. "Me? Working for you? What do you think I am? Stupid?"

"Well, no. But I don't think you'd want to work for them now would you?"

"I don't work for anyone." I say.

I turn and walk away. That was a mistake though. I hear footsteps behind me and I turn around. I instantly break into a run. Evelyn chases after me. I get to the window and jump up. I grab onto the window sill and pull myself up. Evelyn grabs onto my leg and tries yank me down. I shake her off and pull myself through. I drop to the floor. I get to my feet and dive towards one of the tables. I hear a thud and see that Evelyn has made it back inside. I start to run toward Kuvira.

"Kuvir—" I start to yell, but Evelyn catches up to me and covers my mouth with her hand.

Kuvira and Korra stop fighting and look over at me. They turn toward me, but as soon as they make a move, Evelyn pulls out a needle from her pocket and presses the tip of the needle to the side of my neck. "Don't even think about taking one more step." Evelyn says.

Both Korra and Kuvira stop dead.

"Why are you doing this?" Kuvira asks.

"Because I want something." she says.

"What's that?"

"I want you." she says.

"Me?" Kuvira says. "Why do you want me?"

"Because you betrayed me and you need to pay the price for it." she says.

Kuvira steps forward and Evelyn presses the needle in a little bit. Kuvira stops dead. "Evelyn, don't do this. Let Christine go."

"Not until you surrender and hand yourself over."

"No, don't!" I yell. "I'll be fine!"

Kuvira looks from me to Korra and then to Evelyn and sighs. "Alright," she says. "I surrender." With tears in her eyes she turns toward Korra and put's her hands on her shoulders. "Whatever happens," she says. "Just promise me that you'll take care of Christine."

"I promise." Korra says.

Kuvira turns back to us and takes a deep breath. She put's her hands in the air and walks towards us. Evelyn let's me go and I run toward her. I run into her arms and she hugs me. "I'm sorry." she says.

"There's nothing to be sorry for." I say, my voice breaking.

She pulls away from me and I start to run towards her. But Korra holds me back.

Evelyn smirks. "Well, will you look at that. The Great Uniter finally has surrendered. I guess you're not so great after all."

Kuvira pulls out her metal sword. "We'll see about that."

She runs forward and Evelyn twitches her fingers. Stopping Kuvira dead in her tracks. Kuvira groans and I try to run and help her, but Evelyn starts to bloodbend me. She walks up to Kuvira and smirks as she sticks the needle of death serum into Kuvira's neck. Kuvira coughs and collapses onto the ground. Evelyn laughs and releases me. I run towards her and pull out my needle of death serum. I plunge the needle into her neck and she collapses onto the ground. Dead.

I run over to Kuvira and she breathes out weakly. "I'm sorry." she rasps out.

"Its okay." I say, as tears roll down my face.

She put's her hand on my cheek and I hold onto it. "I... love you... Christine." she says, weakly.

"I love you too." I say.

Her eyes close and her hand drops to the ground. Then she's gone.

Chapter 17

*Four years later...*

"Hey, Christine!" Korra says.

"Yeah?" I say.

"Come here, I want to tell you something."

"Coming." I say.

I get up and say. "Mama's going to be right back. Why don't you go play with Suyin?"

My daughter looks up at me and smiles. "Okay." She runs over to her sister. "Hey Su! What to go have a sparring match outside?"

Su smiles. "Sure, why not?"

The two run outside and to start to spar and I watch them for a few minutes as the two shoot out chunks of earth and their metal cables.

I make my way to the living room of our new house, when I get there, I say. "I'm sorry about that. Kuvira really wanted to play."

"That's okay," Korra says. "But I have something to tell you."

"What's that?"

Korra smiles and I instantly know what it is. "You've got to be kidding me." I say, smiling.

"I'm having another baby." she says.

"That's great!" I say and I pull her in for a kiss. When we break apart. I smile and lean my head against her chest. "When are you due?"

Korra smiles. "Sometime next year."

I give her another kiss. "I love you." I say.

"I love you too."

---

Me and Korra smile when the doctor comes into the room. "It's a boy." he says.

"What are you going to name him?" One of the nurses asks.

"I think. We're going to name him Baatar. After Baatar Jr." I say and I look over at my wife.

Korra smiles and gives me a kiss. "I think that's a wonderful name."

---

"Hey, Korra!" I say. "You're never going to guess what happened today!"

"What happened?" Korra asks. "Why are you soaking wet?"

"Well, me and Baatar Jr. were outside going on a walk and it started to rain and it turns out Baatar is a waterbender. He tried to bend the water away, but ended up getting us soaked instead."

The four year old Baatar smiles and rubs his arm. "Well, I'm still learning."

"That's great!" Korra exclaimed.

Baatar breathed in deeply and motioned his hands. The water on our clothes disappears completely.

"See!" I say.

"Wow!" Korra says. "That's amazing!"

Moments later, Kuvira and Su coming running into the house and there's dirt all over them.

"Woah, what happened?" I say.

Su coughs. "Sparring match."

"I see, who won?"

"I did!" Kuvira exclaims.

"Did not!" Su says.

"Did too!" Kuvira says.

The two girls drop into a bend stance and start shooting out metal strips.

"Girls, please," Korra says. "Not in the house."

"Fiiiiine." Suyin says.

Kuvira smirks and shoots out a strip of metal from my uniform. "Woah!" I say.

Kuvira looks at me and puts her hands behind her back and whistles innocently. "Kuvira!" I say. "What did I—" I stop and smile. "Wait, did you just bend platinum?"

"Sure did!" she says.

"Yeah, well watch this." Baatar says and he bends a blob of water from the sink.

"Woah!" Su and Kuvira say.

"Alright guys," Korra says. "That's enough." she smiles at me though. "I have to admit I was not expecting Baatar to be a waterbender."

"I guess your genetics are stronger than mine." I say.

"But you're the Avatar." she says.

"Yeah and so are you. But you have to remember, I wasn't the Avatar to begin with."

Korra put's her hand on her chin. "Oh, yeah."

"So," Korra says. "What are we going to do now?"

"What we always do best." I say, giving her a kiss.

"Ewww! Gross!" the three kids say.

Baatar Jr. pretends to throw up. I laugh.

"Oh, I see." Korra says, pulling me in closer.

I playfully slap her on the cheek. "Not that!" I say.

Korra starts to laugh and my face turns red, with embarrassment. I clear my throat. "Well, why don't we go watch our kids practice their bending?"

Korra grins and gives me another kiss. "Okay."

We follow the three kids outside and watch them spar with each other. Korra puts her head down on my shoulder and I look up at the sky. "Kuvira, I promise that I'll keep everyone safe. I love you and I always will."

Korra looks at me. "She loved you."

Tears flow down my face. "I know."

Korra gives me a hug. "I love you, you know that."

"I know," I say. "I love you too."

Together me and Korra watch the kids spar with each other. Suyin bends out some lava and I blast it with air. I hardens into rock. Su looks at me and whistles. When they're done, me and Korra walk inside hand-in-hand. I smile at Korra and she smiles at me. Not matter what happens we will always be there to protect each other. That's what family does and that's what we are. A family.

The Legend Of Korra Meets The Fate Of The Furious Part 3
(Book 12)

Chapter 1

*Just as Raiko is about to insert the needle, I hear a voice. "Christine!" Raiko stops and we both look up,
Kuvira has woken up and staring at me wide-eyed. "Don't do it!"*

*"Don't do what?"*

*"Don't let him inject you with the serum!" she says urgently.*

*"I'll be fine," I say. "Its just an inoculation serum."*

*I nod to Raiko and he poises the needle over top a vein on the side of my neck. He plunges the needle in
and presses down the plunger slowly. I feel the effect of the serum almost immediately. My mind starts to
feel hazy and that's when I realize that its not an inoculation serum. Its simulation serum!*

*"Christine!" Kuvira yells.*

---

*My mind starts to race. I can't fight it! I think. Its too strong!*

*My thoughts are interrupted though when Evelyn says. "Christine?"*

*I turn to look at her. She beckons me forward and I walk towards her. She pulls out a needle and hands it
to me. I look down at the liquid inside. Its purple. Death serum.*

*"I want you to finish the job." she says.*

*With the needle in hand, I turn towards Kuvira and start to walk towards her slowly. Kuvira starts
to back away slowly. I pick up the pace. Kuvira hits the wall and I lunge at her. She ducks out of the way
and I lunge again. She grabs onto my arm and pushes me backward. I crash into a table, but I quickly
regain my footing. I drop the needle and it shatters when it hits the ground. I bend the liquid into a frozen
spear and throw it. Kuvira dives out of the way. The ice spear shatters against the wall and I let out a yell.
I run at Kuvira and tackle her to the ground. She tries to throw me off, but I hold onto to her. She let's out
a yelp of pain and tries to throw me off again. But I keep my grip on her as tight as possible. I bend the
death serum back into a frozen spear. I jerk my arm upward and Kuvira jumps up to avoid being hit. I
jump to my feet and bend out platinum strips. One strikes Kuvira and she collapses onto the ground.*

*"Christine," Kuvira says. "Please."*

---

*Kuvira runs forward and Evelyn twitches her fingers. Stopping Kuvira dead in her tracks. Kuvira
groans and I try to run and help her, but Evelyn starts to bloodbend me. She walks up to Kuvira and
smirks as she sticks the needle of death serum into Kuvira's neck. Kuvira coughs and collapses onto the
ground. Evelyn laughs and releases me. I run towards her and pull out my needle of death serum. I
plunge the needle into her neck and she collapses onto the ground. Dead.*

*I run over to Kuvira and she breathes out weakly. "I'm sorry." she rasps out.*

*"Its okay." I say, as tears roll down my face.*

*She puts her hand on my cheek and I hold onto it. "I... love you... Christine." she says, weakly.*

*"I love you too." I say.*
*Her eyes close and her hand drops to the ground. Then she's gone.*

---

*"Christine?"*

I open my eyes, my wife is looking down at me. I sit up and Korra sets a tray down on the bed and kisses me on the head. "I made you breakfast."

"Thanks." I say, returning her kiss with one of my own.

Korra sits down next to me and puts her head down on my shoulder. I start to eat breakfast. I let out a sigh.

"What's wrong?" Korra asks.

"Well, it's been ten years since Kuvira's death and I…" I stop and tears flow down my face. "I miss her so much."

"I know," Korra says. "I miss her too." I cry and Korra holds me in her arms.

## Chapter 2

Later that day me and Korra walk to the living room with our kids. I smile at Kuvira. "Happy fourteenth birthday!"

Kuvira smiles and gives me a hug. "You remembered!"

"Of course I remembered." I say.

"Well, you forgot about Baatar's birthday last year." Korra says.

"That was one time, Korra. *One* time!" I say.

"What about me," Su says, grinning. "You forgot about my fourteenth birthday last month."

"*One* time!"

Everyone starts laughing.

I sigh and shake my head. "Oy!"

"Alright, kids," Korra says. "That's enough."

Together we walk out of the house and to the noodle restaurant. We go inside and walk to our tables. We sit down and Bolin walks over to the table and sets down five bowls of noodles. Then he sits down next to us.

"How have you guys been?" he asks.

"We've been great!" Su says.

Bolin nods. "That's wonderful."

"How are things between you and Opal?" I ask.

"Oh we're grand," he says. "Everything has been great."

"That's great!" Korra says.

We start to eat and when I'm done Bolin pulls me aside to talk to me. "What's going on with you?" he says.

"What do you mean?"

"You seem… depressed." he says.

"I'm sorry," I say. "Its just… well even though its been ten years since Kuvira's death, I've had a really hard time getting past it."

"I understand." he says.

He gives me a hug and we return to the rest of the group. After we're done we all go to the train station and get on the train. We arrive in Zaofu. We walk to the Beifong estate and when we get there, I knock on the door. It opens moments later and we walk inside. Lin leads us to the living room and we sit down. I watch as Baatar Jr., Su and Kuvira run outside and start to spar with each other.

"Can I talk to you and Korra for a minute?" Lin asks.

"Sure." I say.

Lin sighs and pulls out a folder and hands it to me. "This was taken a week ago."

I pull out the photo and take a look at it. "That's impossible," I say. "It can't be her."

"I don't know how Su could've survived. But she did." Lin says.

I shake my head.

"I don't understand," Korra says. "How is this possible?"

"I don't know, but what I do know it that I need to keep an eye on the situation and I'll update you on any new developments."

"Thank you." I say.

## Chapter 3

Me, Korra and Lin are talking to one another, when the kids run inside. "Mom!" Baatar says. "You're going to want to see this!"

"What is it?" I ask, glancing a nervous look at Korra.

"I can't explain it," he says. "You have to see it for yourself."

I give Korra another nervous look and we get up. We run outside and Suyin and Kuvira run up to me and give me and Korra a hug. "What's going on?" I say.

"We were sparring with each other and then someone walked up and said that they wanted to see you." Baatar says.

"Where are they?" I ask.

"Over there." Baatar says, pointing towards the sparring circle.

Korra and I start to walk over to the sparring circle and kids start to follow us. Korra turns and says to the kids. "You should probably go and stay with Lin. Just to be safe."
They nod and run back to the house.

Me and Korra continue to walk over to the sparring circle. When we get there start to look around, but we don't see anyone. I turn towards Korra and shrug. I start to leave but then Korra says. "Christine, look!"

I turn around and my jaw drops. *"Su?!"*

"Hello, Christine." she says.

"How…" I croak, but I manage to push the words out. "How are you alive?"

She walks over to me and gives me a hug. "Does it matter?"

We break apart and start to make our way back to the house, but on our way there Su stops me. I turn and look at her and Korra stops as well. "Its okay, Korra." I say, keeping my eyes on Su. "Just go back to the house, I'll be there in a minute."

Korra nods. "Okay."
She leaves and goes back to the house.

Su gives me another hug and I hold her tightly. "I missed you so much." I say.

"I know," she says. "I know, but I'm sorry I have to do this."
I start to pull away and I feel a sharp pain in my neck. I groan and fall to the ground. My eyes start to feel heavy and I pass out.

---

I let out groan as I start to regain consciousness. I put my hand on my head. "Ow!"
Once my vision clears I see Korra lying next to me. I try to wake her up, but its no use. She's out cold.

"Don't worry, she's fine," a voice says. "She just got knocked out. Like the rest of us."

I turn towards the voice and jump back in fear when I realize who it is. "Evelyn?"

"Hey." she says, groaning as she tries to sit up straight.
I drop into a bending stance.

"Woah!" she says. "Calm down. We're on the same side."

"Where's Su?" I say.

Evelyn scoffs. "That was me you idiot. I was dressed like Su so that I could kidnap you, but that didn't work out as well as I thought it would."

*"What?!"*

"Yeah," Evelyn says. "I know. Shocking right?"

"Where are we?" I ask.

"If I knew, then we wouldn't be here now." she says.

*Where are we?*


## Chapter 4

I pace back and forth in the cell. Evelyn watches me for a moment and then glances back at Korra. She still hasn't woken up yet. Evelyn checks Korra for a pulse and she nods at me. I let out a sigh of relief. But I still don't know where we are. Well I know that we're on a train, but I don't know where we're going.

"Do you know where the kids are?" I ask Evelyn.

"They're in a heavily guarded cell on the other side of the train."

"Do you know who took us?"

She shakes her head. "No. I don't."

I sigh and turn back to Korra. I give her a slight shake, but still I receive no response.

I turn back to Evelyn. "We will get out of here. I promise."

"You sure about that?"

"Yeah."

"Remarkable," says a voice. "I never thought that you two would ever consider working together." I turn around and see a women with blonde hair that is tied back into a ponytail and is wearing a gray t-shirt with a black overtop coat. She walks over to the glass and I notice that her eye color is blue. But I still don't know who she is.

"Who are you?" I ask.

"Who am I? I'm the reason you're still alive." The women says.

"Okay," I say. "But what is your name?"

The women laughs. "Now why would I tell you that?"

"Christine," Evelyn says and I turn to look at her. "Don't talk to her."

"Why?" I ask.

Evelyn gets up and walks over and stands beside me. "Because, this women is the most evil, psychotic, manipulative person ever. Isn't that right Cipher?"

"Wait, Cipher?" I say, glancing at Evelyn. "You mean the crazy hacker that can manipulate anything that has a chip in it?"

"Precisely," Cipher says. "Now, I want you guys to work for me."

I laugh. "Oh boy, this again. You know, I've heard this saying a lot, so I'll make this simple for you. No we won't work for you."

Cipher sighs and opens the door to our cell and walks inside. She pulls out a phone and hands it to me. "Oh, you're going to want to work for me. You're going to betray those you love and shatter your family." she walks out of the cell. "Oh and Christine, I wouldn't mention this to anyone in your family."

I put her phone in my pocket and run out of the cell after her. "Let them go!" I yell.

She stops and I jerk my arm forward, but Cipher side-steps my attack and twitches her fingers ever so slightly. My body comes to a jerking halt and I scream in pain. My limbs twisting in inhuman ways. Cipher motions her hand to the left and I fly back into the cell, crashing head first into the wall. I land on the ground with a thud and the last I see is Cipher walking away from the cell. Then darkness surrounds me.

Chapter 5

*"Christine, please wake up!"*

I groan and slowly come to my senses. I breathe in deeply and my eyes flicker open. I cough and roll onto my side. I wince at the pain in my ribs and head and lie there on the floor, hacking and coughing out blood. It trails down my chin and onto the otherwise pristine electrified platinum floor. A pair of arms wrap around me and help me sit up straight. Though my ribs sting and I let out a gasp of pain.

"Hold still for a moment." A voice says.

I feel something cool and soothing on my ribs and the pain starts to subside. At least for now. I look at the women in front of me and I'm in to much pain to be shocked at who it is. "Evelyn?" I say.

"Hey."

"Wha— what are you doing?"

"I'm healing you," she says with a small smile. "Now would you sit still for a moment?"

I stop moving and Evelyn starts healing my head. I let out a sigh as my head starts to feel better. I look over at Korra, she still hasn't moved in the two days we've been here. I groan as I crawl over to her. I check her pulse. Its slower than normal. I gently shake her but there's no response.

"Evelyn get over here!" I say. "Hurry!"

She comes over and kneels down beside me."What is it?"

"I think that her Avatar spirit is weakened and we need to fix it quickly."

"How do we do that?" Evelyn asks.

"I need some of your water."

She nods and bends the water out of her flask. I bend it into my hands and kneel over Korra. I take a deep breath and enter The Avatar State. Soon the water around my hands is covering Korra's entire body and for a moment it glows bright blue. The glow fades a moment later and I check Korra's pulse, it's weaker than before.

I look over at Evelyn. "I'm going to go into The Spirit World to see if I can find Korra, could you watch over my body until I get back?"

Evelyn nods.

I sit down on the floor and take a deep breath. Soon I feel the world fade away.

---

I open my eyes and see the wonderful colors of The Spirit World. I look around and see Korra standing by the tree of time. I run over to her. "Korra!" I yell.

She looks back at me. "Christine!" she yells back.

I run over to her and she gives me a hug. "What are you doing?" I ask.

"Trying to figure out how Su survived." she says.

"Oh... well," I pause, take a deep breath and then continue. "You need to come back to the physical world like now."

"Why?"

"Its hard to explain," I take another deep breath. "But we need to go now."

"Alright." she says.

Soon I feel The Spirit World slip away.

Chapter 6

I open my eyes and look over at Korra. I get up and pull her in for a kiss. She sighs when she pulls away. I smile at her, but she's not looking at me, instead her gaze is focused on something else. She get's up and starts to walk. My eyes settle on her target. I get up and try to block her but she just pushes past me and continues to walk towards Evelyn. I stand, unable to speak as Korra moves closer to her. Soon Evelyn realizes what's going on and she get's up. She begins to back away and soon she's backed against the wall.

"Where's Su and our kids?" Korra asks, angrily.

"I…" Evelyn stammers. "Its hard to explain."

"Where's—" Korra's anger overtakes her and she thrusts her fist forward. It crashes into Evelyn face. She reels back, hitting her head against the wall. Korra brings her hand back again and Evelyn puts her hands up to block the next blow.

Finally I come to my senses and I run forward. "Korra, stop!"

What the hell is going on?" Korra yells, as she struggles against my hold. I push her away and plant myself between her and Evelyn. Evelyn straightens her jaw and starts to walk towards Korra. I put a hand up and she stops. I look at the two women. They're scowling at each other.

"Enough!" I say. "Will you two just listen to me for a moment."

"Fine," Korra growls. "But you'd better have a good explanation for this."

"I do," I say. I look from Korra to Evelyn and back again. I sigh and say. "Well, first off Su never came back. Evelyn dressed up like her so she could talk to me, but it ended being that she knocked me out and she was knocked as well. When I woke up, I was here and Evelyn was with me."

"But that doesn't give me a reason *not* to beat the crap out of her." Korra says.

"I wasn't finished!" I snap.

Korra steps back in shock. "Sorry." she mutters.

I take another deep deep breath and continue speaking. "I always thought that Evelyn was top dog of her group. But as it turns out, there's another person who's even higher up than her. Her name is Cipher."

Korra's eyes widen and her jaw drops. "Are meaning to tell me that Evelyn works for a psychotic computer hacker?"

"I *used* to work for her." Evelyn says, defensively.

Korra glares at her for a second, but then looks back at me. "Where are our kids?"

"From what Evelyn has told me, they're in a heavily guarded cell on the other side of the train."

Korra nods. "Are they okay?"

"I'm not sure." I say.

"Do you know where we are going?"

"I'm not sure, but we need to be careful as to how we plan our escape." As I speak both Korra and Evelyn look up and my voice trails off. I laugh nervously. "Cipher's standing right behind me, isn't she?" I turn around. "Of course."

Cipher just stares at me, emotionless.

I smile nervously. "Hey Cipher, how are you doing?"

"Did I just hear you guys talking about a plan to escape?" she asks.

"No," I say. "Not at all."

I stand completely still for a moment, then I make a break for the cell door, but just as I step out, my body starts to twitch. I groan at the pain and moments later I'm thrown back into the cell. But before I crash into the ground, Evelyn catches me.

"Tsk, tsk, tsk," Cipher says. "Not so smart are you?"
She turns and leaves, locking the cell door behind her and leaving us once again all alone.

Chapter 7
*"Christine?"*
I groan and sit up. My head is pounding. My vision clears and Korra kneels down beside me. She bends a blob of water over my head. Moments later the throbbing in my head disappears. I cough and a drop of blood drops onto the floor. I sit up and lean my head against the wall.

"Where are we?"
"In Erudite headquarters." Evelyn says.
I look at Evelyn and laugh. "Of course."
"What so funny?"
"Well, I just find it kinda ironic that you always put me in here, you know and now…" I chuckle again. "Now we're prisoners in the same cell."
Evelyn rolls her eyes. "Haha, very funny."
I bump her shoulder. "Come on, lighten up. I was just trying to make the best out of our situation."
"Yeah?" Evelyn says. "Well I don't think now is the time. We should probably focus on staying alive."
"Don't worry," I say, turning to Korra. "We'll—" I stop mid-sentence when I realize that she's crying. "Korra!" I say. I kneel down beside her. "Wh— what happened? Why are you crying? Where are the kids?"
Korra wipes her eyes and sniffles. "They're… they're not here. Cipher has them. I don't know where they are now."
I step back, my eyes widen and the feeling of fear creeps its way through my chest. "No."
Tears start to form in my eyes and I collapse onto the ground in a sobbing heap. It felt like it would never end.

---

*"Come on!"* Kuvira let out a grunt as she slammed into the cell door again. "Come on door, budge!"
*Why would someone do this? Why capture us at all?* Kuvira thought. *What would our moms do?*
Kuvira stopped for a moment. *What would our moms do?* She thought again.
She looked at her brother and sister, her brother lay on the cell floor unconscious and Su sat beside him holding his hand. Kuvira breathed in deep and slammed into the door again. This time it opened and she cheered. She ran out of the cell, crashing into someone on her way out. Kuvira rubbed her head and looked up. Cipher stood above her, an evil grin creeping its way across her face. Kuvira started to back away into the cell and Cipher followed.
"What do you want?" Kuvira says, trying to sound as strong as possible, but instead her voice was barely a whisper.
Cipher said nothing, she just stared at the three teens, like a predator trying to decide whether or not to kill its prey.
"What do you want?" Kuvira asked, again.
"I want to make a deal with you guys." she says.
"What kind of deal?" Kuvira asked.
"Well…" Cipher says. "If you guys come work for me than I'll let your parents go."
Kuvira laughed. "Yeah, no." She ran passed Cipher and out of the cell, but then her body came to an abrupt halt. She squealed in pain.

Cipher walked in front of her and held up a needle, it was full of simulation serum. "Aren't you quite the troublemaker. Here I'll make it simple for you. I need to inject you with this."
Kuvira's voice returned just in time for her to scream.

Chapter 8
I pace back and forth in the cell. I take a deep breath and focus on the platinum within the cell. I breathe out and try to bend the platinum away from the walls, but the electricity shocks me and I groan as it courses through me. I hunch forward and breathe out deeply. I shake out my hands and try again. But I receive another shock. I slump to the floor and breathe in deeply.
"What are you doing?"
"Trying to get us out of the cell." I say.
"By doing what?" Evelyn asks. "Electrocuting yourself each and every time you try?"
"If that's what it takes." I say.
"You're pathetic. All you're doing is hurting yourself even more than you should."
I take another deep breath and Evelyn grabs onto my arm. She shakes her head. I sigh and stop. I look over at her and she nods. I sigh and tears start to form in my eyes and she gives me a hug. I bury my head into her shoulder. We break apart and I walk over to Korra. She groans and sits up. I kneel down and give her a hug.
"Hey." she says.
"Hey." I say.
Korra groans again and puts her hand on her stomach. I frown and look over at Evelyn. Evelyn gives me a confused look and walks over to us. She kneels over Korra and bends a blob of water over her stomach. Korra groans again and puts her hands back onto her stomach.
"What are you doing?" Korra asks.
"Just hold still and relax," Evelyn says. "I'm just... oh."
"What?" Korra blinked in confusion. "What is it?"
Evelyn looks at me and then at Korra. "Korra you're..." she takes her hands away from Korra's stomach. "You're *pregnant!*"

---

Kuvira lets out another scream as the veins and muscles in her body bend and twitch. She tries to move but that only made the pain even more unbearable. *"Baatar!"* she screamed. *"Help me!"*
Baatar just stood where he was standing. *What am I supposed to do?* he thought.
Kuvira screamed again and Baatar's heart leaped into his throat. He started to walk forwards toward Cipher and she raised her hand, Baatar's entire body seized up and he groaned as his body bent and twitched. Cipher let out an evil laugh and Baatar tried to move and another wave of pain crashed over him. He groaned.
*"Baatar!"* Kuvira screamed again. *"Help me!"*
"I..." he says, looking over at Kuvira and Su. "I can't. I'm... I'm not strong enough."
"Yes you are," Su says. "You just have to believe that you are."
Kuvira screamed again and Su kept on urging him to do something. He struggled against the bloodbending grip again and another wave of agonizing pain hit him.
"Let..." he groaned again and he struggled again, harder this time. "Let her go!"
He broke out of Cipher's grip and he let out a yell as he charged into her. Baatar slammed into Cipher and she released Kuvira. Baatar charged at Cipher again and this time he was ready for her attacks. He sent out streams of his water and one of them stuck Cipher. She flew back and crashed onto the floor. Baatar let out another yell and twitched his fingers. Cipher came to an abrupt halt and she let out a groan.

Baatar flicked his wrist and she went flying into the opposite wall. She slumped to the floor and Baatar clenched his fingers harder and Cipher screamed louder.

## Chapter 9

My head snaps up at the sound of screaming. I look over at Evelyn. "What was that?"

"I don't know." she says.

Another scream ripped through the train and my heart jumps. I take a step back and charge at the door. I slam into it and it comes off its hinges and I run through the building, Evelyn follows me, carrying Korra with her as we run. Korra jerks awake and Evelyn sets her down. "You okay?" I say, putting my hand on her shoulder. She nods. We turn a corner and I come to an abrupt halt, my jaw drops. "Baatar?"

Both Su and Kuvira turn toward me and they run over to me and give me a hug. "Mom!" they exclaim. I look back and notice that Baatar didn't hear me.

"Baatar?" I say again. Baatar turns toward me and he runs over to me. But his grip on Cipher doesn't loosen and I just stare at her twitching body.

Cipher lets out another scream and Baatar turns around. He gasps and his bloodbending grip on her loosens, he scrambles backwards and I watch as Cipher slumps to the floor.

"Wha—" Baatar says, as he stumbles on words. "What...? Did I...?" He pushes the words out. "Did I just do that?" He looks back at me when he asks the question.

"Umm...," I say. "Well, you kinda, might have, possibly, undeniably, sort of, maybe, done that, maybe. Why?"

"Oh my god!" he says, "I...' his voice trails off and he struggles for words.

"Baatar, sweetie, you did nothing wrong." I say.

"Did nothing wrong!?" He pulls away from me. "What do you mean I did nothing wrong!? I... I almost killed her!"

"Okay, I agree, you almost killed her, but... on the other hand she tried to kill you, your sisters and me and Korra. So in this situation—which was a life or death situation—what you did was technically a good thing, but in any other situation, it wouldn't have been the best option." I sigh and look back at Evelyn. "Can you give me a hand here? I stuck at this."

She nods and as she passes me she says. "You do stuck at explaining this. Honestly, I'm surprised that the kids haven't gotten themselves in trouble yet," She pauses for a moment, then says. "Although this might explain why you've been in so many situations that are exactly like this current one."

"Oh, shut up." I say, with a grin. I bump her shoulder as she walks past.

Evelyn smirks at me and then turns back to Baatar. "Listen, kid," she says. "I know that this is not the ideal situation in which you wanted to be in. Believe me, I didn't want to be in this situation to begin with, in fact I never thought that I would be working with your parents and do you know why?"

Baatar shakes his head. "Why?" he asks.

"Well, once your parents and I were bitter enemies, did they ever tell you that?"

"No." he says.

Evelyn laughs and turns to me. "Well, it seems like you have quite the history to tell them."
I growl, but Korra puts a hand on my shoulder. I take a deep breath and calm down.

"As I was saying," Evelyn continues. "We started out as enemies and you know what I think that we're getting along quite well. Anyway my point is: We all get stuck in these situations and we have to make the best of them and we have to try our hardest, or else, what was the point? What's the point of trying to win? In fact, order cannot exist without chaos, because without either one of them, there is no balance. Do you get what I'm saying?"

Baatar nods and he walks over to me and Korra and he gives us both a hug. "I'm sorry." he says. "Its okay," I say. "Its okay."

## Chapter 10

When Baatar finally lets go, all his tears had run dry and he couldn't cry any longer. He walked over to his sisters and and gave them both a hug. When they break apart they walk over to us. Korra smiles and says. "Hey kids, guess what?"

"What?" They ask.

Korra smiles at us. "I'm having another baby."

"Cool!" Baatar and Su exclaim.

"That's wonderful!" I say.

Me, and the kids start to walk, with Evelyn carrying Korra behind us. We reach the hallway and turn a corner. We reach the main entrance. But just as we push open the front door I hear a gasp. We turn around and I instantly drop into a bending stance.

"Mom!" Kuvira yells. "Help!" She struggles against Cipher's bloodbending hold.

"Let her go!" I yell.

"Actually, I don't think I will." Cipher says, smirking. She pulls out a needle of simulation serum.

"Don't do it!" I yell.

"Mom!" Kuvira yells again. "Help me!"

I don't think I just run. Cipher thrusts the needle forward.

*"No!"* I scream.

I jump in front of Kuvira, pushing her out of the way and the needle plunges into my neck. I slump to the ground, but the serum doesn't take effect.

*Thank goodness,* I think. *But now I have to convince Cipher otherwise.*

"Christine?" Cipher says.

I get up and look at her. I walk over to her and she hands me a pair of electrified platinum handcuffs. She jerks her head toward Evelyn and Korra. I turn to look at them. With the handcuffs in hand, I turn and start to walk toward them. I try my best to act as if I was actually in a simulation. Evelyn, Korra and the kids start to back away slowly. I run forward and the kids scream. Korra steps in front of them and I stare her in the eye. She swallows nervously and I can see the fear in her eyes.

*I wish I could say something,* I think. *But I don't want to blow my cover just yet.*

I turn up the settings on the handcuffs and put them on Korra. She tries to metalbend out of them and they shock her. Her scream makes me want to cringe, but I know that if I blow my cover now, that Cipher will kill them and me. Korra charges at me and I duck as she tries to hit me. The handcuffs shock her again and she slumps to the ground. She breathes heavily and I yank her to her feet. She raises her foot and it slams into my chest. I groan. Korra pushes me back.

"Come on, Christine," she says. "I know you're in there somewhere."

"You're right." I say and I give her a kiss.

Korra pulls away in shock. "Christine?"

I nod.

"But how?" she asks.

"Because I was never under it." I whisper.

"Finish her off!" Cipher yells.

I turn and charge at her. Her eyes go wide, but before I can reach her she twitches her fingers and my body comes to a halt. I groan and I struggle, but Cipher's bloodbending grip is so tight that I can't even break free. She pulls out another needle of simulation serum and I have just enough strength to twist my foot and kick out a blast of fire. Cipher ducks and it misses her. Moments later though her grip on me falters and I drop to the floor. Cipher's body starts to twitch and I turn to see Evelyn bloodbending her. She walks up to Cipher and stares into her eyes for a moment. Then she lowers her hands and Cipher falls to the ground. Evelyn turns to me and gives me a hug. I bury my face into her shoulder, but moments later we hear an evil laugh.

"Evelyn, look out!"

Evelyn turns around and Cipher charges at her. Cipher grabs her and sticks a needle of death serum into her neck. Evelyn coughs and collapses onto the ground. Cipher takes that advantage to jump out the window and disappear.

I start to chase after her, but Korra holds me back. "We'll have another chance to get her." she says.

I nod and turn back to Evelyn, I kneel down beside her and she reaches up and grabs onto my hand. Her voice was raspy and weak. "If my life had no meaning, there was no reason not to end it."

I grip her hand tightly, my heart breaking. "So you ended it?"

"So I gave it meaning."

Evelyn's eyes fluttered and rolled back. Her hand went limp. I just sat there and I cried.

---

*Nine months later…*

The doctor walks into the room and me and Korra smile. "Its a girl!" he says.

"What are you going to name her?" The doctor asks.

"I think that we're going to name her Evelyn." Korra says, looking over at me and giving me a kiss.

---

I watch as all four kids spar with each other. I watch as Su and Kuvira shoot out chunks of earth and both Baatar and Evelyn send water blasts at each other. Korra walks up behind me and puts her arms around me. "Hey." she says.

"Hey." I say.

I turn to face her. She pulls me into a kiss and a moment later we break apart. When the kids are done sparring, we all walk back inside.

Tomorrow we may have to fight again, but for now we'll just have to take what comes and we'll do it as a family.

The Legend Of Korra Meets The Fate Of The Furious Part 4
(Book 13)

Chapter 1

*Five years later…*

I stand by Korra's bed, I hold onto her hand. The kids stand beside me. I take a deep breath and squeeze it. Her hand is ice cold. I look at her face and at the cannula in her nose, I look down at the hand that I'm holding, there's an IV in it. I look from her hand to the heart monitor. I watch as the life-support machine keeps her heart beating. I squeeze her hand again, hoping that it would bring her back. I was at home at the time of the crash, and Korra was on her way back from a meeting. Lin had told me that a car had been going one hundred twenty miles per hour when it T-boned Korra's car. Her car had rolled several times down a hill before coming to a stop. She was unconscious when the paramedics had found her. The driver of the other car fled from the scene after the crash.

"It was probably just an accident." Lin says.

I shake my head. "No. It wasn't. No one drives at a speed of a hundred twenty miles per hour only to crash into a car and then flee from the scene. Someone deliberately hit her." I lean over and kiss Korra's head. "I'm going to find and kill the bastard who did this. I love you Korra." I give her another kiss and walk out of the room. I walk out of the hospital. I get into my car and start to drive.

---

*I give Korra a kiss. "Have a safe trip!"*

*"I will!" she says.*

*She starts to drive away and I watch as her car fades into the distance.*

*"Stay safe." I whisper.*

---

*Korra let's out a sigh as she drives. It was night time. Korra pulls out her phone and dials Christine's phone number and puts it on speaker. It goes straight to voicemail. "Hey Christine," she says. "The meeting ran a little later than I expected, so I'll be a bit late coming home. Give the kids a hug and a kiss for me. I love you. Bye."*

*Korra turns a corner and she could see Chicago up ahead. She turns another corner and a car is driving in her direction. "Oh shit!" she says. "I need to get out—"*

*The oncoming car slams into the side of her car and it rolls off the road and down a hill. Korra starts to scream. Her car comes to a stop at the bottom of the hill. The other car revs its engine and drives off. Korra's vision went black.*

---

I put my hand on my head as I drive. I turn a corner and an oncoming car T-bones me. My car rolls and lands upside down. I gasp in pain. I put my hand on my head and it comes away sticky with blood. I undo my seatbelt and break the car window. I crawl out, but I my ribs scream in pain and I collapse onto the ground. I hear a car door open and then slam shut. Through my blurry vision I see someone walking towards me. I'm lifted off the ground and carried. The last thing I see is the inside of a car. Then I pass out.

Chapter 2

I groan as consciousness returns to me. I roll onto my side and cough. My eyes flicker open and I put hand on my head, pain pulses through my head and I groan again. I put my other hand on my ribs and let out a sharp breath. I sit up and the room spins. I put my hand out and it brushes against the floor. I roll onto my back and close my eyes. A breath hitches in my throat and I groan at the pain again. I pinch the bridge of my nose, hoping that it will help relieve some off the pressure in my head. It doesn't. I look around. I'm in a cell on a train. I know that much. But what I don't know is who took me and where we are going. I get up off the ground, slower this time. When I get to my knees, I take a deep breath. My ribs scream in pain and I gasp.

"Here," A voice says. "Maybe this will help."

I feel an ice pack on my sides and moments later the pain in my rib cage disappears.

I sigh. "Thank you."

"No problem." The voice says.

*Wait.* I think. *I know that voice!*

I jerk away from the person healing me and put my hands on my ribs. I crawl backwards and my eyes go wide.

*"No!"* I scream.

---

Kuvira, Baatar and Su all give Korra a hug and then walk out of the hospital. Korra still hadn't woken up. Lin stayed with Korra to make sure that she was safe. The kids start to walk home. On the way though a car pulled beside them and the window rolled down.

"Hey, kids!" Baatar Sr. says. "I need to talk to you."

The kids jump and then say. "Oh hey, Baatar."

"I need to talk to you guys," he says, urgently. "Get in the car."

Su and Kuvira look at each other and Baatar Jr. and Evelyn do the same. After a moment's hesitation they walk over to the car and get inside.

"What's going on?" Su asks.

"It's about your mother." he says.

"Korra?" Su asks.

"No." he says. "Christine."

"Did something happen?" Kuvira asks.

Baatar Sr. pulls into the driveway of his house and the kids get out.

"Did something happen?" Kuvira asks again.

Baatar sighs and turns to face them. "Your mother's been kidnapped."

*"What!?"* Baatar Jr. exclaims. "By who?"

"I'm not sure," he says. "That's what I'm trying to figure out."

The group walks into the house and Baatar Sr. walks up to Wing and Wei. "How's the search going?"

"Not so good," Wing says. "So far we haven't been able to locate where Christine is or who took her."

"Damn it!" Baatar Sr. says, slamming his fist down on the table. "Well, keep an eye on everything, we'll find her eventually."

Chapter 3

I back away from Cipher and she takes a step forward. I hit the wall and she takes another step forward. She puts her hand on my cheek, turning my head from side to side. "You're not as injured as I thought you would be."

"What are you doing?" I ask, my voice hoarse.

"Making sure you didn't break anything." Cipher says.

"Well, my ribs broke when my car flipped." I say, swatting her hand away.

"Yes, that was very unfortunate, but on the other hand, it had to be done."

"Why?"

"'Cause we have work to get done." she says.

*I know where this is going.* I think

"Why do you think that I am going to help you?" I say.

"You have no other option that's why."

I raise my eyebrows. "But you always used to say that everything is a choice and that nothing is necessary."

She sighs. "I'll admit that is what I used to say, but desperate times, require desperate measures and currently these times are becoming more desperate."

"How about you let me go and leave me and my family alone for once." I say.

"I can't do that." she says.

"Why?" I say.

"Just because, I can't."

I sigh. I hate it when she does this.

"You have to understand that I'm a good person, Christine. I don't mean you any harm."

I scoff. "Right, you won't hurt me. You're going to have to try better than that to convince me that you're a good person."

She sighs again. "I guess there's only thing left for me to say to make you trust me and if that doesn't work... then I'll let you go."

"Oh yeah and what's that?" I say.

"I'm the one who crashed into Korra's car, I was the one who put her in the hospital."

"*What!?*" I exclaim. "What makes you think that I'm going to trust you now?"

"'Cause I'm the only one who can properly heal Korra. No matter what they do in hospital, the doctors won't be able to heal her. Even if she is on life-support and even if the best waterbenders in the world try to heal her, it won't work. I'm the only one who can save her."

I open my mouth to say something, but my words fail me. I sigh and I look at her. "Okay."

She smiles. "I knew you would come around."

I nod. "Yeah."

Chapter 4

Su, Kuvira and Evelyn watch as Baatar Jr. paces back and forth. The kids were just outside the living room in the Beifong estate, waiting for Baatar Sr. and his sons to tell them their mother's location. Christine had been missing for just over a week and Korra was still on life-support in the hospital. The doctors feared that Korra might never wake up and that they would have to take her off life-support. Lin pleaded with the doctors to keep her on it. Baatar paced faster and faster. He was worried for both of his mother's, as were the other kids. The door to the living room opened and Baatar quit pacing. Baatar Sr. walked out.

Kuvira jumped to her feet. "What happened? Did you find them?"

"Unfortunately, no. We're still unable to locate them," Baatar Sr. sighs. "I'm sorry."

"Its okay." Baatar Jr. says.

"Its like she just disappeared." Su says.

Baatar Sr. is about to say something when Wing and Wei come running out of the living room. "You guys might want to come and see this."

Baatar Jr. and his sisters jump to their feet. "What is it?"

"Come on." Both the twins say.

The kids follow them into the living room and they walk over to a computer. "We found Christine." Wei says.

"Really? Where is she?" Kuvira asks.

"Cipher kidnapped her."

*"What?!"* Baatar Jr. exclaims.

"We have to find her!" Su exclaims.

"But we don't know where she is even." Wei says.

"Wait, what?" Evelyn frowns. "But you said—"

Wei interrupts her. "What I said was that we found surveillance footage from where she was last spotted, but we have no idea where she is now."

"Oh," Evelyn says. "My apologies."

"Its okay," Wing says. "On the other hand, at least we now have a clue as to where she might be."

"Well, let's go." Kuvira says, walking to the door.

"Wait, hold up." Baatar Sr. says.

"Why?" Kuvira asks, turning around. "If we have a lead then we need to go."

"Yes, I know," Baatar Sr. says. "But we have to make a plan first. We can't just run off without a plan."

Kuvira groans. "Fine."

---

I let out a yell as I blast fire at Cipher, she uses her water to stop it, creating a cloud of steam. I run at her and tackle her to the ground, but she's too quick and she shoves me backwards. I let out a gasp as I slam into the ground. My ribs burn. I jump to my feet and run at her again. Cipher side-steps me and I duck as she sends out a stream of water. I thrust my fist forward to release a jet of fire, but I'm stopped before I'm even able to make smoke, my arm begins to twitch and I groan in pain. My body lifts off the ground under the force of Cipher's bloodbending grip. I scream in pain as my limbs bend near their breaking point. Dark spots crowd my vision and then everything go black.

Chapter 5

The kids pace back and forth. Baatar Sr. is talking to Wing and Wei about a possible plan to find Christine. Baatar Jr. lets out a frustrated sigh and sat down on the floor. He put his head in his hands. *I need to find mom. I* just *have to.*
The front door opens. Baatar and his sisters look up and see Lin Beifong walking into the house. Lin walked up to the kids and she let out a sigh.

"Any news on mom's condition?" Baatar Jr. asked.
She didn't need to say anything the look in her eyes told them everything, Korra was running out of time. Lin still said nothing. Instead she walked over to the living room doors and pushed them open and the kids watched as she disappeared into the room.

---

"What plan do you guys have?" Lin asked, walking up to Baatar Sr.
"That's what we're trying to figure out." Baatar Sr. says. "Do you have any updates on Korra's condition?"
"Yes I do." Lin says.
Baatar raised his eyebrows in surprise. "Oh," he says. "What is it?"
Lin sighed. "I spoke to the doctors at the hospital, they said that if we can't find a healer in the next week then they'll take Korra off life-support."
*"What!?"* Baatar Sr. exclaimed. "But... but they can't do that, we still need to find Christine."
"Well, then we better find her pretty damn fast because we don't have much time." Lin says.
Baatar Sr. sighed. "Well then let's go."

---

I drive faster and faster, I look at my speedometer, I'm already going two hundred forty miles per hour. However, I lose control of my car and it crashes. I break the window and as I crawl out. I hear a *clink!* I look to the side and see a round metal cylinder rolling to a stop by the side of the car. I hear a beeping noise and I jerk away from the car. The cylinder explodes and the force of the blast sends me flying down a hill. I tumble to the bottom and land with a thud. I hear footsteps and I shoot out a metal strip. I hear a gasp and then something sharp connects with my side. I groan. I try to move but I'm in so much pain. I black out.

---

I jerk awake. Thank god it was only a dream. I roll onto my side and slap my hand onto the ground. I let out a grunt as I push myself up. *That's the last time I'm going to underestimate Cipher's power.* I think. I sit on my knees and hunch forward, my body was still so sore. I hear footsteps and I look up. I see Cipher walking toward the cell. I let out a sigh. Cipher walks into the cell. "Hey." she says.
"Hey." I say, clutching my ribs.
"There's some other people hear to see you." she says.
I frown. "Other people..." My voice trails off when I see them. I watch as Kuvira's parents walk into the cell.
"Hey Christine." her father says.
My eyes go wide and I look from Kuvira's father to her mother. "What are you guys doing here? Shouldn't you be with the Governor, helping him run the state of Yi?"
"Well..." her father says. "We were until Cipher offered us a better job."
"Why on earth would you guys want to work with Cipher?"
"Besides," Kuvira's mother says. "We wanted to help her capture you."
"Why?" I ask.
"Because you killed our daughter!" Kuvira's father yelled.
"I didn't kill Kuvira, Evelyn did." I say.
"You may not have killed Kuvira directly, but you were the reason that she died!" Kuvira's mother screamed.

Kuvira's parents start to walk into the cell and I back up. I hit the wall. Kuvira's parents charge at me and all I can do is watch.

Chapter 6

I duck as Kuvira's parents swing at me. Both her parents take turns trying to attack me. Kuvira's father lets out a yell as he swings his arm at me. I duck and grab onto his arm. I push him back and he stumbles backward.

"Look, I'm sorry you lost Kuvira," I say as I avoid another blow. "But as I've been trying to say, I didn't kill her!"

I block another blow and I kick out a blast of fire. Kuvira's parents jump out of the way and I take that advantage to run out of the cell. Cipher tries to bloodbend me and I dodge the attack. I run through the train. I hear footsteps behind me and I continue to run. I reach the front of the train and I break open the window. I lean out the window and hold onto the windowsill. I'm just about to jump when something wraps around my ankle. I'm pulled back into the train and I thrust my arm forward, sending out a chunk of earth from outside. It slams into Kuvira's mom's chest and she screams. She let's go. I'm about to jump when my body starts to bend and twitch. I scream and Cipher bloodbends me harder. She motions her hand and I slam into the wall. I fall to the ground and I black out.

Something smacks me hard in the face and I jerk awake. I let out a yell. "Ow!" I reposition my jaw and look up. Cipher stands over me. "What do you want?" I say, my voice hoarse.

Cipher yanks me to my feet and I swing at her. She jerks back and curls her hand into a fist, I jerk back just in time. I shoot a platinum strip at her and she dives out of the way.

"I want to make you a deal." Cipher says and I stop my attacks.

"What kind of deal?" I ask.

"How about we call a truce?"

"What!? Why?"

"Well, as I told you earlier I'm the only one that can save Korra."

"Like I would believe you." I growl.

"You have to trust me."

"No way."

I'm about to run at her when I hear a rumbling sound. The rumbling becomes louder and moments later the cell door bursts open.

"Let her go!" A voice yells.

I look over at the person who the voice belongs to. "Junior, Kuvira, you kids are okay!"

The kids all drop into a bending stance. "Let her go!" they yell again.

Cipher starts to run but Baatar Jr. twitches his fingers and Cipher's body seizes up. "You're not going anywhere!" he yells. With a swift motion of his hands, Baatar sent Cipher crashing into the wall.

Baatar and the girls run over to me and give me a hug. "We missed you so much mom."

"I know," I say. When we break apart I sigh. "So... How's Korra doing?"

The kids look at one another. Kuvira sighs and says. "The doctors are going to take her off life-support today."

*"What?!"* I exclaim. Fear pulses through my chest. I grab onto their hands and together we run out of the cell. We run out of Erudite headquarters and towards the hospital. I just hope that we make it there in time.

Chapter 7

Lin ran towards the Emergency Room, she had just got word that the kids had found Christine. Now she needs to stop the doctors from taking Korra off life-support. She bursts through the door, just as the doctors were wheeling Korra's hospital bed out of her room.

"Wait, stop!" Lin says, urgently.

The doctors stopped and looked at her. "What's going on, Chief?"

"We've…" Lin takes a deep breath and continues speaking. "We've found Christine."

"Where is she?" the doctors ask.

"She'll be here soon." Lin says.

---

I run faster and faster. I push open the doors to the hospital and I run towards the ICU. When I get there I see Lin, and the two nurses, with Korra on a hospital bed. "Wait, stop!" I say.

Lin turns toward me. "Oh thank god you're here." she says.

"You can't take Korra off life-support." I say.

"But she's been on it for the past two weeks." One of the doctors says.

"Yes, but I know that I can bring her back." I say.

"Alright. Try your best then."

I walk over to Korra and take a deep breath. I bend out a blob of water and then enter The Avatar State. The water around Korra glows bright blue and moments later Korra starts to cough. When she's finished coughing, she opens her eyes and looks over at me.

"Christine?" she says, weakly.

"Hi." I say.

"Wha— what happened?" she asks.

"I'll tell you later," I say. "There's just too much to tell you."

Korra pulls me in for a kiss and when we break apart, she says. "I love you."

"I love you too." I say.

"Mom!"

Me and Korra look up and see the kids running into the living room. Baatar, Kuvira, Evelyn, and Suyin all give Korra a hug. "We missed you so much."

"I know," Korra says, returning the hug. "I missed you guys too."

---

I finish telling Korra what happened three weeks ago. I tell her about Cipher and Kuvira's parents. I tell her about her "car accident" and then me being kidnapped as well as my constant battle with Cipher. I also tell her about how the kids found and saved me from Cipher.

"Wow." she says.

"I know," I say. "When I arrived at the hospital, Lin was already there begging them to keep you on life-support. I told the doctor's that I could heal you, but they were a little uneasy at first. But they eventually let me do my work and now look where we are," I look down. "Well, I mean you're in a wheelchair."

Korra chuckles.

I laugh. "But what I mean is that, at least you're alive."

"Yeah." she says, pulling me down for a kiss. When we break apart she asks. "So, how long am I going to be in this wheelchair?"

"A few more days." I say.

"Okay." she says.

Moments later our kids run into the room. Baatar and Evelyn give Korra a hug and Su and Kuvira give me a hug. "We love you mom." The kids say.

"We love you too." Me and Korra say.

Chapter 8

Later that evening Lin comes over to check on us. "How are you doing Korra?" she asks.

"I'm doing great," Korra says. "I'm only in this wheelchair for a couple more days."

Lin nods and then turns to me. "Cipher's been locked up, so don't be expecting anymore trouble from her from now on."

I nod. "Thank you, Lin."

"No problem," she turns to leave, but then stops. "Oh and Korra."

"Yes?" she says.

"I just thought that I should let you know that everything in still in order for the trip next week."

"Okay, thank you." Korra says.

Lin smiles and walks out of the house

I furrow my eyebrows in confusion. "What trip?" I ask.

Korra smiles. "You'll see."

---

I wheel Korra into the bedroom and I help her out of the wheelchair and she stands without any problems. She gives me a hug. We hold each other for a moment longer and when she lets go she wraps her arms around my waist. I smile and she grins. My eyes go wide as she pulls me onto the bed. She pulls me in for a kiss and when we break apart she smiles. "I love you." she says.

"I love you too." I say.

---

The next morning Korra and I walk downstairs with our kids and have breakfast. Afterwards, we get ready for our trip. Korra goes into the closet by the door and grabs our winter jackets. The kids put their coats on and Korra hands me mine. "Here you go." she says.

I give her a confused look and put it on. We hear the honk of a car horn and we look outside. There's a car parked beside the sidewalk. Korra walks outside and me and the kids follow her. The car window rolls down. "Hey, Lin." Korra says.

"Hey, guys," she says. "Your already to go?"

Korra nods. "Yes, we are."

We all pile into the car and Korra sits in the passenger seat, while me and the kids get into the back. I get in and close the door. At that exact moment I realize that I'm squished against the door. "Um, Lin," I say. "There's not enough room for all of us."

"Don't worry, I got it." Korra says.

She gets out and I open the door. I hop out and Su hops into the front. I hop back in and Korra gets in as well. "Umm, Korra?" I say. "There's not enough room."

"Don't worry," she says. "There will be in a second." She gets in and she sits on my lap.

"Really?" I say, raising an eyebrow at her.

"I told you there would be enough room." she says with a playful smirk. She starts to bounce up and down on my lap.

"Korra, will you please— *oof!*" Korra bounces down really hard on my lap and I look up at her. "Really?"

She starts to laugh and Lin starts to drive. I enjoy the rest of the ride to wherever we are going.

Chapter 9

We arrive in Zaofu and drive to the Beifong estate. Korra get's out of the car and says. "I'll be right back."

She goes inside the house and moments later she comes back out with Wing and Wei as well as Huan, Opal and Baatar Sr. she talks to them for a moment and then get's back into the car and sits on my lap again. The rest of the Beifong family get into their car and we start to drive.

We arrive in The South Pole and get out of the car. The kids and Lin are trailing behind us. I start to shiver and I take a deep breath. I warm up instantly—one of the upsides to being a firebender is being able to keep yourself warm. We start to walk and I give Korra questioning look. "Why are we in The South Pole?" I ask.

"You'll see." Korra says.

We arrive at the southern spirit portal and I look at Korra in confusion. "Wait, we're going to The Spirit World? What are earth for?"

Korra looks back at us and then at Lin. Lin looks at the rest of us in confusion, but then shrugs.

"Like I said, you'll see." Korra says, grabbing my hand. She guides me into The Spirit World with everyone else in tow.

I look at The Spirit World in awe and I hear the gasps of our kids behind me. "Whoa! Cool!" they exclaim. "I've always wanted to see The Spirit World!"

We arrive a cabin and Korra leads us up to the front door. I give Korra another confused look. "Korra, what's going on?" While we could be here to make sure The Spirit World was safe, that wouldn't explain all the secrecy. Something else was going on here.

Korra smiles at me and takes my hand, leading us towards the front of the cabin. "You'll see in a minute, Christine. I promise."

I look back at our kids and then at the rest of the Beifong family. I turn back to Korra and she smiles and leads us into the house. We walk to the living room of the cabin and Lin still looks confused. "Okay, seriously Korra, what are we…" Her voice trails off and I follow her gaze across the room. My jaw drops. "

Su?!" Me, Baatar Sr. and Lin say at the same time.

Su smiles at us. "Hey, guys."

"Mom?!" Opal and the rest of the Beifong family exclaim.

Opal and her brothers run up to Su and give her a hug.

Kuvira tugs on my shirt. "Who's that, mom?"

"Huh, oh! This is Su. She looked after me when I ran away from home." I say.

Kuvira and the other kids smile. "Cool!"

They run up to her and give her a hug. Su smiles at me and says. "You have kids!"

"Yeah," I say, then I point at Su. "That's Su. I named her after you." I point at Kuvira, Baatar and Evelyn. "Then there's Kuvira, that's Baatar Jr. and that one's Evelyn."

Su is about to say something when a new voice pipes up. "Christine? Is that you?"

I look over at the person who the voice belonged to. "Kuvira?!"

Kuvira smiles and walks up to me, she gives me a hug and I bury my face in her shirt. She let's go and I look behind her. I see the silhouette of another person. The person steps forward and that's when I see him. "Baatar!"

"Hello, Christine." he says.

Chapter 10

I stand there speechless, I try to speak but I'm too shocked. I try again and end up sputtering instead. Baatar Jr. walks up to me and gives me a hug. I stand there too stiff and shocked to move. Soon I relax and I lean into him. Baatar holds me close and when I pull away I smile at him. I turn around and grab onto his hand. With my other hand I do the same thing with Kuvira. "I wanna show you guys something."

We walk over to the kids and I point at them in turn. "That's Su, that one in the middle is Baatar Jr.," I turn back to Baatar. "Me and Korra named him after you," I point at Kuvira. "This one's Kuvira and the one standing beside her is Evelyn."

"Awww, they're cute." Baatar and Kuvira say.

"I know." I say.

"But I have a question." Baatar Jr. asks.

"What's that?"

"If my name is Baatar Jr. and I'm the original one, does that make me Baatar Sr. or Baatar Jr. *Jr.* and if it makes me Baatar Sr. than what is my father? Would he be Baatar Sr. *Sr.?*"

"Uh… I'm not really sure."

Kuvira laughs. "Yeah, so what does that make me? Kuvira *Sr.?* I'm not that *old!*"

I groan. "I don't know. Ugh. You guys are giving me a headache."

"Sorry." Baatar says.

He gives me another hug and when we break apart, Korra walks up and puts her hand on my shoulder. I squeeze her hand. Kuvira walks over to Korra and gives her a hug. "Hey." she says.

"Hey." Korra says.

"Thanks for looking after Christine." Kuvira says.

"No problem."

Kuvira says. "You did the one thing I always struggled with, you kept her safe."

"Thanks." Korra says.

Korra and Kuvira hug one more time and when they break apart, she walks back to me and the kids follow. We walk to the door, but just before we leave Kuvira says. "Hey, Christine?"

I turn around. "Yes?"

Kuvira walks up to me and gives me another hug, when we break apart this time though she pulls me in for a kiss. I flinch but don't pull away. When we break apart I blush. "I always loved you Christine," Kuvira says. "I always will."

"I love you too."

I turn away. Korra and the kids, as well the rest of the Beifong family follow me out of the house. We walk out of The Spirit World and back to our cars. We pile inside and once again Korra sits on my lap. Lin drives us back to Chicago and drops us off at our house and we go inside. We sit down on the couch and I lean my head on Korra she smiles down at me. No matter what happens we will be there for one another. We will keep each other safe and we will be a family.

## Chapter 1

I walk through the police station in Chicago and to up to the front desk, where a man with black hair, a round face and is wearing a police uniform sits. There are police officers milling around near the front entrance. The man at the desk looks up and when he sees me, he practically jumps out of his seat.

"Commander Christine!" he exclaims with a salute.

"Good morning, Sergeant Shon." I nod and return the salute. "Please, just call me Christine."

Shon nods and then asks. "What are you doing here?"

I look around—my heart is thumping hard in my chest—and lean in so that no one else can hear me and whisper. "You can't tell anyone else this, but I need to see a prisoner."

Shon frowns for a moment and then asks. "Which one?"

"Prisoner six-nine-three." I whisper softly.

He jumps out of his seat. *"Prisoner six-nine-three!"*

I cringe and look around the room, all of the officers by the door have jumped to their feet. I turn back to Shon. *"Sergeant!"*

Shon shrinks back in his seat. "But she's a highly dangerous inmate, why would you want to see her?"

"Just let me back there." I say.

He nods and gets up from his seat. He signals for the guards by the door to follow, but I stop him. "No, guards," I say. "I want it to be just me and her."

He nods again, he motions for me to follow him and I do, as we walk past the other cells, he asks. "Does Korra know you're here?"

"No," I say. "I told her that I was going out with some friends. But she doesn't need to know about this."

Shon nods. "Okay."

We stop at a cell, in the solitary confinement section and Shon salutes to the two guards standing there. The guards return the salute. "Sergeant." The two guards walk away and that just leaves me and Shon.

He opens the door to the cell and I walk inside. "Do you want the door open?" he asks.

"No," I say. "Close the door." He nods and the door slams shut and locks.

I look across the room and at the women sitting on a bed at the very end of the cell. Her blonde hair hanging loosely around her shoulders and her hands bound together with metal shackles.

"I guess I should consider myself lucky that the Avatar is here to visit me in my lonely prison cell."

"You should consider yourself lucky that I spared your life a couple of weeks ago." I say.

Cipher scoffs. "Why are you really here?"

"I'm here because you're going to tell me something."

Cipher gets up off her cell bed and starts to walk toward me, but she's only able to walk a couple of feet before the chains jerk her back. She swears under her breath and looks me in the eye. I stand there, unflinching.

"Alright, what is it that you want to know?" she asks, her voice flat and unemotional.

"Where is the Beifong family?"

She smirks. "I don't know."

"Okay, you want to do this the hard way," I say, rolling up my sleeves. "We can do this the hard way."

## Chapter 2

I walk out of the cell and Shon jumps to his feet when he sees me. He salutes and together we walk down the hallway. I shake out my hands and look at them, there are dark bruises starting to form on my knuckles, as well as some dried blood.

"Did Cipher tell you what you need to know?" Shon asks as we walk to the lobby of the police station.

"Yes, she did," I say. "She's probably going to need a healer though," Shon raises an eyebrow at me, but I just shrug. "It was the only way to make her talk."

"So what is your next move?"

"I'm not really sure," I say. "Just because I have the Beifong's location doesn't mean that I can waltz into wherever they're being held. I need to be smart about this."

"Would you like my soldiers to assist you?"

"No, I want to do this on my own."

I walk out of the police station and get into my new car. I turn the keys in the ignition. The car doesn't start. I try again, but still, the car won't start. I let out a sigh. I grab my keys. I get out and start to walk.

---

I arrive at my house and walk inside. The lights are off, which is strange I was pretty sure that I turned them on before I left this morning. I walk around the house.

"Hello?" I say. "Anyone home?"

My voice echoes throughout the house. I hear a creak and look around but I don't see anything. I hear a door slam and I run upstairs but there's no one there.

"Korra? Kids? Anyone home?"

Something wraps my mouth and I tug at it, but it won't budge. Something hard connects with my temple and I groan and grab the side of my head. I feel something grab onto my arms and yanks me to the side. I fall to the side. I hear a click and I stiffen. I try to see who it is, but my vision is blurry. I'm dragged across the floor and I hear the sound of a car engine and I start to thrash. I hear a door open and I'm dragged again. I thrash again but its no use. I'm laid down and I hear a car door slam shut. I try to move, but my body is paralyzed. I hear a hiss and start feel drowsy, I try to keep my eyes open, but its no use. My eyes close and I pass out.

---

I let out a pained groan as consciousness returns to me. My eyes flicker open and I drag my hand across the floor and it jerks to as stop, I can feel a metal restraint on both hands. Once again I was tied down. I hear the squeak of a door and I look over at it. Its open. Someone walks inside and turns on the lights. "Hey." A voice says.

When I saw who it is my jaw drops. *"Junior?!"*

My son, Baatar Jr., walks over to me and stands by the bed that I'm strapped to. I try to move, but its no use. My brain is buzzing with confusion.

*Why was I tied down? Why was Baatar Jr. looking guilty? What was going on?* I shake the thought from my head.

I hear another squeak and I look back at the door. Several other people walk in. I watch as my ex-girlfriend walks inside. "No. Kuvira?"

"Hey, Christine." she says.

Kuvira says nothing. I look at her, still confused. "How...? What are you...?" The words get stuck in my throat. "I don't understand."

Before she's able to answer, three other voices speak. "Hey mom."

I look over and see my three daughters walk into the room and soon after Korra walks in. I try to speak but I unable to form words. I just lay there and watch them.

Chapter 3

I stare at Kuvira wide-eyed. My heart is thumping like mad in my chest. I take a deep breath and it shakes on the way out.

"What are you doing here? *How* are you here?" I finally ask. "You're supposed to be dead."

"I honestly have no idea." she says.

I try to move my hand but it doesn't get very far before the restraint pulls it to a stop. I look past Kuvira and at Korra. Our eyes meet for a moment and then Kuvira steps into my line of sight. Kuvira turns around and says something to Korra, she nods and ushers the kids out of the room. Kuvira lets out a sigh and turns back to me. I look up at her. She reaches down and grabs my hand. She then laces her fingers with mine and pulls my hand up as far as the restraint will allow. She holds onto my hand for just a moment before undoing the restraint.

"What are you doing?" I ask, confused.

"Getting you out of here." she says, as she undoes the last restraint, she helps me to my feet.

Moments later the door to the cell opens and Korra steps inside. She looks at Kuvira in confusion. "What is it you think you're doing?"

"What does it look like I am doing?" Kuvira says with a smirk. "I'm getting her out of here."

"I can't let you do that." Korra says.

"If you want Christine, you'll have to go through me first." Kuvira says.

"Very well," Korra says. "I guess you leave me no choice."

Without warning she sends out a blast of lightning and I jump in front of Kuvira. I don't have enough time to redirect it and the lightning courses through my body. I scream as it shoots across my chest. The lightning explodes against the wall. I land on the ground with a thud and my vision begins to shift in and out of focus. I black out.

---

I jerk awake and sit up. I put my hand on my head. A soft groan makes its way out past my lips. My vision clears and someone puts their hand on my shoulder. I flinch away from it, but the grip doesn't loosen. Through the ringing in my ears, I hear a voice. "Christine?"

I look up at the person standing above me. "Korra?"

"Hey." she says.

"Where are we? What happened?"

Korra takes a deep breath and sits down next to me, she runs her hand across my back and I lean against her. "What happened?" I ask again.

"We're at the police station." she says.

"What?" I say. "Why?"

"Well…" Korra starts to say, but a voice interrupts her.

"You're not plotting an escape with the prisoner, are you Korra?"

Korra gets up and salutes to the person walking towards her. "Not at all." she says.

I turn around and see Kuvira walking toward us with the kids trailing behind her. Kuvira stops and returns the salute.

I look back and forth at Korra and Kuvira. "Wait—" I start to say, but Kuvira interrupts me.

"Ah, ah, ah. Shhh!" She covers my mouth with her hand. She looks over at Korra and nods. Korra walks behind me and puts my arms behind my back. She then wrenches me to my feet. She pushes me forward, forcing me to walk. We turn a corner and walk down another hallway, coming to a stop at a cell at the very end of the hallway. I pull away from Korra and turn towards the cell door. That's when I realize where we are.

*"No!"* I scream.

Chapter 4

Korra and Kuvira push me towards the cell. I turn away from it and they push me forward again.

"Open the door." Kuvira says.

"What?" I say, confused.

"Open the cell door." Kuvira says, pushing me forward again.

"Are you crazy? No, I won't." I say, pulling away from her.

"You will, if you want to see the Beifongs again."

I stop trying to pull away and stare at her wide-eyed. "What?! You're the one who took them?"

"Well, not directly," Kuvira says. "But I did tell Cipher where to find them."

"But, how?" I ask. *"How* were you able to talk to Cipher when she's in prison?"

"The Spirit World, duh." Korra says, with a smirk.

"Wait, *what!?*" My eyes go wide. "She's able to go into The Spirit World!?"

Korra is about to say something, but Kuvira interjects. "Careful," she says. "What are you telling her?"

I look at the two women and then glance at my kids. So far, they have remained silent on this matter. I turn back to Kuvira and Korra. They're staring each other down.

After a long moment Kuvira finally speaks. "Christine, open the cell door."

*"What?!"* I exclaim in shock.

"You heard me," she says. "Now open the door."

*"No!"*

Kuvira sighs and without warning, she lunges for me. I don't get out of the way fast enough and Kuvira slams me into the wall. I grunt in pain and my head starts to feel fuzzy. My vision starts to blur and I struggle to stay awake. But I push through. I swing at Kuvira and she blocks the blow, grabbing onto my waist and throwing me back against the cell door. I slam into the door and then I land on the ground with a thud. I let out a wheezed breath and Kuvira yanks me to my feet.

I put my hands up. "Alright, alright. I'll open the door."

Kuvira releases me and I drop into my platinum bending stance. I take a deep breath and push my hands forward and the door unlocks. I open the door and Kuvira, Korra and the kids walk past me and into the cell. I follow them. Cipher looks up at us when we enter. She grins when she sees me. "Well, hello Christine."

I nod. "Cipher."

"What are you doing here?"

"Don't ask me," I say, bitterly. "Ask Kuvira and Korra, they're the ones who dragged me here."

Cipher nods and looks at Korra and Kuvira. "Everything went according to plan?" she asks. "There are no loose ends to tie up later?"

Kuvira nods. "There are no loose ends. Only this one if she doesn't do what we ask," She points at me. "But I don't believe that she'll... disagree with what we have to ask of her."

"Alright." Cipher says and she turns to me. She smiles at me and then nods at Kuvira. Kuvira takes a deep breath and clenches her fists. The platinum shackles on Cipher's wrists pop off and she smirks. Now free of her chains, Cipher walks over to me and smiles. I subconsciously start to back up and I back into the wall. Cipher nods to Korra and Kuvira, they walk over to me and grab onto my arms. They handcuff my hands behind my back. I try to bend them off, but they shock me. I let out a scream of pain. Electricity courses through my body. I shudder in pain and quit struggling, my body starts to relax and my eyes close.

Cipher nods to everyone else. "Let's go."

Together Kuvira and Korra carry Christine out of the cell with Cipher and the kids following close behind.


Chapter 5

*"Mom?"*

I jerk awake and rub my face, shielding my eyes from the bright lights. I sit up A moment later though, my eyes adjust to the bright, pale lights and that's when I see him. I cough.

"Junior?" I breathe in deeply and it shake on the way out. My head pounds and I let out a groan. I turn my head to the side and close my eyes for a moment. I take another deep breath and look back over at my son.

"Son?" I say.

"Yes, mother?" he says.

"Are we home?" I ask.

Baatar doesn't say anything, for a moment, he just looks down at his shoes and sniffles. He wipes his eyes and looks at me. His eyes are red and bloodshot, probably from crying. He holds onto my hand and looks at me.

"Are we home?" I ask again.

"No." he says, his voice barely a whisper and his head hung low.

"Then where are we?"

Baatar sighs and looks at me again. He didn't need to say anything. We were in Erudite headquarters. I shouldn't even have asked.

"Baatar?" I say. "Where's Korra?"

"She's alright, so is Kuvira." he says, softly.

I nod and close my eyes, trying to keep the tears from falling. "Good."

"Mom?" Baatar says. "Are you okay?"

I wipe my eyes. "Yeah, I'm fine." Baatar nods and laces his fingers with mine. I grip them hard and he looks at me again. "Baatar, sweetie, I need to ask you something."

"What is it mom?"

"Do you know what Cipher's planning?" I ask, looking into his eyes. Baatar just stares at me blankly and I squeeze his hand again.

Junior clears his throat and looks down for a moment. "Um..." he starts to say. "She's, um..." His voice trails off. He clears his throat and says. "You know what she's planning."

I furrow my eyebrows in confusion. "What do you mean?"

Baatar sighs. "She has the Beifongs, you know what she's planning."

"Wait, what? What do you mean she..." At that moment it hits me and my eyes go wide. "Oh no."

"I'm sorry," he says. "Truly, I am."

I hear the cell door open and I see Cipher walk inside with Korra walking in behind her and Kuvira with the Beifongs—Baatar Sr., Opal, Huan and Wing and Wei—beside her.

"Hello, Christine." They all say.

Chapter 6

I look at the Beifong family wide-eyed. I stare at Baatar Sr. and he stares back at me. He walks over to me and stops by the bed.

"Hey, Christine." he says.

I look from him to the rest of the family. I look from the twins to Huan and then finally I look at Opal. "Opal?" I say.

"Hey, Christine." she says.

With tears in my eyes I look over at Kuvira. "How... could you do this? I thought you loved me."

"Well, you see. *That's* what I thought too. *I* thought that *you* loved *me.*"

I furrow my eyebrows together. "What are you talking about? Of *course,* I love *you.*"

Kuvira scoffs and walks up beside my bed. "If you loved me, you wouldn't have *abandoned* me!"

"But I didn't." I look over at Korra. "Go on Korra, tell her."

Korra starts to say something but Kuvira interrupts. "Don't... answer that. Do you know why Korra?" Korra shakes her head and Kuvira continues. "'Cause Christine needs to stand up for herself, she's been hiding behind you and me, for the last fifteen years."

"Alright." Korra says, stepping away from me and walking back to Kuvira.

"Well?" Kuvira says.

I sigh. "Alright, you're right," I look at Kuvira. "You want to know the truth?" Kuvira doesn't say anything.

I swallow hard. "The reason I left you and had kids with Korra was because...," I take a deep breath. "You *died! Your* the *one* who left *me,* what'd you think, that the day you died, that I wasn't going to be with anyone else? That just because you weren't there, that I wasn't going to move on with my life. That's not how life works! You just have to move on."

I breathe in deeply to calm my nerves. I look back at Kuvira and flinch when I see her expression. It's completely blank. I've seen that expression before—It was when she first betrayed me. I smile nervously and say. "So... um, That... um, that came out wrong." I get off the bed and walk over to Kuvira, I put my hand on her cheek. "I'm sorry, okay?"

Kuvira doesn't say anything, she just stares at me. Moments later her expression softens and she lets out a sigh. She grabs onto the collar of my shirt, my eyes go wide. I let out a muffled yelp as she pulls me in for a kiss. I try to push her away, but she's too strong. I try and muster all the strength I have. I shove her away, wiping my mouth with my arm.

"Why did you do that!?" I yell.

"'Cause, I love you!" she yells back.

"If you really loved me you would've just accepted my current relationship with Korra, you wouldn't be working with Cipher and wouldn't have kidnapped me and Korra!" Kuvira starts to walk towards me and I shove her backward. "Leave me alone! I—" The words get caught in my throat. "I don't love you anymore."

As much as the words break my heart as I say them, its true. I'm in love with Korra. I wouldn't have married and had kids with her otherwise. The look in Kuvira's eyes makes my heart shatter and she lets out a sigh. When she looks at me again though, her stare is cold. I back away slowly and Kuvira runs at me. She tackles me to the ground and I let out a strangled scream as my ribs bruise. A breath hitched in my throat and my vision blurs. Kuvira yanks me to my feet and I thrust my fist forward, it strikes her in the face. Kuvira releases me and stumbles backward. Blood is pouring freely from her nose. I look over her shoulder and notice that the Beifongs and Cipher are running out of the cell.

"No, stop them!" I yell, trying to push my way past Kuvira. "Don't let them escape!" I struggle past Kuvira and then run out of the cell. I catch up with them and Cipher skids to a stop. She twitches her fingers and my body seizes up under the control of her bloodbending grip. I scream and Cipher flicks her wrist. I crash into the wall and fall to the ground. I black out.

Chapter 7
*"Mom, wake up!"*

I let out a groan and my eyes flicker open. My vision clears and I see Baatar kneeling beside me, with a blob of water pressed against my head. The pounding in my head disappears a moment later, replaced instead by a dull throbbing.

I focus my eyes on my son. "Junior?"

"Hey." he says.

"Where are your sisters?" I ask.

"There here with Korra and Kuvira," he says.

"Why?" I ask.

Junior helps me to my feet. "Their loyalty is split between Korra and Kuvira, Su and my sister are trying to figure out what to do."

He gives me a hug. I look around. We are in one of the hallways near the lab. I put my hand on the back of my head and it comes away sticky with blood. I start to feel light-headed and I bring my hand up to Junior's cheek. He holds onto it.

"Son?" I say, my voice hoarse.

"Yes, mother?"

"You need to get out of here," I say. "You need to go find Cipher and bring her back to me."

"What about Kuvira and Korra?" he asks.

I grunt in pain as I drag myself towards the wall. "As long as Korra stays here, she'll be safe," I let out a sharp breath. "She too valuable to Kuvira. Both me and Kuvira know that the moment she does something to Korra that I'll be back to finish her off."

"What about my sisters?"

"The same holds true for them as well. As long as they stay here, they'll be safe. Kuvira wouldn't risk hurting them."

Baatar Junior gives me a hug and I grimace in pain, he doesn't notice. He lets go and I notice there are tears in his eyes. "I love you, mom." he says, his voice breaking.

"I love you, too," I say. "Now go!"

He nods and runs off. I breathe in deeply and lean my head against the wall. Tears fall from my eyes and stain my cheeks. I hear footsteps coming from around the corner. I look up and see Kuvira, Korra and the remainder of the kids walking over to me. Kuvira yanks me to my feet and I don't even bother pulling away. We start to walk down the hallway. We walk to the room where I once faced simulation after simulation. Kuvira puts handcuffs on my wrists and attaches a pair of chains to them. Korra walks over to me and gives me a kiss. I try to keep myself pressed against her for as long as possible. She pulls away and puts her head on my shoulder. Tears leak from my eyes and I lean into her.

A moment later she whispers. "I'm sorry."

I pull away. "For what?"

"For what I'm about to do." she says.

Korra pulls away and drops into a lightningbending stance and aims for the chains. She lets out a blast of lightning and it comes in contact with the chains. The lightning shocks me and I scream, collapsing to the ground. My heart flutters and my vision starts to blur and shift in and out of focus. My head pounds and I start to breathe heavily.

"Korra, stop!" I yell. "I thought you loved me!"

The lightning continues flowing. My vision starts to go black and I know I'm going to go unconscious.

*"Stop!"* I say again, my voice getting softer and softer. "Please... stop."

I black out.


Chapter 8

Junior runs to the police station and bursts through the doors. "Lin!" he yells.

The chief of police looks up at him. "Junior?" she says. "What are you doing here?"

"Cipher's escaped. She attacked my parents and now we can't find her. We need your help."

*What?!* Lin exclaims. "Cipher escaped *prison?!* Why didn't anyone tell me."

"Uhhh... I don't know." Junior says.

Lin looks at Junior, but then yells. "Sergeant Shon!" She received no answer. *"Sergeant Shon!"* Still nothing. Lin starts to walk to down the hallway, but a moment later Sergeant Shon appears and salutes.

"What is it, Chief?"

"I have a question for you sergeant."

"Yes, Chief?"

"What's the current status of prisoner six-nine-three?"

Shon blinks at Lin in confusion. "Come again?"

"Prisoner six-nine-three, Cipher, our newest arrival."

"Oh!" he exclaims. "Uh, well... Why are you even asking me this? You know that she's in her cell in the solitary confinement section."

"No, she's not!" Junior exclaims. "She's escaped! Won't you listen to me?!"

Lin looks from Shon to Junior and back again. "Shon, where's Cipher?"

"I already told you," Shon says. "She's in her cell."

"You *lying!*" Lin says.

*"What?!"* Shon exclaims. "Why would I lie to you?"

Junior walks up to Sergeant Shon and drops into a bloodbending stance. "I'll give you ten seconds to tell us the truth," he says and he starts counting. "Ten... "

"I... I don't know!" Shon exclaims.

"Nine..."

"Wait..."

"Eight... Seven."

"Lin... please. You can't let Junior do this."

"Six... Five."

"Lin..."

"Four... Three."

"Wait..."

"Two..."

"Please..."

*"One!"*

Junior twitches his fingers and the young sergeant's body seized up. Shon groaned in pain. His veins and muscles jumped and twitched under the control of bloodbending. Shon let out a shrill shriek of pain, his limbs bending near their breaking point.

"Stop!" Shon screamed. "I'll... I'll tell you what you need to know."

Junior lowered his hands and Shon dropped to the floor. "Where's Cipher?" Before Baatar receives an answer though, something hard connects with his temple and he fell to the ground. He blacked out.


Chapter 9

Lin let out a groan of pain. She coughed and rolled onto her side. Her eyes flickered open and she sat up. She felt light-headed and she pinched the bridge of her nose, hoping that will relieve some of the pressure. It doesn't. Once her vision cleared, she looked around, but all she saw was pale white lights.

She looked to her left and saw Junior sprawled on the ground. Blood was pouring from his nose and mouth. He coughed and a glob of blood splattered onto the floor.

"Oh my god! Junior!?" Lin exclaimed. "What happened?"

"Cipher..." he croaked. "She..." he coughed out another mouthful of blood. "She beat and bloodbent me."

"She did what?!" Lin yelled.

Junior coughed again and put his head down on the ground. His eyes closed and Lin panicked. She could tell by his heartbeat that Cipher had beat him almost to death and the bloodbending almost finished the job. Lin knew that she needed to get him to a healer and she needed to do it fast.

"Hang on Baatar," she says. "I'll get us out of here."

"Remarkable," A voice says. "I'd love to see you try to get out of here."

Lin turned toward the voice. "Cipher." she snarled.

Cipher smirked. "I have to admit, I thought that the chief of police would be more aware of what was going on inside her own station house. I guess you're not the great chief of police that you and your mother thought you would be."

Lin growled. "You don't know anything about me."

Cipher raised her eyebrows in mock surprise. "I don't? Oh, that's a shame. I spend the last five years watching you from the shadows and I don't know anything about you," she smirked again. "Oh, no, Lin, you are gravely mistaken. I know *everything* about you. I know who your team is, I know who your family is, I know your weaknesses. I even know who your newest sergeant is," she laughed. "He even works for me. Didn't you know that?"

*"What?!"* Lin exclaimed. "No, no, no, Sergeant Shon works for me. I did all the paperwork to make sure he was a real worker before I hired him. He works for me," Lin paused. "Unless you have proof stating otherwise."

Cipher nods then calls. "Sergeant Shon!"

A moment later the young sergeant walked into the room. "Yes, ma'am?"

"Show our guests to their new cells, will you?"

"Of course, ma'am."

Sergeant Shon walks over to Lin and Junior. He yanked Junior off the ground and grabbed onto Lin. He starts to drag them away. Lin starts to protest, but its no use.

*I thought I could trust him!* Lin thought. *He betrayed me!*

Cipher watched as her captives were dragged away, then she turned away and started down the opposite hallway. She had a job to finish.

Chapter 10

I jerk awake. I sit up and the room spins. There's the metallic taste of blood on my tongue. I cough and blood dribbles down my chin. I groan and clutch my chest, my heart flutters and I have a hard time breathing. Once my vision clears, I look around. The room I'm in is dark. I get off the bed and start to walk forward. But i'm stopped when something jerks me back. My shoulders ache. I see the glimmer of shackles on my wrists. I walk as far as the chains will allow me and look around. When I'm unable to see anything, I sit back down on the cell bed. A moment later, my cell door opens and I look up. Cipher, Korra Kuvira walk toward me, with someone else trailing behind her. I recognize him instantly.

"Sergeant Shon?"

"Hello, *Commander* Christine." he says in a mocking tone.

"You...," My words get stuck in my throat but I push them out. "You work for Cipher?"

"Of course," he says. "She's the one who got me into the police force to begin with. She knew that I could help her escape," he smirks. "Which worked out quite well I have to admit."

"I thought I could trust you," I say, my head pounding. "I thought..." My voice trails off.

"Maybe you're not as smart as you think you are." he says.

I try to say something but my words fail me. I look from Cipher to Shon and back again. Cipher says something to Shon. He nods and walks over to me. He walks behind me and takes the chains off the cuffs, leaving only shackles. Shon pushes me forward and I have no choice but to walk. Cipher, Korra and Kuvira follow behind me. I try and struggle out of the handcuffs, but they shock me and I shriek in pain. Shon's grip on me doesn't loosen. I struggle again, but I get shocked again. I start to feel drowsy and I struggle to keep my eyes open. My vision is shifting in and out of focus. I fight through the heavy feeling of sleep. I have to. We continue walking down the hallway and we arrive at a different cell. We go inside and Shon lets me go. The cell door slams shut and I look around. As I look around, I hear a voice.

*"Christine?"*

I look beside me and let out a gasp. *"Lin?"*

Lin grunts in pain and walks over to me. "Hey."

"Are you okay?"

Lin lets out a sharp gasp. "Yep, just fine."

She sits down next to me. I bend the water out of my hip flask and put my hands on her ribs. They heal a moment later.

"Is it just you here?" I ask. "Or...," My voice trails off and my eyes go wide. "Where's Junior?!"

"He's here, don't worry," she says. "But he needs a healer."

Lin moves off to the side and I see Junior laying on the floor. His breathing is shallow. I run over to him and kneel down beside him. I lift his head up. "Junior, sweetie, can you hear me?"

Junior starts to cough and I see drops of crimson on the floor. Blood. A moment later his coughing ceased and he focuses his eyes on me. "Mom?" he says, his voice weak. He wipes the blood from his chin and takes my hand.

I bend the blob of water towards him and start to heal his body, though I'm unsure where the bone fracture is.

"You're okay," I say, my voice quivering. "You're going to be okay."

He nods and lays his head back down. His breathing is even more shallow. I try my best to keep the water glowing, but I don't have enough energy to do so. The glow fades and Baatar passes out.

Chapter 11

I continue healing Junior, but there's too much damage to his organs, I won't be able to do this alone. I need someone else for Junior to get better. I need *Korra*. Lin walks over to me and kneels down beside me. She puts her hand on my shoulder and I don't say anything. I just focus on Junior. The water around my hands glows for a moment. The glow fades and a moment later.

Junior opens his eyes. "Mom?"

I sigh in relief. "Thank goodness you're alright."

Baatar sighs.

"How do you feel?" I ask.

"Like I got hit by a train," Junior says, grunting in pain as he tries to sit up. "How are you?"

"Meh," I say. "I'm feeling about the same as you."

Junior starts to laugh and it instantly turns into a coughing fit. He wheezes and I run my hand across his back. He continues coughing and when he's done. He spits out blood. He wipes his mouth and sighs.

"We need to get you to a healer," I say, then I pause, looking at the cell door. "Once we get out of here."

I pick him up and look over at Lin. She walks over to cell door and takes a deep breath. She drops into a metalbending stance and pushes her hands forward. The cell door opens and I cheer.

A voice interrupts our success though. "Don't mean to burst your bubble, but you guys didn't open up the door. I did."

As soon as I realize who it is, my eyes go wide. "Cipher!?"

She smirks at me. "Hello Christine."

She walks into the cell. With Korra and Kuvira, as well as sergeant Shon behind her. I back away slowly and Cipher steps forward. I take another step back.

Cipher smirks again. "It looks like you want to ask me something, so just ask me."

"Um...," I say, my heart pounding. I look at the ground. "Can you...," my voice trails off. I look up at her and take a deep breath. "Can you heal Junior for me? He's on the verge of death and he has internal bleeding."

Cipher tilts her head to the side. "Why would I do that?"

"'Cause I'll quit running from you if you do," I say, my voice quivering. "I'll do anything, okay? Just please heal my son."

Junior coughs and looks up at me. "Mom, no. I'll be okay."

I don't say anything.

Cipher puts her hand on her chin, thinking over the offer. "Hmm, I suppose that I could do that and considering that you've already offered to work for me, I will."

I let out a sigh of relief. "Thank you."

Cipher walks over to me and Junior shrinks back against my chest. Cipher bends the water from her water flask. The water glows brightly for a moment and then returns to normal. "There, that should have done the job. I used spirit water, so he should be fine."

I put Junior down and he's able to stand. "I feel wonderful." he says and he gives me a hug. "I love you, mom."

"I love you, too, Junior."

He lets go and Korra and Kuvira start to walk toward us, but I put up my hand. "Don't," I say, turning toward them. "I have to uphold my end of the deal."

"Christine, no." Korra says.

I walk over to her. "I have to." I give her a hug. When we pull apart, I pull her in for one last kiss. I only pull away when I have to breathe. "I love you, Korra."

"I love you, too."

I turn away from Korra and walk over to Cipher. Sergeant Shon joins us as well. We start to walk and I look at Korra one last time before she disappears from view.

The Legend Of Korra Meets The Fate Of The Furious Part 6
(Book 15)

Chapter 1

*Present day…*

Kuvira, Korra, and Junior stand just outside the police station. Lin had called them there for a meeting. The three walked inside and up to Lin's desk. There Lin sat, scrolling through footage after footage. She had to find Christine and the kids. Lin looked up at the team she assembled, which was consisted of, Kuvira—Christine's ex-girlfriend—Korra and Christine's second youngest, Baatar Jr. The other kids had betrayed them to help Cipher capture Christine, once that happened they stayed with Cipher. Who knows where any of them were now.

"Thank you guys for coming to meet with me." Lin says.

"No problem," Kuvira says. "We couldn't just sit back and watch as the world fell into chaos."

"Well, then," Lin says. "Let's get started."

Lin turned back to the computers when suddenly one of her officers comes running into the station. "Chief!"

"What is it, Sergeant?"

The sergeant saluted and then said. "We've found Cipher and her team."

---

*Three years earlier…*

*I let out a sigh as I pace back and forth in my cell. I don't know where Cipher's taking me, but there's no point in asking. She won't tell me anyway. I continue pacing back and forth, I try to go as slow as possible. I shake out my hands and I receive a powerful shock from the handcuffs on my wrists. My body lurches forward and I groan. The handcuffs beep and I feel something sharp stab into my wrists. I feel a cool liquid fill my veins and that's when I realize that the handcuffs are giving me my daily dose of simulation serum. I breathe in deeply and clench my fists together, the handcuffs shock me again and I collapse onto the ground. The room spins and my vision blurs. I hear the echo of footsteps and I look up. I can see the silhouette of a person walking towards me. I black out.*

---

Lin looked at her sergeant in shock. She looked from him to Korra to Kuvira and finally at the kids. Then she looked back at the sergeant. "You found Cipher and her team already?"

The sergeant nodded. "Yes, ma'am."

"Well, where are they?" Lin asks.

The sergeant was about to speak when suddenly he was knocked to the ground. Lin knelt down beside the sergeant and she noticed a sharp piece of platinum sticking out of his neck. She checked his pulse, but it was too late. He was gone. Everyone dropped into their own bending stances. The door to the police station opens and a group of people walked inside. Soon it becomes clear as to who it is.

Kuvira takes a step back into shock. "Cipher?"

Cipher smirks. "Hello, Kuvira."

Chapter 2

Kuvira stood there unable to say anything. But Korra speaks a moment later. "What are you doing here? Where's Christine? What did you do to her?"

"Christine's with us, don't you worry." Cipher smirked. "I would never hurt her if that's what your thinking."

"Let me see her." Korra says.

"Of course." Cipher says. She whispers something to Shon. He nods and leaves the station.

---

I pace back and forth in my cell. I try to remember what I was doing, but I can't. I can't remember *anything*. I continue to pace, but a moment later Sergeant Shon walks into the cell. "Your presence has been requested."

"By who?" I ask.

"Cipher."

I nod. "Alright, I'll be there in a couple of minutes," Shon starts to leave but I stop him. "Where is she?"

"In Chicago," he says. "She said that you would know where to find her." He goes to leave again but then stops himself. "Before you leave you should probably go get Kuvira, Su, and Evelyn."

I nod and Shon walks out of the cell, leaving the door open for me. I take a deep breath and grab my metal sword and my spools of metal cable. I attach them to my commander uniform and walk out of the cell.

---

The kids and I walk up Michigan Ave. and turn left. We walk to the police station and go inside. Cipher's standing by one of the desks. "Hello, commander." I say, with a salute.

"Hello, Christine." Cipher says, returning the salute.

I'm about to say something when I hear a voice. *"Christine?"*

I look at the person who spoke, she has blue eyes and short brown hair. Beside her, there is another women. She's tall with black hair that's in a bun, she has fern green eyes and is wearing metal armor. Beside them, there's a boy who's about sixteen or seventeen with blue eyes, short black hair, square glasses and a goatee that's just starting to grow in.

I look back at the woman who spoke. "Who are you? How do you know my name?"

"Its me Korra," The women says. "Don't you remember?"

I shake my head and the women—Korra—steps forward again. I step away from her and she steps forward again. I look over at my other kids, they're backing away slowly as well. I watch as the boy with black hair steps toward them.

I look back at Korra. "I don't know who you are." I say.

"I'm your wife." she says. Then she points over at the boy behind her. "He's your son."

"I don't have a son. I only have these three," I say, pointing at the three girls behind me. "I don't have a wife either. She left me three years ago."

*"Christine?"* Cipher says.

I look at her. "Yes, Commander?"

She walks over to me and whispers. "These three are a threat, you need to get rid of them."

I nod and she takes a step back. Korra continues to walk toward me. When she's close enough, she reaches for me. I grab onto her arm and shove her backward. She lets out a yelp and I start to back away slowly.

"Kuvira," Korra says. "Get Christine."

The other women—Kuvira—walks toward me and grabs onto my arms. I break out of her grip and she reaches for me again. I shoot out a platinum strip and it strikes her. She screams and stumbles backward. Cipher grabs onto my arm and together me, her, and the other kids run out of the police station.

Chapter 3

As soon as we get back to the train I go to my personal apartment. I sit on my bed and put my head in my hands. I take a deep breath and it shakes on the way out. I hear the door to my room open, but I don't even look up. I feel someone sit down beside me and give me a hug. I look up and see Cipher sitting beside me. I lean into her embrace and close my eyes. Moments later I drift off to sleep.

---

*I pace back and forth. I shake out my hands and the handcuffs shock me. I groan and hunch forward. I hear footsteps and I look up. Cipher walks into my cell and stops in front of me. I look away from her.*

*"Christine?" she says.*

*I don't look at her. Cipher sighs and grabs my chin and forces me to look at her. I jerk away from her and the handcuffs shock me. I groan and look back at Cipher. She's holding a needle of simulation serum. I crawl as far away as I can. She walks up to me and sticks the needle into my neck. I cough and collapse onto the ground. My eyes close.*

---

I jerk awake and breathe heavily. I put my head in my hands and take a deep breath. Someone sits down beside me and I look up. It's Cipher.

"Are you okay?" she asks.

"Yeah, I'm fine."

"Are you sure?"

I nod.

"That's good." she says.

"Where are we?" I ask.

"Just north of Chicago."

"Okay."

I take a deep breath and look at my shoes. Something pokes at the back of my mind and I focus on it. I can't tell whether it's a real memory or not. The thought makes me panic and I back away from Cipher. She gives me a strange look. I turn away from her and I walk to my apartment door. I open it and walk out. I glance over my shoulder and notice that Cipher is still following me. I pick up the pace and run through the train. As far away from her as possible. I stop at the engine of the train and sit down. I bury my face in my knees. I take a deep breath and I just sit there, alone.

---

Its minutes or hours later—I can't tell—before Cipher finds me. She walks over to me and sits down beside me. I move a few inches away from her. My heart thumps like mad in my chest. I get up and turn away from her, wiping the tears from my eyes in the process. I start to walk away from Cipher, but she grabs onto my arm. I stop in my tracks. "Christine?" she says.

I turn and look at her. "Yes, Commander?"

"Is there something you need to tell me?"

I shake my head. "No." Cipher raises an eyebrow at me. I shake my head again. "There's nothing that I need to tell you."

"Fine, then." she says.

I take a deep breath. I look over my shoulder and at Cipher. "I just need some space."

Cipher nods. "Of course. Take as much time as you need."

I nod and turn away from her and walk toward my apartment.

Chapter 4

I toss and turn, unable to fall asleep. Everytime I close my eyes, all I can see is Kuvira trying to attack me. I try to go to sleep again, but when I finally start to drift off, I hear a voice. "Having trouble falling asleep?"

I jerk awake and rub my eyes. I see Cipher sitting in her chair on the other side of the room.

"Yeah."

"Is there anything that I can do to help?"

I nod.

Cipher gets up and walks over to me, she crouches in front of me and looks up at me.

"What is it?"

I lean forward and put my head in my hands. Cipher reaches forward and removes my hands from my face. I don't even bother wiping the tears from my eyes. Cipher wipes away the tears for me. My eyes meet hers for a moment, then I look away.

"What is it?" she asks again.

"Its...," My voice trails off and I take a deep breath. "Its just... I feel lonely."

"How about I stay for a little while until you don't feel lonely anymore."

I lie back down on my bed. "Okay."

Cipher lays down beside me and brushes the bangs away from my eyes. I close my eyes and drift off to sleep.

---

*"Mother?"*

*I jerk awake and look around. My heart is racing. My eyes finally adjust to the dark and I see three figures standing in the doorway. They step forward and I just sit there, unable to move. The figures walk forward and that's when I see them. My other kids.*

*"Girls," I say. "I miss you."*

*"We miss you too," They say. "But we're sorry we have to do this."*

*Evelyn drops into a bloodbending stance. I don't react in time and she starts to bloodbend me. I let out scream and my vision starts to go blurry. Through my blurry vision I see Kuvira and Su walking towards me. Kuvira shoots out several platinum strips. One strikes me in the leg, the other, my arm and one strikes me in chest. I start to bleed and I let out a scream. Evelyn lowers her hands and I drop to the ground. My vision go black.*

---

I scream and bolt right up. My heart is racing. Something wraps around my waist. I start to thrash, trying to get away, but then I hear a voice. Cipher's voice. "Christine! Christine! Its okay! You're safe! You're safe!"

I stop thrashing and calm down. With one hand Cipher holds my shoulder, while her other one runs across my back. I take a deep breath. I put my head in my hands and tears stain my cheeks. I turn towards Cipher and wrap my hands around her. I bury my face into her shoulder.

"Shhh! Shhh!" Cipher says, holding me close. "You're alright. You're going to be alright."

---

Cipher holds me tight and I try to slow my breathing. I take another deep breath. I pull away and Cipher puts her hand on my shoulder. I look at her and she wipes away the tears in my eyes. I smile and hold onto her hand. She laces her fingers with mine. After another moment of silence, she lets go. Ciper gets up and walks to the door, motioning for me to follow. "I have a surprise for you." she says.

I get off the bed and follow Cipher out of train. Together we make our way back to Chicago.

Chapter 5

As we walk up Michigan ave. I look around, its dark out. We continue to walk and I look over at Cipher. Although she's disappeared. I don't know where she went. I stop and look around. I'm unable to see her. I shrug and continue to walk. As I walk through I hear the sound of footsteps of someone behind me. I turn around, but I don't see anyone.

I continue on walking. While I'm walking though I hear a voice. *"Christine?"*

I turn around. "What are you doing here?" I ask.

Korra walks up beside me and wraps her arms around me. "I came to see you," she says. "I miss you."

"I miss you too."

We break apart and I lean in to give Korra a kiss. But she pushes me away. I look at her, confused. She looks around and her eyes settle on me again. "Christine, you need to…"

*"…wake up."*

I open my eyes and see something covering my face. That's when I realize it's a pillow. I pull the pillow away from my face and see Cipher staring at me. Her expression blank.

"What?" I look at her in confusion and a moment later it hits me. "Oh…," I say. "Sorry."

"No, no," Cipher says. "Its fine."

I just look at her.

Cipher sighs and after a moment of silence, she says. "Let's go for a walk."

Together we walk out of the train.

We walk up Michigan Ave. and turn left. We walk to the noodle restaurant. Cipher leads me inside and we sit down. I look around and laugh. I look back at Cipher. "You booked out the whole restaurant, didn't you?"

"Well, of course, I did." she says with a smile.

The waiter walks over and sets down two bowls of noodles. I pick up the chopsticks and taste the noodles. The moment the noodles hit my tongue, I spit them out.

"Ack!" I exclaim. "These noodles are flavorless."

"Would you like something to help with that?" Cipher asks.

I nod.

Cipher pulls out two salt and pepper shakers and slides them over to me. I take them and dump some into my bowl. I take another bite.

"Are they good?" Cipher asks.

I nod again and dump the rest into the bowl. I take another bite. This time when I swallow though, it feels like something is burning my throat. I try to breathe, but my airways feel blocked. I wheeze and cough. I get up from the table. I run to the bathroom and burst through the door. My legs give out just as I reach the sink. I collapse onto the floor and my head hits the tiles. I black out.

Chapter 6

*"Christine?"*

I jerk awake. I rub my eyes and sit up. My vision clears and I look to my left. That's when I see him, dressed in his Chicago Police Department uniform. He shifts his weight from one foot to the other. I watch him for a moment.

"Shon?" I say.

Sergeant Shon looks at me. "Yes?"

"What happened?"

"I don't know."

"Are you sure?"

"Yes."

I nod and get out of bed. But Shon stops me.

"What are you doing?" I say.

"You should stay in bed." he says.

"Why?"

"'Cause you need to rest, the paralytic did a number on you last night."

I look at him with raised eyebrows. "I thought you said that you didn't know anything about what happened last night."

"I don't," Shon says. "I only know what Cipher told me."

"What do you mean?"

"Well, Cipher told me that you two went out for dinner and when you took a bite of your food, you started to choke on it. She also said that the food had simulation and paralytic serum in it."

"That's what I'm trying to tell you!" I exclaim. "Cipher tried to kill me!"

Sergeant Shon shakes his head. "No, the waiter tried to kill you."

*"What?!"* I exclaim. "Why would the waiter do that?"

"I don't know," he says. "What I do know, is that Cipher wants to talk to you when you have a moment."

"Alright, I'll be out in a minute."

Shon walks to the door and looks back at me before walking out of the room. I put my head in my hands and take a deep breath. It shakes on the way out. I just sit on the bed and don't move I just… sit there. I put my hands on my lap and just stare at the floor. I shake my head and look back at the ground. I take another deep breath and get up. I walk out of the room and to the meeting area, where Cipher is waiting for me. I walk to her and salute. She nods and I relax. We stand in silence for a moment.

"You wanted to see me, Commander?"

Cipher nods. "Yes, I wanted to talk to you about last night."

"Right," I nod. "So what happened?"

"You were paralyzed by the waiter at the restaurant," she says. "I had to save you."

I nod again. "Right. Sergeant Shon already told me this."

Cipher nods and clears her throat. "Okay, I guess we don't need to discuss this anymore."

I nod. "Is there anything else that you wanted to discuss with me?"

"Yes, there is."

"Oh?" I raise an eyebrow. "What's that?"

"I need your help with something important."

"Alright," I say. "What is it?"

Chapter 7

Baatar Jr. sighed as he scrolled through footage of the city. He rubbed his eyes and looked back at the screen. He continued to look through the footage, watching different parts of Chicago. He was trying to find his mother—as of right now Kuvira was his step-mother. Korra was still his original mother of course. Kuvira started dating Korra after Christine left, just so that she wouldn't become lonely—he let out another sigh and put his head down on the desk. Someone sat down beside him and he looked up.

"You okay?" Lin asked.

He shook his head and looked back down at the floor. Lin sighed and gave him a hug. He leaned into her embrace. Baatar tried to hold back his tears. He took another deep breath and pulled away from Lin. The two looked at each other in silence.

After a moment he finally spoke and Lin's heart shattered when she realized how broken his voice sounded. "That wasn't her," he said. "I don't what Cipher did to her, but that wasn't my mom."

"Su would know what to do." Kuvira said.

"No!" Junior exclaimed. "We can't bring Su into this, we agreed on that."

Tears ran down Kuvira's face. "I know."

Junior breathed in deeply and then got up from his chair, he walked out of the police station. Once he was outside he started to jog and soon he was sprinting. He ran toward Erudite headquarters and when arrived, he walked inside. He walked to the lab and went inside. He turned on the light and walked over to the wall panel. He opened it, took out several vials of serum and put them in his pocket. He closed the panel and walked out of the room, turning off the light as he went. He walked through the hallways. Just as he made it to the lobby he heard a voice. "Hello, Junior."

Junior stopped dead in his tracks and turned around. He froze instantly when he saw who it was. He struggled for words. "How...?" he croaked. "Cipher?"

Cipher smiled evilly and walked toward him. Junior took a step back and Cipher continued forward. Junior was backed into a wall and he started to panic. He was trapped. Cipher took another step forward and Junior looked around wildly for a way to escape. He saw an opening and he made a run for it. No sooner than he did that, he was jerked back. Junior tried to break free, but he soon couldn't. He tried to move his arms and legs, but they wouldn't budge. A bending, twitching feeling ripped through him and he realized with horror as to why he couldn't move.

Bloodbending.

Junior screamed at the top of his lungs and vision started to go black. He knew he was going to go unconscious any minute now. He tried to fight through the pain, but it was too much. He blacked out.

---

I walk towards the workshop on the train and go inside. Sergeant Shon is kneeling on the ground with a screwdriver. He grunts as he fastens the bolts and nuts into place. When the bolt is tight enough he moves onto the next one. He moves onto another one and he looks up. "Oh, Christine!" he exclaims. "I didn't see you there!"

"Cipher told me that you needed me for something?"

"Yes," he says. "Can you help me please?"

"Sure."

I walk over and kneel down beside him. I take a deep breath and raise my hands, the bolts float into my hands. Using my metalbending, I fasten the bolts into place. I wipe the sweat off my forehead and when we're done we take a break. After our break, we put the machine on a trolley and we wheel it out of the room. When we reach the hallway we stop in our tracks. Korra, Kuvira, and Lin are standing in the hallway.

"Christine?" They all say.


Chapter 8

I drop into a bending stance and everyone takes a step back. I look behind me and notice that Shon has retreated back to the lab. Good. I think. I look back at everyone. Korra takes a step forward and I pull out my metal sword. Korra stops for a moment and then continues walking forward. I stand frozen. Korra walks to me and reaches for me. I back away. I hit the wall and Korra walks forward again. I start to panic and I look around wildly.

"Sergeant Shon!" I yell.

Shon runs over out of the room and Korra steps back.

"What is it, Christine?" he asks.

"Call Cipher," I say. "Tell her I'm in danger."

Shon nods and runs back into the room. I look back at everyone. My heart pounds in my chest.

"Christine?" Korra says.

"Who are you?" I ask. "Why do you keep following me?"

"Its me, Korra."

"I'm sorry," I say. "But I don't know who you are."

"Then you need to remember," she says. "You need to remember who I am."

"Why?" I demand. "Why do I need to remember?"

"'Cause Cipher's brainwashed you, she's made you think that we're the enemy. But we're not, we're your family."

"Cipher's my family," I say. *You're* the *enemy.*

Korra looks at me in shock and tears flow freely down her face. She takes a step forward, but I can't move. I drop back into my metalbending stance and Korra continues to walk toward me. Though moments later her body comes to an abrupt halt and the same thing happens to Kuvira as well. Her body bends and twitches.

I stare at their twitching bodies for a moment and then I hear a voice. "Christine!"

I turn around and let out a gasp. "Cipher!"

Cipher walks into the hallway with Sergeant Shon beside her. I run up to her and give her a hug. With one hand Cipher keeps her bloodbending grip on Korra and Kuvira. With the other hand, she holds me close. We stand in almost complete silence, aside from the cries of pains coming from Korra and Kuvira.

"Christine?" Cipher says.

I look up at her. "Yes?"

"I'm going to ask you a question and I want you to think very hard before you answer."

I nod.

"If you were given the choice to either be here with me and help save the world, from the likes of Korra and Kuvira or let the world fall into chaos, what would you choose?"

I look over Korra and Kuvira, then back at Cipher. "I'd... I..."

"I'll give you one minute to decide."

I look back at Korra and Kuvira again. "I..."

"Christine," Korra says. "Please."

"I..." I take a deep breath. "I'd say with you and help save the world."

Cipher lets me go and I lace my fingers with hers. "Good choice." she says.

"How could you?" Korra says. "How could you choose this monster over me."

I don't say anything.

Cipher looks over at Shon and nods. "Sergeant, take these two to the prison."

"Don't let them have me, Christine!" Korra screams as Shon drags her and Kuvira away. "Don't let them have me!"

"Come on," Cipher says, once they're out of sight. "We have a job to finish."


Chapter 9

I let out a grunt as I roll the trolley off the train. We arrived in Chicago a couple of minutes ago. Together me and Cipher walk through Chicago and we arrive at Erudite headquarters. We go to the lab and start to set the machine up. As we set it up, Sergeant Shon walks into the room, he salutes when he enters.

Cipher smiles when she sees him. "Ah, Sergeant, please come in."

Sergeant Shon nods and walks into the room. "I just thought that I would let you know that Kuvira and Korra have been put in their cells."

Cipher looks over at him and glares for a moment, then she smiles. "That's wonderful." Shon turns to leave but then Cipher says. "When you have a minute Sergeant, I would like to talk to you outside."

Shon stiffens for a moment and relaxes. "Of course."

I look up and Cipher looks back at me and says. "Continue on working Christine, I'll be back in a minute."

I nod and Cipher leads Sergeant Shon out of the room.

---

Sergeant Shon and Cipher walked around a corner and away from the lab.

"What's this about?" Shon asked.

"I thought I told you not to use the names of Christine's current wife and ex-girlfriend when Christine was around. I worked so hard to get her to work for me and that required a lot of brainwashing and I would prefer if she didn't snap out of it. Do you understand?"

Shon hung his head. "Yes, Commander."

"Good," she said. "Let's get back to work."

---

I let out a grunt as I connect the last of the parts to machine. I wipe the sweat off my forehead and let out a sigh. I look up and Sergeant Shon walks over to me. "How's it going?" he asks.

"Good," I say, as I get up off the ground. "I'm finished the project."

"That's good." A new voice says.

Me and Shon turn around and see Cipher walking toward us.

"Hello, Commander."

I salute and Cipher returns it with one of her own.

"Alright," Cipher says. "Let's get started."

---

Korra and Kuvira paced back and forth in their cell. Kuvira walked up to the door and dropped into a bending stance and thrusted her hands forward. The platinum door didn't budge. Kuvira sighed and walked back over to one of the cell beds and sat down.

"Are you okay?"

Kuvira shook her head and Korra sat down beside her. Korra gave her a hug. Kuvira put her hand down on Korra's shoulder.

When Kuvira finally spoke, Korra was shocked at the brokenness of her voice. "I don't understand," she said. "I don't understand what's wrong with Christine. I mean I know that Cipher brainwashed her, but…" her voice trails off.

"Its okay," Korra whispered. "We'll find Christine, we'll stop Cipher. I promise."

"Thank you." Kuvira said.

"No problem," Korra smiled. "Now get some sleep, you'll need your energy for tomorrow."

Kuvira nodded and closed her eyes. Moments later she drifted off to sleep.

## Chapter 10

I let out a grunt as I lift the machine off the ground and put it on the table. Sergeant Shon walks over and sets a bag down by my feet. I smile at him and open the bag. I pull out the mysterious vials of liquid inside. I inspect them and put them back into the bag. Someone claps me on the back and I jump. I turn around and stand at attention.

"Commander!" I exclaim with a salute.

Cipher smiles. "Hello, Christine. How's the project coming along?"

"Its done." I say, with a smile.

"Good job," she says. "Then let's get this party started."

---

*"Kuvira!"* Korra yelled. *"Wake up!"*

Kuvira shot up off the ground, looking around wildly. Finally she saw Korra and she calmed down.

"What is it?" Kuvira asked.

"We need to get out of here." Korra says.

"What's the point?" Kuvira asked, defeated. "Christine's betrayed us, we may as well quit chasing her."

"You can't give up." Korra says.

Kuvira shook her head and looked down at the ground. Korra sighed and grabbed Kuvira's arm. She pulled Kuvira off the cell bed and pulled her toward the cell door. She took a deep breath and dropped into a metalbending stance and metalbent the door open. The two made their way out of the cell. They turned a corner and continued walking.

"Where do you think you're going?"

Korra and Kuvira stopped in their tracks and turned around. Cipher stood behind them, with Korra's son, Junior in handcuffs. Behind her as well were Korra's daughters. Korra and Kuvira took a step backward.

Cipher laughed. "I'm not here to hurt you or anything. I was just coming to find you so that you can be reunited with Christine."

Korra took another step back in shock. "What? Are you being serious?"

"Of course." Cipher motioned for them to follow. Korra and Kuvira hesitated for a moment and then started to follow her.

---

Shon and I are talking quietly when the door to the lab opens. Cipher walks inside with six other people. I recognize three of them as my daughters. My daughters run up to me and give me a hug. When they let go, I walk over to Cipher and give her a hug. "Thank you for bringing my daughters here."

Cipher smiles. "There's no need to thank me, I thought that you would like to see them again. After all, we've been too busy to see them anyway," I let Cipher go and she adds. "Christine, let's get this party started."

Chapter 11

I pull out several vials of serum from the bag and turn toward the serum detonator. I walk over to it and press a couple of buttons. I turn around and look at Korra and Kuvira. Korra takes a step forward and Kuvira steps forward as well. I take a step backwards. Korra takes another step and then starts to walk toward me. I back away slowly and then I hit a wall. I look over at Cipher and she drops into her signature bloodbending stance.

"Christine—" Korra starts to say, but her body comes to an abrupt halt. She lets out a groan of pain. Kuvira starts her way toward me as well and moments later her body comes to a halt as well. Both Korra and Kuvira twitch and bend in ways that no one should. They both let out a piercing scream. Junior looks from Korra to Kuvira. He drops into his bloodbending stance and twitches his fingers. Cipher's body seizes up and she screams. Korra and Kuvira are released from Cipher's grip and they collapse onto the floor.

"Christine!" Cipher screams. "Help me!"

"Let her go!" I yell as I drop into my signature lightningbending stance.

I charge to the lightning and it shoots out from my fingertips. Korra jumps in front of the lightning and tries to redirect it, but it strikes her in the chest. Korra screams and stumbles backward, crashing into Junior. The two trip over one another and fall to the ground. I run over to the serum detonator and press one of the buttons. I hear a beep and a hiss. The serum starts to fill the air. Korra and Kuvira start to cough. The smell of smoke and spice fills the air. I walk back over to Cipher and she nods. We start to walk toward the door, but our bodies abruptly come to a stop.

"You're not going anywhere!" Baatar Jr. declares.

I try to move, but my body won't budge.

"L-let me go!" I squeal.

Junior clenches his fingers tighter. "No, mom."

I scream louder as my bones bend near their breaking point.

"Cipher!" I scream.

"Christine!"

I try and break out of Junior's bloodbending grip, but its no use. Suddenly, my chi paths become blocked and I'm unable to move. Everything becomes still. Junior releases me and I slump to the floor. My vision blurs. Cipher quits screaming and through my blurry vision, I see her slump to the ground. Her body hits the ground with a thud. She doesn't move. A moment later the realization hits me like a freight train.

"You killed Cipher!" I say, weakly.

Junior walks over to the serum machine and presses another button. The death serum disappears a moment later.

"You're right," he says. "I did kill Cipher and I took your bending away."

My eyes widen. "You did *what?!* You are going to pay for this Junior."

Junior walks over to me and says. "No, mother, you're going to pay for this."

I hear the lab door open and I see the Chief of Police walk in. She walks over to me and picks me up off the ground. I struggle out of her grip and she drags me out of the room. I look behind me and notice that Korra and Kuvira have woken up and are escorting Sergeant Shon and the girls out of the room. I struggle again and Lin puts handcuffs on me. She pushes me forward and I quit struggling and start to walk.

"You're going to answer for everything you've done, Christine." Lin says, looking down at me.

"But I did nothing wrong!" I yell.

I thrash again and then something hard connects with my temple. My vision goes black.


Chapter 12

*"Christine?"*

I jerk awake and look beside me. Sergeant Shon is sitting next to me. I look around and notice that its dark. Then I realize where we are. We are in the back of Lin's police cruiser. I look back at Shon.

"Yes, Sergeant?"

"I'm sorry about Cipher." he says, his voice breaking.

I nod. "Yeah, me too."

"What do you think is going to happen to us?" he asks.

I shake my head. "I don't know. But we should probably expect a steep penalty."

"How steep of a penalty?" he asks.

"At worst, the death penalty. At best, twenty-five years to life in prison."

Sergeant Shon nods and looks down at the floor.

After awhile Shon finally speaks. "I had a daughter you know," I look at him. "Before I joined Cipher, she was all that I had. Her name was Kanna." He sniffles. "She had blonde hair and blue eyes. She was always a good kid, she always wanted to help people. I loved her so much."

I scooch over and sit next to him. "What happened?"

"She wanted to go see the circus, the one in the Fire Nation. So, I bought us tickets and we went. She loved the circus, she always told me that she wanted to be in one," he says, his voice breaking. "So I decided that I would get her a job at one. I talked to a friend of mine and he got her set up in one. On her thirteenth birthday, we went to the Fire Nation and she started her job almost instantly. She was a natural. One of her favorite things to do was walking a tightrope. She was fearless." Shon stops for a moment and breathes in deeply, before continuing. "It was her thirteenth birthday and she wanted me to come watch her. It was her final act, so I went. I remember her being so confident. So for her final act, she wanted to walk across a tightrope over a pit of fire. Kanna was halfway across when the rope snapped. She fell. I remember her screaming. I remember the chaos and the smell of burning flesh and then it was all over. Kanna was gone. Soon after, my wife left me, I was never the same after that. So when I turned thirty-five I joined Cipher and spent the next five years working for her. Cipher reminds me of her, of Kanna."

I put my head on his shoulder. "I'm sorry."

"It's okay." he says.

I'm just about to say something when the cruiser comes to a stop. The back of the cruiser opens. Me and Shon get out and Lin leads us inside the police station. She walks up to the man at the front desk and says. "I need two wooden holding cells."

"For how long?" the man asks.

"About a week." she says.

The man nods and gets up from his desk and he leads us down the hallway. Lin nods. But before we split though, Shon says. "See you in a week."

I nod. "See you in a week."

I turn away from Shon and Lin leads me to my cell. When we arrive at the cell, I go inside without looking back. I hear the door close and lock. I walk over to the cell bed and lay down. Moments later I drift off to sleep.

Chapter 13

*Six and a half years.*

That's what the judge ordered. I'm going to serve a six and half year sentence. I guess its better than what Shon got. He got a life sentence. Although the kids have better. They're free of all charges and are able to go home. Korra and Kuvira will look after them while I'm gone. I shake the thought from my mind and focus on walking. I arrive at my cell and go inside. The door closes and locks. I walk over to the bed and sit down. I look down at my clothes, I'm still in my forest green uniform, the only difference is that it's armor free. I lie down on the bed and stare at the wooden ceiling. I'm about to drift off to sleep when I hear a knock my cell door.

The tiny wooden slot on the door opens and I hear the guard say. "Dinner time."

He slides the tray through the slot and I get off the bed and walk to the door. I grab the tray and walk back to the cell bed. I take a bite of the food and spit it out. I don't know what it is, but its gross. But I know I need to eat so I don't question it. I just eat it. After I'm done I send the tray back and I lay back down.

I'm about to drift off when I hear another knock at the door. The little slot on the door opens and the guard says. "You have a visitor."

I get up off the cell bed and walk to the door. The door opens and my eyes widen when I see who it is. "Cipher?"

"Hello, Christine." she says.

---

I gasp and jerk awake and wipe the sweat off my forehead. I take a deep breath. I sit up and look around the room, making sure that Cipher isn't here. She isn't. I put my head in my hands. I lay back down on the bed. I hear a knock at the door and I hear the guard say. "Visitor."

I bolt right up and drop into a bending stance. The door opens and someone else walks inside. When I see who it is, I tense up a little.

"Christine?" the person says.

"Who are you?" I ask. "Why do you keep following me?"

"Its me, Korra." the women says.

"I don't know who you are." I say, shaking my head.

"I'm your wife." she says.

"What!?" I exclaim, unable to believe that its true.

Korra just nods.

"If you're my wife then who were you with when I first saw you?"

"I was with Kuvira," she says. "Your ex-girlfriend."

"How come I don't remember that?" I ask.

Korra sighs. "I don't know, but whatever Cipher did to you while you were with her, must have messed up your memory."

Something itches in the back of my mind and I try to focus on it. It was what Cipher had told me a couple of years ago. That she was all that I had, that I had no family.

"No," I say, backing away slowly. "No, you're lying."

"Christine—" She starts to say, but I just shake my head.

"Get out." I say.

"What?" she says, stepping back a bit.

"Get out!" I yell, pointing towards the door. "Just get out!"

Korra looks at me with hurt eyes and starts to walk away. I hear the cell door close and lock. That's when I feel the tears come.

Chapter 14

I take a deep breath and look down at the floor. I sigh and shake my head. I look back down at the floor. My vision shifts in and out of focus. Out of the corner of my eye, I see something flickering. I look over to see what it is. I see a flickering blue light. Soon the light transforms into a person, or rather a projection of a person. It takes me a few minutes to realize who that person is.

When I do, I instantly salute. "Hello, Commander."

"Hello, Christine." Cipher says.

I run my hand through my hair nervously.

"Is something wrong?" she asks.

"I think I should apologize." I say.

"For what?"

"For the way that last fight went, I tried everything in my power to save you. I'm so sorry."

"Its alright." she says.

Tears form in my eyes and I break down. My knees go weak and I collapse. Cipher "catches" me and "holds" me in her arms. "I miss you, Cipher," I say. "I really do."

"Shhh! she says. "I've got you, I've got you. Don't worry."

---

When I can no longer cry, and I've calmed down, Cipher "let's" me go.

"You okay?" she asks.

I nod.

"Are you sure?"

"Yeah." I say.

"Well, if you ever need me, you can just call." she says.

"Okay." I say.

Just like that Cipher is gone.

---

"Breakfast."

I get off my bed and walk to the cell door. The guard slides the food tray through the slot in the door. I take the tray and go sit down on my bed. I start to eat and I cringe at the taste of the food. When I'm done eating, I take a shower and change into the clothes I was given at breakfast. I walk back to the bed and sit down. I look around the room and then lay down on the bed. I stare up at the ceiling. My head is swimming with thoughts, specifically one from when I was working for Cipher. That's the only thing that I can remember. I can't remember anything else. Then I realize that maybe the only way to remember something would be to meditate into The Spirit World. I sit down on the bed and begin to meditate. Just as I start to cross over, there's another knock at the door.

"Visitor."

I open my eyes just as the door opens. Someone walks inside and stops a few feet away from me.

"Christine?" The woman says.

"Who are you?" I ask.

"Its me, Kuvira," she says. "Your ex-girlfriend."

Something about what she says triggers my memory and I look at her. "Kuvira?" I say.

Kuvira sighs in relief. "You remember me?"

Just as I start to speak, I hear a voice in my head telling me that she's dangerous. I back away.

"Get out." I say.

"What?" Kuvira asks.

"Get out!" I yell.

Kuvira steps back in shock and with tears in her eyes, she walks to the door. I turn around and sit down on the bed. When I hear the door slam shut, I finally break down in tears.

Chapter 15

I let out a sigh as Lin escorts me back to my cell. I just got back from an afternoon of socializing with my fellow prisoners. According to the prison rules, if you don't cause any problems for a year, you're allowed to visit other prisoners that aren't in solitary confinement. We reach my cell and I walk inside.

Before Lin leaves though she says. "Someone should be here soon, to give you lunch and a fresh pair of clothes."

I nod and Lin closes and locks the cell door.

I sit down on my cell bed and look around the room, some decorations have been put up to make the cell more lively. I lie down on the bed and drift off to sleep.

---

"Christine?"

I sit up and rub my eyes. I stretch and yawn. I look around the cell and I see Cipher in the corner of the room. I get up off the bed and walk over to her. I salute and relax.

"What is it, Commander?"

"How's prison life treating you?" she asks.

I shrug. "Its okay. I'll be out in a few more years."

"That's good."

I nod. "How's The Spirit World treating you?"

"Meh, its okay," she says. "It's not really what I prefer, but it could be worse."

I nod again and then an idea pops into my head. "You know, there is a way you could return to the physical world."

"How?"

"Meet me in The Spirit World and I'll show you."

Cipher nods and moments later she disappears. I sit down on the floor and start to meditate, soon I feel the world slip away.

---

I open my eyes and look around. I'm in The Spirit World. I see Cipher appear a few moments later. I motion for her to follow me. We walk deep into The Spirit World and through a forest full of vines. When we reach the edge of the forest, we walk up to a house. I turn back to Cipher and say. "You should wait back in the forest."

"Why?" she asks.

"'Cause the person I'm about to talk to may not be happy to see you."

Cipher nods and I watch as she makes her way back to the forest. When she's gone, I turn back to the house and knock on the door. It opens a moment later and I smile.

"Hello, Su."

"Hello, Christine."

"May I come in for a moment?"

"Of course."

I walk inside and Su closes the door. I walk to the living room and sit down on the couch.

"What's going on?" Su asks.

"I need to ask you something." I say.

"Okay," she says. "What is it?"

Chapter 16

I walk out of the house and back to the forest. I find Cipher and motion for her to follow. We start walking and we go deeper into The Spirit World. We walk to the Tree Of Time and I go inside. I sit down and begin to meditate. I connect with the energy in The Spirit World and then to the energy of the physical world. It doesn't take me long to locate where Cipher's physical body. When I do, I gasp.

"What is it?" Cipher asks. "Did you figure out how to bring me back?"

"Sort of," I say.

Cipher sighs in relief.

"Unfortunately, you've been away for so long that your spirit can no longer return to your physical body." I say.

"What?!" Cipher exclaims.

"I'm sorry," I say. "I really am."

Cipher sighs.

"Well," I say. "I should be heading back to my physical body before I become trapped in here."

Cipher nods.

I give her a quick hug and then I feel The Spirit World slip away.

I open my eyes and let out a sigh. I look over at the cell door and see that dinner has been dropped off, along with another pair of clean clothes. I grab the food and start to eat. When I'm done, I have a shower and change into the fresh pair of clothes that I was given and sit down on my bed. I stare at the floor. I become lost in thought and my vision starts to shift in and out. My thoughts are interrupted though when I hear a knock at the door.

"Visitor."

I look up just as the cell door is opening. Korra walks inside and the cell door slams shut behind her.

"Hey." she says.

"Hey." I say.

"How are you?" she asks.

I shrug. "I'm okay, I guess."

"That's good."

"How are the kids?" I ask.

"They're fine."

I nod. "How's Kuvira?"

"She's doing okay."

I nod again and Korra sits down next to me.

"I'm sorry." I whisper.

"For what?" she asks, furrowing her eyebrows in confusion.

"For what I've put you through." I say.

"It's okay."

"No, it's not," I say. "I shouldn't have done it. I don't know what's wrong with me."

"Christine—" She starts to say, but I cut her off.

"Do you love me?"

"What?" Korra asks.

"Do you love me?" I ask again.

"Of course I do." she says.

"Then do me a favor."

"What?"

"Make this your last visit until I'm released."

But—" Korra starts to say, but I cut her off. "Please," I say. "I need time to heal."

She nods. "Okay. Anything you need." She leaves and that's when I let the tears come.

Chapter 17

*Five and a half years later…*

I let out a sigh as Lin escorts me out of the police station and to her car. She starts to drive and while she's driving she looks over at me. I look over at her and neither one of us say anything. I look away from her and I look out the window. I watch as the city rolls past us. In the distance, I see Erudite headquarters—the sight of my defeat and downfall. We reach my house and we get out of the car. We walk up to the front door and Lin rings the doorbell. The door opens a moment later and we go inside. Lin undoes the handcuffs and I rub my wrists with my hands, Lin hands me my metal armor and I re-attach it to my uniform. We walk to the kitchen and there I see Korra and Kuvira sitting at the table. When they see me they freeze in place. I see tears starting to form in Korra's eyes and she walks over to me. She gives me a hug and I stiffen for a second. Soon I relax into her embrace. Korra lets me go and I smile.

Moments later I hear a voice. "Mom!"

I turn around and see my daughters running toward me.

"Girls!" I exclaim.

They all run into my arms and give me a hug.

"We've missed you." They all say.

"I missed you too." I say and I let them go.

Kuvira walks up to me and gives me a hug. "Welcome home."

"Thanks," I say, holding her close. When we let go, we walk over to the couch and sit down. I look at everyone."So… What have I missed for the last nine and a half years?"

"Where can we start?" Korra says, smiling.

"Tell me everything," I say. "My memory is still foggy."

"Alright." Kuvira says and she starts to tell me everything.

*Two weeks later…*

I watch Kuvira as she gets ready to move next door. She puts her bags by the front door and I walk up to her and give her a hug.

"I'm going to miss you."

She laughs. "I'm only moving next door."

"I know. But I'll still miss you."

"You can still come visit me."

"I know."

Kuvira gives me another hug and picks up her bags. She opens the door and just before she leaves she says. "Goodbye, Christine."

"Goodbye, Kuvira."

Just like that, she is gone.

Chapter 18

I sit down the couch and lean into Korra. She gives me a hug and I return it. I sigh and let her go. I lean forward and Korra runs her hand across my back. I smile at her and give her another hug. For a while neither one of us says anything. We just sit in silence. I look over at Korra and she smiles.

After a couple minutes of silence, Korra finally speaks. "I have a question for you."

"Okay," I say. "What's the question?"

"Do you love me?"

"I… don't know."

"How do you not know?" she asks.

"'Cause I don't remember much about you."

"Oh, right." Korra looks down at the ground.

"Hey, its okay. We'll figure it out."

I give her a hug and get up from the couch.

"Where are you going?" she asks.

"I'm going to find Junior, I need to talk to him."

I stand outside of Baatar's room. My hand hovers inches from the door. I sigh. I hear footsteps behind me and I turn around. Korra stands behind me.

"Hey." she says.

"Hey."

"Why haven't you gone in yet?"

I sigh. "I don't know, I guess I'm afraid that he's still going to hate me."

"You feel bad for what you did, am I right?"

"That's the thing. I don't know how to feel bad for something that I don't remember."

Korra walks up to me and squeezes my shoulder. "You'll be fine."

I nod and turn back to the door. I take a deep breath and put my hand on the doorknob. I open the door and walk inside. I close the door behind me. When I turn around I see Junior sitting on his bed, looking at the floor. I hesitate for a moment and then take a step forward.

"Baatar?" I say.

He doesn't look up and I take another step forward.

"Son?"

I still don't receive an answer.

I sigh and turn towards the door, but just before I start walking, I hear his voice. "Mom?"

I turn around. "Yes?"

"Is that really you?"

"Yes."

Junior gets off his bed and runs over to me and gives me a hug. I sigh and wrap my arms around him.

"I missed you." he whispers.

"I know, I missed you too."

"I love you, mom." he says and he starts to cry.

"I love you, too," I say, holding him close. "And I always will."

Chapter 19

Me and Baatar walk out of his bedroom and I see Korra standing in the hallway. She walks up to us and gives us a hug. When we break apart, we walk downstairs and sit down on the couch. We watch TV and when we are done, we have dinner. After that, all of us go for a walk. We go to millennium park. I watch the kids spar with each other. Korra walks up behind me and gives me a hug. I turn around and give her a kiss. She pulls me in closer. When we break apart, I look into her eyes.

"I love you." I say.

"I love you, too."

We turn back to the kids and as I watch them something pokes in the back of my mind. Its a memory. I focus on it. When I realize what it is, I gasp.

"What is it?" Korra asks.

"I remember." I say.

"What do you remember?" Korra asks.

"Everything, I remember everything."

"Do you remember what Cipher did to you?"

"Yes."

"What did she do?"

"She brainwashed me right after I left."

"Do you remember how she brainwashed you?"

"She, uh, she would inject me with simulation serum every day and while I was in the simulation she would tell me what was right and what was wrong. So if I brought you up in any conversation, she would inject me with the serum and tell me that you were the enemy."

Korra's eyes widen. *"What?!"*

"That's why I would attack you whenever you showed up and that's probably the reason why she let me see you."

Korra puts her head in hands and I notice that she's shaking. I give her a hug.

"I'm so sorry." I say.

"Its okay." she says.

"Korra?" I say.

She looks at me.

"There's something I need to do and I need you to trust me."

"Alright. What is it?"

"I'm going to go into The Spirit World and get rid of Cipher once and for all."

Korra stares at me blankly.

"Korra, do you trust me?"

"Yes, of course."

"Then I'll be right back. Watch over my body while I'm gone."

She nods and I sit down on the ground and begin to meditate. Soon I feel the world fade away.

Chapter 20

I open my eyes and look around. I try and remember where I last saw Cipher. I start to walk. As I walk I call out for her. I walk toward the last place that I saw her. I call for her again. I still receive no answer. I continue walking around. As I walk, I hear a voice. "Christine?"

I turn around and let out a gasp. "Cipher?"

Cipher smiles. "I wasn't expecting you to be back so soon."

"I originally wasn't planning on returning at all."

"Why are you here?"

"I need to ask you something."

"Okay, what is it?"

"Why did you brainwash me?"

Cipher looks at me in confusion. "What are you talking about?"

"I remember everything, I know you brainwashed me. So all I want to know is why."

"I can't answer that."

"Fine, then maybe you can answer this, why did you come after me in the first place? What caused you to do this?"

"I don't think you can handle the truth."

"What do you mean?"

Cipher walks up beside me. "If you think that the first time we met was the first time you saw me, your dead wrong."

"What are you talking about?"

"I'm surprised you haven't figured it out yet."

"Figured what out?"

Cipher sighs. "Do you remember when Baatar first released the serums on Chicago?"

"Of course," I say. "I almost died that day. Why?"

"I was the one who told Baatar to release them. The only difference was I told him to release the death serum, but he went behind my back and released the paralytic serum instead. So when that plan failed, I went to Zaheer and asked him to take care of the problem. When that failed I teamed up with Baatar again, I posed as the female bandit. Then when Baatar failed to kill you that time, I went and teamed up with Zaheer, Raiko, and Evelyn. I've been there since the beginning. You just didn't realize that until now."

*"What!?"*

"Shocking isn't it?"

My shock and anger takes over and grab Cipher by the collar of her shirt and yank her forward.

"I'm going to make you pay."

Cipher smirks. "I'm already dead, how are you going to make me pay."

"'Cause there's one other place that I can take you, where you will never be able to come back to the physical world."

"Where's that?"

I smirk. "You'll find out in a minute, oh wait, we're already here."

Cipher looks over her shoulder and then back at me, her eyes go wide.

"Welcome to The Fog Of Lost Souls," I say. "You'll never escape."

I push her backward and she screams as she falls. I watch as she disappears into the fog. I take a deep breath and turn away. Then I feel The Spirit World slip away.

---

I open my eyes and look over at Korra. I get up off the ground and walk over to her. I kiss her and she kisses me back. When we break apart I smile.

"What is it?" she asks.

"I got rid of Cipher once and for all."

"That's good."

"I know." I say.

"What should we do now?"

"How about we go home?"

Korra smiles. "Sounds perfect."

---

When we arrive at the house, we sit down on the couch and I tell Korra what Cipher had told me.

"Wow," she says. "I didn't realize that she had been here since the beginning."

"Neither did I."

I lean over and give her a kiss. Moments later we hear the kids gasp. I pull away from Korra. "What?" I say.

The kids laugh. "We just weren't expecting that you two were going to be back in a relationship that quickly."

"Well, apparently we are." I say and I give Korra another kiss.

When we break apart. The kids walk over to the couch and sit down next to us.

Baatar Jr. gives me a hug. "I love you, mom."

"I love you too." I look over at the girls. "I love you all."

---

I have learned a lot over the decade. Especially what is important in life. What matters to me the most out of everything is family. Family is what kept me going through my toughest times and no matter what I will always be there to protect them because that's what family does and that's what we are. A family.